The Call of the Earth

The Call of the Earth

a Novel by

EVANGELOS
AVEROFF-TOSSIZZA

Translated by
André Michalopoulos

CARATZAS BROTHERS, PUBLISHERS
NEW ROCHELLE, NEW YORK
1981

The description of the public activities of the Roman Legion and the actions of the Italian Forli Division, and of the resistance offered to them, strictly conforms to reality.

Published in the English language by

Caratzas Brothers, Publishers
481 Main Street (P.O. Box 210)
New Rochelle, N.Y. 10802

ISBN 0-89241-134-1

Part One

ALONG THE PATH OF DECADENCE

I

Here even the trains were worse. They vibrated more, and he couldn't keep from bumping into the walls of the corridor as he walked back to his compartment. Why on earth didn't they put the diner next to the sleeping car?

What could one expect? Once you were in the Near East everything began to go wrong. He shut the door behind him and looked at his watch: only nine o'clock, Since his nursery days, he couldn't remember having breakfasted at this ungodly hour. In the civilized world of the West no one woke you for breakfast on a train unless you were approaching your destination. There ought to be an international rule—

Well, never mind. What was the use of thinking about rules when one had crossed the Serbian border? The dining-room staff were good locals, no doubt, who got up at crack of dawn. For them this would be very late in the morning. And that was that.

In bored distaste, Nikita Coletti took off his grey traveling gloves and sank back in the corner of the green plush seat which now replaced the bed. It had taken just one trip to the diner to ruin his clean gloves with filth. "That's because the trains in this country don't run on electricity," he thought. "The coal they burn is probably foul, and the engines ready for the junk-heap where they would have been long ago in a prosperous country." It was obvious that they were passing through the Balkans, those filthy, uncivilized Balkans, that had set their stamp upon his nice gloves.

Tonight then he would be back in Greece. In fifteen or sixteen hours he would stand on Greek soil. How strange it seemed. He had been away for almost twenty years, and now that he was returning he felt absolutely no emotion. For the first time in so many years he would be in Larissa again and, after a few days, in Athens. Yet nothing stirred within him. Neither joy, nor curiosity; no feeling of any kind, not even a heartbeat quickened by old memories. If he had to force himself to find some sensation within him, it would be one of denial, of revulsion.

He curled into the corner of the seat by the window, and looked out absent-mindedly at the dullness of that November day in 1939; he thought it was quite natural that he should feel so ill disposed toward the land of his birth.

People said he had a great fortune in Greece. Well, good for them! From the time that poor old Panayioti died they hadn't sent him a penny! Exchange regulations, they said. But it was his fault, too. Partly through indifference and partly because of the advice of relatives, the only thing he had bought in Paris was the apartment in which he lived. He had left everything else in that wretched country. So there he was, while this great war—phony though it was—had broken out, and one didn't know when it would flare up and in which direction it would spread.

What if it spread to Greece during the few days or weeks that he was there? The thought paralyzed him.

"An uncivilized place," he reflected. "From the time I was able to form my own judgment, I have felt nothing but impatience and loathing for it. Is there one good thing I can remember about it?"

Faint scenes of bygone days flitted through his mind.

Lessons, all kinds of tutors at home, his famous grandfather who wanted to make a man of him while he was nothing by an anemic boy. And then, when he was thirteen or fourteen, that tragicomic event when all the notables of Larissa were invited to Pteliona by Grandfather to see the wonderful grandson fire an army rifle for the first time. The recoil of the gun had given him such a stab of pain, and he had been so terrified by the sudden roar in his ears, that he had thrown down the Mannlicher and had run sobbing to the arms of his mother. He had just had time to see the angry flash in his grandfather's eyes as he jumped to his feet. A few moments later, with a sidelong glance, he had seen the old man leave in silence and go into the house.

For all present it had been ridiculous and unfair, a tragic, harsh scene. Might it have been the prelude to what was to come? Was it an omen? The next day they left for Athens, on the day after that his father and mother were buried, both at the same time.

"The barbarian, the vile drunk," the old servant had told him. "He killed her and then committed suicide."

He would wake up in the night and scream, until at last his

grandfather ordered an employee of his bank to take him to France, where he was placed in a school near Versailles.

How cold life was there too! And after the disaster of Asia Minor it was worse still. Defeat, flight, streams of refugees, charity from foreigners. He couldn't stand the jeers of the other boys.

It was then that he began to understand that all he had heard from his grandfather and his Greek teachers about the power and glory of Greece was nothing but a silly fairytale invented by the Greeks in order to cover up their miserable condition or to console themselves for it. What a disillusioning discovery! Because, while he of course was no eagle, he had taken comfort in the thought that he belonged to the most glorious race in the world!

Those were dark years, dark indeed and cold. Nothing but bitter memories.

"What would have become of me," he reflected, "if my first poems hadn't received a prize. The reward was my salvation."

He had been a lonely stranger in a foreign land among indifferent folk; then his life changed suddenly. He had a splendid position, he was sought after, invited to parties, and surrounded by friends. And he hadn't made the slightest effort.

It was true that many critics found fault with his work. They said his poems were the outpourings of a diseased mind and would have a poisonous influence on young people. They went so far as to condemn the distinguished literary committee which awarded him the prize. But why should he care? Those who praised his work were numerous too. The discussion which was provoked by the controversy increased the sale of his book.

On the title-page of his collection appeared a line of Verlaine, *Je suis l'Empire a là fin de la décadence*, which represented his feelings exactly: worn out nobility in the last stages of disintegration. Let others think as they pleased and follow their chosen paths. This was his mood; this was how he chose to live. He liked comfort and elegance, he liked to be free from worries and violent passions. He adored the company of a certain type of woman—refined, intellectual, sensuous. As a young man he had been overcome by spiritual *ennui* and disillusionment, and now that he was nearly thirty-five he did not feel differently. But he found no cause for anxiety in this, just so long as his comfort were secured during this senseless journey through this world.

He was infuriated by the thought that he might not be successful in the business that took him to Larissa and Athens. What if there were delays, if the war were to spread and he found himself stranded in Greece?

Horrible thought! He was no longer in any way attached to the country of his birth; he could not bear the idea of being boxed up there and prevented from leaving.

Hoping to get rid of his mood, he looked out the window. What he saw only increased his depression. The train was passing through a Serbian village. Nikita noticed how small and low the houses were—depressingly low. The men outside them had not shaved for days, their clothing was patched and their feet were covered in sheepskins tied with thongs. They were surrounded by innumerable pigs which roamed about freely. Men and pigs alike were caked with mud. There was mud and filth everywhere giving the whole village a sordid look. Over the low walls of the houses the eaves extended lower still and gave him the impression that the whole village worshipped the bog. If the pigs had been goats, this might well have been Greece.

"Somewhere this side of Croatia," Nikita reflected, "runs the line which separates the Balkans from the West. From here southward everything is uncivilized and dirty. I'd rather kill myself than have to live here." The thought came to him that the character of a locality is defined by its natural features, the conditions of life which prevail in it, and the intellectual development and values of its inhabitants. Above all, one is made conscious of it by means of the people with whom one comes in contact.

What contacts were left to him in Greece? Actually none.

On rare occasions, when relatives or old school friends sought him out in Paris, he received them without relish as he would receive total strangers. He had never struck up any friendships with Greeks abroad, not even that pale, inconsequential, but enduring kind of friendship which he maintained with a few other people; he never spent holidays or a week-end in any

Greek's country home or shared the slightest familiarity with any of his countrymen. How was it possible, then, not to feel that he was coming to Greece as a stranger, an exile?

No, there was no room for doubt. There was only one thing for him to do—to get away as soon as possible from these uncivilized and detestable Balkans, and to return to the city of light, to civilization and comfort.

* * * * *

Vassili Manoussis signed the order without even looking at it and gave instructions that he was to be left alone.

"I have to write a letter to the Governor. I do not wish to be disturbed. I'll ring if I need anything." Manoussis had no letter to write to anyone. He wanted to be left in peace. Something was worrying him and he needed to be alone to give it serious thought. For some time past he had been vaguely disturbed—perhaps a little frightened. Last evening, when just before midnight his daughter Katie and his brother Nikos had left the Vlach celebration he had organized, his apprehensions had crystallized into a feeling of real fear. Surely he was right about this.

It had looked as though the two of them had deliberately intended to show their contempt for all the guests at the party. At that moment the orchestra had stopped playing and the dance floor was empty. They had crossed it with arrogant strides and departed without saying good-bye to anyone and without giving him any explanation. They were always scornful when they spoke about Larissa, and last night during the whole time they were at the celebration they had refused to take part in the dancing and plainly showed that the gathering was distasteful to them. When they left in that provocative manner they appeared to indicate that they considered everybody present to be unbearably inferior.

So it was quite natural that his latent anxieties should come to the surface. In fact he hadn't been able to get any sleep all night. He adored his daughter and his brother; they were the only people he loved. For them he had endured many privations and had built up dreams for the future—dreams that sometimes seemed about to be realized.

As a small boy he had come on foot all the way from Samarina to Larissa. That giant of a man, old Nikita Coletti, had made it possible for him to get through high-school; after that he had taken him on at the bank. Vassili didn't imagine then that he would ever go very far. But he had been successful. He was now a branch manager and had acquired a tidy fortune. He had put his brother through law school and had given his only daughter a good education.

These were the results of hard work, thrift, patience and application. He had also been skillful in his private enterprises. Now, at last, when he hoped to reap the fruits of so much effort, he saw his brother, for all his talents, withdrawing into a kind of isolation, and was disturbed by his pretty daughter's stubborn resistance to marriage. She was twenty-six; few girls had failed to find a husband at her age.

"It's that foreign school in Athens that has spoiled her," he thought. "Those rich friends of hers and the summers she used to spend in their homes at Glyfada and Kifissia. She's the victim of her own charm. As for him, he's too bright and his former misguided connection with the Communist Party hasn't done him any good. Well, now it's my duty to protect them against themselves. If they go on as they are, they're heading for certain disaster.

He got up and started pacing the room. "I'm going to put my foot down," he said aloud to give himself courage. "After all they do depend on me. They've got to listen to me and I'll have to be more strict with them. I've been too soft."

The door opened and he heard a familiar voice.

"We've all been too soft these days, my dear Vassili.'

He turned and saw his old schoolmate Hadjipyrros, a colleague of his brother in the bank's law office. Vassili felt uncomfortable not knowing how much his friend had overheard. He told him that he had been annoyed by a customer's insolence.

"We shall be needing our severity for another kind of customer," the newcomer said.

"What do you mean? What's going on?"

"Tonight, at midnight, the grandson arrives from Paris."

"You mean the poet?" Vassili asked, surprised.

"Yes indeed, the poet who bears the charmed name of his grandfather. The Governor phoned me. He wants us to go to the station to receive him and to do all we can to counteract his plans."

He explained that young Coletti was coming to sell all his possessions in Greece and to take out all that he could get for them. He was determined and he was in a hurry. His uncle, Spyros Coletti, governor of the bank since the death of his grandfather, was furious. He didn't want anything sold.

The young man's idea is not such a bad one," the banker replied cautiously.

"You're joking, Vassili."

"Well, he's getting a very small income on the capital invested," said the branch manager without too much insistence.

"That is not the question. Might I point out that as matters stand today, and in view of the young man's impatience, he will probably sell out at half price. Furthermore, a war has begun, and in war it's better to have real estate than cash and paper. Still more important, whatever he realizes will be held here and will be useless to him abroad."

"Well," said Vassili, "we can always help him to get part of it out of the country."

"We'll never assist him in any such illegal action, particularly as the Governor disapproves of it. And what's more, let me tell you that I feel badly about the grandson coming back to liquidate everything that that grand old man left him. That good-for-nothing!"

Vassili Manoussis had gone back to his desk. He looked at the floor.

"You're very hard on him," he said softly. "Every man follows his own path. He didn't follow in his grandfather's footsteps, but he has become famous in France, and that reflects honor on Greece."

"Which he hasn't deigned to visit even once, and to which he refers in his poems as if it were a foreign land, a land of antiquity. What's more, as you know, in France he is condemned as 'the poet of corruption and degradation'. I worshipped the other Nikita; this one I despise. The very thought of him disgusts me."

He got up to leave, but he stopped because the expression his friend's face annoyed him. There was a new gleam of satisfaction in his eye; his crafty mind was absorbed by thoughts which were clearly not disinterested. And yet they were, all of them, creations of the legendary grandfather, and he ought to be disturbed when something in the family was going wrong. Friendship does not die with the man! It continues in his memory.

The lawyer felt the urge to irritate him in return. Standing in the doorway he said, "Last night I came to the Vlach celebration for your sake, but I've come to the conclusion that with all the Rumanian propaganda that's going on so actively, it's time we disassociated ourselves from the Vlachs."

"But there's no connection Taki."

"We are giving him an excuse to say that there is and that we are different from the rest of the Greeks. But it was something else I came to say. The organizers of the gathering were all friends. Did you have to invite Ropotika?"

"He's a customer of the bank, Taki, and an important cattle-man."

"Yes, and your partner in private deals, and also a former bandit, damn it. Do you have to bring him to our social gatherings?" And he added with a sarcastic smile, "I hope that was the reason why Katie and Nikos left early and so scornfully."

* * * * *

Mourayias stopped at the end of the field, laid the plow on the ground, and put the team out to graze by the grassy ditch. He sat on the bank, took out his pouch and started to roll a cigarette. He cast his eye over the cloudy sky and calmed down a little. It was not likely to rain, at most there might be a drizzle. But the trouble was that the weather had to hold for days, for November was here and the sowing had not begun.

What could he do? How could he work any faster with the tractors locked up and rusting in the barn at Pteliona? How could he manage with only four pairs of oxen? How could he drive all the furrows and cover the seed that was sown by hand now that the machines were no longer available? Every year fewer crops were planted, more carelessly, and the neighbors prospered more, while Pteliona, once so splendid, went downhill and many of its fields remained uncultivated. The animals, too, were badly fed and growing weaker. It was impossible to get them to plow from dawn to dusk and expect them to stand on their feet. He was about to get up, but the beasts grazed greedily and he decided to wait a little.

"It's too much for me," he thought. "I can't stand it much longer. It isn't as if I hadn't worked hard to keep things the way the Old Man who was a father to all of us had set them."

God only knew how hard Mourayias had tried to persuade Uncle Panayioti, while he was still alive, to get a tractor, to use fertilizers, to rotate the crops in order to give the land a rest, to feed the animals well, to do this and to avoid that.

"We can't afford the expense from the two thousand stremmata left to us by the expropriation," Panayioti had said. "forget the good old days. Today we have to be very thrifty if we are going to make ends meet. I have a lot of expenses. I have to send the boy money, and life is not cheap in Paris. I am forced to sell off land from time to time."

He was a good man, God rest his soul. A good man, but nothing like his father. He let his eyes wander over the endless plain. On the horizon, in the gathering mist, visions of the past seemed to rise.

The Old Man had wanted the first band of volunteers for the Macedonian struggle to go out from his village. One of his men had arrived at Syrrako, then in unliberated Epirus, a stone's throw from the old border, and had secretly called for volunteers. He remembered the two months he had spent just over there—he glanced at a hill in the distance—at St. Elias' Monastery; he remembered the exercises and the marches through the rain and the dark nights. He remembered the time when the Old Man himself came and, standing by the Beautiful Gate, distributed the rifles and the crossed cartridge-belts. There he had stood, tall, straight as a rod, with his eagle eye and long silver-white beard, and he seemed like an archangel, like someone who, when he wanted to could speak with God. He remembered the unforgettable song that Father Modestos had sung that night for the first time and which they had sung hundreds of times on the crags and in the swamps outside Salonika when they were battling with Turks and Bulgars. He gazed at the old border which he had crossed with his company, and the tune came back to him. Overcome by a wave of nostalgia, he now sang it softly to himself.

For forty years I've battled here
    On Macedonia's plain,
And now that forty-two have past
    I'll see it free again.
Wake up, poor slave, wake up! Arise!
And look at freedom with new eyes!

He smiled to himself as he thought of the good old days. It was no use complaining. He'd had a good life, thanks be to God.

Only these last years, why he wondered, did everything seem so black? Never before had he felt like this. What could be the reason? He tried to figure it out but couldn't come up with an answer. Could it be his daughter's grief? No, it wasn't that. All the things he thought of were over long ago or were nothing to worry about. Suddenly, in a flash of understanding and memory, it came to him. He stood up and glared wildly at the badly plowed fields and the bony animals. "My heart's not in this work any more" he said to himself, when it's this way the poison that's eating me spreads to everything around. The boy is coming from Paris tonight. If he doesn't change things at Pteliona, I'll finish the seeding and then I'll find a job somewhere else. I've had it."

He took a couple of steps toward the oxen and stood still, wrapped in thought. "I must talk to Phrosso tonight. If I put it off, I'll startle her when the time comes."

With the metal handle of his whip he rubbed the dirt from the plow, called out to his faithful beasts, and began plowing again, his head bent toward the ground.

Phrosso tried to make him change his mind, but she did not insist. She told him they were comfortable in their little house and that he wasn't a young man any more. But she spoke halfheartedly, for she knew her father. She knew his moods and understood his grief. She didn't want to upset him. Already she had given him enough cause to worry.

"Allright, father," she said after a moment's hesitation. "You're quite right."

Her father went out to see if the farm-hands were looking after the animals, and as he passed her he stroked her hair. She took up her knitting but couldn't go on with her work. The needles got tangled in the yarn as if she were a novice. She dropped her knitting in her lap. She realized that her father felt the need to leave, but she was afraid of the unknown future. What was in store for them? Here at least there was comfort, habit. The city was hard by and across the river, at the Agricultural College, she had found a friend. No, Alexis was more than a friend. He was like a brother. Now where would they go? Her eyes filled with tears. Why was fate driving her so hard? Why?

Phrosso was indeed an unlucky girl. She hadn't felt the loss of her mother. Her father's tenderness more than made up for it. The first years of her life at Pteliona were like a fairytale, and later the short distance from the farm to Larissa made it easy for her to go to school there. She enjoyed school because she was gay and cheerful, had a lot of friends, and was a good student. Her ambition was to become a lawyer, the first woman lawyer in Larissa, and her father raised no objections; on the contrary, he was proud of her. Everything was going well, until the last year in high school, when suddenly a new dream came true and upset her whole life.

One evening she was coming back from school with two other girls. It was election time and, as they passed through the main square, a political meeting was in progress. They stopped to watch and have some fun, and they saw that Notis—whom all the girls loved for his masculine enthusiasm which made him different from others—was speaking. All the girls were jealous of Katie Manoussis, who was the only one in the class to whom Notis paid attention.

From time to time Phrosso had met him on the street; they exchanged formal greetings nothing more. But on the day of the political meeting the three girls had literally hung on his words, as had all the crowd. He was frequently interrupted by applause and, as he spoke, with a few wide gestures of his hands, his eyes uplifted he filled the audience with enthusiasm.

"For how long are we going to remain the slaves of habit, the slaves of petty ties and senseless prejudices, indifferent to the misery around us? How long will we go on refusing to overcome it, when we know that the misery of the masses, the misery that we all share can be overcome? How long are we going to see the wealth around us not being equally distributed to all, since we all are born equal and alike? My brothers! My oppressed, weak, wronged brothers, rise up! Follow us! The hour of liberation for the slaves, the hour of revolution, the hour of justice has struck."

"He's a Communist," said one of the girls.

"Let's get out of here," said the other. "This is a Communist meeting. There may be trouble."

They left, but Phrosso found it impossible to go. Something attracted her and she drew nearer. She felt everything go limp inside her; her heart was ready to burst. She'd never felt anything like this before. She grew limp, her flesh seemed to fall away from her, and she was spreading her wings to the sun. And when Notis finished and came away amid the cheering of the crowd, she caught him by the arm and cried, "Notis, you were wonderful! Wonderful."

He stopped in surprise, and said with delight, "Little Phrosso, are you one of us?"

"Of course I am," she answered impulsively.

"Tomorrow night I'm speaking in Philippoupolis. Do come. It's not so much that I want you to hear me again as that I shall be so happy to see you."

The Philippoupolis settlement was a good distance away on the other side of the Peneus River. But even if it were farther she would have gone. She would have gone to the other end of the city, to the end of the world. Hadn't he said he would be happy to see her?

And she went three and four times. And the first kiss came, the first surrender, the trips to Salonika and Athens. Paradise, the perfect paradise, had come down to earth—until one night in Athens, when Notis did not come back to their room. She found a note under the door. He was going abroad; he couldn't say where he was going; he was afraid he would be away a long time. He added a few tender words of love and vague hope. That was when the misery, the great misery began. A child was born. She had to work for a living, and everywhere in her jobs she was exposed to the crude advances of men. Then the baby died and a succession of black, hopeless days followed. She returned to Pteliona where she found comfort and understanding in her father's arms.

Now everything had quietened down. Even the hatred which had taken the place of love had passed and given place to indifference. The earthly paradise was gone, but in its place was tranquillity—even a kind of happiness. And, apart from that, there, across from Pteliona, there was the warmth of a friendship. But now? Now, if they were to leave, what would happen? Where would they end up? "It's in God's hands," she whispered. "The straws blown by the wind will settle wherever God wills."

She waited for him until very late. As soon as she saw him she understood. Mourayias came in with head bowed, rolled a cigarette and began to smoke in silence.

"It's a black day," he whispered after a while. "And he looks exactly like his grandfather. If he had a beard he'd be the spitting mage of the master. An accursed day!"

"What happened, father?" Phrosso asked.

He didn't answer. He bent lower and his wrinkled face looked more worried than usual.

"We're leaving, Phrosso," he said. "When the seeding's over we'll go. On Sunday I'll go into town for work. It's got to be this way."

II

Nikita walked swiftly, as though he were on some mission as though he were going toward a specific objective, toward something that was waiting for him. But in reality he was without purpose and didn't know where he was going.

After a frightful night, after the drink and sleeping pills which followed the arguments about his financial situation, after all this, the house was choking him. The old-fashioned furniture, those heavy curtains, the dark, dull colors that pervaded the house, all caused his heart to contract and filled him with a sudden panic. Without knowing why, as though driven by fate, he rushed out.

Perhaps a little light, a little movement, the green of the trees would clear his head of the noise and confusion which filled it, an take away the bitter taste from his parched mouth, and ease the contraction of his heart.

He walked fast and, looking at everything around him, tried to drive away the thoughts about his tangled finances. God! Why couldn't he get rid of these ugly thoughts. Ever since he had stepped on this wretched Thessalian soil, they had churned incessantly in his mind. Facts he had known nothing about until now, obstacles in the way of selling and transferring funds abroad, kept coming into his head and torturing him. But what was the use of thinking about all this? What could he do? The language he had spoken with these people was entirely foreign to him and seemed to belong to some other, unknown world.

"Whatever we get from Pteliona and from the stores in town will be placed in a blocked account. That's the law. It's explicit and it's strictly enforced." the lawyer had said.

"Why don't we register false sales prices, and take out the surplus secretly? Or why don't we try to sell the property to some Greek abroad who would give me most of the money outside Greece?" he had asked. "You'd lose everything and go to jail besides," the attorney had answered drily.

"Well, let's see," the banker had said. "Maybe something can be done."

"Nothing can be done," the lawyer had insisted coldly. "Besides, who would be willing to get mixed up in this sort of dirty business and compromise himself?"

"How can I go on living in Paris? Your precious laws don't take this into account," he had retorted angrily.

With an insulting look the attorney had given him an insulting answer.

"The Greek laws are interested only in how Greeks will live in poor Greece with Greek money."

Was he to go on thinking about all this? No, no! He must think of something else. He must look around. He would give his banker a power of attorney for the Larissa property and would go straight to Athens. There too he would have problems with his possessions, but at least he would be away from the mouldy narrow-mindedness of provincial people. He would find some comfort and variety, and more hopeful prospects, in the atmosphere of a big city. Here all he could get was fresh air and nothing else. He might as well enjoy it. He quickened his pace, driven by a need to get as far away as he could from that house—a haunted house it seemed to him, the source of his intolerable aggravation.

Ah! there was the wood, Pteliona, and the house and barns near the river. The other wood, the smaller one, Little Pteliona, was far away at the foot of the hill where St. Elias' Monastery stood. Here was one of the places of which Grandfather was so proud. What enormous trees, what a vast, dense green dome above his head!

Grandfather had bought the estate at the time when Greece took over Thessaly in 1881 and his first act had been to plant these two woods in the treeless steppe around Larissa. Niketa remembered his grandfather's words which had been repeated to him many times, for people considered them wise and impressive:

"I'll never live to see a real forest," he had said. "But I'm comforted by the thought that the greatest and most beautiful works are those that a man accomplishes with the knowledge that he is not destined to see them completed himself, but that future generations will."

Nikita's face took on a sarcastic expression.

"The elms fooled you, Grandfather," he said to himself. "They grew fast. You saw them become a forest, and so not even this work of yours was great and beautiful!

"Poor Grandfather," he went on after a while. "Everything fooled you. People said you would live to be a hundred because even death was afraid of you. But it seems that he was fooling you too. He was late in coming not because he was afraid of you, but so as to pull a fast one on you. And so you lived long enough not only to see your nurseling forest grow up, but your son become a murderer, and your eaglet-grandson a quiet little bird fluttering in an alien cage, and to see that Hellas of the Five Seas, as you called the imperial vision, was nothing but the whipping-boy of the Great Powers."

Jeering at his grandfather relieved him a little and he went forward with a lighter step. The autumn afternoon was beautiful in the wood, and as he walked he forgot his troubles. He lingered looking at the giant trees and at the Peneus as it rolled muddy and lazy at his side.

Suddenly, he stopped short. At first he thought he heard singing, then he was sure. Now he saw her. In a small clearing a girl was singing an aria from Madame Butterfly in Greek. Her voice was untrained, but it had an extraordinarily wide range with great possibilities, and it was unbelievably sweet and warm. Further away, leaning against a tree, hands in his pockets, stood a young man.

Nikita was amused by this scene and hid behind an elm. The young woman was tall and rather plump, and was dressed in an olive-colored raincoat and blue skirt. There was a grace and charm about her which he hardly expected to find among the peasantry of Thessaly. She seemed to have a pretty face. He couldn't see too clearly but her skin appeared to have the tawny dark glow of ripe wheat, her eyes large, her mouth full and generous. Her chestnut hair fell over her shoulders in a rich mass.

The man was quite different. He was dark, squarely built, and the lines of his face were sharp but well-balanced. His hair grew back from his forehead and was unkempt. He wore a grey turtle-neck sweater, and his general appearance gave the impression that he issued from the primal forces of mountain and plain.

The girl stopped singing. The couple exchanged a few words, and then the man took her in his arms and kissed her on the mouth and on her cheeks and neck. She received his kisses passively at first, then slowly lifted her arm and ruffled his hair with her hand; then with her two hands she drew his head towards her and kissed him on the mouth.

Now they were talking animatedly. Something annoyed the girl; she stamped her foot on the ground and he, with a sorrowful look, put his arm around her waist and led her to another part of the wood.

A strange couple, Nikita thought. He didn't like them. He was put off by their youth, by the strength that radiated from them, and he felt humiliated that he, the owner of the place, had hidden guiltily behind a tree, while they, happy and carefree, were kissing in the clearing as if the wood belonged to them, as if it were quite natural that they should stand there among the elms, proud and erect under the lofty trees.

But there was one consoling thought. They had quarreled. She had poisoned his happiness, and that strong, hardy man had looked at her in sorrow without answering her. He had bent before the whim of a woman.

''One can never escape from weakness and pain,'' he said to himself with a bitter smile. ''They're ever-present. Strength and joy are only a façade.''

He looked disconsolately toward the path leading to the town which the couple had taken; suddenly the man returned alone and Nikita hid again behind the tree.

The stranger didn't seem very cheerful, but there was nothing weak in his bearing. He was walking with big strides, stopping to cut away the thorns in his path. When he got to the river he leapt down the bank, got into a boat that was tied to the shore, and rowed across to the other side. There he climbed up toward the Agricultural College and passed out of sight.

Without any apparent reason, Nikita started to run in the opposite direction from which he had come. Behind him were the house, the other buildings of the property, and further away the town—all the ghosts of the past. And around him was the damp, sunless wood, no longer familiar for it filled him with fear. On the other side was the broad meadow free from shadows and terrors. He would run that way. Some fate, some unknown purpose seemed to be drawing him thither.

When he emerged from the wood he saw that his instinct had guided him well. He took a few deep breaths. He felt better—freer and once more in control of himself. The horizon around him was boundless. How beautiful the plain was! All green meadowland and plowed fields, stretching as far as the eye could see! And far away in the distance to the right was the incomparable slope of Mt. Olympus, an eternal concept and a wondrous sight—glory of Greece and the abode of the gods, ancient gods unsurpassed in beauty.

''And that too is a product of antiquity,'' he reflected scornfully. But, at the same moment, he was overwhelmed by the sight of those familiar, proud lines, sweeping majestically in one great curve from the plain to the heavens on high, to the clouds. Bewitched by the divine mountain, he stood motionless, avidly gazing at it

But what were those small black lines above the plain? They moved towards him an for a moment he thought it was an illusion, that his imagination was playing tricks on him and that messages were coming to him from the gods. But it was no illusion. These lines were real and moving. Now he saw clearly: they were birds flying south on their autumn migration. They flew onward in arrowlike formation, onward, majestically ever onwards. From time to time gusts of wind caused the arrowheads to waver, but straight away they recovered their perfect triangular form.

Gusts of wind indeed! What he saw, or rather what he sensed, were gentle caresses to these birds. Who knows from what distant northern lands they had started out, what mountains and ravines they had crossed, what rain and storms they had come through! They had their resting places, of course. But after each rest, up they went again high into the sky to face new storms as they winged their way over more peaks and valleys, pressing ever forward on their long, long journey across trackless paths—proud, strong, indomitable birds!

"Don't they ever get tired," he wondered. "Are there no weaklings among them?"

It seemed to him that he got his answer from the first group that approached. He could hear the beating of their wings, and their wild cries, cleaving the wind, seemed to say, "No, there are no weaklings among us. The weaklings die. And when they fall, we who are strong cry out at the top of our voices, 'Let them die! Those who are overcome don't deserve a roosting place in the reed-thicket. Let the victors go forward! Let the others die, die, die!'"

Other arrowheads of birds passed in quick succession with the same raucous, triumphant cries. Louder and louder they shrieked: "Let them die, let them die, let them die!"

It seemed to him that they did it on purpose, that some other-world spirit had sent them to make him understand that he too was one of those who had no right to a roosting place.

The birds came on in greater numbers and their shrieks mounted in an infernal crescendo: "Let them die! Let them die! Let them die!"

He shuddered, shrugged his shoulders instinctively and bent his head. From the moment he had arrived in Greece a thousand details, a thousand signs had made him feel that he was one of the weaklings, one of the defeated, one of those who could be "left to die."

He came out into the open plain, but here too the same indefinite, bitter anguish overtook him once more. He tossed his head back, thinking of all the people who talked about him and admired him in France, and he walked toward a field where three yoke of oxen were plowing. He might as well go and watch them. What the hell. Just because he had run up against some difficulties in a wild and uncivilized place, he was not going to give in to feelings of inferiority. That would be utterly unworthy of one who had won an established position in the most refined circles of the civilized West.

Lately he had been drinking a lot and taking too many sleeping tablets. He must find the strength to break this habit. It dulled his mind—it was dull now.

When he reached the field he stopped short. Wheat seeds were strewn along the furrows, and he wondered whether he had the right to step on them. All around him the seed was spread in his own fields, in those of the neighbors beyond, and perhaps in the fields belonging to the village in the distance and through the length and breadth of the whole plain. God! What patience was required for the earth to conceive and bear the wheat. What labor in opening up the land slowly with the plow—the whole land, all of it, so that not one inch should remain unturned; and then a second and perhaps a third tilling. And then the toil of walking over it from end to end casting the seed! And more toil yet, for the soil must be turned over again, all of it, for the seeds to sink in, and the farmer must walk slowly patiently, driving the plow into the womb of the earth.

He had forgotten this whole procedure or, rather, when he was a child, he had not paid attention to it so as to realize the amount of labor and courage demanded by this simple work.

The teams passed by him, Mourayias and the other farmers

greeted him, and he saw clearly how hard men and beasts toiled over this monotonous endeavor. He couldn't have stood it for an hour or even fifteen minutes.

The plows had opened up three new furrows in front of him and he smelled the odor of the damp, newly turned earth. What a strange odor. It wasn't really an odor; it seemed like some living essence which came out of the torn entrails of the earth. It was something that couldn't be defined. He felt that this exhalation was, as it were, a very tender expression of life, a mysterious message of life. Or was this a complete delusion? Was his dulled mind deceiving him under the influence of the alcohol and drugs of the preceding night?

His brain clouded. Without thinking, as if it were the most natural thing in the world, he crouched down and took up a handful of freshly turned earth. He raised it to his nose and smelled it. It was years since he had known that strange smell which seemed alive, seemed to give him a message full of mystery. It was a weak and delicate smell, yet so pervasive that it seemed to permeate his whole body, to penetrate to every cell. He threw away the earth he was holding and picked up a large lump with both his hands. He smelled it, breathed it in, absorbed its spirit, its life force, its message.

Then, without realizing how or why, he fell prone in the nearest furrow, pressed his head into the freshly turned earth, turned his face right and left—almost rubbed it—in the bottom of the furrow, and took several deep breaths with all his strength so as to absorb as much as he could of this unknown, newly-found life.

How long did he remain in this position? A few seconds? An hour? He could not tell. All he knew was that at some moment he heard steps nearby and got up. He shook himself, picked up his cap, and saw the teams at a standstill at the other end of the field. Mourayias hurried toward him with big strides.

"There's nothing the matter," he said. "A dizzy spell...I'm better..I'm all right now."

Mourayias looked at him straight in the face and a strange brightness shone in his eyes, a flame full of mystery and love.

"It was no dizzy spell, master" he said. "It spoke to you."

"What spoke to me?" the young man asked in surprise.

"The earth, master. The earth talks, but not to everyone. Blessed is the one who is able to hear."

* * * * *

Never in recent years had the teams turned from the fields so late at night. Phrosso had begun to get anxious, wondering whether anything had happened to her father or one of the men. But she forgot her worry the moment she saw her father coming through the door looking more alert and cheerful than he had for many a day.

"Phrosso," he said, "You don't have to fret any more. We're not leaving."

"Why father? Are you doing this for me? I had made up my mind about it and was thinking about getting a job at the Agricultural College or somewhere else."

"I'm not doing it for you. I've changed my mind. We're fine here. Come, let's eat."

III

Nikos Manoussis went into the bank, without greeting anyone, went straight to the manager's office. In a dark mood, he sat opposite his brother.

"For your information, I'm telling you that I've been having a lot of sarcastic comments about our Vlach affinities which I had begun to forget."

Vassili looked at him patiently.

"I wasn't intending to come to see you today, but a little while ago, just outside, the District Attorney made some annoying remarks, and I've come in to tell you what a ridiculous idea it was for you to organize that country dance the other night."

"It wasn't my idea, Nikos."

"You agreed to it, you contributed, and you insisted that the family go in full force."

"My dear boy," Vassili said with an embarrased smile, "You don't know my real reason for doing this. You are one of the cleverest fellows in Larissa and one of the best lawyers. But your youthful mistake in cultivating left-wing ideas, even though it was a long time ago, has stood in the way of your advancement. I thought it would be a good thing to win over the Vlach element in the community. It is dynamic, influential, and includes a great number of people.''

''In 1925 I was a candidate for election in Trikkala, not here. I chose Trikkala because there were many Vlachs there, and yet not a single one voted for me because they did not lean to the Left and because they lacked a sense of solidarity. Most of them no longer spoke Vlach in their homes. Do we ourselves, who were brought up with Vlach as our mother tongue, speak it to day?''

''But they do say 'I'm a Vlach' with pride. They have a clear sense of identity. And we should encourage them in order to draw them to us. As for the language, maybe we don't speak it ourselves, but there are tens of thousands that do.''

''Nonsense,'' said Nikos impatiently, ''There never was a Vlach conscience. And even if there was it was created quite ineffectually by the vast sums spent by Rumanian propaganda and because a few ragged beggars wanted to emigrate to a richer country. It's true that many speak the language, but it's only a miserable dialect that serves the primitive needs of undeveloped people. For any kind of civilized communcation and activity a deficient language is useless. It is only the intelligentsia that has any influence in any social group and can create sectarian or even national movements. The intelligentsia of the Vlachs was always, and still is, Greek in language and in sentiment.''

Don't kid yourself, my dear fellow,'' he continued. ''This is a lot of romantic stuff invented by people who are as Greek as all the rest, but who, just because they come from mountain and sheep-farming districts, occasionally wear goat herd's shoes, carry a shepherd's crook, and pretend they are Vlachs. Now, I ask you, don't these very same men boast with pride that they are the compatriots of Coletti, of Lambros, of Crystallis and of so many others who were fanatical Greeks?''

At the mention of these names Vassili Manoussis's expression changed.

''By the way, I want to talk to you about young Coletti,'' he said with sudden animation. And thus the conversation turned to a subject which had preoccupied the banker for the last few days.

"Young Coletti," he said to his brother," may know a lot about poetry, but he knows nothing about finance and law. To get money out of the country he would be willing to sell his property at a third or even a fourth of its real value. And the worst is that I have promised to help him."

His brother quickly retorted, "Couldn't we find a way of buying the stores he owns in the center of the business district? We have some cash and we could borrow the rest, and there must be some means of getting the money out. It's the best real estate in Larissa."

"I know that, and although it's difficult I think it could be arranged. Did you forget that the Governor of the bank is related to him, and if the old bastard learns that we have bought the property, or even that I had any part in a bad sale of such valuable family possessions, I stand a good chance of losing my job."

"He can't fire you so easily. He might transfer you elsewhere. But once you've got hold of the kind of real estate you can afford to retire. Besides, with your years of service, you'll be getting a good pension."

A cunning smile came to Vassili Manoussis' lips.

"I've thought of something better," he said.

Then he unfolded his master plan. It seemed to him that Coletti was in a daze. It was clear that everyone and everything was strange to him and annoyed him. What if he got to know Katie? He wasn't able to leave for France since he hadn't any longer the means to live abroad. In his exasperation and loneliness he would seek comfort in Katie and he might fall in love with her. That would be a marriage suited to her, the kind of marriage she herself dreamed of. She must be made to realize its advantages and then, she could be trusted to do the rest, herself.

"She didn't do very well with the other fine marriages she went after in Athens," Nikos said. "You live in a dream world; You have a habit of mistaking your desires for reality. In a few days the musty atmosphere of the provinces and the boredom of Pteliona will drive our poet away from Larissa. And because he won't be able to go abroad, he'll go to Athens where a superficial and empty-headed society will acclaim him with a show of enthusiasm, with parties and women, and will make him forget not only Larissa and one of its charming girls, but maybe even Paris. Besides I believe that Katie is cooking up something with that professor at the Agricultural College."

"But there's no possible comparison. You're talking nonsense, Nikos."

"There may be no comparison, but a little while ago I saw Katie crossing the bridge and hurry out to the wood at Pteliona. I know she meets him there. So forget your dreams, Vassili. Can you get your hands on the stores? That's the burning question. Life does not wait for dreams to come true. It's implacable and can only be mastered by force and money. And both depend on the capacity to exploit a good thing when it turns up. Years ago we missed the bus because Greece then was not drawn into Communism. If it had been, with my joining the party when I was young, you'd see where I'd have been by now. But let's not waste time on lost dreams now and miss a chance that leads to money. Are you listening to me? In our small world such an opportunity may never come again. Why are you looking at me in that distant manner? Do you disagree with me?"

Vassili Manoussis did not disagree. On the contrary, he found his brother's words reasonable and, above all, he concurred that a rare opportunity of speedy enrichment presented itself. There was a different reason for the strange look he gave his brother. Something Nikos had said about Katie had suddenly aroused his dormant suspicions and he was startled.

"I don't disagree, Nikos," he said. "I was thining of something else. You said she was going toward the wood. Do you really think she meets the teacher there?"

"I have reasons to be quite certain she does."

"So, this summer when she wanted to visit her friends in Athens, was this in her mind? Do you think her long walks and bicycle rides are excuses to meet him?"

"Her trip to Athens had nothing to do with last year's episode. She told us that and I believe her." But the so-called long walks are a cover for meetings with Alexis Stournaris. Of this I'm certain. Have you noticed that these walks always take place at dusk?"

"That's because it's hot in the daytime."

"The heat let up long ago. It's November now."

"Well then, Nikos, what happens at these meetings?"

Nikos didn't answer.

"And there's something more," Vassili, went on. "This is the first time I mention it. I haven't had the courage to say it even to myself. At times when she curls up with that strange languor in the armchair, or talks vaguely about sex and sensuality, or reads us some poetry, I think,..I think,..well, not quite, but I fight off a rising thought that maybe..."

"I've thought of that too, Vassili. Her whole manner has changed. Even her body seems to speak. Those summers at Kifissia and Phaleron have done something to her."

"But that's terrible! It's impossible!" Vassili Manoussis cried. He got up from his desk. "And that's what may be happening now, over there in the wood with that man, while we're talking here."

He sank into his armchair, leaned against his desk and pressed his hand to his forehead.

"My God, my God," he whispered, "why do you torture me so? What shall I do? What can I do?" Rousing himself violently he banged his hands on the desk. "No," he cried, "my Katie couldn't do this to me. Nikos, we've got to find out exactly what's going on so that we can decide what to do."

"What do you think you can do? Are you going to beat her? Or do you propose to send one of them into exile?"

"I'm in no mood for jokes or arguments. If what I'm afraid of turns out to be true, I'll put my foot down and make her marry Stournaris as soon as possible. That's why I need to know what's going on. Listen, Nikos. You talk to her about all kinds of things. See her and try to find out."

"I'll try. If necessary I'll speak to her openly, but I think I can approach her indirectly. But let me tell you something. You talk like any provincial Greek father, and I confess that I too should prefer our suspicions to prove unfounded but, if they should turn out to be correct, don't imagine that a terrible catastrophe has happened to her. This is 1939. Times have changed. For our generation more than for any other. People no longer think and behave as they did in the past. If you want proof, take the case which faces us. Others share our suspicions about Katie; perhaps all of Larissa does. And yet you know that young men of the best familes have asked for her hand. We live in an age when new values are replacing the old ones, when the taboos of the past are fading away, when people say one thing and do another and, above all, when the new ideas have not crystallized. Everybody pretends he believes in the old superstitions but behaves according to the new ways; they do what they please. But don't be over-anxious. And I'll tell you something else; if what we're afraid of about Katie is true, then she is more likely to hook our wealthy and experienced friend Coletti.

* * * * *

She got up to greet him and settled back in her armchair.

Her gait, her habit of curling up in a corner like a voluptuous cat, her silence after the first few formal words—all this gave the impression that she was deliberately trying to create an atmosphere. But it wasn't so, because for him she had never tried to put on charm or play at being coy. Her attitude was completely natural and this was part of her strength.

"I've interrupted your reading," he said, as he saw her put down a book. "What are you reading?"

"Oh, nothing. An insignificant book which one of my friends in Athens sent me. It has had a great success in London and is now being widely read in Europe. Yet it's only a commonplace social novel without any depth, without a message, and not too well written at that. But the plot is interesting."

He gave her a friendly smile.

"Do you mean to tell me that we here in the sticks understand it, while in Athens, London and everywhere else people are incompetent to judge it?"

"That's what I'm saying, uncle Nikos. But I don't give Larissa credit for that. Only you and I who are suffocating in this dreary place."

He stared in front of him with a hard look. "We really are suffocating. I understand you so well."

"What are we to do, uncle? We're still young but the years go by and I shudder at the prospect of spending our lives buried in this frightful atmosphere. What can we do about it?"

"Nothing. We started in a swamp and we want to reach the peak. Such an achievement depends on exceptional opportunities—opportunities to be exploited in time and to the full. Where and how are such opportunities to be found?"

A strange gleam came into her eyes.

"War has broken out," she said, "and war brings upheaval. What changes do you think it will bring to Greece and how will they affect our life?"

"You're much younger than I and a very unusual person; you could look forward to certain prospects. There are none for me and, what's more, I'm afraid that because of me the war may wipe out your prospects too."

She was surprised and told him that he had connected totally unrelated things.

"Quite the contrary. The most important recent events—one to which the world has not paid sufficient attention—was the signing of the Ribbentrop-Molotov agreement between Germany and Russia. One of two things is certain: either Russia is very weak, has no alternative, and is playing for time, or she is very strong and aims by this agreement to hurl the Germans against the British and French and to tear them to pieces when they are all involved in destroying each other.

"But they have signed a mutual non-aggression pact."

"According to the principles laid down and enforced by Lenin, agreements are signed only to be broken if and when necessary. I'll explain this to you some other time. But to return to my argument. If I've judged matters rightly, in a few years one of two things will happen: either Hitler will prevail if Russia is weak, or Stalin will prevail if she is strong. We, a small, insignificant fringe country, will bow to the powers which rule Europe. And in either case I'm lost. To the extreme Left I'm the traitor who deserted it, and to the extreme Right I'm the suspect who was once a Party member. I know that I played my game and lost. What I didn't know until now was that that game could have permanent consequences for myself and the few people I love."

An awkward silence followed. She gave him a look which contained new fear, censure, and compassion.

"But, uncle Nikos, you have so many fine qualities. What a pity! Often when I think of your lot and mine, I feel I could scream and smash everything round me. It is as if we were omnipotent, and as if a host of weak and stupid dwarfs had bound our hands and feet with heavy chains."

"Never mind me. It's you we have to talk about. That's why I asked to come an see you alone. Well, what are your plans? You won't be young for ever, you know."

She answered him in fast, hard tones:

"What do you expect me to do? I tried in every way I know for a 'brilliant' marriage and failed. Then I wanted to study for the opera abroad or even in Athens. Everyone said I had the greatest chances of success. But all of you stopped me. "An actress," you said, "what a disaster."

"I didn't say that."

"You weren't quite so outspoken, but the others. My mother went so far as to curse me on her deathbed if I did this. And I, young and inexperienced, was paralyzed by the ridiculous superstition of a mother's curse. So my career was ruined. I should have left home, taken a job and studied."

Her eyes filled with tears and she asked him angrily, "So now you ask me what my plans are. What do you want me to say? What can I do now?"

"You're twenty-seven now. Make up your mind and get married."

"Do you really see me as the wife of some lawyer or doctor in Larissa, as father would like me to be? Can you imagine me fussing over a brood of children and spending every day, all day, in the kitchen, doing the washing, going to the market, gossiping with the neighbors?"

"Kitchen and children and all the rest are not inevitable."

"Of course they are, for that's the kind of lord and master I'd get. That's the sort of wife he'd expect to get and, once the honeymoon is over, that's the kind of wife he'd require. He wouldn't know any better, for around him his brothers and his cousins and his friends would all have the same image of a wife. In other words, he would draw me down into the swamp of the provinces. But I would explode, because swamps don't fit into my pattern of life. As things stand now, at least I'm free, I do what I want, sometimes I take a trip, I often rebel, but at least I'm not suffocated day and night. Occasionally I feel oppressed, but at least I'm free and independent. I'm not tied down to a bunch of insufferable people. If one has to suffocate, it's better to suffocate alone."

He tried to calm her and to reason with her. He agreed with her on many points but said that as time went by things would become more difficult; he could not see how her dreams could be realized and insisted that marriage was the best solution for her.

"Since we are speaking of marriage, what about Stournaris? I have a notion that you like him."

"Alexis," she said pensively. "Alexis is an interesting man. He's handsome and strong and very much in love with me. But he would be unbearable as a husband. He's very poor, but it doesn't bother him. In fact he's not in the least conscious of his poverty. He thinks of himself as very rich, for to him other things constitute wealth. He has deeply rooted convictions which belong in another age. As a friend he's wonderful—better than any. As a husband he'd be terrible."

"Darling Katie, I'm going to ask an indiscreet question which no provincial uncle would ever dare to ask of his niece."

He stopped, and she remained silent. Without making a movement, she lifted up her eyes which, until then, she had kept stubbornly fixed on the floor, and looked at him with defensive insistence.

He broke the silence.

"My little Katie, tell me, how far did you go with Stournaris, with others, in Athens?"

"That's a question which no one—neither an uncle in the provinces nor the most sophisticated uncle in the world—would ever put to his niece." And after a short silence she added somewhat aggressively, "And you have no right to ask it. You've no right to ask a girl something so personal."

"So you refuse to tell me?"

"Yes."

"You realize that your refusal gives rise to a particular interpretation?"

"Uncle Nikos, you're making a great mistake. Just as I

would hate to think that you were sure that your facile interpretation was right, I should equally hate you to know that I'd never been touched. This is my business, nobody else's."

"What about you father?"

"With regard to you and me, my father is like the broody hen who has sat on eagle's eggs and gets flustered and scared when she sees that she has hatched eaglets. And the eagles pity her because they've come forth from her warmth, but they can't turn into chickens. If he's asked you anything, tell him what you want, but don't interfere anymore."

Flushed with anger, she stood up and added with some venom, "Have I ever questioned you about your relations with Phoula? All the town is talking about it, as you must surely know."

For a moment Nikos was on the verge of losing his temper, but he controlled himself. In fact, he admired the girl's spirit. At that moment, more than ever before, he saw her as flesh of his flesh. She seemed to him to be his daughter rather than the daughter of poor old Vassili.

"If fate had been good to us, what couldn't we have accomplished together! Come, sit down. I haven't come here to torture you. I've got something else to say to you."

She sat down again without a word. She looked at him, a defensive expression on her face. But at her uncle's first words, she relaxed and listened with interest.

"I've got to tell you that all of a sudden there's a splendid opportunity for you..."

"You wouldn't be the man I've always considered you if you hadn't mentioned it to me."

"And you wouldn't have been my niece if you hadn't thought of it already." At first I considered it very unlikely, but on thinking it over I believe that it's a real opportunity."

"I hear he wants to leave for Paris soon."

"He may want to, but he won't be able to go. The Governor of the Bank in Athens has blocked his income, just as his rents have been blocked here. He gets nothing out of Pteliona. If he sells, I don't see how he'll manage to get his money out; in any case it would only be chicken feed. So what will he live on in

Paris?'' And sooner or later Paris will be bombed. Here, on the other hand, he can have all the money he wants, because if it's to be spent in Greece, the embargo on his accounts will be lifted. As for the war, it's likely that we shall be just spectators, and in the end we shall peacefully and quietly submit to the victor. It's logical to assume that he's here for the duration—for two, three years or even more.''

He was silent and noticed that Katie was smiling with an air of satisfaction and gratitude.

''The danger lies elsewhere,'' Nikos Manoussis continued. ''He won't be able to stay in Larissa. He'll go to Athens where the Athenians will go out of their way to smother him with their attentions. He may stay there and then you won't be able to reach him.''

She answered him simply, as if they were discussing some ordinary topic.

''You're quite right. That's where the danger lies. And it's a pity, because with him I could make my dreams come true.''

''Not all of them because, while you're a restless and energetic young girl, there's a side of you which is all woman. But, in any case, he can offer you much more than all the doctors, lawyers and professors of agriculture in Larissa. Think what you can do, lay your plans, and if I can help you let me know.''

He went out leaving her deep in thought. Katie curled up again in the armchair and remained there motionless for an hour. Her face was almost expressionless. It would have been difficult for anyone to guess whether it showed bitterness or joy, pessimism or hope. But it was obvious that her brain was working, that she was restless— was devising ways and means.

At last she rose and walked swiftly to her bedroom. She sat down before her mirror and, with deft motions, began changing her coiffure, trying out one style after another. She carefully studied the changes in expression and personality which each new hair-do produced, giving her the appearance now of an old-world romantic girl, and now of an ultra-modern popular novel heroine. At last she let her silken hair fall loose over her shoulders and became once more her everyday self. But the mirror no longer smiled back at her. The pretty image it reflected was that of a bored and unsettled young woman; in it there was perhaps an added touch of hatred.

As she stood up her eye fell on the ikon of the Holy Virgin. Alexis had given it to her on the day he proposed. He had been very insistent. How closely he had held her to him. She remembered the thought running through her mind at the time: 'He's going to crush me, this man of steel with so much determination, such a passionate nature.' And under the delicious wave of pleasure which came over her she'd almost wished he would.

"But he's so poor!" she whispered to herself hopelessly, "and so peculiar and unsocial."

She remained wrapped in her thoughts for a few instants. Then she crossed the room obstinately, locked the door with a quick gesture, and began pacing back and forth nervously striking everything that stood in her path. She wanted to find release in tears, but when she realized that the tears wouldn't come, she threw herself on the bed and began to claw and bit the pillows furiously.

IV

That afternoon at the Agricultural College, Alexis Stournaris usually so composed and orderly, collected his papers somewhat untidily, finished his business in a hurry, and started off in the direction of the stable. The days were growing shorter and he would have to hurry if he was going to take a walk in the meadows and go over to Pteliona. Phrosso was expecting him and he was going to meet the newly arrived grandson of his benefactor.

He went into the stable. As soon as the horses saw him they began to neigh and frisk and paw the ground with their hoofs. It was not just an affectionate greeting. The animals knew he was going out for a long ride and each wanted to be chosen.

They were well-fed, unruly steeds, and few had the courage to come near them in their iron stalls; fewer still dared to ride them. They knew Alexis, who was the only one that took them out regularly for long rides, free of all restraint. With restive impatience each strained to be chosen.

"Quiet now!" he called to them. "Everyone gets his turn. This evening I'm taking Pegasus." Raising his voice he called his favorite horse:

"Come, Pegasus, come along now!"

The great grey horse, its nervous body trembling with joy, responded with a loud whinny.

Every afternoon, as soon as his work was done, Alexis Stournaris hurried in the stables, chose a horse, and rode it out on the plain. The animal felt his master firmly seated upon his back, fearless in the face of obstacles, a sure and determined guide over rough ground, and broke into a gallop, stretching out his powerful body, and rushing forward at top speed until his strength ran out. Alexis never wearied of riding. It was his passion—a kind of intoxication.

A quick turn, a vigorous jump over a hurdle, a fast gallop or a dancing trot..Between his knees he felt the horse's strong breathing as it marked the rhythm of the animal's great lungs under a breast taut as a steel spring. He was aware of the horse's every movement, every quivering reaction, and his own firm and competent riding. Wonderful thoughts that flashed through his mind as he rushed along; thoughts of demigods, of the lion-hearted heroes of the Revolution, of hopes and dreams for the country. It was a strange intoxication with its own peculiar flavor which came over Alexis only when he was on horseback. At times, he said, a "centaur feeling" enveloped him.

He wore a pair of old breeches and rode bareback. He clung tightly to the horse and demanded all it could give—lightning speed, sudden swift turns at right angles, dangerous jumps, and an occasional bold response to the rein which caused it to rear up on its hind legs. At such moments his mind was empty of thoughts and he wished it so.

He wanted his mind to be completely vacant, so that he might become a primitive man, almost an animal, governed by instinct alone and by nothing else. Governed by the instinct for speed, uncontrolled speed, the double beast, the centaur, was measured against the immensity of the plain and merged with the vastness of Nature itself.

This emptying of the mind, this unreserved and complete return to primitive instinct was a kind of rebirth. It was a deliverance from man-made thoughts and cares and a return to all that Nature alone had created.

Whenever he experienced that deliverance, he felt afterwards that he could face everything with greater strength and calmness. That is why from time to time, quite suddenly and without any definite reason, he sought to become a centaur and, fusing his body with that of his horse, let himself fly across the plain.

People stopped to admire this fearless and impetuous rider flashing across the plain, and their thoughts naturally went to the famous Thessalian cavalry of antiquity, to those men who, with their horses, leaped over ravines and rivers, to men of other days who instead of being weighed down by fears, subdued nature and beasts. On the days when he had this feeling he usually rode to the monastary of St. Elias for a talk with Father Modestos about Greek history.

This was the life which Alexis Stournaris enjoyed. His work in the classroom, the laboratories, and the fields gave him many satisfactions. It was a quiet life but one that was pleasant and full of purpose, since his mission was to educate young people and to improve the soil. And, seeing that he was allowed complete independence in his work, and could take whatever initiative he chose, he was a hard, passionate and tireless worker.

In the evenings, in his rooms at the College, books took him on long journeys through unknown worlds and to provocative intellectual spheres. And as if this were not enough, the College possessed for his moments of leisure the means of satisfying his passion—horses such as no one in Greece owned, and possibly only a few of the princes of wealth in Europe. His health was good, he had a purpose in life, he was of a cheerful disposition, his life was full and pleasant. He had everything. What more could he desire?

Now, however, everything around him was enveloped in a new light—a light that was sometimes bright and powerful, at other times dull, so dull that everything seemed different. New meanings attached to things. Values which had seemed unshakeable and well ordained, seemed to be falling out of place. They had become mixed up into an amorphous mass before one face which dominated everything.

Women had never before disturbed Alexis' life; they had

merely been the object of prosaic and inconsequential physical experiences. But now, recently, there was one woman. Alexis was often struck with terror! Here was a whole life, settled and full of serious purpose, and it was being disrupted. What was the force that could bring about so great a change?

Was it a disease of the body, a disease of the mind, astral magnetism, the will of God? It must be something definite. Simply because people said the phenomenon was inexplicable, or because simpletons simplified it, it didn't mean that it didn't exist. It did exist. He saw it; he was living it.

* * * * *

Nikita Colletti had gone up into the tower of the mansion. It was a small room, above the roof, with windows on all sides, built by Grandfather so that he could have a better view of the plain, Mt. Olympus. Pteliona, the Agricultural College and the town. Nikita used to go there when he was a child, not to look at high mountains and broad meadows, but to hide from the others, to be alone and to give himself over undisturbed to his small, childish dreams. Now, bored, weary and without purpose, he went up to pass the time of day, to take another look at his old refuge, and to see the countryside around him.

It was afternoon. One of the first things he saw on the far horizon were the long arrows of migratory birds. Big white clouds in variegated formations floated down from Olympus and Kissavo and moved slowly across the sky. Among them one could see the sharp, angular formations of the birds, flying hurriedly, as if they were trying to conquer as great a distance as possible before nightfall. When the moving black line happened to stand out before a low cloud, one saw clearly how the big birds advanced faster and the line fluctuated as it was struck by sudden gusts of wind. There was grandeur and meaning to the scene.

But today something different and very strange was happening. A cloud of dust rose from the ground and followed the birds. It seemed to be chasing one arrow after another. At the head of the dust-cloud was a black spot which was raising the dust.

He took the largest binoculars in the tower, cleaned them

and took a good look. He saw something unusual. Down in the plain a horseman followed the course of the birds in an extraordinary manner. There he was! He had just passed the flock of birds he was chasing. The horse came to a halt and reared up on its hind legs two or three times, beating the air with its forelegs in a kind of dance; then it shot forward again to pursue another flock of birds going in another direction. What lightning speed! What a horse!

The rider had bent over the outstretched neck of the horse, the animal's legs gathered themselves and shot out again like lightning in rhythmic motion, as man and beast, in one swift harmonious surge, advanced as one body leaving in their wake a long, trailing cloud of dust.

See! Once again they got ahead of the flock of birds above them, and again the horse stopped, reared up on its hind legs, dancing and tossing its head, and then again started off tempestuously in another direction, galloping at headlong speed.

Why was this man chasing wild birds in such an extraordinary manner? He wasn't shooting them. It was quite evident that he had no gun. What was the meaning of this impassioned hunt?

It must be some madman...or perhaps the man was playing a game.

No, this was not a game, nor was it madness. Nikita understood. Instinctively it came to him. It was the response of the mighty of the earth to the mighty of the heavens.

Yesterday he himself—he was more consciously aware of it now—had been disturbed by the grandeur of the scene, had bowed his head, had felt something akin to humiliation.

Not only did the horseman not feel humiliated, but he provoked and conquered the conquerors of storm and mountain. And the horseman's provocation and victory humiliated Nikita once again and even more deeply.

He was amazed! He was aware of his pessimism, his permanent state of disillusionment—of his weakness. This he accepted as part of his nature which he couldn't change. It had never troubled him. But at this instant he felt that it humiliated him in his own eyes and now he understood that from the time he had arrived in Greece he had sensed at moments a certain diminution in himself.

How very strange! Could it be that in the inner recesses of his soul he fostered unknown ambitions for power? Otherwise why this disagreeable sense of diminution? A thought to be dismissed with ridicule and irony.

He lowered the binoculars and continued to watch the rider until he saw him take the road to Pteliona. He looked through the lenses again and saw the man advancing at a graceful trot; then he recognized him. It was the man he had seen yesterday in the forest with the girl.

He was shaken by a sudden and violent reaction of hatred against that man. And yet there was no reason for this. Or if there was, it was the kind of reason which influenced other sorts of men—not a refined and weary man like him, who looked upon his weakness, provided that it was protected by luxury and ease, as a natural and pleasant refuge.

What was the matter? Was it a reaction to the practical difficulties that beset him, or to the behavior of certain people who according to his standards of fastidious politeness, were very vulgar. Was it because for the first time he was coming into direct contact with strong, primitive people? Or could it be—according to vague new theories—that the environment of the neighboring mountain of Epirus and the Thessalian plain continued to affect his consciousness because it derived from so many generations born and bred there?

He shuddered at the idea that there might be any likelihood of truth in his last thought. It would mean that his cells were related to those of his grandfather, and that nothing could cause them to respond in a manner that was Greek.

Such a possibility was distasteful to his feelings and to his mind. He loathed and detested the idea. He didn't belong to this miserable country. No, he certainly didn't belong here.

* * * * *

Alexis Stournaris handed his horse in at the stable, have orders to have it rubbed down and fed, and went over to Mourayias' cottage.

"I haven't come to stay, I've got to see Coletti later." he said to Phrosso. "I'm a mess. Give me a brush and tell me where I can go to wash up."

"You've churned up the whole plain," she answered, laughing, "Which horse did you ride?"

"Pegasus."

He's a fine beast. Come to the head of the stairs and I'll brush you down myself."

"Yes, I'll come to the stairs, otherwise I'll fill the living-room with dust. But I'll brush myself."

"Certainly not. That's woman's work. And you know I'll enjoy doing it for you."

A little later they were sitting at the table with two cups of coffee in front of them.

"I got your message and I'm here," he said.

"I'm sorry I wasn't able to get in touch with you to tell you that it wasn't necessary for you to come after all."

She told him about her father's behavior. They discussed the matter for a while, and talked about Pteliona's new master who had made a very poor impression on Phrosso, and then she said, "Well, you've wasted your time coming."

"Aren't you ashamed to say such things? We're having coffee together; what better reason could I have for coming?"

"I see you've learned to pay compliments," she mocked him.

"Yes, compliments are my specialty," he said laughing. "But I never pay you compliments, little Phrosso. I feel that if I had a sister I wouldn't love her more than I do you. And I want you to know that your troubles worried me more than they worried old Mourayias himself."

"I know it, and I'm grateful," she said. "Our friendship is a great comfort to me. I'm alright now. I can even say that I'm happy. I lead a calm life, I adore the old man, and what with the English lessons I give to a few high school girls, and my knitting, I earn enough pocket money to buy books; I even bought a radio. What more do I want?"

She smiled at him. "I have no ambitions. All I ask for is quiet and a little comfort. Have you got a good radio? I wonder how many people in Greece have one?" And with a pensive look she repeated, ''I wonder how many people in Greece possess a radio.''

With equal seriousness he replied, ''Phrosso, you're either trying to fool me or you're talking nonsense. You're still very young; you're an attractive woman and you've got brains; it's not possible that the things you've mentioned could fill your life. We've only disscussed these things once, but we must discuss them again some time. I'll tell you what I think with complete frankness. Notis was a good, strong fellow; he was in love with you, but he went astray. If he hasn't given any signs of life, if you have no hope of finding him again or of finding in him the sort of man he was, then you must find someone with whom to build a family. That's the only way in which you'll have a full life.''

He followed her with his eyes as she turned to the window and watched the clouds scudding across the sky. What a good girl she was! How pleasant and sensible. He noticed her upright, somewhat fulsome form, the healthy flush of youth in her cheeks, her full lips which, when she smiled, revealed her strong white teeth, her large brown eyes, the braids of her hair plaited into a crown above her forehead, and he realized that Phrosso was not ony pretty. She had a natural air of grace and authority about her.

After a while, she broke the silence.

''Don't speak about Notis, Alexis. You know as well as I do that he can't change. A man, who is willing to accept that the orders of the Party should overrule love and family ties and everything, is not a man with whom I could be close again, even if he were to come begging. Anyone who accepts that others should make decisions for him about the most intimate, the sweetest things in life must be suffering from a grave and incurable illness. I saw this illness in Notis, and lived with it, Alexis, so don't talk to me about him any more. As for making cold, calculating plans to marry some other man—I couldn't ever do that. It is a very serious thing to take a man to one's bed, to share everything with him—the very breath of life—to live with him continuously, forever, to bear children. Such matters are not decided by cold logic. They're decided by all one's being or perhaps by fate.''

"By fate! Did you say fate? Am I hearing right?"

"Yes, you heard all right."

"That's a new one! What's the matter with you today?"

"Nothing's the matter with me. I've thought about all this for a long time."

"You must be crazy. Are we really to believe that decisions are made for us by some unknown power? Of course not. We govern ourselves and determine our actions."

She answered him softly, with a far-away look in her eyes:

"Many of our actions we do decide for ourselves, but not all Just think a moment. Consider instinct. Doesn't it seem to you that it is governed by fate? And there are so many other unknown things within us. I must confess the more I live and the more I think the more I believe that we do not control the tangled mysteries of our nature. They are controlled by something else about which we know nothing. And when that 'something else' seizes hold of the reins, we follow its course and not that which we would have normally chosen. . ."

This time he didn't answer her, for his thoughts went to his confusion over his own emotional disturbance, his own private illness.

Sensing his need, Phrosso instinctively felt that her words had affected him and, in a more direct tone of voice, she continued.

"Until now you weren't aware of it, were you? But now you too have discovered it, and I'm afraid for you, Alexis."

"Afraid for me? Why?"

"She's extremely clever and very beautiful, but she's a strange girl. Notis never would tell me the truth about her, but I'm under the impression that because of her, and reacting against her bourgeois mentality, he sought an escape in the opposite direction."

He stared at her in amazement and asked sharply, "She knew Notis? Was there ever anything between them? Why didn't you tell me?"

"We never happened to speak about her," she replied. "They were very much in love from the time they were in high school, but I never knew the details. I only know that the affair lasted two or three years. They broke up because she didn't want to get married and Notis, with his stubborn character, refused to see her again. And then I came along, his other great love from whom he parted also, but for other reasons."

A heavy silence fell between them; then Alexis rose. He was thoughtful but soon recovered his lively expression.

"Well, we'll have to talk this over again, little Phrosso, when we've got more time. Now I must see Coletti. Will you let him know that I'm here?"

Alexis was somewhat startled when Nikita sent word that he would come down into the garden to see him; he had expected to have a long and cordial conversation with him. He didn't at all suspect the cold reception that was awaiting him. Nikita Coletti, looking like a foreign mannequin in his deliberately casual clothes, stood before him and asked him, with marked indifference, why he wanted to see him.

He wasn't a bad looking fellow: tall, broad-shouldered, with a long face and high forehead. He had black eyes, a determined chin, and rather full lips. He looked very tired. Everything about him exuded a kind of fatigue. His shoulders were hunched forward, his face was lined and pale, there were lines under his eyes, and his wide mouth drooped in a bitter curve. Alexis thought he looked ill, bored and unfriendly. He didn't answer him at once. For a moment Alexis Stournaris felt like turning his back on him and walking away. What a deterioration, he thought. Was it possible that this miserable creature was the grandson of a man who for fifty years had fired the imagination of the Greeks, that grand, upstanding old man whom Alexis remembered as a kind of legendary hero with his flowing white beard, his eagle's eye, and that deep, warm voice.

Dusk was beginning to fall, casting its gloom over the clumps of trees, and the dampness of the autumn dew made itself felt. Alexis pulled himself together and introduced himself.

"Your grandfather was very kind to my family. He took great care of me from the time I was a little boy, and provided for my education in his will. The province owes him a great deal. I came to tell you that if I can do anything to help you with the farming of Pteliona, I am entirely at your disposal."

"Prayers should be offered up for the repose of my grandfather's soul, and speeches should be made in honor of his memory," Nikita Coletti replied. "As for me, I have lived for so many years among people who didn't know him, didn't know him at all, that I have come to feel that friendship for me has nothing whatsoever to do with honoring my grandfather's memory."

These words went through Alexis like a knife. It was not so much the arrogance that hurt; he hardly noticed that. But he remembered something else. Yesterday in the forest, after the singing that had so enchanted him, after that last passionate kiss, Katie had told him that young Coletti had arrived, and he had said that the whole community were so indebted to the family that everyone should offer to help him. And Katie had stamped her foot and said to him, "If we have obligations, then let's have prayers said for the old man and hold ceremonies to honor his memory."

The same words, the same temper, the same mean reactions as those of this degenerate poet of decadence. Yet surely his suggestion deserved warmer consideration. It occured to him that maybe, without meaning to, he had given Coletti the wrong reasons for his visit and that the offense he seemed to have taken was genuine. With this possibility in mind he tried again:

"I've come to offer you my services in all sincerity," he said.

"I suppose you have," Coletti replied in the same hostile manner. "But in this case help is superfluous. I live permanently abroad and, with the crooked dealing that prevails in this country, it's impossible to hope for good management of the Pteliona ranch.

Alexis' face flushed with anger. He saw that Coletti was determined to insult him. In his mind the Old Man's image faded suddenly, for in front of him he saw a man who had nothing whatsoever in common with him.

"You've been away from Greece a long time," he said raising his voice. "Too long to be able to know what prevails here. I'm sorry I've wasted my time. Good night."

That evening, on the return trip, Pegasus didn't run as briskly as usual. The loyal and noble beast was bewildered by the sudden jerks on the bit, the sharp strokes from a stick which his master carried for the first time, by the heavy weight of the rider slumped on his back. Pegasus imagined that he was somehow at fault; maybe he had not performed adequately in the afternoon's bird-chase. So he trotted quickly but dejectedly, with neck outstretched, looking neither to the right nor to the left, dispirited and listless as night closed in dark and gloomy.

V

The countryfolk of Theasaly looked upon the Monastery of St. Elias as a flame which warmed their hearts in the freezing wintertime, and as a cool spring which refreshed them in the burning heat of summer. For them it was not so much a venerable pile of buildings as an idea—an inspiration.

During the countless years—the centuries—that had passed over it, there had been times when the freezing cold and the scorching heat had been unbearable, and the flame had gone out and the spring run dry. But even when St. Elias had happened to be little more than a ruin, it still stood against the horizon, a symbol of faith and worship, of holy protection, of immortality. For the monastery never died. It always rose again on the top of the hill, filled with new life, spreading comfort and hope.

Some said it came to life again because of a miracle; others that it was revivified by the love of the faithful which never waned. But no one could say when it was built nor how many times it had been resurrected. Many had tried to investigate its history, but the Archdiocese in Larissa and the Patriarchate at Constantinople had been burned down several times, and no records were found to reveal the age and history of the monastery.

The only thing that everyone knew was that over the centuries one generation told the next that the monastery was of great antiquity, that it reached back to the days when the Byzantine Empire ruled the land and even to classical times since, at the same spot, there had once been a temple, with marble columns, and there had been winding underground passages—labyrinths of pagan worship. It was not the memory of man alone that bore witness to these beliefs; the stones themselves were silent witnesses, because one could see, embedded in the walls, marble slabs on which lines, circles, birds, and strange beasts were engraved.

The last resurrection of the monastery had taken place when it was rebuilt after the disastrous war of 1897.

At that time it had been in ruins—a deserted refuge for the goats of neighboring farmers. It was then that old Nikita Coletti had chanced to visit it. He had found the courtyard overgrown with brambles and weeds; thick soot coated the whole church and its creviced walls—soot from the oil lamps and the candles, and from the fires kindled in the abandoned sanctuary by goatherds, refugees, camping troops, or even brigands. Coletti noticed that there was the red paint under the thick soot and brought in experts to remove the dirt. When he saw the paintings that covered the walls of the ruined church, he had it restored and he rebuilt the monastery as it had been in its days of grandeur.

The faithful, as they bent to pass through the low arched gate by the bell-tower, said that he had been inspired by a miracle to restore the monastery. A miracle, they said, as they entered the narrow-paved courtyard surrounded by high walls and low buildings with domed windows. A miracle, they repeated, as they made the sign of the cross in the quiet atmosphere of peace and serenity, and their thoughts went to days gone by, days of piety and prayer. A miracle, when they went out onto the hill covered with green clover, and gazed at the ancient plane-trees, their trunks so great that it took seven men with arms outstretched to encircle them. When they were in leaf these majestic trees looked like green mountains, and when their leaves fell they seemed like giants buried to their necks in the earth, lifting a thousand tortured arms to the heavens.

But the resurrection of St. Elias was completed only when the new abbot was installed. Father Modestos came from the same town as Coletti; he too had gone through high school with the old man's help. One year after he entered Athens University he disappeared from sight. No one knew what had became of him. Rumors spread that he had run off to Constantinople with an actress, he had been seen in Marseilles, in Paris, and Bucharest. Then, after a lapse of ten years, he turned up at grandfather's house wearing monk's robes. He humbly asked the old man's pardon for his youthful errors and told him that he had graduated from the Theological School at Halki, and that the Oecumenical Patriarch had wanted to keep him as an archdeacon at the Patriarchate. However, he preferred to enter a monastery.

Thus it happened that St. Elias, which had just acquired a material body, now, in the person of its new abbot, acquired a living soul.

One felt that every building, every stone, every inch of land had come alive. And indeed it had, for when a man's spirit burns with the flame of true inspiration it communicates its enthusiasm to everything around it and draws a kindred response. If the flame is removed, either by death or for any other reason, everything changes: the stones lose their glow, the trees stretch forth their branches listlessly, the farm animals become sluggish, even the earth is slow in yielding its fruit.

"These are things unfathomed by knowledge and science, but things that manifestly exist," grandfather used to say.

Thus, under the new abbot, St. Elias had come to life again. Situated close to the old frontier, it took an active part in the glory of the Macedonian liberation struggle. Later, through the years, the abbot gave assistance to the poor, comforted the persecuted, and welcomed discussion with men of culture.

Father Modestos had a warm affection for Alexis Stournaris. Alexis often visited him and spent Sundays at the monastery, offering his expert advice on the cultivation of the monastery's lands. But above all he loved the long discussions with the abbot, often extending long into the hours of the night, on every kind of subject, from matters of local interest to subjects of the most general interest.

That Sunday morning Alexis opened his burdened heart to Father Modestos. He told him all the details of his visit to Pteliona, and spoke to him of Katie.

"What's happening to me, Father? For some time I've felt that I was out of my depth. But now all kinds of doubts are assailing me, and I'm lost—I don't know what's happening to me. Until now I've sought your company. Now I need your help. Father, help me."

"How can I help you, my son? First of all the experience of other men is useless to us. It is a precious thing, but it is not given out as a gift or a loan. And, as for me, such experience as I have was acquired a very long time ago; it is almost forgotten and has been muted by other things that are deeper and more important. Furthermore, you are so greatly enslaved by your passion that my spiritual means would be little more than a drop of water in a parched field.''

''Never mind. Give me that drop of water. It may lead me to the discovery of a spring which will refresh me.''

''No, my son. If you were some unknown person who came to me for confession, I would speak to you of sin, give you strict injunctions, and write out the usual prescriptions. But in your case, it's not quite the same. The Church has created molds in keeping with the Lord's dispensation, but they are intended for those who are made to fit into molds, and for those whom we, the worthless and feeble interpreters of the will of God, have not the time or the ability to understand fully. However it may try, whatever prescriptions it writes out, religion does not conquer the man who has thought much in his life, who has felt deeply, and who has a vitality of his own.'' And the abbot continued with warm emotion.

''The only thing that masters him is the revelation of blind faith in the sovereign will of God. On your behalf I shall resort to other means—the greatest at my disposal: I shall pray for you with deep fervor and with all the power in my soul.'' There was a burning quality in the abbot's words, but the young man looked at him in surprise.

''But do you really believe that your prayers can change my fate? Do you really go that far, Father?''

The abbot's eyes reproached him before his lips spoke.

''Stop. Do not blaspheme. I am willing to accept that you should practise your religion after your own fashion, but not that you should blaspheme.''

''I'm not blaspheming, but what you say does not come within the bounds of logic.''

The abbot pondered for a moment.

''Man has made rules of logic to the measure of his puny brain and says that whatever is not encompassed by them does not exist instead of saying that he cannot attain it.''

''Father, I am a believer. You know that. But there are scientific truths, there are matters that have been resolved, there are mathematical laws which are confirmed even by the movements of the stars. We cannot allow our speculations to go counter to such scientific data."

The abbot smiled at him with the tender affection of one dealing with an unreasonable child.

"You're right up to a point. But think a little deeper. Every now and then one scientific truth is proven false by another, new scientific truth, which in turn may be proven false later. Therefore, some of these truths of yours are worthless and, indeed, deceive you. In the field of these matters which you say have been resolved, science in its progress discoverd new unexplored regions which are often vaster than anything of which the scientists were previously aware. The more science progresses the more it realises that it is advancing into the unchartered regions of divine creation. You yourself admitted this when you spoke of mathematical laws in relation to the stars. The few laws which have been discovered prove that there are many others, complex and most accurate, which govern the whole universe. Not just the few stars we know but the infinite multitude of stars—galaxy upon galaxy. And men have sought to discover these laws for centuries and haven't succeeded. They have made statements about the universe, but they cannot define it, they cannot define the inconceivable idea of infinity—of that which never, nowhere and in no direction—do you hear me—never and nowhere comes to an end. And not only can they not say, but they can't even conceive of the manner in which these laws came into being, or how these ideas were created which our mind cannot attain or contain. How then can I compare even the whole wide extent of science with the inconceivable mass of divine creation and the ocean of mysteries which it conceals? But why am I saying all this, my son? How can one talk of the light of the lamp or the flicker of the candle in a monk's cell when one looks at the undying glow that suffuses the universe, the universe—do you hear me—which never and nowhere has an ending? When you contemplate that glow, then you believe that your prayers can influence everything, since it brings your soul into harmony with the powers that govern the universe." He paused, glanced at Alexis, and continued.

"Don't be surprised. Whether that harmony, that communication is made by etherial waves which the scientists are studying, or by angels or other souls that float in the upper air, I do not know. I only know that it exists. And if only you can establish communication then all is possible, even the most unbelievable miracles."

He paused, gave Alexis a strange, warm, inspired look, and took his hand. He then resumed with new fervor which gathered strength as he spoke.

"I have often talked about prayer. But there is something else which I have never told you. On rare occasions, when I am troubled by some great grief, I lock myself into the church, fall prone to the ground and pray with my face pressed to the floor in front of the altar. Many times nothing happens; but there are times when I feel the flagstones trembling beneath my body. Then I pray with even greater intensity, I struggle to embrace the stones, I moan and writhe, and I pray to the Lord of the Universe; I pray with redoubled intensity, with deep veneration. And naturally I don't embrace the flagstones but the more I struggle to do so the more powerfully they tremble. When this happens I know, because the throb of the earth against my face and breast tells me so—I know that my prayer has reached Him or someone near Him, and that some good will come of it."

He was exhausted by his inspired effort and as he stopped talking he was breathing heavily. He turned to the young man and said, "That is how I'm going to pray for you."

Alexis Stournaris looked at him in amazement. "Are you going to pray for me that way," he asked, "because you have a fatherly fondness for me, or because you think my predicament is very serious?"

The abbot thought for a moment, gave Alexis a look of great affection, and whispered, "For both the reasons you mentioned, my son."

Alexis answered him crisply, almost peevishly.

"I'm very greatful to you, Father Modestos, but I don't think God meddles in the lives of human beings."

The Father remained wrapped in thought for a while.

"Alexis, when man's thought advances far beyond those things for which his mind was created, then it is inevitable that there are many things he is unable to understand. If he insists on presuming to understand and explain them, it means that he resorts to a method of simplification which reduces things that are infinitely great and complex to the puny scale of his own comprehension. Last Sunday you explained to me how the radio catches invisible waves in the air and turns them into words and music. Another time you showed me diagrams proving that a microscope magnifies things invisible to the naked eye and makes them visible. I got a general idea of these things. A primitive human being would not be able to understand them. But he could be educated gradually to the point where he too would understand. But if you were to take any animal, whatever you did to it, it would never understand any of these things because its mind cannot reach that far. So it is with man. Much as he may wish, whatever he may do, he will never be able to comprehend any of the mysteries for the understanding of which his mind is not equipped; he cannot even tell with any degree of approximation what is their form or substance. You say to me; "God does not meddle in the life of man." How can you say that, since we can't even say what God is, by what means and to what purpose He acts, not only on earth, but in the universe—among the millions of stars, and in that sky which scientists tell us has no ending in time or space? As regards God's interference in human affairs, I will offer one surmise, or rather I will tell you what I believe, blindly, without having inquired too deeply, without logical reasoning. I don't believe that He interferes in everything, because in that case men's evil deeds would be His work. But I do believe not only that He can but that He does sometimes take an interest in small personal affairs. Don't ask me how and why. I don't know. Perhaps because of prayer which is a most powerful force generated by the intangible flame that vivifies His most select creation, man."

Alexis interrupted him.

"And why should man be His most select creation?"

"For many reasons. I'll give you one which is related to our discussion. I believe that, in some manner which I am not able to define or even to comprehend, in a very general way He concerns Himself with the progress of man, the favorite object of His creation. And at the present time, He is possibly taking a greater interest in man than before, is more urgently pursuing some greater, some tremendous objective. In all of divine creation, mineral, vegetable and animal, man alone has evolved greatly. He alone, to a great degree, has become spirit, he alone is incapable of living as mere matter, and continually augments in his life that part of his being which is spirit. Furthermore during the past fifty to eighty years I have seen in the proportion of spirit to matter certain changes in human beings that are many sided and surprisingly rapid, such as were not seen in the preceding five thousand years. Just think. How many millions of human beings who lived their whole lives like beasts are now entering into the spheres of knowledge—in the countries which are called civilized. And in the others, they are coming up. They will approach us with hundreds of millions of eyes seeking the light of knowledge for the first time. Consider also, that in recent years man has begun to master matter. He is mastering distance, discovering and controlling micro-organisms, overcoming disease, postponing death, governing heat and cold and developing his powers in many other extraordinary ways. On the one hand the spirit is spreading, on the other, matter is being brought under control. In one century there has been greater progress than in five millennia. Why now? Why when so little was accomplished before is so much being accomplished now in such a concentration of progress. I believe that this is the work of the Lord. I believe that this rapid evolution is leading somewhere and that in the not too distant future—not in thousands of years—He will transform His chosen creatures into a being in which spirit predominates over matter, and that He will mold the society of man into a dominion of God and Justice. Who knows?. . .It's quite possible."

Alexis listened intently to the abbot. When he concluded, Alexis said, "Once a rich nucleus of knowledge was discovered—electricity, for example—it was natural for the mind of man to exploit it for further discoveries. It needed no special help."

"This is possible, of course. But there was not just one nucleus. There were a great number and they were of all kinds. Moreover, why were these nuclei not discovered for so many thousands of years or if they were as in the case of electricity, why wasn't the slightest advance made? But we'll talk about all this again some other time. Now tell me what's going on in the world. Occasionally I see a newspaper. Do you think that war will again strike our unfortunate country? What's your opinion?''

A change of expression came over Alexis' face. The signs of his inner conflict disappeared and he spoke with serious and determined interest.

''Nobody really understands what is going on at the fronts opened by Germany. It seems that the giants are probing each others' strength and are weighing and preparing their forces.'' Then he continued with thoughtful deliberation.

''As regards our position, I've spoken with officers of the General Staff who are friends of mine. They consider it impossible that we should stay out of the conflict. Greece stands at the crossroads of the continents and seas. The General Staff expects a double attack: by the Italians through Albania and by the Bulgars, or the Germans and Bulgars combined, through Bulgaria.''

''And what, in their opinion, will be the outcome?''

''That we will resist and that they will not pass.''

''And how can that possibly happen?''

Alexis tried to explain. His arguments were more emotional than reasonable, and the old abbot couldn't agree with him. He said that this would not be a war like those which had gone before. We would be attacked by the most powerful air forces in the world, and by vast land armies.

Alexis appeared to be annoyed by such talk and said, with a touch of ill-humor, ''When our men are determined not to abandon our mountains and our fortifications, there is no air force or artillery or any other means that can open a passage for the enemy.''

The old man sank into a deep reverie.

''My son, I don't think it will be as you say, and I am deeply perturbed. I am perturbed because this time our nation finds itself in great peril. If Germany wins, and if Bulgaria is her ally as she will be, then the country will be controlled by those who for centuries have been enemies of the Greeks. The Slav will plow through the country and leave it in utter ruin. And the worst is, my son, that we stand alone. We have no brothers or cousins. If you look at any other people you will see that they have a family and are bound by various ties. The Anglo-Saxons, the Slavs, the Scandinavians, the Moslems are great families, sometimes happily united, sometimes less so, and if one of the brothers is brought low, the others survive. But Hellenism has no family. It stands alone. And what is worse is that the mighty branches of the tree of Hellas, which for centuries extended over the whole Balkan area, over Asis Minor and as far as the Black Sea, have withered and are no more. Gone are Monastiri Stenimachos, Philippopolis, Constantinople and Smyrna! It was fated that the face of our nation was to change forever in our time. The great expansion is over. We are hemmed in on this range of mountains. And if the Slav overruns the only land we have left and holds it for several years, what will remain of the shining dream of Hellenic splendor? I have never before felt so afraid, my son."

Alexis received the old man's words with an intentionally loud laugh.

"Your fears are unwarranted, Father," he said. "The young men of Greece will not allow them to come true. When the hour strikes you will see that no mortal power will make them yield."

"I have not forgotten another generation of Greece's young men. They fought like lions all the way from Mt. Olympus to Odessa and Ankara. They fought and they were winning. And then you saw what a disaster overtook us."

"Yes, I know, but now it's different. This time we won't be rushing barefooted in pursuit of a dream. We shall be fighting on our own ground in defense of hearth and home." And Alexis went on to describe the enthusiasm which would burn in the hearts of the young fighting men of Greece. Modestos' eyes sparkled with a new light.

"I hope to see all this, Alexis," he said. "The fervor with which you talk leads me to believe that for all that we shall eventually be forced to bend before the superior numbers and strength of the enemy; if we manage to stand fast for a little time and acquit ourselves with courage, sacrifice, and honor, the nation may again emerge strong and healthy for a long time to come. Because sacrifice and glory mold and strengthen souls, and numbers and military force never succeed in subduing the soul. For soul is not matter to be broken and lost. But how long can we hold? You saw how heroic Poland fell. How much fire and metal will they pour over us? How many will fall upon us?"

"Poland," Alexis retorted, "was attacked on all sides; the country is one vast plain and it was overrun by thousands of tanks. Here we are surrounded by sea, and England is the mistress of the seas; the front may be an extended one but it is made up of mountains and fortifications." And he concluded, laughing "Would you be satisfied if we hold out for ten years?"

Modestos didn't laugh. "If the fanatical Bulgars fall upon us," he said gravely, "and, above all, if three million bayonets and two thousand aeroplanes are thrown against us, then ten days will be enough for glory and the future."

A young monk interrupted their conversation. He bowed to the abbot. "Father," he said, "a carriage is coming up the hill. Have you any orders?" They looked out of the window across the plain.

"It is coming here," Modestos said.

"It's one of the carriages from Pteliona. Do you think young Coletti is coming to visit the monastery? I'm not anxious to see him."

"I hope it is Coletti. I very much want to meet him. But whoever it is, let us go to welcome him."

Alexis was in no mood to go and stood at the courtyard door. The abbot went out alone.

Coletti alighted from the carriage. Modestos, visibly moved, stood in front of the Old Man's grandson; lifted his hand and made the sign of the cross over him in blessing. In a voice vibrant with emotion he said, "Blessed is he that cometh. Welcome, my child, to the land of your ancestors which has been awaiting you for a long time."

But Nikita Coletti was not the only visitor. Alexis, responding to a kind of premonition, moved back a step, and without apparent reason, he felt his heart contract. Then he realized that his premonition was correct. Not just because Katie, her father, and uncle got out of the carriage, but because of certain little details—insignificant things. No one else would have noticed them. But Alexis could not help noticing, since they led to conclusions which affected him deeply.

Details. In a song two discordant notes are mere details, yet they can ruin it. And the little things he had noticed tore with strident dissonance through the sweet song that had been Katie's and his.

Coletti seemed lighter and gayer than before, and stretched out his hand to help Katie as she got out behind him. She took his hand and thanked him with a smile that was infinitely sweet. Alexis had never seen her smile so charmingly. She stood beside Coletti and again smiled at him in the same way and gazed into his eyes. The others exchanged a few words with the abbot and the poet glanced absent-mindedly at the view over the plain. Katie went up to him and again her expression was one that Alexis had never known; it was full of concern—almost of longing. She took Coletti by the elbow, turned him toward the fountain at the foot of the giant plane trees, and with an expansive gesture showed him the monastery and its grounds.

At that moment she saw Alexis. Surprise showed on her face—and embarrassment. What good was her embarrassment to him? What comfort would it bring him? He had known her joyful smiles and had often seen her eyes kindle with desire. But never had he seen anything like the effort she was now making to appear very sweet, this intensity she was showing to make the other man understand beyond any doubt that she was interested in him.

Katie couldn't possibly have fallen in love with this lifeless puppet! She couldn't have forgotten their love, the bond that united them! What he was seeing couldn't be true! It was all a pretense that was being enacted before his eyes while she was in love with him. And only a few days ago she had told him that Coletti filled her with disgust that even the great shadow of the Old Man could not dispel. A great weariness came over him. The anguish he felt was such that he couldn't think, he couldn't even try to find an explanation for it all.

Some moments later Katie came towards him. "I followed your advice," she said. "Last night I went with father to call on him."

Alexis looked at her in bewilderment and felt a bitter stab of pain. Those were the blue eyes in which he had first discovered paradise, and now her false words filled him with bitter disillusionment. He remembered what Phrosso had said to him, and again recalled that Katie had never spoken to him about Notis.

Without stopping to weigh the wisdom of his words, he said to her calmly, "Why are you lying? In any case, you do exactly what you want and think only of your advantage." Her eyes flashed. "You are the only one in a position to know that when I do what I want to, I do it without any thought of advantage."

"When one is in love one can't possibly think of selfish interests."

Her eyes flashed again, but she laughed with a carefree lightness which belied her angry look. "I'm laughing," she said, "so that the others won't notice that I'm telling you you're spiteful and vulgar."

Alexis felt that he was going to lose his temper. "What a perfect actress you are," he said, and added calmly, "I hadn't realized it before. I'm glad I see it now so that I may recover."

He noticed the anger fading from her eyes. She seemed distressed now. She spoke to him more naturally. "But, Alexis, what has annoyed you so much? Why are you so cruel to me? You haven't seen anything terrible!"

"I'm not cruel. I am my own self. And you're mistaken. I have seen something terrible, to use your expression. I've seen deceit. It only takes little things to reveal it. And your behavior couldn't have been more clear."

Her voice was soft again; there was a note of entreaty in it. "Stop playing the philosopher, Alexis. You know I love you. You know it very well."

But she didn't continue. The others called to her to go and see the frescoes in the church, and immediately she forgot the emotion that was beginning to play upon her features. Light and airy and charming, she joined the group and he was left alone with his sorrow.

"I used to read about such things in novels and made fun of them," he thought. "A couple of glances, a couple of smiles, a few bitter words are enough to cast a full-grown man into the fires of hell. I used to find such things unbelievable or, at any rate, ridiculous, and now they are happening to me. What kind of illness is this? What is this power love has to paralyse one's thoughts, will, manliness—everything?"

He saw them all come to the arched doorway of the church.

Before entering, Katie turned and gave him a last, long look. He drank it in thirstily and for a second felt something drawing him to the others; he took one listless step toward them, and then turned suddenly away and, running quickly out of the courtyard, untied his black horse, Thunderbolt, and without putting his foot in the stirrup leaped onto his back.

He gave the horse a hard kick in the flanks, and pulled sharply at the bit two or three times, called to him gruffly and started galloping down the hill. Clinging to the body of the maddened beast, his eyes straight ahead of him, he devoured the space before him, galloping insanely off the trail and through the fields, leaping over hurdles and ditches as he shot in a straight line toward the College. Only when he approached the river did he pause to guide his frothing steed to the shallows. He crossed the river at the same swift pace.

The horses neighed when he entered the stable, and his beloved Pegasus stamped his hoof on the stone slabs. But Thunderbolt showed his anger. Even when Alexis was wiping away the froth which the saddle had left on his back, he refused to calm down. He pawed the pavement, shook his powerful body they way and that, tossed his head, and seemed to breathe flames from his nostrils. When Alexis finished rubbing his back, he put his arm around the broad neck crowned by a flowing mane, and spoke to the horse that seemed to understand him. The noble animal seemed to sense his master's pain. He grew calm, turned his head towards Alexis, pawed the ground with his foot and whinnied softly several times. As Alexis left the stable all the horses neighed sadly as if to show him that they loved him and understood his sorrow.

VI

Nikos Manoussis' office was like most attorneys' offices in the provinces. It was just an ordinary store; it might have been a grocery, a barber-shop or a butcher's shop. But it was a law office, as attested by the sign on the door, a desk, a few chairs, and a dark wooden bookcase on whose shelves stood bound copies of

The Law Journal and a dozen other legal books. It was a bleak setting, exposed to the scrutiny of passers-by through the wide store-window. This was where he had to try to concentrate, to study his briefs, to prepare his legal documents, and carry out all his professional work.

It was a far cry from the offices of some of his colleagues in Athens, and from the sumptuous quarters of the great lawyers of Europe which he had seen in movies or read about in novels. His only luxury was a curtain which he drew occasionally in order to be able to have some privacy when he lost himself in mournful thoughts about the bad luck which had clipped his wings and had condemned him to be a poor, frustrated provincial lawyer without any satisfaction and without power.

"Well, I might as well sit down and prepare my brief in the case of that derelict shack and forget about all those dreams that never came true. The whereases about the shack will bring in a drachma or two, while dreams will smother in bitterness.

He glanced at the file and started to write; at least he had the satisfaction of feeling the pen running smoothly over the paper without stopping. But before he came to the end of the first page, he jumped to his feet. Phoula had come into his office. She had dashed in, excited, as if she were being pursued.

"You must be mad!" he cried. He crossed the room quickly to draw the curtain and to lock the door.

"What on earth has happened? Why didn't you wait at least until it was dark? You know all the gossip about us; you never should have come. What's the matter?"

The girl sank into a chair in the darkened corner of the office, passed her hand over face, and remained silent for a while. Standing in front of her, he asked again harshly, "What's the matter?"

"I don't know, Nikos. Maybe I have gone mad. But I had to see you. I had to tell you, and I knew very well what I had to say. But now, after running all the way here and sneaking into your office, and with you standing over me so furious. . .I can't seem to gather my wits together."

He sat next to her, anxious and displeased, but tried to hide his feelings in an attempt to calm her.

"Yesterday I received a note from Katie asking me to come with Costa to have dinner at your home tomorrow to meet Coletti, the poet. I was very upset. I don't want to come."

"Why?"

She looked at him and her eyes were brimming with adoration and despair.

"It's so long since I've seen you, Nikos. And I love you, I want you, I think only of you every moment of the day and night. You know it, you see it, I tell you so in my letters."

"Yes, but you also know the difficulties we have to face."

"If you were as eager as I there wouldn't be any difficulties. But never mind that. There's gossip and we've got to be careful. At least spare me the torment of coming to your home and seeing you in front of the others. It's an insult to Costa. He may be. . .whatever he is. But don't you understand? I love you and yet I'm sorry for him. We're causing him enough trouble. At least we oughtn't to force him to give people the impression that he associates with you, and indeed that he is doing you favors."

Nikos tried to comfort her and make her change her mind. They were inviting them to a family dinner, he argued, and it could be taken as proof that there was nothing between them. There was nothing in the invitation that was humiliating to her husband or could be misconstrued by public opinion. His closest friend, Dr. Raptis, and his wife, would also be present. As for themselves, he preferred to see her with other people than not to see her at all.

"And now that we are alone you haven't kissed me yet."

He took her in his arms and kissed her.

"Nikos," she whispered, "let's go to Athens, let's go to Salonika, please, please, let's go somewhere where nobody knows us."

"You know how much I wish we could," he answered. "You know that in the hopelessness that chokes me you are my only comfort. But if we both leave Larissa at the same time, the gossip will flare up again, and they'll do everything to destroy us and our families."

"Oh. Nikos, I beg you. At least we'll be happy for a few days and afterwards the memory of that happiness will console us. Do make the decision."

He insisted that this was wrong and reminded her that only a few moments before she had said that they must not humiliate her husband. He made a vague promise for the summer when many people left on vacation. He refused absolutely to leave now.

"You've made such a fuss about my not coming here late in the evening in spite of all the precautions I take. If this is how it is, I prefer not to see you at all, and I'll wait until we can meet somewhere else. I'll be able to bear our separation better. And I won't come to your dinner. Invite another couple."

"Whom shall I invite? At least Raptis has studied abroad and speaks a foreign language. We may have an interesting discussion. Besides, I don't want the rumor to get around. . ." He was at a loss and hesitated.

"You don't want the rumor to get around, "Phoula broke in, "that you've got something in your head about Katie and the poet."

"Nothing of the sort!" he said sharply, "how could you imagine anything so absurd?"

"I didn't imagine it. It's the talk of the town."

"This blasted town," he said angrily. "It's full of spite and distorts the slightest happenings. Don't mention the dinner to anyone," he added hastily.

"And do you think no one will see Coletti going through your doorway? If only one person sees him, it will be enough to start a rumor."

"Well, anyhow, don't you say anything. It'll be better for you, for the reasons you've mentioned."

"But they'll see us also, Nikos. That's why I don't want to come. We mustn't come."

He took her in his arms. He didn't tell her that it was important that they should come because it was impossible for Katie and him to be alone with Coletti and it was almost impossible to invite anyone else. Whoever was there would carry tales about everything that was said, exaggerating and gossiping about it. He talked to her sweetly, soothingly, stroked her and kissed her and, intent on making the dinner-party a success, told her how much he loved her and promised that they would meet soon. And the girl left, after saying that she and her husband would come to the dinner and would do all they could to make the evening pleasant for the young poet.

* * * * *

From the day when they met at the monastery, Katie was out of her mind. She was torn between her desire to make the big catch and her anguish at the prospect of losing Alexis.

If she did manage to get Coletti, she would still feel the loss of Alexis very much, but at least the prize would be worthwhile. But what if her scheme did not succeed and she also lost the man who attracted her so much?

What a fine, strong man Alexis was! When he drew her close to him, she tried to gather up and contract her body the better to feel his strength. He had powerful muscles in his arms, legs and all his body; his face reflected his unpetuous strength and drive. In his every movement one saw a man capable of mastering wild beasts. Even his thoughts, which were strange and belonged to another era, were attractive because of their manly forthrightness. He had the mind and body of an animal that had been tamed, but still retained the power and characteristics of its wildness.

No, she certainly didn't want to lose him. The ideal solution would be for her to be able to attain her other objective and still continue to see Alexis. But now these dreams were far away. Alexis was angry, almost without reason. If he heard that the poet was going to dine at their house tonight. . .

She thought for a while and then got on her bicycle and went up Epirus Street. At this time, until noon, Alexis would be at the College. He would either be in class or somewhere on the premises. She had to see him; she must talk to him and win him over.

* * * * *

A message was brought to him that Manoussis' daughter was waiting for him in the pine-wood outside the main gate of the College. He was startled and annoyed. In spite of the fact that this was the first time that this had happened, it wasn't right. It set a bad example for the students. Furthermore he was in such a state of mind that he would have preferred not to see her for some time, however much he missed her. But he hurried out, not wishing her to be seen waiting at the College gate.

"I'm going crazy," she said, "you were so cruel to me. I can't bear it."

He looked at her in silence, and wondered what he felt. Was it love or hatred? Was it admiration and desire for this beautiful girl or fear and disgust at what he suspected she might really be? Was it joy because he was wrong about her or sorrow because he was right?

She took him by the arm and drew him further away.

"Alexis, why don't you speak to me? Why do you look at me in that way? After all, what's so terrible about what happened? You and father and Uncle Nikos all told me that we have obligations to him, that he is alone here and that we must entertain him. I've merely followed your advice. What's so wrong about that?"

He stopped, took her by the shoulders and looked into her eyes.

"Katie," he said, "I'm very unhappy. I'm in love with you. I wish you'd tell me the truth."

"If I wasn't telling the truth would I be coming here publicly in the middle of the day for no other reason but to see you and put a stop to your anger?"

He wanted to draw her to him, to kiss her, to whisper a thousand words of love to her, but the bitterness and suspicions of the last few days held him back.

"Why were you so sweet to him?" he asked calmly.

"I behaved towards him just as I would to anyone else."

His suspicions got the better of him once more. She was usually most indifferent, almost arrogant, in her behavior to others. She had been different with Coletti. She was lying.

"You were giving him very tender looks and smiling at him lovingly."

"You're jealous," she retorted sharply, "and you can't see clearly. I looked at him and smiled in a perfectly natural manner. Would I be flirting with him when I have you, a man among men, masculine from head to toe?"

She was still lying. He was absolutely certain that she had been leading Coletti on. He didn't have time to tell her so because she pressed against him, leaned her head against his neck and whispered, "You're crazy, Alexis. I love you. Can't you feel it? I love you."

How wonderful it was to feel her pressed against him and to hear her saying these words with so much passion. Maybe he was crazy.

"I love you," she repeated. "I've never felt like this—only with you, only for you."

His suspicions began to fade, but her assertion that he was her first and only love suddenly reminded him of a name. The warm feeling that had come over him left him. What about Notis? She had explained her meeting last year with Coletti's cousin in Athens and he had believed her. But the affair with Notis had lasted two or three years. It had been enough to drive a man of strong character to despair, but she had never said a word to him about it, and now she was telling him that she had never been in love before. And yet she spoke earnestly; her words, her voice, her straining body—all seemed to attest to her sincerity. He was almost sure that she was lying. What a mass of confusion man was! How could he sift out the truth? How could he sacrifice his happiness if he chanced to be wrong? He pushed her away from him and held her by the shoulders.

"Listen, Katie," he said. "A lot of thoughts are running through my head; I'd like to tell you about them, to sort them out, and find out what you think. But there's no need for me to think of you as a complicated person or even as an insincere person, nor is it necessary for me to try to discover whether jealousy obscures my thoughts. All this can be dealt with very simply. You know that I'm in love with you. You say you love me. So let's get married now."

She wanted to avoid his eyes but knew that it would be a mistake. She looked at him and tried to assume an expression which would conceal her confusion.

"I am yours and I love you. We can be together as often as we want. Why should we get married?"

"Because it's not the same," he replied. "I want you near me all the time, I want you naked in my arms, I want to have children with you. I've saved some money; we can build a small house. Come, let's get married tomorrow."

There was a silence. He pressed her shoulders hard and said more firmly, "Tomorrow, or in a week at the most. I'm ready." He gave her a hard look. "Say something. Answer me!"

She was hard pressed to find an answer and couldn't think of any excuse.

"But I'm not ready for such an important decision," she whispered in a feeble voice.

"And yet you say you love me very much."

She recovered her voice and with her usual warmth answered at once.

"I adore you. I adore you."

He pushed her away. "You lying bitch!" he cried. "If you loved me you would marry me tonight."

He turned and left without so much as looking at her again.

* * * * *

She leaned against a pine-tree and felt a wave of despair coming over her. She knew intuitively that she would never recapture him as she had known him—warm, in love, her man. It was the second time in her life that love had slipped away from her, and in the same manner. "Let's get married! "You lying bitch!" And yet it wasn't so. She did love him sincerely, but things were not as easy for her as they were for other people.

And now what would she do? Only Notis and Alexis had caused her to respond, body and soul—Alexis more so because she was more mature and conscious of her feelings. What was she to do?

She walked to her bicycle, her head bent toward the ground. "I've burned my bridges here," she reflected. "But tonight, when Alexis would have liked us to get married, if I succeed in making an impression on the wealthy poet. . .if luck is with me. . ." She smiled to herself, lifted her head, took up the bicycle with a swift movement and rode back to the city.

* * * * *

With quick strides, Alexis walked back to the College buildings. He wanted to forget those stormy moments by losing himself in some occupation which would absorb his thoughts. Later in the evening, maybe, when he was alone and undisturbed, he would be able to think about what had happened and come to some conclusion.

He came upon Mourayias sitting on a doorstep.

"I've come to you for advice," Mourayias said. "Phrosso read me an article in some foreign magazine which said that they plant wheat stalk by stalk and get a tremendous crop. I thought I might take a chance, and I'm trying out this method on a couple of acres. It's a funny business. What do you think about it?"

"I've tried it myself this year, and it ought to be good in this region where we have a lot of workers and few fields. But it needs a lot of hands. Just think what is means to plant thousands of stalks of wheat one by one. It would be about a hundred thousand stalks for each acre. This would be possible only where a whole family worked together. It's not for you."

He noticed the doubtful look on the old man's face and added, "This sort of thing wouldn't have been possible even in the old days with Grandfather at Pteliona; it certainly can't be done with the Paris playboy there."

Mourayias glanced down for an instant, then he looked Alexis in the eye and said, "He's heard the call of the earth, Alexis."

"The earth calls to everyone, Mourayias, but few realize it, and still fewer have ears to hear,"

"But he did hear, Alexis. He may not have understood too well, he may not have believed, but he heard and he was startled. I know what I'm talking about."

"You're dreaming, Mourayias. Dreaming dreams of days gone by."

"A poor bed brings rich dreams, my boy." And he went on to talk about the experiment in transplanting wheat which he was intent on trying.

* * * * *

Late at night when the door closed behind the last guest, the three of them stood still for a moment and looked at each other.

Maybe they were not yet certain that they were alone and were waiting for the last guest to get out of earshot. Or perhaps they needed a short breathing-space to recover from the difficult evening and to think what they should say after that unusual dinner. At any rate, they stood silently looking at one another. Their eyes were bright, smiles of satisfaction played upon their lips, their faces clearly showed that they were pleased.

Vassili Manoussis rubbed his hands and said, "Well, the evening was a great success. I'll swear to God, Katie, I didn't recognize the house. Flowers, service, excellent food, good conversation—I couldn't believe my eyes and ears. We must have made a very good impression on him."

His brother, who obviously was also very pleased, could not refrain from a little sarcasm, "I'm sure he thought he was in Paris, or in some French chateau.

"My dear Nikos, I didn't say anything about Paris or chateaux. But if you want to know, as far as conversation goes, you were perhaps better than Paris."

Nikos abandoned his sarcastic tone, sat down in an armchair, and said without conceit, "Yes, the conversation was good, and it must have impressed him to find it in a Greek province. There was quality to it."

"Well, it was thanks to you and Katie."

"Not at all. Everybody did fine. I was particularly impressed by Dr. Vaidis. For a puny little man his conversation was certainly very meaty. But his meek and unhealthy looks are not very pleasant."

Katie interrupted him impatiently. "Leave the man alone, Uncle. You can afford to let him be ugly since he can't compete with your good looks! What we're interested in is your opinion of our foreign friend. How do you find him?"

Nikos noticed that Vassili gave him a meaningful glance. He said, "Well, I must admit that he's a handsome man, a charming gentleman, and has excellent manners."

Katie broke in, "That kind of appraisal," she said in an exasperated tone of voice, "is unnecessary and unworthy of you. Didn't it seem strange to you that he asked whether he could hire a car to go to Athens because he was afraid of the bridges and tunnels on the train route?"

Vassili looked at his brother anxiously.

"Yes, perhaps it did. But you remember that he hastened to

explain as soon as he noticed our surprise; he said it was something left over from the impressions and fears of childhood."

"How do you find him as a man, as a thinker, as a conversationalist?" Katie asked.

Her father hastened to answer. "Splendid, my dear, splendid. Didn't you notice how he was in on everything, discussed everything?"

She did not feel any need to hide her disappointment at her father's pronouncement and turned again to her uncle. "You tell the truth, Uncle Nikos. How do you find him?"

"I'll tell you. With regard to everything he said about the impregnability of the Maginot Line and at the *Pourquoi?* being quite natural in a civilized people, and that it would not prevent the French from fighting as well as they did in 1914, and everything he said about France's predominant position in Europe, it was nothing more than one would expect from someone who reads the French newspapers regularly. But his remarks about the intellectual world and about literature and poetry show that he has a good mind and that he possesses the culture and sensitivity of taste.

Vasilli spoke again enthusiastically.

"Your criticism of his poems was astonishing. I couldn't believe my ears. How did you know all that? Where did you read it?"

"Did we have to read it? Wasn't it enough that we'd read his poems?"

He didn't understand his brother's irony or the meaning of his words, and continued. "And as for that translation of Katie's—how well you managed to bring it into the conversation, Nikos. You're a wily devil. But the translation was amazing. You two kept it a secret from me. He was astounded that Katie had translated him, and you noticed that he said that perhaps the translation was better than the original. Even I who don't understand these things liked it. I must say I liked it a lot. Recite it again, Nikos."

"There's no doubt that the man paid her a compliment, but there's also no doubt that the translation is good."

He began to recite:

"I want to wander aimless o'er the peaks
    Where wild winds blow,
Seeking the traceless trails that no one seeks,
    The trails that nowhere go
In dusk ne'er followed by a dawn's tomorrow—

And if may aimless path should chance to lead
    To some uncharted bourne,
I pray my wayward steps at last may tread
    The quiet depths of some ravine forlorn
And find in darkness solace from my sorrow "

Nikos laughed. "The trouble is that out of the twenty-odd stanzas which must be taken as a whole, we had only translated two. If he had asked us to go on . . ."

Katie was very annoyed and got up. "I suppose you think it's very important for us to repeat everything we said and to make a few silly observations in order to conceal our real thoughts. And yet we might have some interesting things to say."

Vassili Manoussis looked at his daughter with new eyes. He saw before him a positive, imperious, self-willed young woman. How different from himself, he thought. Different in physique too—so much more robust than he—she was tall, had a healthy body, strong thighs and taut, well-developed breasts. How proudly and gracefully she moved. As he looked at her with adoration and melancholy, he realized that she was no longer a little girl. "My darling," he thought. "How proud I was of you when you were a child. How my heart melted when I helped you to put on your school uniform, or when I took you by the hand and we went to the church together on Sundays. Why, oh why have you grown up? And now what a problem you are to me. Darling child, how you torment me!"

He rose, rubbed his hands together and looked around disconsolately.

"Very well, Katie dear," he said. "Let's not go on now. It's time for bed. There's work to do tomorrow," He made a movement toward the door, but turned back. He stood awkwardly in the middle of the room.

"I heard him ask you to go to Pteliona to discuss literature. Because . . .because of possible gossip, and above all because of the impression it will make on him, I don't think you ought to go alone. It would be better if Nikos went with you."

"Yes, Vassili," Nikos said. "We'll go together. Don't worry."

When she was left alone with her uncle she said, with a note of suspicion in her voice, "You didn't seriously mean what you said to father?"

"Of course not. Although . . ."

She interrupted him and sat down. Her blue eyes had become cold as ice.

I'd like to discuss that 'although'. Which is better? The well-educated, pretty, untouched little provincial girl who is easily impressed, or a girl with some experience in life, who may also be impressed but also cannot resist the temptation of a handsome man?"

Nikos Manoussis was not at all put out by the fact that his niece spoke to him in a way that no other Greek girl would have spoken to her uncle. He gave her his opinion bluntly: the middle road was best. Lead him on gradually. "But on no account allow him to quench his passion until has has led you to the altar," he concluded.

"That's what I expected you to say. It's the only way to handle the matter. But there's one thing I'm afraid of. You said 'lead him on gradually' and you were right. But if I'm not able to meet him at least a few times, how am I going to light the kindling? When the bad weather comes and he leaves, I may not have had the time to accomplish anything. That's the problem."

* * * * *

The first winter rains always deluged the plain for two or three weeks — sometimes more. The rain fell in a steady downpour night and day; it came in torrents or in a continuous drizzle, but it never stopped. The waters of the heavens were inexhaustable, and the black clouds spreading above the plain were so thick that they seemed to reach to the uppermost limits of the firmament. A grey and heavy sky closed in upon the earth almost touching the tops of the trees and the roofs of the houses. Olympus to the north was invisible; Kissavos to the east could not be seen; the craggy ridge of Kozakas to the west was hidden from view. Even the low hills and the wide spaces of the great plain were hard to discern. A dark, grey impenetrable mist covered the earth from end to end.

You could hear the rhythmic beat of the rain the whole night through. Sometimes the rhythm might change as the downpour grew stronger and the spattering of the water on the roof-tiles and on the ground echoed louder.

At such times, when the clouds poured forth their furious cataracts of water, you would gather yourself up beneath the blankets and pull them over your head so as not to hear the noise, for a panic fear came over you. Maybe the mythical words of the ancient prophets were coming true; maybe this was the end of the world—a second Flood. Maybe the mountains might collapse, the plain sink into the abyss, or some other horrible disaster, some unprecedented phenomenon, come to pass.

The earth, damp from the first rains of autumn, now spewed forth in a few days the water it could not drink into its depths. The rivers flooded, the dry torrent beds filled and roared in wild turbulence, the ditches overflowed, and the surface of the ground was transformed into an endless sea of mud. It was impossible to walk through the fields—one's boots would sink deep into the mud—and solid paths were few. Beasts remained in their stables, and men went out only if it was absolutely necessary and they knew of some safe, trail that would get them through.

Overhead was nothing but the grey, dank darkness; underfoot heavy mud as far as the eye could see. And to the predicament of the present was added the anxiety for the future. If the waters did not recede rapidly the seed would rot in the ground and the crops that had already come up would be ruined.

Body and soul were tormented by the rain, the damp and the cold. And from every side prayers went up: Christ and the Holy Virgin help us! Grant us a clearing of the weather to save our crops, to allow us to bring out our beasts to the pasture and to save us from the dampness which cuts into our bones.

It was thus that the rains came towards the end of that autumn to put an end to the late summer weather for Larissa. They changed the pleasant course of life and ushered in days of weariness and boredom. Rain all the time; rain, rain and mud everywhere, mud, mud, mud.

Everyone stayed indoors. Those who lived on farms and ir villages and had houses in town came to Larissa. The few who could afford to left hurriedly for Athens.

* * * * *

Nikita Coletti also left for Athens, driven away by rain, damp and mud. He had also been driven away by the silence on the farm which had been interrupted by only two visits from the pretty girl. But what good were these two brief interludes in that depressing silence? Not a sound in the house, not a sound around it, not a sound at night, in the daytime, at any hour or any minute. Not a soul to talk to.

Hurry! Hurry!

Hurry away! Hurry away to the great city!

Part Two

A PAUSE IN THE JOURNEY

DAY OF THE HOLY VIRGIN

AUGUST 15, 1940

At sundown the heat which from early dawn had penetrated everywhere and tormented everything, came out from all its hiding places and made a last effort to hold the day under its domination—to torment it to the end. And so, when one began to hope that the day's suffering was over, one was deceived; there was always a last flaming hour to endure. Breathing was difficult, one took short breaths, as if to avoid inhaling the fiery flame which continued to burn up the endless Thessalian plain.

Such was this stifling August day which seemed to have no ending.

They had closed the shutters for him and sprinkled the wooden floor boards two or three times with water, but no relief came. How could man remedy this evil which nature had created? Only Nature, either with the coming of night, or with her breezes from the north, could drive away the searing breath that poured over the plain. From dawn to dusk, the heat—terrible, merciless, indifferent to the suffering of men—crowned and paralyzed everything.

But it was not only men that suffered, he thought. The beasts too felt the torment as they stood motionless in shady spots, breathing heavily, their tongues hanging out of their mouths. Even the trees were affected as they stood erect, their leaves withered and crumpled, covered in dust. And the plants and grasses were yellow and lifeless, dried up by the hot rays which had burned the plain from end to end.

Scorched earth! Scorched earth!

He had often heard that expression, but he had never understood what it really meant. Now he knew, having seen Thessaly in the heart of the summer. It meant parched land everywhere, dry, naked earth on the plain, bare rocks without any moss, at the foothills, a few burnt weeds here and there, a few desolate trees, a surfeit of white, binding light, and the absence of any living thing. Because whatever lived and breathed took shelter to recover from its exhaustion.

Scorched earth! Scorched earth!

And to think that at this same hour Parisian parks were fresh and green, that at the French resorts it might be hot, but that it cooled off quickly, that there were frequent showers and that all around everything smiled at you with a cool, joyous, green smile.

Nikita Coletti threw the sheet off his emaciated body and in the gloom cast by the closed shutters reflected upon the *impasse* to which he had come in the past months and days.

Athens was no solution, but life there had been bearable. Apart from a few blocks of civilization at its center Athens was a wretched city, but the hotel was good. It provided comfort; one could live there. The people were a mixed crowd: there were good people and bad, proud and servile. Among the women some were facile, others difficult, and the girls, true to their reputation, had looked at him as an eligible bachelor. There had been receptions and dinner parties every day, most of them boring; but a few were pleasant. The papers discussed his poetry and were not sparing in their praise or blame. He went sometimes on picnics with girls he had been fond of when he was a boy—the men were either ridiculous or too coarse for his taste. But these excursions took him to interesting places which were not really attractive to him because they offered no civilized amenities.

He had not been able to do anything about his financial situation because everybody—and especially his uncle—had been utterly negative. But for his expenses in Greece he was able to unblock whatever money he needed and life flowed on. It wasn't the life he fancied, but after all it was a life he could put up with.

That was how he felt until the Germans attacked, broke through the defenses of Holland and Belgium, brought France to her knees and drove the British from Dunkirk. Paris, beautiful, glorious, proud Paris, was under Hitler's boot! Everything was lost! No one would be able to speak and breathe freely any more; Europe was enslaved; everything would be determined by the harsh orders of the barbarians in the black and brown shirts.

Europe in subjection, and France, the land of freedom, graciousness, and light, in chains! What would become of the world? How would aesthetes like himself be able to live? No one would be able to conquer the two dictators who, with their steel-girded might, occupied the whole of Europe.

A heavy night had fallen over the world he knew.

He was seized with despair. He felt as if a thunderbolt had struck his mind and spirit. What did he see before him? He would have to forget the places he loved and the life he enjoyed. He was henceforth caught in this trap—a prisoner in Greece. And this miserable and ill-omened Greece would also cease to possess even the little charm it had until now.

The Greeks were stark, raving mad. They presumed to pass judgment on everybody. They cursed Leopold of Belgium who was the first to withdraw from battle and said that he could not possibly be the son of Albert, the Soldier-King. They heaped abuse upon the French for being defeated so quickly and did not forgive them because some of their famous generals either did not fight or capitulated to Hitler. On the other hand they extolled the British, praised their defeat and flight at Dunkirk as if it were some glorious undertaking, and said that Britain, as always, would win the last battle and would annihilate Germany.

And they supported all these statements with arguments and with absolute conviction—as if the world-shaking events of the times, of the the eastern front in the autumn, and of the western front now in the summer—were not the result of the insuperable power of the Nazi war machine, but due only to the moral weakness of all other Europeans or to chance mishaps and secondary errors.

They hadn't the slightest idea of what was happening. They didn't understand that Europe was lost, that nothing could save it, that their turn would come soon, because it was not possible that Hitler's Europe should tolerate an Anglophile excrescence such as Greece. The Rome-Berlin Axis would not dare to attack Greece for fear of breaking its own neck!

These stupid discussions enervated him beyond measure—still more so because he felt that some were talking like this for his benefit, as if he were among those responsible for France's defeat. His uncle Spyros had said as much in no uncertain terms. One day he invited all his sons and nephews to his home and, standing under the portrait of Grandfather, gave them hell.

"The Colettis in the old days used to build," he said. "Today they only defile and destroy." The wars had taken all the tough Colettis. Theodore, the captain, had been killed at Kilkis when the Bulgarian resistance was broken; Anastasios, the major, fell at Skra. Demetrios, the colonel in the war in Asia Minor, surrounded on all sides, took the chaplain of the regiment, seized a standard and, revolver and sword in hand, attempted to cut his way out and fell dead. Thus only the weaklings were left to produce today's miserable specimens.

After indulging in a tirade of pleasant remarks of this nature, directed at the assembled group, he began taking them apart one by one, starting with his own sons. When it came to Nikita's turn, Spyros remarked that he had "condescended to set foot on the land of his creative ancestors for the sole purpose of attempting to break its laws." He added harshly, "You're very proud of your poems. You seem to forget that this is the kind of stuff which gave rise to the *Pourquoi*? and destroyed that fine and glorious country." Nikita had not been able to stand that and had risen to go, but his uncle had had time to say angrily: "Get out. Go and live with the people you have poisoned. In this country men struggle and, if need be die. They don't say *Pourquoi*?"

Perhaps this scene with his elderly uncle, the last pillar left standing amid the ruins of his family—a scene which had its comic side and its tragic side too—was instrumental in forcing him to a decision.

He restrained himself, and he didn't drink as he usually did when he was upset. He spent the evening calmly reviewing his predicament.

Even if he were able to return to France he ought not to do so. For many reasons it was impossible for him to live in France for the time being. On the other hand, there was no doubt that sooner or later Greece too would fall and Athens would starve. He remembered how, when he was a child, people had gone hungry during the blockade in World War I, and the whole family had left post-haste for Pteliona. How would the great city be supplied now when the Germans took it? The fields of Attica were sparse and poor. The potatoes which, under the Metaxas dictatorship had begun to be grown, in the few parks of Athens and in Constitution Square, would not go very far; nor could on count on Axis charity, for the invaders would have their own supply problems. The Athenians would surely die of hunger. So he would have to go to Pteliona.

He would make up with that wild fellow at the College of Agriculture. He would apologize to him and ask him to put the ranch in order. In this way at least, during the long, black night ahead, he would want for nothing. He would repair the house, secure some comforts, buy a few trunk-loads of books, and enjoy the company—perhaps more than just the company—of that pretty girl with whom he had kept up a regular correspondence. He would try to build up around him a circle, however small, of people whose society would be bearable. If travel remained open, some of his Paris lady-friends could come and visit him. Why not? Particularly those who hadn't any money. In Paris they would have to face all sorts of difficulties, whereas with him they would have everything they needed. There was no doubt that he must go to Pteliona. This was the only thing he could do. Anything else would be disastrous. And he must go at once because when things got bad it might be impossible to get to Larissa.

And so he left. Before May was out he was gone. Everything came about as he had planned.

At first he encountered an unexpected obstacle. He smiled as he thought of it. Just fancy, at the beginning Alexis had refused to see him or to have anything to do with Pteliona. He had gone to call on him at the College, Mourayias and his daughter had spoken to him, but he had not given in. In the end, without Nikita knowing it, the Director of the Agricultural College had intervened. He was an elderly, much respected man, and as Alexis admitted later, he had taken him almost by force and brought him to Pteliona.

"My friend Stournaris and I", he had said, "want to help you to revive this historic ranch. Do you agree?"

"Do I agree?" he had exclaimed. "There's nothing I would like better!"

Forcing himself to be polite, he had added, "I have already asked for Mr. Stournaris' assistance. He is a man who inspires me with the greatest confidence."

"However, I have to tell you something," the Director had said. "Your ranch is in a worse condition than any in the region. Radical changes involving considerable expense will be needed. New machinery and other equipment will be required. We want to restore Pteliona to its former condition. In your Grandfater's time it competed with the College farm and, in certain areas, was superior to it. Indeed we were envious. Stournaris must have complete freedom of action.

Nikita had accepted everything. He was very gracious to them, entertained them and subtly flattered them.

Every evening Alexis threw himself into discussions and plans. Only in his personal relations with Nikita did the rough farm specialist show little enthusiasm. He called on him regularly, reporting on his plans and submitting estimates of costs. His attitude was that of an employee and he kept his distance. But Nikita, partly because he needed Alexis and partly because he was lonely, was pleasant to him and every time he came Nikita kept him a little longer than was necessary, showing great interest in the work going on at the ranch. Alexis changed gradually—very gradually. It would be more accurate to say that he was becoming politer, and did not avoid Nikita as much as before.

Eventually a day came when the change in the two men became more marked. At first the discussion was very formal. Alexis had opened it by talking about the call of the earth. His attempt to make it appear that the subject had come up naturally was clumsy. No less clumsy was Nikita's attemt to show that he did not understand. Was there such a call? How could the earth speak?

Alexis had heard it. He knew what he was talking about. He almost held conversations with the earth. Nikita wouldn't admit that this was possible, but in the end he was obliged to confess that the first day he had gone out into the plain some months previously, when Mourayias had found him in the field, something strange had happened. He hadn't heard a voice, but something like a new life, like an otherworldly message, had come out of the freshly turned earth and had sent a shock through his whole body. That was all. But after all, it could have been nothing but a false impression created by a dizzy spell or some emotion.

For the first time Alexis' eyes lit up. "The emotion of the receiver." he said. "Messages of all kinds, from the simplest to the most mystifying, are being sent all the time, but only those who are proper receivers can capture them."

Nikita pretended not to understand. Alexis explained. "A deaf man doesn't capture the closest and clearest words spoken to him because he is not a receiver; similarly the most grandiose symphonies by Beethoven have no meaning for one who is not attuned to classical music."

From the following day his attitude towards Nikita changed completely. He became warm and friendly. And in a thousand ways it was apparent that his friendliness had nothing to do with Nikita's relationship to the Old Man. It sprang up because he was the man he was, because it happened this way. As he instinctively had a feeling for the crops, the meadows, the animals and the equipment of Pteliona, so now he became instinctively solicitous of Nikita's comfort, his health and his peace of mind.

What a strange thing this was! Were there actually people who took an interest in others unselfishly, without any particular reason, simply out of what was called friendship? He couldn't believe it! Up to this moment friendship, to Nikita, meant company, a defense against boredom, small politenesses to others to ensure reciprocal politeness from them. It had not meant a lively interest, a true sharing of joys and worries. He had believed that such a thing only existed in fiction, not in real life, or if it did exist in life it was only when love united two human beings, and even love was an unknown quantity. Yet all this was present in this rough man. So there was such a thing as friendship in life! But he —this he admitted only to himself— had never felt it. All he felt now was a satisfaction, a certain gratitude and sympathy for Alexis, but he couldn't feel that natural warm interest which the other showed towards him.

The new and simple warmth of which he was the object might not be anything very significant, but it was something when one was alone, an exile on a farm in Greece. It was comforting, in the midst of the upheavals which had changed the pattern of life so drastically.

Furthermore, the friendship was useful.

Whatever happened, whatever disasters overtook Greece, and however great the privations that came with them, if Pteliona prospered he would lack for nothing. He would have all he needed to live on until the end of the war when he could go back to Paris.

There was no doubt that at the beginning all had gone as he had foreseen, in some ways perhaps better. The only thing he had not forseen was the possibility of the serious illness which struck him down.

He had been told in France that he had a weak liver, had been troubled by it, but had never suffered such pain as he did now. A severe attack came over him bringing with it not only acute, unbearable pain, but also high fever, fits of vomiting, delirium, and hours of fatigue when he hadn't the strength to lift an arm. The disease hit him in full force. Worst of all was the hateful diet imposed upon him and complete abstention from wine or liquor. At the time when he most needed his dear friend, the doctors forbade him to see him.

In the hours of his great weakness, when he was forced to stay in bed in the gruelling August heat and time seemed to stand still, he had for all comfort, to put up with the company of a very few people—most of them not on speaking terms with one another. At last he began to feel better. As this thought passed through his mind he felt light shivers going through his body and drew the sheet over him.

"All I have to do," he thought, "is to think I'm getting better, and it all starts up again, How am I going to come out of this? Perhaps I should ask for another examination, another treatment. I'll suggest it tonight. What a pity I'm obliged to see Katie and Alexis separately. It would be much easier to talk things over if they could come togehter."

He hoped desperately that the accursed fever would not come over him again bringing on the sweating and the bouts of delirium. What a torment it was, especilly the delirium. During the attacks, and after he came out of them, he could never be quite sure if the ravings were all fantasy, or whether they had some connection with reality. There was no doubt he was raving when he thought he was engaged in conversation with his French friends and reliving past memories. But those terrible discussions with Alexis, once a useful acquaintance and now a close friend, were those discussions the product of deliriium, or did he deliberately sort them out and go over them again in his feverish moments?

He could not be sure. But why should he want to repeat

those discussions which had interested him at first and then been a continuous annoyance to him afterwards when he thought about them? Perhaps they came to him again when the fever was upon him exactly because they had a tantalizing bittersweet quality.

"You take a spark," he would cry, "and in your imagination you turn it into a flame! You take a star and turn it into a sun!

"No," Alexis would answer calmly. "This is not imagination. History is our witness, and the lives we live and others see us living. It is a great, a unique thing, Nikita, to be a Greek, and to carry forward in yourself, in your body and your soul, three thousand years of a history that has known heights unknown to the rest of the world.

"And now Greece is experiencing a decline also unknown to the rest of the world."

Alexis resumed quietly. "In between times of extraordinary brilliance, we have often gone through dark periods which were much worse than this. But the splendid and difficult goal which lies before us is this: that we who are the living continuity of the past, should prepare, and perhaps realize a new and genuine Hellenic resurgence."

"Alexis, you don't know what you're talking about. Have you any notion of what the West is? It's a thousand years ahead of this impoverished and wretched country."

Again his friend answered him with conviction; "The greatness of Greece is not to be measured against that of other countries; not by buildings, roads, or giant machines. Those things are fine, and we'll get them eventually. But the greatness of Greece has always been measured by the greatness of the mind and soul. And it is by these that we shall measure once again; we shall test them and find that their standards are still high."

This kind of talk got on Nikita's nerves. Alexis' enthusiastic way of speaking had a certain charm and gave a kind of nobility to his words. But there was so much exaggeration in what he said, and Nikita, a man who denied everything and above all the country which gave him birth, found it hard to accept. He was put out by Alexis' words, but somehow they kept coming back to him when his mind was clouded by the fever, perhaps even more in his delirium than at other times.

He didn't want to think about all this now. Chills and fever might return with greater force if he were upset. He would try to keep calm. He would be patient; it would not be long before the heat died down and in the evening Katie was coming to keep him company

* * * * *

He asked her if she was ready and went into her room for a talk.

"How come you're so early, uncle Nikos. Normally you'd still be taking your siesta at this hour. Is anything happening?"

"I might ask you the same question. You've been getting ready for a long time. Is anything happening?"

She answered him wearily that she was following her regular schedule. He had no business joking about something she didn't like to be teased about.

Nikos became serious. "I haven't come to tease you. On the contrary I've come to talk to you about your 'regular schedule' It's been going on for a long time, and occasionally there are extra visits in the morning. This business has gone on too long; gossip is rampant. Have you any hopes, at least?"

In her light, white dress which contrasted with her dark complexion and her ash-blond hair, with the beauty and health which radiated from her fulsome form, with her mocking expression when Nikos first came in the room, one would have thought that this was a happy girl who enjoyed her life to the fullest. But as soon as her uncle began talking to her, her expression changed: it was that of a woman in despair unwilling to admit defeat.

She became sullen and sat on the edge of the bed, resting her arms upon her knees and clenching her fists.

"I'm conscious of the gossip and sometimes I even hear it. But I don't care. The trouble is that on the one hand I'm bored and am beginning to be disgusted, and on the other I'm not at all sure that I shall succeed."

In answer to his questions she told him that Coletti was a

weak man and that his illness had further weakened him, physically and mentally. At the beginning, the hours she spent at Pteliona were devoted strictly to nursing. Later, friendship developed but she found it boring. There were times when they had interesting discussions on literature, but on the whole she found Coletti timid, negative and weak. Companionship in these circumstances was neither inspiring nor pleasant; it was very tiring.

"But the man's ill," he said.

"He's ill in his mind. He's a neurotic."

"Hasn't all the attention you've given him for so long aroused any feelings on his part? Hasn't he said anything?"

She became more despondent. Leaning forward with her head supported on her arms, she said in a low voice without raising her eyes, "Yes he has said something. And up to a point he may be telling the truth in explaining why he depends so much on me and Alexis. But in the last few days he's been asking me to go to bed with him. That's the extent of my success." she said bitterly.

Nikos cautiously suggested that this was not so terrible. He said that of course she must not do such a foolish thing, but that she could certainly exploit the young man's eagerness to further her purpose.

"My purpose..." she murmured with the same despondent expression. "I'm beginning to ask myself whether I want him after all. I'd gotten this idea into my head because I thought he would be able to give me what I was longing for all these years. But where are my dreams now? We have to forget about Paris for many years to come. He's already tired of Athens, and the most I can hope for is for an occasional trip from Larissa to Athens. And with whom? With whom shall I be spending my nights and days?"

She got up, took a couple of steps, and clutched the back of her chair.

"When he takes my hand," she said, "and tries to draw me to the bed with honeyed words and all sorts of arguments why he should get his way, believe me, I am nauseated." She had worked herself up into a rage. "I really can't understand what a lymphatic and degenerate youth gets out of making love. And that's what he wants to do with a girl like me, after all. Anyway, he makes me sick and I feel like telling him so. I'd like to put an end to this comedy."

Nikos rose from his chair, took her by the hand and soothed her with a few sympathetic words. Then he added, "You know, the 'comedy' has been going on for quite a long time. You can hardly quit now. You're being talked about in every house in Larissa, and this isn't the first time. You've got to go through with this thing. You can't afford to fail. Once you're married to him there will be plenty of ways for you to get what you want. Please believe me. You know I'm very fond of you and that I speak without prejudice. There is no other way out for you. Or, if you prefer, the other ways are worse for a person like you. You must go on."

They couldn't continue their conversation because, at that moment Vassili Manoussis came in. He seemed worried, and his first hesitant words showed that he was trying to say something. At last he pulled himself together and said.

"Today is the Feast of the Holy Virgin. Everyone who's still in Larissa will be out on the piazza tonight. Why don't the three of us go and have an ice-cream and mingle with the people walking up and down? What do you say, Katie darling?"

She noticed how troubled he was and the note of entreaty in his voice, and was sorry for him. However she refused.

"Father," she said gently, "you know I hate these evening parades and never go to them."

"Yes, child, I know. But the 15th of August is a very special day. Can't we for once be like other people?"

She was really sorry for him now and she heard her uncle Nikos agreeing with his brother, so she relented a little. She said she would try to leave Coletti a little earlier and, if she could, she would join them for a walk in the piazza.

And she left to go to Pteliona.

* * * * *

They heard the sound of hoofbeats and paused in their conversation. The rider approached at a quick gallop and stopped abruptly under the window. Who else could it be but Alexis?

And yet it was not likely that he would come at that hour when he knew that Katie would be at Pteliona. That would be contrary to the tacit agreement which had been established between them. Nikita and Katie were amazed, and before they had time to say anything they heard heavy footsteps on the stairs. The door was flung open and Alexis appeared with a strange expression on his face. Without greeting them, he said, "I've come at this unusual time because something terrible has happened. They've torpedoed the *Helle*."

"The *Helle?* Which *Helle*?"

"Where? How did it happen?"

"I don't know too much about it," he answered. "Two of my colleagues insisted on taking me to a village feast near here. No sooner had the dancing begun than the police suddenly stopped the music. They said that an order had come from Athens to stop the festive dancing all over Greece because this morning a submarine sank our cruiser in the harbor of Tinos where it was anchored for the feast of Our Lady of Grace. I asked the head constable about it, but all he knew was that there had been victims."

Nikita's pale and emaciated face turned even whiter. In a weak voice he asked, "Was the submarine seen? Could it have been an explosion on the ship and they're saying it was torpedoed?"

"Impossible. It is a big ship, the second largest cruiser in our navy. It wouldn't have sunk from an accident on board. Besides, the authorities don't lie about things like this."

"It must have been an Italian submarine," Katie said.

"That's the most likely supposition, and that's why I came to tell you. The damage to us is great because we haven't many ships and this was a splendid vessel. But what is more important than the damage is the significance of this cowardly act. I don't think they are trying to frighten us and take the wind out of our sails. They know us too well and must realize that this sort of thing gets our blood up. Considering their other provocations I can only guess that they are going to attack us soon, maybe even tomorrow. That's what everyone thinks. They must have wanted to begin by depriving us of one of our best ships, without risk to themselves.

The sick man sat up in his bed, leaned upon his arms, and turned an anguished face to the other two. They looked at him in silence and this seemed to disturb him. Katie smiled at him and pressed his hand. This comforted him a little and he was about to give expression to the panic that had come over him, but he was ashamed and merely said, "Tomorrow! As soon as that! But what you say is terrible."

"Yes, it is," Alexis said, and with a sudden movement he broke the switch he was carrying across his knee. "And to think that I'm officer-in-charge of a machine gun squad of the Eighth Division of Epirus, and now they want to keep me back as an indispensible expert for agricultural cultivation. A thousand others could do this work and leave me free to go to my post at the front. I telephoned Divisional Headquarters before coming here and was told that they have no orders to mobilize us and furthermore, a friend of mine informed me that I'm on the list of experts reserved for agricultural development, and that therefore I shall certainly not be called up before the fighting actually starts."

He happened to look at Katie and saw on her face an expresion of love and admiration which made him shiver. Could it be that she was still in love with him? He was suddenly filled with great joy. But her expression changed immediately. With an ironic smile she asked, "Will you be in time to go?"

He looked at her with surprise and annoyance. "What do you mean? Of course I'll be in time."

"Eight million bayonets," she replied, "and the greatest air force in Europe. We are only a drop in the ocean, Alexis, and Italy is a great power. If she attacks she will flood Greece with her army, she will bomb roads and bridges, and Divisional Headquarters will be blown to bits before it has time to send you the orders you expect."

He was standing in front of her and gave her a furious look. "Our people are well aware of the various possibilities," he said. "But even if things turn out as you say, then every Greek, without waiting for orders, will spring forth, up from the rivers and down from the mountains, and go on foot, wherever he must in order to stop those, whoever they may be, who attempt to invade our homes."

The smile still played on her lips. Pretty and provocative, she started to speak, "I think..."

"You don't have to think anything," he interrupted her angrily. "And if you know what's best for you, you'll refrain from making this kind of defeatist remark anywhere else, or you may find yourself in jail before you know it."

In a fit of temper she stamped her foot on the floor. She turned to the Nikita, gave him a hasty smile and pressed his hand, then ran to the door and left.

Alexis had turned toward the window and stared through the slats of the closed shutters. There was a painful silence.

After a while, Nikita Coletti said, "You've embarrassed her greatly. Without you and her, I don't know how I would cope with my illness and loneliness."

They spoke a little about what had happened without going too deeply into the matter of the relationship between the three of them. At that moment this was not the question that interested them. Nikita was thinking about the war, the war that might start tomorrow plunging him into adventures which he had never imagined possible and now was afraid to contemplate. He hesitated to voice his fears, but he had no one except Alexis from whom to ask advice. Sheepishly he said, "And if war, an invasion, comes tomorrow, what do you think will become of me?"

Alexis looked at him as if he had not understood the question.

"Do you think I should stay here?" he asked again. "Or shall I leave for Athens?" Then as if a bright idea had suddenly come to him he continued in a more lively tone. "Or I might go to some island. I had forgotten that Larissa is the headquarters of an Army Corps, and a key-point in communications."

Alexis looked at him in surprise but remained silent. He went to the window and flung the shutters wide open. Light and heat poured in from the burning furnace of the plain and dispelled the sickly gloom and the fetid dampness. The blazing fire of earth might well melt down the weak, but it turned the strong into tempered steel.

Alexis, strong in his male vigor, gazed steadfastly before him. "If war is declared, Nikita Coletti has only one place to go to—to the place where the Greeks will be fighting to save their country."

Nikita again raised himself on his bed, and this time, he spoke with some animation. "But I'm sick," he said. "Cut out all this patriotic talk when you're speaking to me. All this time you've been like a brother to me, and I've done everything you said because I trust you, and I know that you are strong and that I am weak and desperate. But now you are carried away by your patriotism and you are talking nonsense."

"Half the people in Greece suffer from malaria, others from tuberculosis, almost all from undernourishment. You don't suffer from any of these things. You've had a bout of liver trouble because you haven't taken proper care of yourself, but now all the symptoms of your illness have receded. You've returned to a normal state of health, as the doctors would say. All you have to do is to watch your diet. In other words there is nothing the matter with you."

"But I'm ill, I'm weak, I'm exhausted. Besides, have you considered what you said? How shall I go and fight? As a foreign Greek I'm not liable to conscription; I don't belong to any unit. I've never been trained. I know nothing about war and firearms."

He saw that Alexis was watching him without being in any hurry to answer him and he added impatiently, "I don't suppose you want me to take up a shotgun or a knife and start out alone for the front!"

Alexis, leaning against the window, spoke in the same calm manner as before. "You know Italian," he said. "You know other foreign languages. If you volunteered they would use you to examine prisoners, and for liaison work with allied officers and newsmen. Weakened and untrained as you are, you can still help, Nikita. What I should like very much to do is to get you a job on a regimental or, better still, on a battalion staff."

"What's the difference?"

"At the battalion level you would be doing an interpreter's work but you'd be near the scene of battle, you would be part of it, and you might at some time have to take hold of a rifle."

Nikita did not understand at all. It was true that Alexis loved him; he had proved this many times. He loved him like a brother, he had stood by him in his troubles, had spent whole nights at his bedside, and had displayed a tender compassion that one would not have expected to find in so rough a man. But now this same man who had done all he could to comfort him, now when it was proper and normal that he should either stay at home or go to some quiet place in the country, this same man was telling him that he should go out and suffer hardships and maybe be killed. How could that be possibe? It seemed that even patriotic fervor had a kind of professional deviation and that beyond a certain point it perverted a man's reason.

"You must be crazy," he said impatiently. "But there's something else I'd like to know, since you're so eager for me to get into battle. Aren't you afraid? Have you no fear for yourself?"

"Yes, I am afraid," Alexis answered in the same calm voice, but with an anxious expression in his eyes. "And I'm especially afraid of being disabled, of losing my eyes or my legs. That must be terrible!"

Nikita felt better. His morale was restored as he felt that some sort of equality existed between himself and his friend, and he spoke more cheerfully.

"Yes, it certainly must be terrible. And you want me, without my having any obligation, to risk being disabled or killed? It's the first time I've known you to be unreasonable, Alexis. If I leave this place, it will be to go somewhere where I'll be more secure." And he added in a louder, somewhat hysterical voice, "I'm untrained and I'm ill. I'm not going to do anything foolish."

Alexis looked at him and said nothing.

"Why are you staring at me with that accusing look? What you say is madness and you can't help knowing it's madness. Isn't it true that I've never been a soldier? Isn't it true that I'm a sick man?"

Again Alexis said nothing. He crossed his arms over his breast and looked out of the window. He stared at the sky and remained silent. Nikita could not bear the tension; he got out of bed and approached Alexis barefoot. "I've enough troubles, Alexis," he said. "Don't condemn me; don't make things harder for me."

Alexis gave him a friendly look then turned his eyes again to the blue sky. Maybe he hesitated to reply, maybe he was wondering what he should say.

Nikita went on; "Don't compare me with yourself. You are strong. You are an elemental force like rain or wind or lightning."

Still staring out the window, Alexis now answered him. "Every man is, or should be, a force of nature, should be as the wind or lightning. The difference is that one man is stronger than another, or that he becomes stronger, according to the callenge that he has to meet."

Nikita couldn't believe that by any stretch of the imagination he himself could be compared to lightening!

"No," he said, "it isn't so. Few men are elemental forces of nature and they sustain the others; they defend countries and uphold ideas. I am nothing but a sick man."

Alexis' eyes met his. There was steady purpose in his gaze.

"In ten days, when you've recovered your strength," he said, "you'll be stronger than before. But even if you are ill, you must consider that now many strong men are going to be killed or disabled. What excuse is your puny little illness?"

Nikita found it difficult to answer. Shamefacedly he said, "Why do you want to humiliate me by making me repeat what I've alread said. I'm not like you. I'm afraid. I'm scared of everything. I'm a weakling. Why do you insist?"

Alexis took him affectionately by the arm and drew him to the bed.

"Lie down, and I'll explain to you." He covered him with the sheet and sat by him.

"You're not a weakling," he said. "You're among the strong. But during the many years you spent in the loneliness, the mists, and the rain of Paris, your mind grew sick. As soon as you came back here, even before you opened your eyes to the sunlight of Greece, you heard the call of the earth!"

"Here we go again!" Nikita interrupted.

"If you haven't realized yet the meaning of your experience on that day, you will sometime. The earth does not call to the constitutionally weak. It only calls to the strong. And if you did try to shake the dust of Greece off your feet and everything here seemed to you foreign and uncomfortable, you came back and all alone without being forced by anyone who chose to respond to the call you heard. That is why we at Pteliona all love you."

"I don't understand," he murmured. "I tell you truthfully, I don't understand you."

"I'm telling you again. You may not be fully conscience of what happened to you. That time will come. But don't interrupt me. I have more to say."

His expression was gentle; there was something slightly mystical about it as he went on firmly and with growing earnestness. "Can we refuse, when we are given the opportunity to repeat Plataea and Thermopylae? Don't you understand that if we are attacked and we throw up our hands in despair, we and our children will no longer be Hellenes?"

"I understand," he replied. "But you don't know, and you haven't ever understood what I am. I'm more a Frenchman than a Greek; I'm more an invalid than a healthy man; I'm more of a weakling than a strong man. I'm not strong at all. I'm weak, very weak, hopelessly weak."

For the first time since they had become friends Alexis looked at Nikita harshly and Nikita felt it.

"I don't think that I've been mistaken about your inner private world," Alexis said. "And you won't like what I'm going to say. France is a great and proud country. You have seen how a few Frenchmen in London and all of them in the provinces are going on with the war and calling upon the Parisians to take up arms again. And I'm sure they will. When Paris is liberated and you return there, everyone will turn their backs on you. You will be the foreigner who, as some have already written,poisoned the minds of a whole generation with decadent verse. You will be the foreigner who refused to defend his mother country—one which bore so glorious a name. You will be an outcast there and an outcast here. And here you will be doubly condemned, because you aren't just any Greek. You bear a name which has set an example and stands as a symbol. If you go into hiding many will ask why *they* have to face danger in order to protect *your* land and *your* wealth.

Great beads of perspiration stood out on Nikita Coletti's forehead, and when he heard the bitter words about his position in France he was overcome with anguish. When Alexis had finished, he leaned back on his pillows, closed his eyes tightly, clasped his emaciated fingers and said: "Maybe you're right. But I can't, I can't! Your'e asking for more than I can give! I can't."

Alexis sat beside him on the bed and took him by the shoulders.

"Nikita," he said. "I always wanted to have a brother. God gave me one in you. I wouldn't have loved you as I do if you had an incurably tainted soul."

He rose and dampened the edge of a towel and wiped the sweat from Nikita's face. "Unfortunately I have to leave you now," he said. "It will be dusk soon. I have to go to the monastery and get back to the College before the boys go to bed. If there's important news I'll come back."

* * * * *

When he arrived in front of Mourayias' cottage, holding Pegasus by the bridle, Phrosso was going out.

"If it is not absolutely necessary, please don't go now," he said.

He told her briefly of the torpedoing and of what it might mean to all of them. Then he added, "You would do me a favor if you went up to the house. I've upset him with everything I told him, and also with a quarrel I had with Katie."

A pained expression had come over Phrosso's face. "Alexis," she said, "since war is upon us, sit down and let me look at you. It's you I want to see. What can I say to the man up in the house? What have I to do with that aristocrat who looks down on me as if I were a Cinderella? Do stay a little please."

"I'm sorry. I have to go to Father Modestos, little Phrosso." She gave him a look full of tenderness, and he spoke more gently to her.

"I may have something important to tell you, and then I'll come back. In the meantime, please don't disappoint me. Do me the favor I asked. Don't think about the 'aristocrat.' Think of the man who lies on his bed and suffers. I think we upset him very much. Do go to him, please."

He did not look at her again. He took hold of the reins with one hand and the pommel of the saddle with the other, bent his knees and leaped lightly and easily onto his horse. As he galloped out of the gate his feet found the stirrups.

She stood watching him as he went until he was lost on the edge of the horizon. He seemed to be snatched up in the cloud of dust which he raised as he went, to be taken off by a whirlwind sent down from the heavens. She felt her heart tighten. She imagined that the cloud which enveloped him and took him away was not just a cloud of dust but an incandescent mist, woven around him by fate, which would take him far, far away. And she, petrified and powerless, watched him as he disappeared.

When she could no longer discern the black speck in the luminous cloud that was fading out of sight, she felt weak and lost. She ran to her room, flung herself face down upon her bed, and without knowing why burst into tears, sobbing disconsolately.

* * * * *

Nikita was told that Mourayias' daughter wanted to see him. He did not answer at once. This visit seemed very strange to him. The plowman's daughter wanted to see him? This had never happened before. Very strange indeed!

Alexis had spoken to him about her and had told him her story; he seemed to have a kind of admiration for her. Nikita had noticed her. She was neat and pretty, and there was a country freshness in her face. But she was still only a plowman's daughter.

His first reaction was to refuse to see her, saying that he did not feel well, or to see her for a minute and send her away. But he changed his mind and was ashamed to realize that he felt an expectant pleasure. Only a little while ago hadn't he been terrified that he would be left alone again all evening, all night? Oh, that loneliness,that excruciating loneliness! He could not bear to be alone in his room, particularly during the long nights of torment. There were the short periods of respite, visits from Alexis, Katie, the doctor, and then the loneliness again, the suffocating company he kept with his own weary self! How then could he react negatively to the visit that was now announced?

He received her with joy that she didn't recognize him. She was startled. Alexis had told Phrosso that he had been upset and was torturing himself; and yet this was the first time she saw him free from his usual cold indifference, from the almost contemptuous manner in which he usually said 'good-day.' He spoke to her with lively interest about several little things. It was true that when he spoke about the war and his health he appeared to be terrified and this disgusted her. Otherwise he was quite pleasant.

Could it be that this degenerate man who played the aristocrat and had forgotten his humble ancestors, the poor mountain herdsmen, was coming out of his torpor? Could this really be possible? Could this callow youth really be turning into a man? Alexis thought so, but she hadn't believed it. And yet now, apart from the things that frightened him and made him ridiculous, he was taking a lively interest in talking with her late into the night. He seemed to be a very ageeable person.

When she saw he was getting tired and got up to go, he said to her politely and with sincere friendliness. "Please do come again. Your visit has done me a lot of good."

As she went out into the warm night and crossed the big garden under the stars, she had a strange feeling that while one heavy hand was tugging at her heart-strings, another softer one was caressing her. At one and the same moment a harrowing intimation seemed to be coming to her from one quarter, while from another there was, as it were, a distant premonition of well-being.

She stood still and looked up at the night sky. Could she find an answer up there? She saw the vast black dome studded with innumerable stars and divided by the fantastic trail of the Milky Way, and realized that no answer was to be found there; on the contrary, in the starry heavens there resided an even greater mystery, unanswerable,—the greatest mystery of all.

"How strange," she thought, "that one should be overcome with grief at the thought of losing a friend as noble and proud as a golden eagle, and at the same time to be happy at the thought of gaining a friend as helpless as a molting sparrow. Who can ever fathom the human soul? Who can ever understand the decrees of fate?

* * * * *

As she passed through the piazza, Katie saw that the evening promenade to which her father had set his heart on taking her, was in abeyance that day. In place of the laughter and chatter that was usually heard at this hour, there was hardly a murmur. Only a few people were out for a walk, and there were no girls among them, those quiet, well-behaved girls of the provinces who usually came out to show off their best frocks and their charms as prospective brides, or to exchange rapid glances with their loved ones or even, if they were very daring, fleeting smiles. Few men were walking. They were standing around in small groups. They were engaged in discussion, and from their faces it was evident that while they were not perhaps afraid, they were determined and angry. Their attitude was restrained but it was clear that something very serious occupied their thoughts.

As she crossed the piazza, many turned to look at her. Some greeted her with pleasant smiles; others paused in their conversation and very obviously started to gossip about her. Not even the fear of war was sufficient to curb the sensuous desire she aroused in the men. Nor did the danger that was imminent put a stop to the wagging of tongues in this small town.

"Why am I dogged by this accursed fate?" she thought. "And from now on who knows whether it won't get worse?"

* * * * *

Her father and her uncle Nikos were talking seriously and when she entered the house they didn't pay any attention to her, which was most unusual. They said hello and went on with their conversation. She sat down in a corner.

"What a pity we've extended ourselves in making those recent loans to the farmers," her father was saying. "Of course, the interest we're getting is extraordinarily high and how could anyone have known that things would turn out this way?''

''We must start calling them in tomorrow and try to collect what we can,'' her uncle said. ''We can reduce the interest if we have to. The point is that we've got to forget about interest and invest all the bank's funds in pounds sterling. As of tomorrow the price of gold is bound to start going up.''

A smile of cunning satisfaction crept over her father's lips: ''Gold started to move up some time ago,'' he said ''and I've kept my eyes open. We are well covered. I've been buying pounds and tin steadily.''

''Tin?'' Nikos asked in surprise.

Once more her father said with smug satisfaction, ''I know this from the last war. In wartime nothing appreciates like tin; you can't get any on the market. So since last September, I have been quietly buying tin from merchants and tinsmiths, and I've collected quite a stock down in the basement.''

''Wouldn't this be an opportunity to acquire a building or two?'' Nikos said. ''People in need of money who don't understand the situation might be willing to sell.''

Katie got up and came toward them: ''I'm surprised at you,'' she said. ''This is no time to buy; this is time to sell this house and the shop on Main Street.''

They looked at her in astonishment. Nikos smiled at her sarcastically: ''I knew you were a woman of musical and literary talents,'' he said. ''I didn't know you were an economist as well.''

''My dearest Katie...'' her father mumbled.

''It doesn't take much wisdom to see what's going to happen,'' Katie said. ''Larissa is our greatest military center and is the key-point of two railroads and of our principal highways. When war is declared the town will be bombed and reduced to ashes. The only difference for us, if we survive, will be that we shall be scrounging among the ruins to find the melted gold sovereigns and the melted tin that father has collected.''

The two brothers looked at each other. Vassili Manoussis grew pale and his expression of cunning shrewdness turned to one of anxiety. Nikos stopped being sarcastic. He frowned.

''Well, what do you propose? What do you think we ought to do?''

"We ought to find somebody who doesn't understand what's going on, sell all our property, and go to Athens or some island with our sovereigns and our tin."

"But that's impossible! Impossible!" her father cried, very perturbed.

"If I'm right, why can't it be done, father?"

Taking his head in his hands Vassili Manoussis said, "You may be right, but how can I leave my work? They'll fire me! I've spent a whole life-time building up my position in the bank. And what about the house and the store? I've economized on food, even on coffee in order to buy them and improve them. How can I sell them, how can I possibly get rid of them in a hurry in order to buy gold which will go up even more in price tomorrow?"

There was such hopelessness in his voice that his brother was sorry for him. He turned to Katie and said to her severely, "Sit down and listen. If Larissa is reduced to ashes the whole country will be involved in such disaster that no plans or predictions will hold good. We shall act with reasonable foresight. Your father and I know something about wars and finance and many other things which a young girl, however clever she may be, has not the experience to understand. I've discussed the whole situation with your father and we have come to the conclusion that at this uncertain time we have to be cautious and not expose ourselves. On the other hand, we see that our compatriots are fit to be tied. They're afraid all right, but they've been seized with patriotic hysteria. We've got to go along with them somehow. And that's where you can help us, and it will do you good as well. Starting tomorrow you'll go the a clinic to take a course in nursing, so that if war is declared you can volunteer for service at the Military Hospital."

"You mean I'm to go among sick people and all that dirt?" she cried.

"It is necessary. It's the only thing that will not expose us when the Italians come and at the same time will bring us into line with our patriotic fellow-citizens."

"So I am to go and empty chamber-pots and clean up all those filthy men for the sake of a bunch of fools? I won't do it. I have enough troubles as it is."

Her father stood up. His face was wet with perspiration: "I

can't stand it,'' he said. ''I'm going crazy. I'll take a walk. All this is too much for me.''

* * * * *

Tonight again Pegasus couldn't understand his master's mood.

Early in the afternoon when they first went out his master wanted to play games. At times he would put him to a light trot, then he would break into a gallop, or jump ditches, or make him dance on his hind legs, and then ride slowly with the reins loose ont he horse's neck. On the return to the familiar house and its big trees, he rode him at full speed, striking him with an osier switch. They galloped without pause in the heat and arrived swiftly at their goal.

Now as they went toward the lush clover meadows where the sound of the monastery bells was often heard, he rode listlessly and let him go wherever he wanted. Whether he went at a gallop or at a trot, his master as usual sat firm in the saddle, but he seemed to be indifferent to the gait, as if he didn't know he was riding, as if he were lost in a dream.

And then, later, when the master suddenly made him feel the bit and broke into a gallop again, Pegasus did not at all understand what he wanted. He took him off the trail and made him run across unplowed fields. And yet they were coming to the hill where the ravine was, the dry torrent which was very deep. The bridle-path came down sideways to facilitate the crossing and went up sideways on the other side. Why had he left the path? Why was he riding furiously at an ever increasing speed? Pegasus couldn't figure it out.

And suddenly, when he struck him and spoke to him and urged him on with all his strength as they were nearing the ravine, Pegasus understood. His master for the first time wanted to clear the torrent at one jump. He understood and the froth came to his mouth. The torrent-bed was deep and the leap would have to be made from some distance away from the crumbling edge which would not afford a foothold. But Pegasus was not frothing because he was afraid, but because the leap was dangerous, it was a magnificent jump. This was splendid madness! How it excited him! How wonderful of his master to have thought of it!

The horse knew that the rider was competent and felt his desire to make a clean jump. Never had he sat so light on his back. Not for a moment did the horse feel any weight in the saddle and his spine moved freely, rippling like a snake. The master supported himself in the stirrups and with his knees and legs pressed hard against the horse's sweating shoulders, and he bent far forward over him; as if he was being supported by his very breath which Pegasus felt, pouring over his neck and through his mane, like fire.

So Pegasus galloped on, galloped with all his might, his head stretched forward. He galloped madly, trying at every step to gather his feet under him faster, and to put more spring into every stroke of his feet on the ground which shot them further forward.

And as the iron hoofs trod the dry, stony earth faster and harder, harder, harder, and the rush of air became ever more violent, the echo of the hoofbeats on the earth and the whistling of the wind filled the hearts of man and horse with a paean of impetuous passion and strength which caused them to beat in even greater unison than before.

They came to the edge of the ravine, and at the moment when Pegasus realized that there was room for only one more step, his master gave him a rough command and gave the bridle a hard upward pull. In that instant Pegasus felt that he and the man who rode him so brilliantly were one body governed by a single fate, and he struck the ground with his hoofs with more strength than ever before and, stretching out his neck and head and bringing his legs up beneath his belly, he sprang into the air with an impetuous force which gave his leap to victory an upsurge as though he were borne on wings. When he landed lightly on the other side and was carried forward by the impetus of his spring, he realized that in his jump he had spanned almost twice the breadth of the ravine.

Then he heard a wild cry—a long, boundless cry such as he had never before heard from his master. It resounded and cut the air as if it came from a trumpet, as if it was meant to strike the mountains beyond and call forth an echo. What was this strange cry? Why had his master cried out so loud? Why was he still crying out? At last he realized that it was a cry of triumph, for now the rider was laughing with broad wide-echoing laughter, and then he started crying out again.

Without receiving any sign or command, Pegasus stopped,

stood up on his hind legs, stretched his head toward the heavens, and started to neigh with all the force of his lungs, as never before.

As he was in this upright position he felt a hand caress his neck and a kiss that was born of fire and love. He gave one or two great leaps in joy, and stood up again beating the air with his front feet; his eyes flashed and his nostrils dilated, and with his head lifted high he neighed madly while his master continued to let forth wild cries of triumph over the blazing plain.

Thus on that evening, when Greece was expecting war on the morrow, when the sun marked that expectation by dyeing the broad skies of Thessaly with its last streaks of blood, the hill of St. Elias for long moments threw back to the great plain the echoes of victorious exultation.

* * * * *

In the ancient church Father Modestos sat in a pew and followed the evening service. He was an old man now and left the officiating to younger priests. From time to time he let his glance fall on the lower row of frescoes opposite him. There he saw the warrior saints, St. Demetrios, St. Nestor and others who stood with their swords in their hands. He looked at the saints and they seemed to look back at him. At times they seemed to converse with him and to look at him with complicity when he reviewed all that had happened during the Macedonian campaign. How sweet was that reverie in loneliness and isolation, in the atmosphere of his monastery, where bygone ages blended with present times. As his eye wandered from one painting to the next, the thoughts of the old abbot travelled along the paths of the past. Suddenly he grasped the arms of his pew. What was this? A vision sent to him by the Lord?

Opposite him, the lower row of the warrior saints was interrupted at one point by the arched doorway, left open in the summer because of the great heat. But now, as he looked, the open door did not create a gap between the beautiful young warriors bearing arms. The space had been filled by a figure—a tall, motionless, calm male figure crowned, as if with a halo, by the arch of the door. His aged eyes were not deceiving him. The row of saints had been completed.

He made the sign of the cross. "This vision is the Lord's will."

He looked more closely and observed that the new saint looked at him and smiled. He understood and was deeply moved. Why was he seeing his beloved child among the warrior saints who had retained their youth through the ages?

He went to him and together they walked to the covered porch of the church.

In a few words Alexis told him the news and said that everyone believed that war was imminent. The old abbot listened to him intently but did not interrupt him. When Alexis finished, the abbot remained thoughtful for a while, and then removing his cap, he lifted up both arms and looking up to the heavens, intoned passionately the Byzantine prayer: "Lord! Lord of the Powers. Lord, preserve Thy people and bless Thine inheritance, granting victories to the emperors against the barbarians."

Then he knelt on the pavement of the porch, leaned his forehead on the threshold of the ancient church, crossed his arms over his breast and prayed with fervor. He breathed heavily as he prayed and an indistinct murmur issued from his lips. Before rising he once more lifted his eyes on high. His visage was calm and his expression was one of complete serenity. Fixing his gaze on one point he stretched out his arms and said, "Neither in arms, nor with horses, but in the name of our Lord shall we be magnified. Our enemies have stumbled and fallen, we have risen again and have been established. Lord we pray Thee, in Thy almighty power, make this psalm of David come true for us. We pray Thee, O Lord!"

They walked a few paces, and Alexis said, "Father, I should like to confess to you; I need your advice again."

They went to the abbot's cell. "What is it my child? I'm listening."

"Father Modestos, I don't know exactly when, but I shall soon be leaving for the war. I am content, I have no complaint against life I have lived. It was a fine life. I have only one sorrow—a deep sorrow—that I have no children of my own, no son. And the thought that I may never return makes my grief all the greater. In fact it is quite unbearable." He stopped speaking and looked ahead of him deep in thought.

"So then? the abbot asked.

"If there's enough time, I plan to take out a marriage license tomorrow and come here to have you marry us."

Very surprised, Father Modestos asked, "And who may the girl be?"

"I'm thinking of proposing to Mourayias' daughter, Phrosso. We're very good friends, and she is a wonderful person—a fine woman. I think she'll accept me. If I come back from the war we'll build up a good life together and have a family. If I don't return she will get my pension, and the child which, if God wills, she'll carry in her womb, will grow up."

He saw that the abbot had turned his face away and seemed troubled. he asked him, "Father, you seem to disapprove. Why?"

"Because, my son, marriage is one of the great mysteries of the church—the greatest perhaps, and it is fulfilled at the bidding of the Lord whose spirit enters into the union of his creatures for the creation of new life. Don't be influenced by the fact that the laws of men have turned marriage into an act of everyday life. According to the will of the Lord marriage is no such thing. Marriage is an overpowering surge, an inestinguishable flame that issues from all the cells within us; it is something that God alone can ignite within us since, in an inscrutable, divine manner we are given strength to create new souls. That is why couples, united by this divine flame, even out of wedlock, when they lie together are fulfilling a holy mystery. Don't imagine that at that hour they are playing. They are fulfilling the most sacred and the most beautiful act of their lives and they are accomplishing it according to the prescriptions of the Lord. And you, a man of honor and integrity, cannot wed in any other way."

Alexis was not expecting a reply of this kind and was at a loss. The old man continued: "The other girl—the one you love—doesn't she want to marry?"

Alexis' voice was harsh as he replied. "No, she doesn't. And I don't think I want to marry her either, because she's not fit to bring up the kind of family I dream of having." He continued more calmly but no less earnestly. "But I want to ask you this, Father. If my passion for her is a message from God, if it is a surge and a flame come to me for an unworthy woman, or at least why did not the Lord imbue her with the same feelings in the same form and with the same intensity?"

Father Modestos stroked his beard, passed his hand under it

and, as was his habit when he had a difficult question to answer, he lifted it up over his face up to his eyes. Over the edge of the white beard his two black eyes lit up with visionary brightness.

"My beloved child," he said after a pause, "if I could answer your question it would mean that I was in close communication with the Almighty. Hidden are the purposes of the Lord, my son. I myself was once puzzled by the same problem—you are the first to hear of it—when as a young man I ran away from home and family to throw myself at the feet of a woman whom I adored but at the same time despised. And when I came to, when I saw the Great Light, when I learned at last that all the hidden purposes of God are formed in wisdom, I still occasionally sinned and asked myself the question you now ask. Only later did I understand...maybe I understood."

"What did you understand?"

"Robust and full of life as I was in my youth, I was drawn into the whirlpool of life and, if I had not gone through the agony of passion, if I had not fallen into sin and blindness and worthlessness, I should never have seen the Great Light. Maybe the will of God deliberately bent me to a life of false values in order to enable me to see the light and enjoy that great privilege. I don't know. It is possible."

After a short pause, Alexis said, "My case is different. I am a believer and I go to church, but I haven't seen the Great Light, as you call it. And now my problem is simple: I feel a great need to leave children behind me. It is about this that I need your advice."

"I have given you my advice; it is the only advice I can give to a man like you. The only way for you to have children is the way I told you. The rest is nothing but egoism and does not become you."

They exchanged glances and Alexis said, "This time, I don't know if I shall follow your advice, Father."

"You will act as you choose, my son. Each of us has his own mind and his own nature. If you have made your decision, you have my blessing; but I will not marry you."

"But how can that be? You surely won't refuse!"

"I love you, Alexis, and I give you my blessing. But do not ask me, a humble believer, to take part in the parody of a holy mystery."

Before Alexis left, Father Modestos took his hand and whispered to him in the darkness. "I'm an old man, and you will go off to the war, very soon perhaps. We are the only people who know about the crypt. We must tell someone—more than one person.''

''What is in the crypt now?''

''Very little. The gold napoleons were spent for the refugees of '22. Since then I have added a small bag of sovereigns. There are a few arms, Garand Mannlicher rifles in good condition, and a number of cases of ammunition. But it is not what is in the crypt that worries me. It's the entrance which is very hard to find. It may be needed...Who knows? To whom shall I reveal the secret?''

''To Nikita Coletti'', Alexis replied without hesitation.

''My son,'' Father Modestos exclaimed, startled, ''that's the last name I expected to hear from you.''

''Tell him, tell him before anyone else. The only thing is that if war breaks out, I think he'll go too. In that case tell Mourayias and his daughter, Phrosso. If Nikita goes, rely on her above anyone else for whatever may be necessary, Father.''

* * * * *

In the light freshness of the night, Pegasus once more felt that his master was indifferent to his gait. As always he sat firmly on his back but seemed not to be aware that he was riding; he seemed to be in a dream. The proud animal did not like this. He liked to be ruled and to carry out commands, especially the commands of this capable horseman, for they were always swift, precise and bold.

He gave one or two loud, persistent whinnies to wake him up and to lead him on to some game—any game, but without success. His master stroked his neck; that was all. His whinnying drew no echoing response from heart or hill—it was lost in the silent darkness of night.

Part Three

THE PATH TO RESURRECTION

I

War did not come on August 16th, nor on the 17th or 18th, nor on any other August day. Only its shadow became heavier, its threatening rumblings louder, and anxiety chilled men's hearts. There were no threats, no sensational accusations, provocations or insults to indicate that was was approaching. It was approaching but it did not come.

Every evening the wide heaven over Thessaly was streaked with red from west to east. But this happened every summer. However this summer, after the Feast of the Holy Virgin, the red streaks in the sky were broader, more brilliant, and before the first shadows of night took the last light of the sun, the redness became dull and took on the evil, dead color of stale, clotted blood.

Some people, worried by the distant sounds of war, said that the sky took on that color because the blood which was shed in other lands deepened and increased its red tint. Others maintained that the flames kindled by war in other places were reflected in the sky. Still others believed that this was a heavenly omen sent by fate to warn its chosen people to be prepared for the approaching struggle. But each dawn heralded a golden day, luminous under a blue sky. And evening followed once more red and bloodshot.

Far, far away, a deluge of fire and metal poured down on the one country that had refused to bow to the aggressor. All heard the terrible news from abroad; they looked at the red sky and held their breath.

War is coming! It is coming!

If only a miracle would happen and it wouldn't come after all to this poor land buffeted by so many storms, to this exposed land which, in its poverty, could not endure any more cloudbursts of disaster. But what hope was there? War is coming! It is at hand!

Lovers hastened to get married, brave young men clenched their fists, shrewd business men shuddered and tried to put their affairs in order. All held their breath.

There were times when the fatigue of expectation and the anger at the insult were so great, that they all said: Well, let the war come after all! Let the great storm burst! It would be better to stand up and fight than to go on putting up with the torment of this savage premonition of disaster.

Nikita Coletti was the only one who never spoke like this. He was wrapped in his own selfish thoughts. Paralyzed with fear, he secretly prayed with all his heart that the war might never come. And when the first rains fell and the rivers swelled, making things difficult, as they said, for military operations, when the weather cooled off and the meadows grew green again, bringing some solace to the soul, Nikita began to hope. Perhaps the war would not come! Or at any rate not for a long time.. Who could tell? There might be some hope.

Not that life at Pteliona was pleasant. But at least he was alive, and the days rolled by, and later...later things might change. That was all. Nothing more. If the great danger which had made him forget everything else and put up with his lot had not existed, he would have cursed the day when he had shut himself up in this ranch which had brought him nothing but unbearable weeks of boredom. The terrible monotony suffocated him. And as he had no inclination to read and still less to write, only the company of pleasant, familiar people could have distracted him. But where could he find them? The few people he knew had grown fewer. Even Katie, since she had started her course at the clinic, came far less often and seemed strangely absorbed in her own concerns.

Thus he had come to depend upon Alexis and upon the people at the ranch. But he was obliged to dissemble with them, for all the things that interested them were alien to him. It was true that gradually he had been carried away by his dissimulation, and had begun to feel a slight curiosity about two subjects that filled their lives: the country and the land. But it was no more than curiosity that he felt. How could such things fill his life which was so different and which now dragged itself out in loneliness, fear, and boredom!

But it didn't matter! No! It didn't matter. The days rolled on quietly. All he wanted was to gain time—plenty of time—if only war were not to come.

But a black morning arrived when he was awakened by the thunderbolt of disaster. He felt someone shoving him and opened his eyes.

It was still dark. Dawn had not yet broken. A flashlight cast a dim light over the room. Alexis was holding him. He was neither smiling nor cheeful. He seemed determined and serious and there was a hard, luminous gleam in his eyes.

"I have come to say goodbye," he said simply.

Nikita understood and grew cold. But the hope within him refused to die.

"How? Why? What's happening?" he asked in a faint voice.

"We've all been instructed to open our marching orders. I am leaving at once by the first available means.

In a still fainter voice Nikita asked, "Has war been declared?"

"It seems that since midnight and for the last five or six hours we've been attacked at many points on the Albanian border."

Nikita sat up in bed and remained speechless for some moments.

"Goodbye, Nikita. So long."

"No, Alexis, don't go. Stay a little.Do you mean that they were ready and surprised us? What will happen now?

"What will happen? They'll break their necks!"

"But they've got an army of eight million men. They've got an air force."

Alexis interrupted him sharply: "They can have whatever they like. I guarantee you that they're going to break their necks."

"Alexis, I'd like to discuss this."

"No, Nikita, I've no time for talk. Every minute counts now."

He stretched out his hand. "I have to go. Take care of yourself."

He jumped out of bed and took him in his arms. For the first time in his life he felt a spontaneous emotion welling up within him. and he said, "You have been like a brother to me, Alexis.

I'll never forget it as long as I live. I'll never have another friend like you. Please write to me regularly." They embraced again and Alexis looked at Nikita with new warmth: "I'll write to you, Nikita," he said, "but maybe not for long. I hope...no, I feel sure that we shall meet in Epirus soon."

After he left, Nikita went to the window. In the cold twilight of the dying night he heard a wild whinny and a brisk gallop fading into the distance.

At the moment of separation Nikita Coletti had not wanted to disappoint the friend of his dark days, and so he had not told him how ridiculous was his hope that they would meet in Epirus.

"I volunteer?" he said to himself. "I'll never commit such folly."

But as the days passed, the pattern of life changed. The "folly" gradually began to present itself as a way out, the only way out. A strange fever had come over the Greeks. They all wanted to fight, they all wanted to become heroes, to die in battle. How could anyone dare to speak of fear? All those who were able to fight had disappeared. Phrosso had gone with some organization that would work for the wounded at the front, or something of the sort—he was not quite sure what. Mourayias had made desperate efforts to enlist but they wouldn't take him. Katie had become unattainable; she was shut up in the Military Hospital where she was a volunteer nurse.

All those who had stayed behind talked only about the war. And all looked at him strangely and were cold to him. Some made insulting innuendos about him. The atmosphere around him was cold and heavy; his isolation was total. And the situation became worse after a few days when the Italians were encircled in the ravines of Pindus, when it became evident that Kalpaki, the key post in the defense line was not going to fall, when the enemy was retiring on all sides, and the Greeks, for all their restricted means, were beginning to take the offensive along the whole front.

"We'll throw them into the sea! We'll crush Italy! Let the Germans come! We'll smash them too! What does it matter if we are alone. This is Hellas! Here on our rocks the waves of the oceans are shattered! We were aiming for a Thermopylae and we've won another Marathon! Forward for Plataea! Forward for Valtetsi!''

These were the slogans. A kind of delirium had come over all the Greeks. A madness. And they were winning. A wave of heroic inspiration spread among the people, as if God for a brief moment had replaced the ordinary hearts of the Greeks with the hearts of lions.

Now everyone looked with unrestrained hatred at Nikita Coletti who was the only one whose weak, unmanly spirit seemed unaffected by the general enthusiasm.

One day when the good weather had returned and the earth was beginning to dry, he went for a walk on the plain. Once more he saw the birds starting out on their long autumn migration. The arrows of their flight advanced majestically across the blue sky, driven by the north wind and the icy storms. They flew on proud, strong, and beautiful. He stopped and looked in awe at the impressive sight. The birds, as they approached, seemed to cry out the same message he had heard a year ago.

''For the vanquished there shall be no resting place among the reeds. Let the victors go forward, ever forward! The rest can die, can die, can die!''

And the cries increased in volume. From all the formations came the words, ''They can die, they can die, they can die!''

He shuddered, pulled himself together, and as the thought came to him that he too was among the weak, among those who ''could die'' as those horrible cries proclaimed, he instinctively shouted in anger. ''No, they must not die! They have no strength and fear weakens their wings. It is a shame, it is unjust that they should die!''

He had not noticed that the three ox-teams from Pteliona which plowed the fields for sowing every day when the earth was ripe, had approached. The first team driven by Mourayias passed by. The old farmer's head was bent; he said nothing. The other two teams stopped beside him. The white-haired men in charge of them looked at him with astonishment. Their faces grew red and one of them said in a loud voice, ''Why shouldn't they die? Let them die!'' Unused to answering back, Nikita avoided their eyes. He understood why they had contradicted him so brusquely. They thought he had been talking about the Italians. He noticed their hostile expression, and saw that Mourayias had moved on without saying a word. Nikita turned his back on them and walked quickly to the house. As he started off the two farm hands shouted after him angrily, "We say they must die!" "Yes, let them all die, the bastards!"

He advanced through the damp air which was becoming mistier. His quick footsteps seemed to echo the fierce cries of the men, and their harsh verdict. "The bastards must die, the bastards must die, the bastards must die!"

He stopped short so that the echo should cease. He no longer heard his footsteps but the sound of those words and the hatred persisted. Now something else was bringing them to him...was it his dormant conscience speaking to him? There they were again, those hateful words, maybe he was losing his mind.

He started running.

On the following day, when someone in the town slighted him, he went straight to the recruiting office and enrolled as a volunteer. He was accepted as an interpreter. Frightened, but somewhat relieved, he left for Janina.

* * * * *

On the 8th of March Alexis came down the rear slope of the hill for a conference at battalion headquarters. Every time he had to make these visits he sought out Nikita, and their meetings gave them both great pleasure.

When he arrived at Janina, Nikita thought that his knowledge of languages would ensure his being retained at General Headquarters in the city. But no sooner had he presented himself than he was placed with a battalion. He had objected timidly, saying, "I speak four languages. Wouldn't I be more useful here where a lot of foreign newsmen and officers will be coming?"

They refused to listen to him and told him that his business would be to examine prisoners. Thus it happened that he found himself in the battalion of which Alexis was artillery commander. It was obvious that this posting had been pre-arranged.

They spent the first evening reminiscing over the past and talking about the present situation. At one point in their lively conversation, Nikita was so carried away by Alexis' high spirits that almost without thinking he asked to stay overnight with hm and his men, to see how it was on the other side of the hill. He was at the front, had heard the sounds of artillery fire and rifle fire, he had spoken with a great number of prisoners, but he had not yet seen the enemy lines. He would like to come and see them and could return the next morning just before dawn. Alexis was delighted.

"You'll get to know my fine fellows," he said, "and you'll see our trench which has a deluxe shelter which you'll like."

And so they went. Taking many precautions, bending down, almost crawling at times, they got to the trench before twilight.

"It's so quiet here", Nikita said. "It's as if we weren't at the front — the real front."

"Yes," Alexis said, "for several days now there's been a dead calm. But there are many signs which show that they are preparing something big. We shall see."

He introduced him to his men, showed him the Italian positions, took him round the trench, explained in detail the operation of the machine-guns and rifles, and took him to the shelter whose only luxury was a roof and a storm lamp.

Everything seemed simple and peaceful. It was hard to believe that war had anything to do with this place and that death often stood waiting around the corner. At dinner, conversation was trivial and casual, not, as Nikita had imagined, full of bragging talk about heroic deeds. Only a few simple words about their action were said in passing, when Nikita, on arrival, out of politeness paid them a compliment.

"I didn't believe you, Alexis, when you told me the Italians wouldn't pass. But you've managed it. They haven't passed."

"How could they pass?" said a young private from Konitsa. "What d'you think we are? A bunch of puppies? No, sir!" And instead of boasting about their exploits they just laughed.

Nikita insisted. "Yes, but I'm impressed, because they have so many weapons."

A corporal who came from Janina replied, "They haven't yet found a weapon to put a stop to our determination to fire back.

And it's impossible for them to kill us all. So how can they pass? There will always be someone to shoot at them."

After dinner Alexis detailed men for night sentry duty, and all the rest settled down to sleep in the shelter. Alexis, the lieutenant, slept with his men and no distinction was made for his guest. Their peaceful, contended sleep was broken at dawn by a terrible awakening. A deafening roar shattered their ears; explosions in rapid succession were heard along the line, some of them very near, and they never stopped. The ground beneath them shook. The rocks and the earth to which they were clinging quaked violently at intervals. Earth and rubble poured down through the roof of the shelter filling the air with dust and making it hard to breathe. Suddenly, the roof burst open and a volcano of fire and stones and ashes erupted in their midst. Groans of pain were heard, and when the dust cleared, there was blood everywhere, and on the rocks pieces of human flesh.

Alexis and Nikita had fallen to the ground near the doorway. "Let's get out into the trench, Alexis said, "I have to look at the machine-gun." In the midst of the terrible upheaval. Alexis dragged himself cautiously to the embankment and pulled himself up to examine the heavy machine-gun.

Nikita was trembling. He was experiencing a feeling which was new to him — something he could not define. It seemed to him that his blood had frozen in his veins, that his heart, although it was beating hard, had grown as heavy as stone, and that his vitals had contracted into a lump and were being pushed out of his mouth. His ears were ringing and sore.

He had stayed close to the inner side of the trench and was lying very low. He was surprised when he found he had no difficulty in raising himself to make the sign of the cross. He, who since his boyhood had never crossed himself, was now repeating this gesture again and again. Only his brain, within a fiery circle of terror and despair, was functioning actively.

What a fool he had been to stay there! Why hadn't he left last night when he had heard that "they were getting ready for something"? He had run into a trap full of fire, lead, blood, and pain, from which there was no escape. How unpardonably stupid he had been! Help me, O God! Death was near, very near; and if not death, then butchered limbs, disembowelment, pain, amputated legs. How horrible! How could he get out of there? How?

Was it possible that such a disaster had befallen him? It must be a bad dream. He who was so cautious, who was afraid of the tunnels and railroad bridges near Lamia, could he now be here, mercilessly gripped in the vise of death...death...death... butchery...and not be able to get away? There wasn't any way of escape, none, not even if he gave up half his fortune. No way at all. He was condemned...imprisoned here. He couldn't stand it...he would go mad...everything pursued him...shells, death, fear...

He noticed something on his hand as he was crossing himself. It was damp and warm. Blood. A cold sweat came over him and he thought he would throw up. He heard Alexis next to him.

"The machine-gun is in order," he said briskly.

What did he care about the machine-gun? It could be reduced to ashes as far as he was concerned.

"I'm going to take a look at the boys," Alexis went on.

"I'm bleeding," Nikita said faintly. "I've been hit."

"Have you been hit badly?" his friend asked with warmth.

"I don't know," he murmured. "There's blood on my face."

Alexis spoke with concern but with authority. "Move your head around. Can you move it freely?"

He tried. "Yes," he answered.

"Can you talk freely, without any bubbling in your throat?"

Again he replied affirmatively.

"Now pass your hand over your stomach. Is there any blood there?"

"No. there isn't."

"Then there's nothing the matter with you. It's just a flesh wound on your face. I'll wash it out for you to prevent infection." Alexis went and came back staying close to the ground. He brought a little bag with him. Suddenly the terrible din around them ceased. Only the whistling of shells passing high above them could be heard; and far behind them were the explosions, some heavy and others dry and crackling as if a thousand metal drums were bursting.

As Alexis washed out the wound on Nikita's right cheek below the ear, he said with some concern, "They have raised their sights and are striking at the rear with artillery and mortars to prevent reinforcements reaching us."

Nikita had gained a little courage. Now that the noise had subsided and there were no explosions near by, he felt safer.

"I like it better this way," he said.

"Yes, but the infantry will attack us, and we've sustained many losses. There are gaps in the line."

Several shots were heard. At that moment Alexis had applied a drug that smarted so much that Nikita had no time to worry about what he had heard. From the slope below them a cry was heard, "Get that machine-gun going! They're coming up!" Without another word Alexis left him and got up. From his prone position Nikita followed his movements. He saw him look through the loophole between the sandbags and the earthwork, lower the gun, and fire. It was the first time he heard the familiar sound so near and so loud.

Rat-tat-tat-tat... How horrible that sound was! It registered the flow of bullets and they dealt out destruction, smashing metal and maybe men's bones. Was that the sound death made every time he struck? It was enough to drive one mad.

Now a general quiet followed. Occasional crackles — messengers of death...

Alexis looked through the loophole again, shifted the barrel of the gun and fired. The firing from below, to right and left, increased. A third and a fourth time Alexis fired; his expression was very serious — very serious indeed.

From a neighboring trench a cry went up. "Aerrrra!"

Alexis lifted his head slightly above the sandbags, and placing his hands like a funnel in front of his mouth he shouted in a voice which seemed to be endowed with the force of thunder. "Aerrra! Hit them, boys!.... Hit them hard!..."

From all the trenches along the slope echoed the cry, "Aerrra!"

"Aerra!... Aerra!"

The sound of shots burst fourth anew, and again Alexis' machine-gun spat forth bullets.

Timidly Nikita looked toward the end of the trench, hoping

in his desperation to find some way of getting back to the other side of the hill, hoping against hope, seeking to clutch at any straw. Leaning against the side of the trench was the corporal who had spoken last night. He was aiming and firing. A damp, red blotch marked his shoulder, another long streak of blood showed on his right thigh down to his knee. "They can't break our determination to fire at them. They can't kill us all..."

Yes, but they might kill Nikita Coletti. That was all he cared about. How could he get away? How?

He looked toward the other end of the trench and saw the young private from Konitsa. At dawn, Alexis had placed him there on sentry duty. Now he was dead. He had fallen backwards, his lips parted, his eyes wide open, and his hands spread out against the wall of the trench, as if he had stretched them out in a gesture of appeal and prayer to heaven before dying.

His childish face, streaked with blood and earth, was frozen in a look not so much of fear as of surprise, infinite, unfathomable surprise. What was it that had aroused such surprise in the beardless young here before he died? Was it something concrete and down-to-earth which appeared strange to him? The unbelieveable din, perhaps? Or the shells that exploded on the rocks? Or the metal that was disgorged from the blazing mountain-sides? Or was he struck, perhaps, with surprise and bewilderment because the incredible passage from the carefree joyousness of youth to outer darkness was so sudden and so swift?

In the shattered shelter wounded men moaned piteously. Nikita again felt like throwing up, but was ashamed of doing so in front of Alexis.

"I'll go and see if I can help the men in the shelter," he said.

"Not now," Alexis said in a tone of harsh command. "Come here and hold up the ammunition cases for me."

Nikita made a superhuman effort, dragged himself toward him, and did as he was told. Alexis was calm and fired conservatively now, as the machine-gun was almost empty. He loaded it quickly with Nikita's help, stooped to look through the loophole, and took up his field-glasses.

Then the great disaster happened.

The dry whistle of bullets, like the whirr of wasps' wings, was heard very close. Later Nikita understood that they were bullets fired by expert marksmen. One or two shots passed above their heads, a few more came to a stop in the sandbags in front of them. Suddenly Alexis' erect body jolted backwards against the wall of the trench. He leaned against it for an instant, then slid down slowly to a sitting position. Nikita ran to him. He had forgotten his fear and he stood up in the trench.

"Alexis!" he cried.

Alexis gave him a forced smile. "It's nothing," he said in a weak voice. His eyes blazed for an instant, then seemed to lose their lustre.

Nikita took him by the shoulders: "Alexis," he cried desperately. "Tell me what you want."

"Nothing. I don't know..." he murmured. "There's nothing the matter with me. Don't be afraid."

Nikita started to unbutton his tunic.

"You've been hit. Let me find the wound and wash it out."

Alexis said nothing. He just looked at him with affection, and for the first time he seemed to be begging him forlornly for something... to perform a miracle perhaps...Nikita saw the supplication in his eyes.

At that moment from below came the familiar cry, "Get that machine-gun going! The bastards are perking up!"

The wounded man's eyes brightened again; an angry expression came over his face. More shooting broke out, and more cries were heard. "They're coming at us! Machine-gun!"

"Where's that machine-gun dammit?"

And then a louder cry. "They're advancing without cover. Give'em the works!"

Alexis leaned on his hands, gathered up his feet, and a spasm of pain came over his face. He struggled to get up and managed to stand up straight, very erect. But his legs didn't obey him; they seemed rooted to the ground. His taut body jerked forward a little then swayed backwards toward the wall of the trench. Nikita came forward to support him. To think that that weak reed should be supporting the might oak!

Alexis leaned upon his arm. He looked deep into his eyes, penetrating his very soul. "I am going," he said. "It's your turn now. You fire at them."

His voice was not faint as before; it was deep. Something within him seemed to be boiling up and bringing his words out.

"But I don't now how," Nikita answered.

Alexis let go of his arm, he leaned back a little and fell against the trench wall. He slid on it lightly and sank to the ground.

From below the cries redoubled. "Machine-gun! For God's sake get that machine-gun going. They're eating us up!"

Alexis gave Nikita an infuriated look. "Of course you know how. Just do what I did. Immediately! This is an order!" And then in a gentler tone he added, "Hurry, my dear boy! Fire at them! Quickly!"

Nikita could not stand his words, his voice, his look, that furious look which gradually had become soft, gentle, and distant. He felt that he could not withstand the command he had received; that his friend had passed him a torch which he must take in his own hand, since there was no other living hand there to seize it. It became imperative that the torch held by the manly strength of the Great Plain should not fall to the ground and burn out. It could not, it must not be extinguished.

He hesitated, looked around him in distress, glanced at the machine-gun, looked at Alexis again and saw in his eyes that insistent command and the earnest entreaty. He lost no more time in thought. He looked through the loophole and saw the Italians running up the hill. They were not covered by protective fire.

Acting by instinct, without conscious thought, Nikita lowered the machine-gun and aimed at the point where the enemy were most numerous. He pressed the trigger and made the motions he had seen Alexis make.

Looking through the loophole again, he saw the bodies of men who had fallen. Italian soldiers struggled to rise and fall again, and many more who were either took shelter behind rocks or fled. A few still moved forward. He fired on them and then turned the heavy gun to the right where another line was moving forward uncovered, as if they were not in a war, as if death were not there watching for them, as if the men were engaged in peaceful mountain-climbing exercises, vying with each other in being the first to reach the top.

Again bodies rolled on the ground, men fell, and the advance was stopped.

"Aerra!" The battle-cry went up on the right.

"Aerra!"

"Aerra!" they shouted from other trenches.

"Hooray for the Captain!" someone nearby shouted.

Then Nikita, forgetting his friend, his brother, forgetting that he had killed human beings, forgetting all danger, stood up on a rock, leaned over the parapet of sandbags, and waving his steel helmet high in the air, shouted at the top of his voice. "Aerrra! Give it to 'em, boys! Give it to 'em!"

With only one brief lull at noon, when reinforcements arrived, and a few fresh troops slid into each trench, only then was Nikita convinced that Alexis, his beloved brother, was really dead.

He went to him and, overcome with emotion, spoke to him and caressed his cheek. Alexis was still sitting against the rear wall of the trench. Hanging down by his sides the strong hands lay powerless and dry. His lips were slightly parted, and his manly head was bent back. Only the gaze in those wide open eyes refused to die. It strained upward, very high, to the mountain-tops and to the blue heavens. Next to him, flat on his face, his tunic drenched in blood, lay the corporal who came from Janina. In the turmoil of the action Nikita had not seen him die.

They buried Alexis before dawn, and laid over him a cross made of stones. There were many dead to be buried, and maybe it was more urgent to bury the dismembered bodies which were so gruesome to the sight. But Nikita hastened to bury Alexis first because he did not know if there would be time for all to be buried, and he did not want that giant of a man, now that he was dead, to be exposed to the men's eyes. He did not want the rising sun to see that once erect and noble body with the proud soul beginning to dissolve in decay.

II

They had been marching for five days almost without a stop. Their shoulders ached from the weight of pack and rifle, their feet were lacerated by the holes in their boots which had been split on the hard rocks, their bodies were suffering, but still they marched on and on and on, halting briefly from time to time to take a drink of water and to munch a crust of bread. They were very tired. But what difference did that make? They had to go forward to the end. Since they had to, they would. Their feet moved automatically, their knees shot forward as if they were attached to bolts and worked by springs, their minds occasionally entertained some fleeting thought.

In the daytime these bodies stood upright only to allow the legs to move under them like automata. At night, the darkness made it impossible for the feet to move, so the bodies lay down wherever they were, like dry sticks, and stayed there until dawn, as if they had no life in them.

The last battle had been fought on Albanian territory a few kilometers beyond Konitsa, to cover the regiment which was falling back with all its equipment. Was it the 20th, the 21st, or the 22nd of April? He couldn't remember. A few forces continued to fight in order to enable the main army to retire in good order. That morning rumors had circulated that the German forces had entered Janina, that they had encircled the whole Army Corps fighting in Albania, and that a truce had been, or was about to be, signed with the Germans.

Their captain had told them that these were only unsubstantiated rumors and that they would continue to cover the retreat. Every day they were to take up new positions further to the rear, and if he did not, in the meantime, receive new orders, they would carry on the fight until they reached the only road which joined Salonika with Epirus, as far as Metsovo. There they would see what they would do, maybe they would receive orders to disband and go home.

But on that morning the Italians harrassed them for six or seven hours with a maddening bombardment by mortar and artillery and, while they had held back the enemy's infantry attack, they discovered at nightfall that the company no longer existed as such and that they were cut off from the battalion. Their officers had all been killed and the losses among the men in killed and wounded were heavy.

The few that remained got together to talk things over. They were in no condition to withstand the slightest attack on the next day. To the rear there was no longer any army or, at any rate, it was for away. It was out of the question to transport or care for the wounded. They all agreed therefore to follow the only possible course: each able-bodies non-commissioned officer would take a group under his command and proceed south until they met some army unit.

While they awaited daybreak, they gave summary relief to the wounded and left them bread to eat until the Italians found them. They hung up some shirts on tree-branches to serve as white flags, and just before the first light they left. After five days of tramping through mountains Nikita's group hadn't come across any army, Greek, Italian, or German. They had passed through three villages without getting any news, for no-one knew what was going on; so they had continued to go forward. The villagers had told them that they were going in the right direction.

One of the group, Mitsos, a muleteer from Syrrako, knew the territory fairly well and had guided them through wild gorges, through forest and meadowland, and through bare stony tracts. He had kept them on the right track as they wandered through ring upon ring of mountains, which appeared to be interlocked in a kind of wild and confused circular folk-dance, and had finally gotten them on the path to Metsovo where they would get news and decide upon their future action.

They came out of a dense and tangled forest into the deepening dusk. After hours of walking through the dismal and sunless rows of giant pine-trees, they were relieved at the sight of the pleasant meadow which lay before them where, at the edge of the forest under a great pine, a small spring bubbled. They gazed in amazement at the pine-tree whose trunk was so immense that the outstretched arms of two men could barely encircle it.

As they paused to survey the scene, Mitsos said, "It's about three — or at the most four — hours from here to Metsovo. The way lies through open meadows where the ground is soft and easy on the feet. I suggest we stop here."

"Good idea," said one of the others. "We can light a fire in the forest where it won't be seen, there's good water here, and if we push off early in the morning we'll be in Metsovo with a whole day in front of us to organize."

"What say, Corporal?" a beardless country youth asked in a heavy dialect. "The ole guts are bursting. What say we unharness our packs and give the ole carcass a rest?"

"O.K." said the corporal. "We'll camp here."

They unloosed their packs and rifles and took off their boots. Then they drank the cool water and bathed in the spring and gathered around it to eat a crust of bread and a few olives or a piece of cheese.

One of them, an excellent fellow, was a student from Janina. He broke the silence, saying, "Now that we've come out of the wilds and are close to civilization, I must tell you something that's been bothering me. I am scared at the thought that when we arrive at Metsovo we may be held as deserters and be court-martialled."

The men were startled. The peasant boy broke in with alacrity. "What d'you expect from a guy who's had a college education? Who'd dare to call us deserters, you bastard? Haven't we been fighting from sunup to sundown, and all night too with never a stop?"

"I know we fought, Gongos," said the student, "but a day came when without firing a shot we up and left. And we've been going since." And he added seriously, "Until the day he kills, the murderer is innocent and until the day he steals, the thief has nothing to fear."

"For Pete's sake, will you be calling us murderers and thieves, now? You'd be better off coming to Syrrako to look after my goats!" Gongos said indignantly, and he added, "What the guy gassing about, Corp? Could anything like this happen to us?"

The corporal did not feel like arguing but he sensed that the suspicions of the young man from Janina might become contagious among these rough and simple folk. "I'm not too well up on Army law." he said gravely. "I suppose it's just possible that questions may be asked, particularly if other units are still fighting. But I'm convinced that they certainly won't court-martial us; on the contrary I believe they will commend us. After all, we were subjected to a terrible bombing, and in spite of our small numbers we did stand up to a furious attack. And after being decimated we carried out the last orders we received. We are retreating with our arms intact and looking for a place where we can get new orders. If there's any responsibility to be assumed I alone will assume it, but I don't think anyone will be found to tell me that I should have disobeyed the orders I received and that we should have been taken prisoner without reason."

"You two-bit pencil pusher," Gongos cried out excitedly, "can't you see we've got a great guy for a leader? A great guy, I tell you! Decorated for bravery, promoted to corporal in the field, recommended for further promotion! D'you think anyone's going to court-martial *him* and us with him?"

* * * * *

They lay down for the night, and sleep came — swift, sudden, and heavy. Only the corporal could not sleep. On previous nights he had fallen asleep as soon as he stretched out, slept well, and awakened with the rest of the men at dawn. The fatigue, the immense fatigue, the body's total exhaustion left no room for emotion and memory. The parties, the drinks, and the pills that he once needed to combat his insomnia seemed ludicrously insignificant tranquillizers when compared with the kind of fatigue that paralyzes the body and the mind.

But now he could not sleep, for this night seemed to be the last of this adventure. He remembered what the young goatherd had said earlier and smiled bitterly: decoration for bravery, promotion, that he was a hero and a leader! If only these poor boys who trusted him knew what a coward he was and that these things had happened by chance, by accident, and that there was no bravery involved, no enthusiasm, no patriotism. Of course, he wasn't the old Nikita Coletti, the bored and negative Parisian aesthete, but he certainly wasn't the hero, patriot, and leader that these simple fellows, who were real heroes, believed.

He recalled the chain of events which led to the most recent incidents. Fleeting images of his last days at Pteliona passed through his mind; some of those moments had been very painful. Then he remembered his life with the battalion during the hard days of the advance through the snow and ice in Albania, the uncomfortable, unbearably cold halt before Tepeleni, and the tragic days of March.

"Oh, Alexis, Alexis, I miss you. Nothing will ever take away the bitterness of your absence. Nothing will ever remove the pain in my heart. To think that you should be dead, that you should have been buried by your faint-hearted brother in the rocky wastelands of Albania. How could it be possible? You were one of those men about whom it is impossible to believe that they ever die. You were one of those men about whom one could say, however unreasonably, that they over-come death, that they cannot possibly be stretched out on the ground without the strength to leap up again in the glory of their manhood, without the strength even to open their eyes or move a hand. You were strong, the embodiment of all that is strong in spirit and in body." "Alexis, my brother, my beloved brother Alexis, how can you be dead?"

Alexis dead, and he himself alive and supposedly a hero! He knew he was no hero. He was not even a patriot. He knew it. But now and again he had felt wild, primitive enthusiasms—fleeting feelings. As for the rest... The first time, on the 9th of March, he had fought because he could not oppose Alexis' command. From weakness, and perhaps from shame. Perhaps also because the shouts of the man made him understand that if the machine-gun stopped firing the Italians would kill them all.

After that he fought because he could not do anything else; because the image of Alexis who still had the strength to give him orders as he was dying, was present in his mind; because he still felt the weight of the dead man in his arms; because he had become inextricably involved and all the men round him expected him to fight; and because even if he wanted to run away, it had become impossible to do so. All these things impelled him to go on, but he had not felt any inner flame fire his spirit. He had not felt the passion and élan that inspired all these boys — uncultured village lads or educated town boys; he felt no devotion to country or love of freedom. Those boys were real heros for they knew what they were fighting for and why they were risking their lives, and they accepted the challenge with some fear, but with faith and enthusiasm. He was no hero who had borne himself manfully only because he chanced to be in a critical position, had received a command from a giant of a man and had not been able to oppose it. Everything had been a matter of chance.

And now, now that he was stretched out under this old pinetree and was ready to lose himself in a heavy sleep, what did he want now? Did he want to fight again? To become a hero once more? Oh, no! A thousand times no! How awful if they sent them to fight somewhere else tomorrow, because he would have to go too. How could he avoid it?

What he wanted was to return to Pteliona. How was it that for so long Pteliona had seemed to him unbearable and uncivilized? How could he have been so blind and have failed to see all that Pteliona had to offer? If he was lucky and was free again he would go to the house which he had formerly found old and uncomfortable, he would peel off his uniform and the underclothes which stuck to him, stinking with sweat and filth, he would take a hot bath and luxuriate in the warm water perfumed with scented oils from Paris, and then he would wrap himself in a spotlessly clean robe, take a good French book, and drink a cup of boiling-strong aromatic coffee!

How had he never before understood the pleasures Pteliona could give him?

And Katie would come to him! Only Alexis wouldn't be there.

"Oh, Alexis, Alexis, how deeply I feel the pain of your loss. There is such hopelessness, such tragedy in the thought that noone will ever see or hear you again; that you, so strong and perfect, who seemed immortal, are dead, buried in the wastelands of Albania. How wonderful life would have been with you at Pteliona...with Katie...with a warm bath...clean underclothes...white sheets...and a French book."

Then sleep sank heavily upon him and closed his weary eyes.

* * * * *

At Metsovo they came into contact with the world again and learned the news.

The defense works at the Bulgarian border had been overwhelmed by flame-throwers. A few men, disfigured by burns, came out alive. The Germans drew up in line and saluted them, presenting arms.

The Germans, in a surprise attack, had broken through the unguarded Serbian frontier line and had taken Salonika, the key-point of the Greek defense, on the second day of their offensive. There was no hope of further resistence.

They had shattered the slender Greek reserves and a division of Australians. the only foreign help, had advanced swiftly into Thessaly, and from there were marching into Epirus and on Athens.

Their air force had savagely bombed all the towns in their path.

Everything was disrupted. Some generals in Epirus had disobeyed the King's command and signed a truce. That was exactly seven days ago.

Hitler announced to the German Reichstag that from the Greeks alone among his enemies he would take no prisoners in order to honor their courage.

The Germans were entering Athens that day or the next. The King and the Government had already left for Crete. Greece would go on with the war from there.

The army had been disbanded and the men were returning to their homes by any means they could find.

They discarded their uniforms and put on civilian clothes provided by the villagers. Nikita divided all the money he had on him among his men — he would find all he needed at Pteliona. They embraced and parted.

He was sitting on a pile of boards which a truck was taking to some town in Macedonia, and now he was approaching Larissa. He was overjoyed and anguished; he wanted to get home as soon as possible.

He got down at the Agricultural College. Pteliona was opposite, across the river. If he wanted to find a bridge he would have to go into the town and that would mean making a wide detour. He was impatient. He wanted to get back at once. He ran down the slope to the river where there was a crossing; the waters of the Peneus were not so deep there. Nevertheless he found himself up to his waist in water.

Was it the cold which struck him all of a sudden and the eddies which whirled around him and buffeted him? Or was he dizzy after the hours he had been sitting perched on those boards as the truck rattled over bad roads? Why did the elms look so strange and dim? Could it be that his eyes which had never wept since he was a child were filling with tears now that he was coming home? Nonesense! His eyes never filled with tears; they were dry and clear.

As he climbed the bank and saw the wood and the meadows he realized what had happened. Large holes, like small craters, broke the level expanse wherever he turned his eyes. At the edge of the wood, under cover of its shade, trucks, artillery pieces, tractors were spread out in indescribable disorder — overturned, battered and blasted. Obviously a Greek or allied unit had encamped there and had been struck by heavy bombs of the enemy air force. He approached the spot where, a year and half ago he had seen Mourayias plowing with his team. He felt his heart tighten, and for the first time in his life a kind of anguish lay heavy on his breast.

Giant trees had been cut down and had been piled upon the ground. Others had been uprooted but still remained upright, their branches entangled with those of other trees, as if the living ones had wanted to hold up to heaven those that had died, as if the dead trees refused to fall down. The greater number still stood upright, strong, proud and straight, but the mighty elm wood, the pride of the plain, had suffered a disaster. It was unrecognizable.

He clenched his fists. He felt anger rising within him.

"The barbarians," he said to himself in a fury. "The barbarians! Why did they destroy the few things we were able to build up in our poverty? Why should the wealthy come with their iron machines and strike at the barefoot wretches who sweat to earn their bread. Who will punish them, and how?"

How he hated them! How he hated them! But hatred was not for long the dominant feeling within him. Another thought came to him which made him shudder. If the giant elms, so deeply rooted in the earth, had suffered such destruction, what might have happened to the house, the barns, and the stables.

There had also been the earthquake in February. They had written to him that it had caused slight damages at Pteliona. Perhaps they had not been telling the truth.

Without further thought he began to run. Dodging the fallen trees and craters in his way, he ran, panting and apprehensive, like a madman. He came to the large enclosure. At the other end the tall, two-story house was still standing, but the roof had fallen in and in one of the corners the wall of heavy chiselled stone blocks had collapsed. To the right the barns were leaning back, as if a gigantic hand had pushed them; to the left nearly all the stables had been levelled to the ground. The shed where the machines were kept was ruined and empty. Only the little cottage in which Mourayias lived appeared to be undamaged.

He was breathing hard and felt a lump in his throat. He approached the house. Not a soul was in sight; all was ruin and desolation.

He shouted. "Mourayias, Phrosso!" Then he cupped his hands in front of his mouth and shouted louder. "Mourayias! Phrosso! It's me! I've come home!"

No answer—only an echo in the deathly silence. "I've come home...come home!"

Yes, home. But to what?

His eyes grew moist and dimmed. This was no trick of the imagination now, no mistake. They grew moist sweetly, his body swayed, his spirit seemed to be softening, to be melting sweetly, gently, very gently. He sat down on the ground, covered his face with both hands, and began sobbing. His palms were drenched in his tears.

He wept, wept unrestrainedly, this man who had never wept since his childhood. And what joy this abundance and warmth of weeping brought him! What depth of meaning it held for him! Now, suddenly, amidst the loneliness and the ruins, he understood many of the things his unforgettable friend had told him, things which had once seemed so mysterious to him. Now he understood. And now he was able to understand why in the end he had fought with passion. He hadn't fought by chance and against his will. He hadn't fought simply because that was what his beloved friend had wanted. No! He had fought for something else too. Because, without realizing it, he loved, he adored this tortured but blessed land.

He looked around him with eyes dimmed by tears, saw that all was still quiet around him, and stretched out on the ground — on the earth which, however much it had been torn apart, still struggled to feed a few shoots of grass. With tenderness and love, he stroked the earth with his hands, yes, with love — a love greater than any he had felt for a woman. He kissed it again and again pressing his cheek lovingly on its flesh of soil and grass. He closed his eyes and drew his cheek once more across the earth.

He felt a deep otherworldly pleasure. There he was alone, entirely alone, in that wide embrace. All around was disaster. There he was exhausted, extenuated; and there was the earth, torn and wounded. Yet the fatigue, the exhaustion, the calamity, and the sounds were all healed by this embrace. this love of desolate man for naked earth. As though he held beneath him the most passionate of woman, he rubbed his cheek against the earth's flesh again and caressed it tenderly with the palms of his hands.

And the beloved broad Earth responded to the lover's caress! She leaped beneath the weight of his tired body. She told him that if his love was great she would conceive a thousandfold, that her bare surface would be reforested, that their love would be deep and fruitful, and it would bring joys hitherto unknown and undreamed of, that it would never, never end, not even in death. He closed his eyes tighter as though he were afraid they might open. He wanted to enjoy this unprecedented erotic intoxication, this revelation of love which, in absolute solitude, brought with it so much sweetness, so much joy and a riotous feast of luminous resurrection.

How long did he remain thus? He could not say. But he did not move until he thought he heard the sound of sheep-bells, the grinding of wheels coming to a halt, and then hurried footsteps coming in his direction.

Nikita got up and saw Mourayias, Phrosso and the two middle-aged teamsters. He seemed a changed man at all. His stance was erect, his skin was rough and deeply tanned, his expression was virile, and his look was warm.

The head teamster spoke first. "Glory be to God, master. glory be to the Lord! We heard that you were wounded and that you fought like a lion. Glory be to God that you're back!"

He embraced his friends and the teamsters warmly. Then Mourayias spoke.

"When the first bombs began to fall, I took the herds and all the valuables the carts would hold and went to St. Elias' Monastery. Phrosso came and found me there. But, Master, you see what damages has been done to Pteliona!"

Nikita threw his right arm round Mourayias' shoulders, laughed aloud, and making a sweeping gesture with his other arm, said, "We'll build it all up again, Mourayias. We'll bring Pteliona back to life and it will become the pride of the plain once more."

III

The Italian troops entered Larissa, the boys who had fought in Albania and Thrace came back, and the normal flow of life appeared to be starting again.

In the town the people struggled to repair the houses which had been damaged by the earthquake or the bombs, and to rebuild those that had been destroyed. In most cases they managed to put up one or two rooms on the ground floor and so to get protection against the approaching winter. Builders and carpenters were in great demand and most people put a hand to the job themselves.

In the villages and in the town the merchants who usually served the farmers got ready for the harvest and the threshing, but there was a dearth of machines, spare parts, and a host of other necessities. More than ever before, all the grain had to be gathered in, for it was evident that corps would be valuable and essential for survival through the winter.

Thus, as the daily effort was redoubled and cares of every sort were faced, it seemed that life had returned to its old rhythm.

The tension of the war had passed, and when the intense enthusiasm as well as the danger had subsided, people began once more to remember their petty hatreds and to foster new ones; they pursued the needs of today and tomorrow, they thought about love, their small sorrows and their even smaller joys. The old and the infirm died, children were born, and occasionally, but much less often than before, there were weddings. This is what appeared on the surface.

But in all cities and at all times there are surface appearances which are more or less like those of former times. Now, in the cities of Greece, life on the surface appeared to be not so different from the life of the pre-war years. But that was as far as it went. A glance below the surface would reveal a very great change.

First of all, an unbearably heavy weight pressed down upon the hearts of the people in Larissa. The whole Greek people strained under this pressure. How was it possible that these Italians whom we beat roundly yesterday should now so insolently and harshly lord it over us? How would this insufferable slavery end? And when? No one could speak freely, no one could travel, no one was master in his own country or secure in his own home.

At first, arrests were frequent. There were interrogations and sometimes those being investigated were beaten. This was forbidden, that was prohibited; the restrictions and prohibitions covered everything — even the most trival things. And this was only the beginning, the first weeks of slavery. What would happen later if the slavery went on? The news concerning the duration of the tyranny was not good. At first a part of Greece had remained free. In Crete the fight had continued. Then Crete too fell.

The few who had been able to listen to broadcasts from BBC London had said that the island was unharmed, that the King had left for Egypt and would carry on the war from there with the navy, the air force, and units of the army. Poor comfort indeed to a dying man! Naturally the King would continue to fight and one day would win at the side of the British. But when would that day come? When? When indeed, seeing that Britain was now at bay and our new ally, the Russian giant, was retreating all the time and was waiting for 'General Winter' to come to save him.

They would have to steel themselves against reality. The black night of slavery had descended heavily upon them.

Nowhere was a star to be seen. Yes, in the end we would win. But in the meantime what sufferings must be endured, and how many would survive to see Greece free again? In Athens and Piraeus, on many of the islands and in the mountains, the pinch of privation was felt. Food became scarce; even bread was hard to get. From these places relatives and friends wrote begging for a little food. How long could their hearts endure such oppression without breaking? How long would their enfeebled bodies be able to hold out? The unspeakable tyranny of bondage was like night of impenetrable darkness within whose folds each man and woman wished, was determined to hope, but could not descry, through the endless blackness, even the flicker of one humble altar-lamp.

Nikos Manoussis was startled as the Carabiniero entered his law office.

"My hour has come," he thought. "They must have my past record. They're going to arrest me."

But he calmed down as soon as the interpreter spoke and told him that Diamantis was inviting him to the house where he was staying. He even had the *sang-froid* to ask the interpreter: "Are you or this gentleman Mr. Diamantis' messenger?"

The interpreter was about to answer, but the Carabiniero asked what he was saying and seemed to be angered by the question. He answered in an irritated tone of voice, and the interpreter translated, "He would not have taken the trouble to come with me to your office if he was not intended to give you the message himself. Have you any objection to his being the Commendatore's orderly?"

The Italian was not a man to argue with. Manoussis smiled and said politely, "Not at all. I asked because I wanted to know to whom I should address a second question. When does my old friend wish to see me?"

"At once."

"Very well. I'll finish something urgent and be there in ten minutes."

Left alone, he reflected that he did not at all like that hasty invitation, particularly as it was transmitted through the Gendarmerie. What could his fellow-townsman, the foxy adventurer Diamantis want with him? Diamantis had a bad name in

Larissa. He had been an Italian agent in World War I and later one of the strong-arm boys of Rumanian propaganda. Since Italy's attack on Greece in October 1940 his movements had been very suspicious. Nikos Manoussis would have preferred to have nothing to do with this character. Times were bad, he couldn't refuse. But he must be careful, very careful.

Alcibiades Diamantis received him at home but he was not alone. There were two other men there whom Nikos Manoussis saw for the first time. Their names meant nothing to him. Diamantis was very friendly, asked about his family, and mentioned Samarina, the village from which they both came. Then, without beating about the bush, he came straight to the subject at hand.

"I have called you in, Nikos, because the time has arrived for a dream to come true. The great powers have decided to found a Wallachian Principality."

He perceived the surprise on Nikos' face and, smiling, continued confidently. "It is natural for you to be startled, but I assure you that the time has come. Because I trust you, and know that you are capable and ambitious, I want you to become my first and principal collaborator. I am going to tell what only a few outsiders know as yet. Our principality will not be confined to the Pindus areas as was the plan in 1917, but will include the greater part of Epirus, Western Macedonia, and the whole of Thessaly."

"As far as Domokos," the two young men added, speaking at once.

"As far as Domokos," Diamantis repeated.

"Just a moment," Manoussis observed incredulously. "Most of these areas don't include a single Vlach village. Don't forget that we are living at a time when the patriotic feelings of the Greeks are intensely strong."

Diamantis again smiled confidently. "Do you imagine I don't know this? Everything has been taken into account, the plans have been laid, and you'll hear what will happen. But don't interrupt me. First let me give you the general outline and then we'll come to details. Well then—the Wallachian Principality has become indispensable to the Axis Powers because the Greeks are incorrigible and fanatical Anglophiles. Greece will be cut up. It will revert to the frontiers of 1880. Albania will take Tsamouria, Bulgaria will get Thrace and a part of Macedonia and will reach as far as Salonika. Our principality will get the rest because they want it to be viable so as to become a Latin link between Italy and Rumania."

"Fine, but how will it become a Latin link when it's inhabited by Greeks?" Nikos Manoussis repeated in a milder tone so as not to provoke the others.

"First this will happen because it is the will of those who have brought the whole of Europe and North Africa to their knees and are now bringing Russia to hers. Second, all the village councils will be replaced by our men, and they will proclaim whatever we tell them to, beginning with a statement that the inhabitants are Latins."

"Rumanians," one of the young men interposed.

"Yes, that is to say Vlachs. Third," Diamantis continued, "the nucleus of the new state will be constituted right away. It will be called the Roman Legion. It will have its own army and will collaborate with the Italian occupation forces, and by degrees will take the place of the Greek state. For example, in the summer the occupation authorities will order us to proceed with the concentration of wheat in Thessaly. Before that, with the excuse that there is a shortage of salt, all the milk in Thessaly will be turned over to men of the Legion to be made into cheese. We will carry out some public works; we'll extend the railroad from Kalabaka to Grevena."

He came to a stop and Nikos Manoussis remained thoughtful and silent. The plan was impressive; it was also crazy, dangerous, and doubtful for a host of reasons. It made one dizzy to think of it. Did Diamantis know what he was talking about or was he bluffing?

"I understand what you are thinking," Diamantis said. "You hesitate to believe that such a bold plan can be carried out. Whenever you wish, a higher officer of the Italian Divisional Staff will confirm what I have told you. Moreover, you will be convinced when you see the central offices of the Roman Legion opening tomorrow."

"Here in Larissa?"

"Here, on Athanasios Diakos Street."

"But there are very few Vlachs here, and they are all loyal. Wouldn't it be better to have the center at Trikkala or Grevena where at least there are a certain number of Vlachs?"

"No, that's impossible," Diamantis answered somewhat sharply. "The Forli Division has been ordered to enforce the plan and its headquarters are in Larissa. The Pinerolo Division with headquarters at Trikkala, and with Grevena under its jurisdiction, is not considered capable by the Blackshirts of carrying out such an undertaking."

A short silence followed. Nikos Manoussis' brain worked furiously. The plan seemed crazy, but if it was confirmed by a higher Staff officer, it couldn't be ignored. This was no bluff. The heads of power must have come to some decision.

Nikos was weighing the pros and cons of the matter and was wondering what Diamantis would require of him and what he would reply. He had no cause to say anything. Diamantis broke the silence. His manner was hard and determined.

"In a few days I shall call in the principal Vlach professional men in Larissa and, by preference, our fellow-citizens from the village of Samarina. I'll put the question to them abruptly. But first I wanted to talk to you because you are the most capable and a man of initiative. In the new state I shall be the Prince and I want you to be my Prime Minister. At the present stage of the undertaking I shall assume the title of Leader of the Vlachs of the Balkan Peninsula, and you will be the President of the Legion."

Nikos Manoussis was scared. For the first time he lost complete control of himself and said, "But I'm not prepared for such a role. Give me time to think. I don't know if I have the necessary qualifications."

"You have. Only one drawback presented itself in your case and this caused the Divisional Authorities to hesitate. But I gave them my personal guarantee, and assured them that all that was a forgotten youthful error. I am sure that when as a young man you wanted to become mayor, and didn't give considered thought to the people with whom you were associating. I'm quite sure of your opinion. You're no Communist. And I stated this in the proper quarters."

Manoussis felt a cold sweat come over him. The threat was

only too clear. "I'll give you my answer tomorrow," he said.

Diamantis smiled pleasantly. "Nikos," he said, "you can't afford to refuse, and you can't betray your own blood. I know that you are a good Vlach, so don't miss your opportunity. Tomorrow I'd like you to come with me to meet the Italian officer."

"What is he? One of the higher commanders, did you say?"

"The Forli Division is under the formal command of General Fuggiero, a nobleman who doesn't count for much. The real commander is the Chief of Staff. That's the man you'll see."

After a short silence, Diamantis began speaking fast and passionately. He punctuated his remarks by repeatedly asking Nikos, "Isn't that so?" and poured out all the poison of Rumanian propoganda. It was the Vlachs who had made Greece what it was in war and peace. The Greeks had cheated them and never given them their freedom. The Greeks had not respected agreements, and terrorized them so as to prevent their children from going to Rumanian schools. Under Greek tyranny no Vlach could make headway in his career. The minority system would not work. Only under an independent regime would they find a place in the sun and, since they were capable and energetic, they would achieve great prosperity among their Rumanian brothers and Italian cousins.

The eyes of the young men flashed. They stared at Nikos intently and from time to time gave vent to indignant expletives. Nikos Manoussis didn't know what to do. He had occasionally heard all these crude lies, so contrary to the facts of everyday life, but he hadn't realized that there were men who actually believed them. These two appeared to believe them with virulent hatred. And now they were supported by Italian bayonets. They would become dangerous.

What a pity he had come unprepared. He could not make up his mind as to the safest course to take, but he had the feeling that his attitude so far had left him exposed. He must put things straight, he must give them some satisfaction and, in case he should become involved, must make a good impression.

So he launched into a shrewd analysis of the world situation, saying that on the one hand were the forces of constructive discipline and hard work, and on the other a luxuriance of ideologies and material interests. Now, he asserted, there was a unique opportunity to perform a social duty in bringing to light the vitality of the Vlachs. The faces of his hearers showed clearly that he had succeeded in his purpose.

Without making too many excuses Diamantis tried to get rid of the two exuberant young men. As they got up to leave he asked them mockingly, "Well, boys, is the President I have chosen a good one?"

One of them answered with some reserve. "His actions will tell."

The other was more outspoken. "He's exactly as you described him. He seems to be serious-minded and energetic. But all this time we've been speaking Greek. Doesn't he know our language?" He then spoke to Manoussis in Rumanian. Nikos replied in Vlach. He told him he knew this language well but didn't know Rumanian.

The young man answered impatiently in Rumanian at first and then switched to Greek. "Rumanian and Vlach are the same language. What you know is a corrupt, Hellenized Vlach." A short discussion followed about the local variations in Vlach and the relationship of the language to Rumanian. The young men became more and more restless. Diamantis tried to ease the situation by tending to agree with the youths. Manoussis remained silent for a while. He felt that if he was to become involved in this business he must take a more dynamic stand and clear up any doubts which might stand in his way.

"I'm with you," he said, "but I don't propose to take an active part in anything unless we are going to be realistic. Go ahead and make speeches in Rumanian in the Vlach villages and nobody will understand a word of what you are saying. But everyone will understand me. So take your choice. That the language needs cultivating, refining and enrichment is another matter. It will be achieved gradually through the schools. It cannot be attained by emotionalism and commands." He saw that his words had made an impression, and added firmly, "This is my opinion and no one can change it. Obstinacy and a refusal to face reality will only be harmful to our people and rebound to the advantage of our enemies."

The young men left. Then Diamantis leaned over and said to Nikos in a confidential tone; "You were quite right to be firm with them. Their fathers and brothers are nothing but ragged and barefoot goatherds, but they were sent to school and to the universty. You see how they listen to everything that comes out of Bucharest. I am broadminded and a realist. And as to all the 'history' I was dishing out to you, I'm well aware of how much is right and how much is wrong. But I wanted them to hear it from you and also to hear that you are a fanatical Vlach. But I had more to tell you on the subject and that's why I asked them to leave."

In a still more confidential tone he continued. "The project will succeed, Nikos. There is however one point which is delicate—very delicate. Bucharest wants the movement, and later the new state, to be Rumanian. There are seventy years of endeavour and expense behind the scheme. Rome, on the other hand, wants a Latin state under its control—*Mare Nostrum* and all that. A tricky business."

Nikos gave him a knowing smile. "Brothers on the one hand, cousins on the other. You've found a good formula."

Diamantis laughed and winked at him. "Yes, the formula's good alright, but the trouble is that the Italians want to be the brothers and pass the cousinship to the Rumanians. The matter needs careful handling; it's not easy."

"No, it's not," Nikos said after a moment's reflection. "However, so long as the war lasts it won't be to difficult for you to follow a middle course by telling the Rumanians that nothing can be accomplished without the help of the Italians, and telling the Italians that we have to rely on the pro-Rumanian element if the project is to succeed."

Diamantis winked at him again. "In other words both are to be brothers. I prefer my own formula presented in reverse to each."

"They might both be indignant if they found out about this presentation in reverse."

"It's a question of handling.. Anyway that's the difficult point. You'll see it tomorrow when you talk to Pazzipolino."

"Who's Pazzipolino?"

"He's the Divisional Chief of Staff."

"But, Alcibiades, I haven't accepted yet!"

Diamantis got up and gave him a friendly thump on the back. "Come on, Nikos! Don't be childish. You know there's no other way out for you, and moreover this road will lead you very far, very far indeed. You know where the other road leads."

Nikos was about to say something but Diamantis didn't give him an opportunity. He went on. "I have spoken to you like a brother because I know that you're going to become my right hand man. You'll see how I'll speak to your other colleagues in a few days. Take care not to make a mistake. It would be particularly disastrous for you." Then he changed his tone and with a superior and somewhat indifferent air, continued. "I have something more to tell you which you should bear in mind during tomorrow's conversation. You realize that the cheese production, the public works, and so forth will be a tremendous enterprise. Tremendous even by wider European standards. All the milk and wheat in Thessaly will pass through our hands. You see what that means. So, there are several Italian officers who are already plainly saying that they expect a cut. I don't know whether they're also covering up for some of their superiors. I'll help them out. I'll see how I can manage to cover up for them, and I'll also help my principal assistants to make a penny or two. I personally am not interested in money. I want as much of the profit as possible to go into the Legion's treasury. A state, or the nucleus of a state, without funds would be an absurdity. When you're talking with Pazzipolini there are two points you should keep clearly in mind: first our Latinity, and second business. The line to follow is that we don't want any profit for ourselves; the profit will go to the Legion. Business enterprises are essential in creating a *de facto* situation which will enable us gradually to supplant the Greek State."

* * * * *

As soon as Nikos left Diamantis' house he looked at his watch. It was eight o'clock. He would be just in time. He hurried to his office and telephoned Katie.

"Come to the office at once," he said. "I want to talk to you without being interrupted by your father."

While he was waiting for his niece, a veritable maelstrom of conflicting thoughts whirled through his brain. Sitting stiffly behind his desk he kept his eyes fixed in a hard stare upon the opposite wall as if he were trying to read the future there. The door opened and Katie came in, an airy, pretty, dainty apparition wearing a tight-fitting light blue dress which suited her golden-dark complexion.

She looked at him and said, "And I thought that you had heard about my visits to Pteliona and that like the bourgeois uncle you arc, you wete becoming anxious."

He mustered his sarcastic expression and remarked, "The way you said that would make one think you didn't believe it any more. Why have you changed your opinion?"

She gave him a long look and replied, "I've rarely, if ever, seen you with that expression on your face. Something now must be afoot."

"What's the matter with my expression?" he asked with interest.

"The sarcasm's gone out of it. And then you always had a rather hard expression but now it's particularly hard. Furthermore, how shall I say it? While you seem perturbed and frightened there's a gleam in your eyes. You're very strange this evening."

He looked at her admiringly and kissed her. "You don't know how well you've hit the mark. You're quite a witch! I was right in thinking that you were the only one to give me advice. Here's what's happening.'

He told her about his visit to Diamantis. He related every detail of the conversation with the precision of a recording machine and without making comments.

"As you see," he concluded, "I have refrained from giving you any opinion because I want your completely unbiased view."

She had listened to him with close attention and growing intentness as his story unfolded. She didn't answer him at once.

"Well?" he asked with a trace of anguish in his voice.

"I think you made your own decision before you called me in. However I'll give you my opinion: I believe that the outcome of the venture will depend upon who wins the war."

"I don't think there's any doubt about that," her uncle said. "The problem I'm up against is more immediate. Everyone in this town, whether Vlach or non-Vlach, will turn against me. How does that strike you?"

With a grimace of disdain she retorted, "Here we are talking about matters of world-wide significance and you are reducing the discussion to the petty level of Greek provincialism. I never bother about public opinion in this place; you know how I constantly scandalize people with my antics. Are you going to be stopped by what people may think when such an opportunity that comes your way—when you're actually being offered the most astounding opportunity that could be offered to any man, and particularly to one who in the past has been given a raw deal and has been the object of contempt?"

The double sting in Katie's last words nettled him. "You're right," he said. "However at this particular time everyone is in a state of patriotic intoxication."

"They'll get over it," she answered coldly. "All these timid little homebodies will become totally deflated when the allied situation goes from bad to worse. At first they'll give you the cold shoulder, but by degrees they'll all come crawling to you. For this reason I think it might be wise if you moved out of the house during the fist stage of the operation; that would give us a chance to give out that we're not in agreement with you."

"But that's outrageous," he whined plaintively. "It would give the impression that you were setting an example for others to ostracize me."

"Yes, but in this way father will be able to keep his job and will find it easier to swallow the bitter pill, particularly when he realizes that he'll be able to play both sides against the middle—a line of conduct quite in keeping with his character. We shall also be able to get all the news from the opposition and feed it to you regularly. When most of the people come over to your side—or maybe earlier if we find it expedient—we shall declare ourselves openly."

"I don't like these tactics," he remarked drily. "Things will be hard at first and I shall need all the support you can give me. Besides, I have a feeling that in dealing with the Italians you could be of great help to me."

A cold silence fell between them. Then Katie spoke with slow deliberation. "I believe that by following the course I suggested we shall be giving you the best possible support. On the other hand, this artificial solution suits me personally because I'm not sure that I want to give you my help. I'm beginning to take a serious interest in Coletti."

Nikos Manoussis was amazed. "I don't see the connection," he said. "Besides, Coletti has gone rustic. Have you seen him walking around town in farmer's clothes? I really don't understand you."

"He's become a man," Katie said dreamily. "A real man and handsome too. He also is in a state of patriotic intoxication. I hope he'll soon get tired of all the things he's doing so enthusiastically at the moment. Maybe he will when the rains and the winter mud come. If this phase passes and he limits his activities to a keen interest in Pteliona, I'll marry him. That is why I require this breathing space. If it turns out that he doesn't change intention to be nothing but a farmer then I'll find the strength to break with him. Then..." she continued with an embarrassed smile, "then, I shall be the Prime Minister's niece. I have charm and brains, and you'll find me an Italian officer and I'll be able to get away from this loathsome and benighted place."

She stood up, enervated, and added, "I can't stand any more of this. I can't go through it for a third time."

Nikos stood up too and took her in his arms. They were both conscious of great affection between them; neither of them was capable of much affection for others. He said to her, "What is it you can't go through for a third time?"

She seemed pained but she didn't react emotionally. She stood still and silent. "Nothing," she said. "My grief like my nature cannot be shared with anyone."

She freed herself from her uncle's arms, turned lightly, and said mockingly, "If I need you as a marriage broker, Mr. Prime Minister, I'll let you know in good time. And then I'll help you with all my heart." For a brief moment he remained motionless, silent and expressionless. Then he said, "For the time being don't breathe a word of all this to anyone. I'll keep in touch with you and tell you what's going on, and you will let me know everything you see and hear. I'm aware of all the difficulties, but just think, Katie, what I'm aiming for. If the Italian Chief of Staff confirms my appointment I shall be the ruler of Thessaly and, later, of all the area from the Adriatic to the Aegean and from the northern frontier to Domokos."

"Maybe even more than that," she said eagerly.

"What do you mean by that?"

"If all goes well and Diamantis should die..."

"Stop it! And for the moment keep your mouth shut except when you're with me."

IV

Heavy indeed is slavery! Its night is black, impenetrable, fathomless! It winds around you like a snake, especially when you have small children you are struggling to feed and to educate! As if the sufferings which increased day by day for everyone were not enough, they had to sustain an even harder blow, one which was still obscure but which was humiliating and perhaps dangerous.

What was this Roman Legion? What was the meaning of the command, in the form of an invitation, which the Carabinieri brought to them from that adventurer and traitor, Alcibiades Diamantis? How was he able to have the Carabinieri at his beck and call? And why did they call him Commendatore, a title which his friends said was the equivalent of Your Highness? What did he want with them? What would he say to them? It would be no good, anyway. What kind of adventure was he leading them into?

These were the thoughts running through the minds of the lawyers and doctors of Vlach stock as they walked to the offices of the Legion outside which a few Carabinieri loitered. They were perplexed, anxious and indignant. They soon found out what he wanted of them.

They were not kept waiting in the anteroom. They were ushered into a hall where, behind an impressive desk, Diamantis was standing. Behind him to one side, to their astonishment, stood their friend and colleague, Nikos Manoussis. Diamantis was ill at ease; Nikos, somewhat paler than usual, was calm.

cold, and supercilious. When Diamantis started to speak, Nikos crossed his arms over his chest and remained thus throughout the conversation, looking at the visitors with an arrogant sidelong glance.

From the beginning Diamantis spoke to them abruptly and angrily. He began by berating them for not coming to call on him of their own accord; he gave them the usual propaganda line about past history and announced that the Wallachian Principality was now established, in essence, with the Roman Legion. Nikos Manoussis would be the President; Larissa would probably be the capital of the Principality and would attain great prosperity; Samarina would be the summer capital. In conclusion he said that he expected to have their support and that they would be appointed to responsible positions.

They were thunderstruck. What sort of outrage was this? They were all middle-aged, they had homes and families to support, but they were all Greeks and proud to be so and had always detested Rumanian propaganda and had fought it on their own without anyone to guide them because they believed that national conscience was not something that could be bought and sold.

How could they switch their loyalty? And yet they had their families to consider. The prospective Prince banged his fist on the table and shouted, "Well, say something. Have you all been struck dumb?"

One of them spoke. "Alcibiades, we have lived a good life in this country. We started out poor and we made good careers for ourselves without any hindrance; we don't feel like strangers here."

"Aren't you Vlachs, you fool!" Diamantis bellowed angrily. "Aren't you Vlachs every one of you? Aren't you Vlachs?"

"Yes, we are Vlachs," the speaker answered in a gentle but firm voice. "But we are Greek Vlachs. At home we speak Greek and you yourself are talking to us in Greek."

The leader of the Balkan Vlachs foamed at the mouth.

"I spoke to you in Greek," he shouted, "because I know that some of you have become corrupted. But I have come to save you. I have come to make human beings of you. From Monstir to Domokos, d'you hear me? If that bull-headed doctor has been deluding you, I'm telling you that he'll come along too and dance to my tune."

He was banging his fists on the table, blurting out his words spasmodically, and foaming at the mouth. He went on even more furiously. "Whoever comes with me will prosper. Whoever refuses will be sent by the Italians to the road repair gangs to break stones. D'you hear what I say? You'll be breaking stones out in the desert. I give you forty-eight hours to bring me your answers. Now get out! Get out!"

One of the group paused as he was leaving. "We have families, Alcibiades. Leave us alone to take care of our homes and cope with our troubles."

Without moving, Nikos Manoussis answered him arrogantly.

"You are either with us or against us. That is our policy."

"Get out!" the Leader roared. "After you've thought it over we'll talk again.

* * * * *

On the next day a non-commissioned officer and two Carabinieri accompanied by the indispensable interpreter went to the surgical clinic of Dr. Nikos Raptis. It was situated near the central piazza. The clinic was modern and had been completed just before the Italian invasion. The damage it had sustained from the earthquake had just been repaired at great sacrifice.

The Carabinieri went in to see the doctor. "The Commendatore is expecting you," they said.

"I have to see my patients."

"You can see them later. You didn't go yesterday when he summoned you. We have orders to escort you to him. Immediately."

He went. He knew he was outspoken, he himself admitted it. This time he would have to restrain himself even though he was choking with indignation. He was a family man and had gone into debt to build his clinic. He would not give in, but he mustn't provoke them. Fortunately Nikos Manoussis was an old friend; fortunately too he himself was not unprepared, since the others had told him what had happened and he knew what he would hear and in what atmosphere he would find himself.

Yet, in spite of the fact that the Commendatore was not in an angry mood today, the doctor felt the blood rising to his head and his temples throbbing, as the men developed his revolting thesis. This was unbelievable! This was utterly dishonorable! How could his frined Nikos be abetting such a shameful thing?

When he had concluded the description of his plans, Diamantis did not request the doctor's help. He asked him with a self-satisfied air, "Well, how do you find all this?"

"I am astounded," the doctor replied coldly.

"Astounded that the Vlachs are seeing the light at last?" Diamantis remarked suspiciously.

"No. On the contrary. Astounded because the facts are not at all as you say they are, and because I never expected that we should be seeking to dismember Greece ourselves."

The Leader did not explode as on the previous day. He put his hands behind his back and, bending forward with an evil expression, came and stood in front of the doctor.

"Tell me, doctor, aren't you a Vlach?"

Nikos Manoussis had also approached. The doctor controlled himself with difficulty and managed to reply calmly. "I am a Vlach, a Greek Vlach. I learned to read and write in a Greek school, I served in the Greek army, and from the time I first saw the light of day, I knew only one flag: the blue and white flag of Greece."

Two sharp slaps resounded on the doctor's cheeks as Diamantis shouted, "Now you'll see another flag!"

Manoussis leapt forward and caught hold of his leader, telling him that he shouldn't have done that; then he rushed toward the doctor who was furiously brandishing a chair and about to bring it down on Diamantis' head.

"For heaven's sake, doctor! Calm down, I beg you!"

"Shut up, you traitor!" the doctor shouted. "Shut up, you stooge of this bloody bastard! Get out of here!"

But Manoussis had gotten hold of the chair and, in the meantime, the Carabinieri, hearing the commotion, had come in and pulled them apart. The infuriated leader, who was also a bit scared, said something to them in Italian. They dragged the doctor to the door and told him to leave.

Diamantis, who had gotten behind his desk, called out to him, "You'd better look out or you'll get into trouble—very bad trouble."

"I don't give a damn!" the doctor shouted as he was being hustled out of the door. "You'll never make a Janissary of me!"

* * * * *

The two heads of the Legion were now alone and Diamantis noticed that Nikos Manoussis' look was cold and heavy. He avoided his eyes. He clasped his hands behind his back, walked up and down the room two or three times, and then stopped in front of him.

"We're going to have some difficulties," he said.

"Yes, we are."

"I wasn't expecting this."

Nikos remained cold and silent. Diamantis still avoided looking straight at him as he repeated, "I wasn't expecting this."

"Why not?"

"What do you mean, 'Why not'? I'm making their dreams come true and they're resisting me. How can you ask 'Why not?' "

Nikos remained silent.

"Maybe you don't agree with me either," Diamantis continued.

"If I didn't I wouldn't be here."

"That's true. But what's the matter with them? Am I or am I not making their dreams come true?"

"Perhaps they have other dreams."

"Impossible. They are Vlachs, and most of them from Samarina."

"Your father too was from Samarina."

"What of it?"

"He named you Alcibiades and your brother Thrasybulus. Why?"

Diamantis got angry: "You mean that he was a Greek? He wasn't. He was drugged."

"Drugged? How so?"

"By religion. By the priests and their Greek Bibles and schools."

Nikos tried to conceal his sarcasm, but couldn't.

"I never thought that you would quote Karl Marx."

"Why? What did Marx say?"

"That religion is the opiate of the people."

Diamantis, still angry, took a few steps, and then faced him again.

"You can tell Marx with my compliments that that is nonsense. Religion and Country, Family and Property are not opiates. They are the foundations of society."

Again he avoided Manoussis' eyes. He looked at the ground thoughtfully and changed his tone as he spoke again. "Never mind my father and Marx, Nikos. Tell me what you think. What's the score now? Could I have been wrong in slapping that pig-headed fellow's face?"

"Maybe you were wrong and maybe not."

"You're a great help!"

"I mean to say that there are two ways of looking at the question. However, that was only a minor incident without any real importance."

Diamantis seemed genuinely startled.

"Of course it's not important," Nikos went on coldly. "Between ourselves, we've got to realize that we've embarked on this business against the will of the people. But since we have embarked on it and have shown our hand, we've got to go through with it. Now in order to succeed with the people against us we must have recourse to a great number of devices. In this context who cares about a slap? It may even prove useful as a small warning of bigger blows to come."

* * * * *

He decided not to abandon his law practice. This would be unwise. In the first place people would say that he no longer needed it, and both his prestige and the movement would suffer. Second, he needed it. Third, if the Legion failed to yield other advantages quickly, his premiership would certainly augment his business. But he would have to take on an assistant, or maybe make a deal with a colleague to whom he would pass on his cases and with whom he would share the profits, so that his name need not appear at all.

No indeed, he must not abandon his law practice. Besides, it was a habit with him and one that would be useful in those turbulent times. At this moment, for instance, after the disagreeable incident with his old friend Raptis and the stupid discussion with that idiot Diamantis, what a comfort it was to be going back to his office, where he would be examining familiar files and working out legal arguments.

But as soon as he reached the small side-street where his office was located, his temporary relief vanished. In the twilight shadows he recognized Phoula's silhouette. He saw her from afar as she walked slowly, passed the office and turned back again. She was pretending to be passing by, but actually she was waiting for him. And, certainly she too would condemn him. He was annoyed.

He knew that Phoula adored him, that he meant everything to her. And he was by no means indifferent to her. She was a woman who attracted him more than any other ever had. She loved him with all her heart as well as with her body; he loved her physically only—maybe a little with his mind too. Not that Phoula was a woman made for a prosaic love affair. She was attentive, cultivated, clever, emotional and, while she could not be compared with Katie, she was one of the most alluring women in the city. No, she was not to blame for the quality of his love. It was his nature. He could not love in any other way.

She heard him coming and adjusted her pace so as to arrive at the office at the same time as he did, and scurried inside. The curtains were drawn. As soon as he locked the door she clung to him in terror.

"Nikos, my darling Nikos, what have you gotten yourself into? How could you have done such a thing?" she said to him in anguish.

He scowled at her. "Have you come here to upset me too? I have enough worries already." She stroked his hair and his cheeks.

"No, my darling, I don't want to worry you. I've come because I'm afraid. The men who were at the meeting don't speak out in public but they told my husband what happened. It was a terrible scene."

"You should have seen what happened today—just a few moments ago. It was much worse."

"Who was there today?"

"Only one. Nikos Raptis."

"My husband's closest friend," she whispered, startled. "They work together."

After a brief pause, with real anguish in her voice, she added, "What's going to happen, Nikos? All the world will hear about it! Go away at once while there's still time. You can say that you disagreed and had the courage to leave. If it's any help to you, I'll come with you. I implore you, Nikos, get away!"

Frowning and obstinate, he said, "I won't leave. I have a mission to accomplish. If they don't fully understand it now they will later. I shall protect and exalt the Vlachs."

"Nikos, do you remember what you used to say to me about the Vlachs? Tell me the truth."

"I'm telling you the truth. I'm convinced that in spite of exaggeration there's much that is right in what's being said. There's no doubt that the Vlachs have been pushed aside. Besides, Salonika and a large part of Macedonia are threatened by the Bulgars. If they are saved it will be by us alone. We shall be a Latin state on the surface but in reality we shall be on the side of Greece."

She passed her hand over her face and gripped her chin. She looked at him in terror.

"Nikos, my darling," she murmured. "What are you saying? All that about...as far as Domokos...is that true?"

He answered harshly. "Yes, it's true. From Monastir to Domokos."

She was on the brink of tears and turned to leave. He caught her by the arm, drew her to him and held her.

"But don't you understand that I have to gamble for high stakes in supporting the movement or else I shall be sent to rot in prison as a former Communist? Don't you understand that at this difficult time I need you more than ever?"

He looked deep into her eyes. There he saw terror, disapproval, adoration, and despair. He felt passion stirring within him and kissed her on her mouth and neck. She felt her body respond to his, but she wanted to resist. Something told her it was not right, that it was not the same as it had been before. But her passion was stronger than her will. She couldn't think clearly anymore. She found herself on the floor, on the dirty mat in front of Nikos' desk.

* * * * *

He arranged his clothes and his hair, and tried to put his thoughts in order. He didn't seem to be able to. He lit a cigarette and attempted to review the events of the last few days. He tried to separate the pros and the cons, but found he couldn't think clearly. He picked up the telephone and, although it was now late at night, asked Katie to come quickly to the office. She was calm, extremely calm.

"You must have been upset," she said. "The beginning wasn't too good."

"Very bad. And you should have seen what happened today."

He told her everything.

"A lot of blustering," she remarked. "It's just the beginning. These men are still intoxicated with what is poetically called the Epic of Albania. But the wine is thin, the thirst is great, and the hunger even greater. And now the antidotes against the intoxication are coming in from all the countries of Europe which have sworn allegiance. After a little more bravado our friends will calm down and get used to the situation. Don't be afraid of them."

"I'm not afraid of most of them, but I am afraid of a few."

"I think you're wrong. I think that all men at all times surrender to money or fear. Any kind of fear: fear of starvation, imprisonment, or death. You will have at your disposal both means of bending men to your will. That is why I want to hear the only news that is in the least bit important: has the Chief of Staff confirmed Diamantis' offer?"

"More or less," he replied with some hesitation. "The establishment of the principality is on their agenda, but without definite frontiers, and it is to be linked with Italy, not Rumania."

"It's better so."

"Naturally. As regards the Legion, there too the situation has not been clarified. It is not at all certain that it will substantially supplant the State in its functions even if it is entrusted with the concentration of argicultural produce and all that. It seems that they are interested in this and want it. As regards our army, it appears that they will create a civil guard of two or three thousand men."

"On the whole the news is good," she said thoughtfully.

"The mission of our army will be to search for hidden arms."

"That's not so good. But what do you care? You've taken the plunge; you can't go back. The Axis is winning, so go ahead. Don't be afraid of the cowards. Their only courage is that they don't admit their fear."

"You're a clever girl," he remarked, "But you're young and have a tendency to generalize. I agree with what you said about money and fear bending the will. But it doesn't apply to everyone. Don't forget the idealists." And he added in a rasping somewhat tremulous voice, "I mean the real idealists."

"They do exist, but they're very rare," she said. "In all my life I've only known two. Nothing can influence such exceptional beings—neither fear, nor money, nor even love."

Nikos understood that she regretted having mentioned love, and said, "When love is fulfilled it dies. It loses its power."

"I don't know. It's possible...but I don't believe it. It may acquire more power." Then more briskly she said, "Anyhow I've known two exceptions. Perhaps I'm about to discover a third."

"Do you know that he too is a Vlach on his mother's as well as his father's side? Diamantis is always referring to the Colettis in his propaganda verbiage."

Katie got up somewhat abruptly, took a few steps with her eyes lowered, sat down again opposite him, and asked him quietly but firmly, "Have you bothered him?"

"No, not at all. Diamantis is not even aware of his existence. Nor are the others."

"Listen to me, uncle. I'm levelling with you. If you call him in you'll be harming me in something I've set my heart on. If you threaten him, you and I will quarrel for the first time in our lives. Besides, he's not interfering in anything. He doesn't know what's going on. If you call him in, he may become your worst enemy."

He smiled at her condescendingly.

"All right, all right, don't worry. We won't bother him. But as for being our worst enemy—that baby, so far removed from the hard facts of life and from the soul of the Vlachs...."

She made no sigh of protest, but stared abstractedly in front of her. "He's no stranger to the vagaries of this crazy life, nor to the even crazier enthusiasms of some Greeks. He's changed very much."

"Have you spoken to him about the movement?"

"I have only prepared the ground. I told him that we had had a quarrel and you had left the house. Out of discretion he refrained from asking why." Then in a livelier tone she added, "However, if he hears what you're doing, believe me he'll become your enemy and a formidable one."

This time her uncle laughed heartily. She changed her tune and said, smiling, "The one who's pleased is father."

Nikos was interested. "Tell me about him," he said.

"He has a great admiration for you. He says that you couldn't have acted otherwise because you past was a dangerous threat to you. He says that it's not true that Diamantis called you in, but that you cooked up the whole business so as to find yourself on top. He says too that in times of trouble prudent people act like this, half of them on one side of the fence, the other half on the opposite side, so that in the end both sides take care of each other." Katie laughed, but her uncle was solemn.

"Such a division can't last forever. We are playing a difficult game for big stakes, and they'll pin me to the wall. Other people won't follow me if my own people boycott me."

"You're right," she said. "But there's no great hurry. In a month or two I'll tell you which side I'm on."

V

However one looked at it, Pteliona was different from the old well-organized ranch with the tall house and the many sturdy buildings which had known days of pride and had then sunk into decadence. Everything was smaller, improvised. Livestock and material possessions were fewer than ever before.

But a more careful scrutiny would show that the greatest change had occurred in the character of the place. Because now it seemed to have a soul which activated all who lived and breathed there; a soul which made them all strive to restore the ruined farm.

From dawn to dusk all threw themselves into their work without a word and without the need for orders or instructions. Among Nikita Coletti's best workers were his army comrades who had come to help him in his hour of need and to eat in their hour of hunger. But none could be called 'best worker'—all worked with equal zest. Mourayias beamed with joy, and Nikita himself moved all over the place and overcame all the difficulties created by the lack of materials. No, there was no better or best. All that could be said was that there was one person whose abscence would have made life difficult for everyone, and that was Phrosso. She was willing, nimble, and thoughtful, and with the help of a single servant girl, made them all feel comfortable and at home. Many foods and a thousand other things were lacking, but somehow she managed to provide for their needs, and the storehouse which had been repaired had now become a cheerful kitchen and a pleasant living room where the men gathered when it rained and after work.

On one particular autumn evening, long before the others came in, Mourayias went into the kitchen. He asked Phrosso for a glass of *tsipouro*, and exchanged a few words with her with an air of indifference. But Phrosso understood that he had something on his mind which was bothering him and that he wanted to unburden himself. She smiled at him.

"Father," she said, "what are you trying to hide? I know there's something you want to talk about. If you dont't tell it to your daughter to whom will you tell it?"

"No, my child, I'm not trying to hide anything. There would be no point in my telling anyone else. It's for your ears alone. But, well, I'm embarrassed."

She was disturbed and went to sit down by him. "For my ears alone?" she asked. "What's the matter?"

He looked at her with infinite love and compassion, and said very slowly, "I heard the news several days ago, but I wanted to be sure. He's come back. He's here."

She understood but was dazed, and feeling her heart contract she asked in a faint voice; "Who has come back?"

"Your husband. He's in Larissa. He's also been to several villages. But he doesn't show himself in public. He seems to be on his guard. I was told he asked after you."

After a short silence he asked her timidly, "What are you going to do?"

"Nothing."

"What if he comes looking for you?"

With an animated expression she said energetically, "You said 'my husband', and now you ask me what I shall do if he comes here. Do you imagine it is possible for me to live with him again? Father, as far as I'm concerned that man is dead."

Mourayias looked at her sadly, but he was relieved. "Yes, but he's not dead, and he's nearby."

"Don't worry, father. Seeing that I have absolutely no feeling left for him, he can't disturb our quiet life. I only hope he doesn't cause some other greater trouble. Why has he come back at such a time? Where has he come from? And since, as you say, he's lying low, why is he going round the villages?"

Mourayias made a gesture of acceptance and indifference.

"I don't know about that. All I ask is for him not to upset things here."

He took a couple of sips from his glass. "Everything's going so well for us. With all the misery and upheaval around us, we couldn't have hoped for better luck."

They remained silent for a few moments. Mourayias rolled a cigarette and lit it. "I sometimes wonder," he said, "why there are troubles in the world; and why sometimes without any particular reason an unbearable anxiety comes over us."

She took his hand and smiled at him. "All I want is for you to have no worries."

"As long as I have you near me, healthy and attractive, I have nothing to worry about. I was talking about other people. How much pain there is in life! Why should this be? You've been to school and read books. Tell me why. Why must there be so much grief? Why must some people be born unhappy? Why from the moment we are born are some of us this way and some that? Why must this be?"

"Father," she laughed, "even those who are far better educated than I couldn't answer your question. Talk to me about simpler things. When will you begin sowing?"

They talked about the farm and at one point Phrosso said to him, "It's my turn to ask you about something which I can't explain. Do you remember the measly young man who came here from Paris two years ago? Do you remember that when you first saw him you wanted us to leave Pteliona? How could such a change come over him? Have you any explanation for that?"

The old teamster's eyes brightened and his face shone.

"It's easy to explain, my child. The earth called to him—so loud that it shook him."

"Father! Do you really believe that the earth has a voice?"

He gave her an aggrieved look.

"Neither you, nor those who know a lot more than you do, can answer the simple question I asked. How can you well-read people say that the earth has no voice when so many of us illiterate fellows hear it? It's not a voice like the human voice. It's different. We don't understand it very well, and educated people understand it even less. But then, do we understand the songs of the birds? Does anyone know what the sheep bleat about, or what the other beasts area saying? We who hear the earth calling understand it about as much as we understand the birds and the beasts. And then, sometimes I say to myself, "Why should not God have given the earth a voice, once he gave her so many other vital and incomprehensible things which no one, educated or illiterate, will ever be able to understand?"

"Like what, father?"

He remained wrapped in thought for a brief moment; the shadow of a smile played on his lips. He seemed to have a thousand examples to give and to be enjoying the difficulty he had in deciding which to choose.

"Just think," he said, "that without science and wisdom, the soil by itself, with one seed and a half-dozen roots, turns into fruit, any kind of fruit you want; it turns into a plant or a tree, into scent, sugar and color—the dark color of the poppy, the cherry or the plum, the tender color of the flowers. The soil...all by itself becomes all these things—fruit, scent, color. The soil! Have you thought of that?''

He became quite animated, and seemed to be almost a little angry as he continued. ''How could you ask me if the earth has a voice. Of course it has and you know it! You've seen it, and the master heard it. You yourself saw him too, lying on the ground, talking to her.'

''It's true, father, I saw him in the spring talking to her joyously in the middle of the barreness and ruin left by the earthquake and the war. And the call of the earth must have startled him much more than others.''

''But it was not only that which changed him,'' Mourayias said, looking straight ahead of him as if he were reading some oracle in the gloom of the old storehouse. ''It was one of those decrees of the Lord about which no one knows how and why they come. His own blood changed him, for if old Grandfather's blood didn't run in his veins, he would never have heard the soil talking to him. And at that very time Alexis stood by him, and Alexis himself was a voice of the earth. Many things were working for the change which came over him. It was the will of God.

* * * * *

The sky had cleared, no one could tell how long the good weather would last, and for days everyone had been in the fields hurrying to get the sowing done as fast as possible.

Phrosso had finished her chores and had gone over to the cottage. She was reading when a knock at the door startled her. She got up and opened the door. There stood Notis, whom she had once idolized and loved. He had not changed much. He was a little thinner, one or two wrinkles had appeared, and his expression had hardened. But he had the same handsome, virile face, the same bright, romantic eyes.

Like lightening, the memory of forgotten ecstasies flashed through her mind, and she became all the more infuriated with this man who had given her so much joy, had betrayed her shamelessly, and now returned to remind her of the past.

Meanwhile he said, ''My little Phrosso, I'm so happy to see you again.''

''Why have you come?'' she asked him harshly.

"I was in Greece, in Larissa. Shouldn't I have come to see you?"

"No, you shouldn't."

"Why?"

"You should be ashamed to ask, particularly as you never bothered to think that I might be dead, that our child, that little angel, might be dead. How dare you come back. What do you expect to find?"

Embarrassment showed on his face; he dropped his eyes before her hostile glance.

"I can't tell you how sorry I was; it would be useless for me to describe it. But it's my duty to sacrifice myself and to sacrifice others when it's necessary, because I'm fighting for something incomparably greater than myself or my family."

"That's your privilege. I remember that humanitarian fairy-tale of yours. I learned it all to well and paid for it dearly."

"It has to be paid for very dearly. It is full of a bitter sweetness, and that sweetness, Phrosso dear, is most intense when you torture yourself and, if necessary, torture others to make the fairy-tale come true!"

She shouted at him in fury. "All right, go ahead then. Fight for mankind by killing man! I've never done anything for humanity, but I love my fellow-men. Leave me alone! Get out!"

She started to close the door on him but he leaned against the door frame. Phrosso was frightened. His expression was calm as if nothing disturbed him, as if he knew that he would get his way. He was good-looking, athletic, and determined, interested only in one thing—doing exactly what he wanted.

She felt then that she understood why she had loved him and also why she had come to hate him. But the time was not propitious for such thoughts. Other worries pressed down on her at that moment. She was alone in the house. Suppose he insisted on coming in...Suppose he tried to take her in his arms...Her fear grew greater.

"I'd like to sit down and talk to you."

"We haven't anything to say to each other."

"There's a lot to talk about, a lot. I've never stopped feeling a great affection for you, and you haven't changed a bit. You're still a very pretty girl."

She felt the blush come to her cheeks and was more embarrassed than ever, because she was afraid that he might misinterpret her blushing as weakness or as a reawakening of love. She struggled with herself to find something to say which would make him leave as quickly as possible. But before she had time to speak he asked, "Has anyone else come between us?"

"There's no one," she said angrily and felt that she was blushing again.

"I heard there was someone—Alexis."

"You heard wrong," she shouted at him. "Now go? Do me the only favor you can any more. Get out of here!"

She was standing in front of him in a state of fury, and he was looking at her quite calmly with a trace of affection in his face.

"If it was Alexis," he said, "I can understand your grief. He was a real man. I too was moved when he died. But he's gone. I would find it quite natural if there was someone else. If there is, say so and I'll go."

"There's no one else because I'm a dead woman. That's another reason why I don't want you. Will you please go now."

He continued undisturbed, "I might have been suspicious of your new master, but I hear that he's involved in a love-affair with Katie. She'll give the aristocrat a fine run-around!"

"I see you've found time to check up on your old girl friends. Congratulations."

"The only person I've been checking up on is you because I'd like us to get together again."

Phrosso stepped back, dug her nails into the palms of her hands. "Have you gone mad?"

"Not at all. I want to come here to stay. I want to be with you."

She had a flash of intuition. She knew now why he had come. She composed herself as best she could and asked him quietly, "So you would like to come and live with me here at Pteliona?"

"Indeed I would. It would be wonderful!"

"It would be a wonderful hide-away for you, wouldn't it? Get out of here at once. Haven't I made it clear that there's no place left in my heart for you?"

She rushed forward gathering all her strength and pushed

him out of the door which she locked behind him. She didn't even bother to look out of the window to see if he was going away, but sank into a chair and burst into convulsive sobs. She didn't quite know why she was crying. She had a vague feeling that she was crying over love that had flown—the old familiar love, betrayed and cast away, and subsequent loves which had flashed through her subconsciuous but which she had not recognized until now, or which she had not been willing to admit to herself.

* * * * *

That evening she told her father everything. Before they parted she said, "Father, don't you think we ought to tell Nikita?"

"I don't know. Why should we?"

"Well, after so many years, Notis has come back. He certainly hasn't come back because he chose to. He is lying low—he's up to something and has some reason to be afraid. He's wandering around the villages, which means that he's laying some plan. It seems to me that all this points to danger. Now he's come to Pteliona. And formally he is my husband. If he is engaged in some dangerous undertaking, Nikita should be told. Just imagine if something happens and he hears all this from others."

"You are always right, my dear child. He must learn it from us."

"You tell him, father, tomorrow."

She said this rather excitedly, and Mourayias was surprised. He looked at her intently.

"Some of the details are rather complicated. You had better tell him."

"No, no, father..."

Her refusal was energetic and final. She perceived her father's surprise and hastened to remove it.

"It is embarrassing for me to tell him that I threw him out. But he must know that too. For our own security it is absolutely necessary that he should know that I threw him out. Only you father, only you can talk to him."

Mourayias promised but did so with a heavy heart, because he felt, without being quite clear in his mind about it, that there was something just a little fishy about this business.

VI

During the summer when Nikita was ill, Alexis, as he was keeping him company, had said, "This land is so rich in tradition that you will find some special significance, some symbolic meaning, in whatever spot you choose."

Nikita had not answered him but had feigned fatigue and closed his eyes in order to avoid telling him what had come into his mind. As a reaction to Alexis' statement which had seemed an unbearable exaggeration to him, he had thought of the rocky crags of Greece—naked, grey, jagged stones, with a few inches of soil between them, a few tufts of dry grass, and an occasional thicket. What significance could be attached to such things, what could they possibly symbolize? Nothing, or at most poverty: barrenness, decline—and worse than that, a decline that was permanent and irremediable.

And yet now that he had become acquainted with the forests and the meadows, the rocky hills and the plains from Tepeleni to Larissa, he understood at last that these rocky places had meaning and were symbols of something beautiful.

One day he was standing in front of an immense bare mountain ridge and for a second he fancied he was seeing some supernatural creature which had reared up in a rage and had arched its stony vertebrae in order to block an attack which threatened forests and meadows, plains and cities. And in truth wasn't this strange, imaginary creature endowed with mystical powers? Hadn't it time and again risen in defense of the land? Time and again among its sharp-edged vertebrae, where there was a little dry grass and a few briars, where a few men eked out their hard, frugal lives, and abstained from trickery and error (for there the penalty of error and trickery was death); time and again among those rocky vertebrae and with their protective help, that handful of barefoot men had fought against hordes of armed invaders in order to live free! Time and again waves of invaders had been broken by them or turned into receding foam or swallowed up by the gaunt and bare rocks! Now for the first time Nikita realized that throughout Greece's history of three thousand years, its rugged rocky regions were the lasting symbol of health and frugality, of strength and freedom—freedom above all!

That evening, alone in his now modest house, Nikita remembered these thoughts that had gradually ripened in his mind. He resolved to spend one of the long winter nights when he usually read or worked at his desk, in jotting down these thoughts with the idea of developing them into the book he planned to write about Alexis.

Again the yearning for Alexis came over him. Memories were but poor and bitter comfort. There was not cure for his grief, he thought, for with death there was no compromise. It was a state that was unique, inexorable, permanent, absolute. And so, he reflected with anguish, his friend who had brought him back to life would never witness the resurrection. Alexis, who had guided him, would never know that, although he was dead, he was still guiding him.

Nikita remembered that Alexis had laughed, but in reality had been saddened, when one night at the front he had told him what had happened to him with the birds. Alexis would never know, he reflected sadly, how he had behaved a few days ago when he encountered them for the first time this year. They were always majestic and impressive. They repeated their usual pattern of flight and once again they cried, "They must die! They must die!" It was true that he had not followed them riding Pegasus! It was also true that he had not called out to them, as Alexis might have, "They must die! The strong of the earth respond to the strong of the heavens, to the conquerors of the storm. They must die!" But he hadn't humiliated himself this time. He had held his head high and rejoiced in the powerful and graceful passage of the birds.

"Oh, Alexis," Nikita cried out in his solitude, "you will never see my salvation, you will never know that even in death you are the beloved brother who guides and inspires me!"

Nikita had also begun to feel the stirrings of another kind of yearning, a pleasant yearning which could be satisfied. It was taking a strange turn and he didn't know what to make of it but that same night, he gave it some thought.

"It must be love; it must surely be love," he reflected. Not just because he desired her, nor because her kisses aroused his passion, nor because she maddened him by smothering him in kisses and caresses and then would let him go no further. It was more than this. He found that he thought of her all the time, and constantly sought her company because he wanted to make a home with her and be the father of her children. He had never felt anything like this before with any other woman.

On the other hand, she surely must love him also. Not because she desired him too, returned his kisses with warmth and loved to feel her body tightly enfolded in his embrace. There was something about her look, her voice, her words, a thousand little details in her behaviour, there was a quality in her that turned winter in spring—all these things seemed to indicate that she loved him.

Then why didn't she want to get married? He couldnt't puzzle it out. She made a number of excuses. "Who knows what disasters the war will bring...It's a crime to have children in the times we're living through...I'm sometimes so nervous, so afraid at the idea of marriage...The solitude of the plain drives me mad...I loathe the provinces."

Hadn't she spent all her life in Larissa? Wasn't she a healthy woman full of vitality? Was she incapable of facing life with quiet confidence? What could be the real reason for her attitude? He couldn't imagine. There must be some mysterious cause for this. Maybe the same that had made her break up with Alexis.

Should he talk to her about him? Should he tell her that when he first arrived in Greece he had seen her in the forest with Alexis? He had thought of doing so but had always rejected the thought. He didn't like using his dead brother to clear up his own love affairs; especially he shrank from using him in a way that might unleash bitter words against him. But what should he do? What should he do?

Now that Pteliona, after so much effort and hard work, was back to normal, and it had been cultivated and would produce enough to get them through to spring, he had explained to her all the difficulties he had overcome and had tried to make her see its beauty and to bring her to love it. On the days when the rains had kept them indoors, he had talked to her about subjects in which she was interested—literature, music, and many other things, he had told her about Europe which she had never visited. He had talked to her about the past and about his dreams for the future. He had done everything he could to show her how well they got on together and that life would be pleasant if they embarked on it together.

She was pleased, she took and interest in everything, she had changed completely, she was no longer the condescending banker's daughter who had taken care of him when he was sick. No, indeed. She sought and enjoyed his company, and very probably she loved him. And yet when he spoke to her of marriage...

Someone was knocking at his window. He heard the sharp taps and was sure he was not mistaken. Who wanted him at this hour on this cold December night? Who could it be?

Whenever he was not in town on business he spent all of his time at Pteliona. He was friendly with everybody, he was fond of them all, and with Phrosso, the only woman among them and the most cultured member of the group, he would often pass the time very agreeably. On occasion—on feast days particularly—they all took their evening meal together and chatted about anything and everything. But on other evenings he retired to the two rooms he had made tolerably comfortable for himself, and nobody disturbed him.

He opened the window and saw Mourayias and Mitsos standing outside. He let them into his apartment and threw a log on the fire.

"Mitsos was in town and heard a lot of strange things. I thought you ought to be told at once."

Then Mitsos, a sound and serious-minded fellow, who had fought with him in the mountains, began to tell him all that he had heard about the Legion. The door opened and Phrosso came in.

"May I hear what you're talking about."

Nikita smiled at her. "Come on in. You're welcome. Sit down."

She didn't take a seat, but stood leaning against the door, listening to their conversation.

Nikita sat opposite her, on the couch which he used as a bed.

From where he sat he could see her fulsome figure and she seemed taller than usual. While the others talked, his eyes from time to time fell on her and his mind wandered. He followed what they were saying and joined in the conversation but now and again, when there was a pause, he would say to himself, "Surely this is an optical illusion. She looks taller than usual...A beautiful figure...Her hips are a little broad...What a fresh complexion she has. There's something special about her...But Katie is much prettier...People would find Katie pretty anywhere in the world."

But his thoughts soon ceased to wander because the things that Mitsos was saying were very alarming. At one point he mentioned Katie's uncle. Nikita now listened intently. Not a word escaped him. He listened but he couldn't believe what he heard. This was outrageous!

But when Mourayias told him about the old days and said that during the Macedonian campaign they had found themselves face to face with many pro-Rumanian Vlach informers or guerillas, and when Mitsos pinpointed those who had given him various pieces of information, when he told him that whole trainloads of corn had been sent from Rumania to be distributed in the starving Vlach mountain villages around Trikkala—when they told him all this he was compelled to believe them.

After a tense silence, Mitsos asked him, "What are you going to do?"

"I don't know. What can I do?"

"Well, we're all Vlachs around here. We've got to do something."

"Yes, but I'm trying to think of something that we can do."

As they were reflecting in silence, Mourayias murmured, "Something's got to be done. I think we might..." He didn't finish his sentence, but burst out angrily, "Damn the bastards! Damn them!"

They were silent again. Then Phrosso spoke slowly, with some hesitation. "Is it so necessary that we should do anything?"

They all turned to look at her. "Of course it is!" Mitsos said sharply, "These men pretend to be speaking for us. We're Vlachs too."

"Nobody's threatening us," Phrosso replied in the same quiet voice. "Nor has anyone mentioned that Legion to us."

"But we do know," Nikita said, "that treason and tyranny are taking place, and that what is being done is being done in our name."

"Have you ever thought you were a Vlach before this moment?" she asked him.

He laughed. "No, Phrosso, I hardly knew that Vlachs existed. But as Mitsos says, I'm a Vlach by birth, and as you've heard my name is mentioned as being a Vlach name. So now, at this particular time, it seems to me that I've got to become a Vlach again, even if I'm not one. It's the only thing to do. Even if I don't believe it, I've got to say to myself that I am a Vlach."

A strange expression came over her face—an expression of sadness and dread.

"But aren't you a Greek?" she asked.

"The Vlachs are Greeks," Mitsos replied angrily.

"To be able to assert that the Vlachs are Greeks, I must be baptized a Vlach, or rather I must remember that I am one. Don't you understand Phrosso?"

She gave the three men a long and anxious look, pulled her shawl over her head tightly, and said, "Maybe you are right. But I'm afraid we may get into trouble. But that's fate, I suppose."

She slipped away quietly as she had come without saying anything more, not even good-night.

It was late at night when Nikita got to bed. He could not sleep for a long time, aand when sleep came at last it was troubled and full of nightmares.

The blood and sweat of generations had fashioned this land, and now a handful of men wanted to dismember and despoil it without a fight, by sheer bullying. They claimed to be speaking in the name of all the Vlachs and they mentioned the Collettis. They spoke for Alexis—what a blasphemy—because he had been of Vlach stock on his father's and his mother's side and had known the Vlach language himself. And Alexis was no longer there to answer them.

"The greatness of Greece has always been measured by standards of intellect and spirit. It is a great thing, Nikita, to be a Greek," Alexis had said.

"Yes, Alexis," Nikita thought, as he lay awake in bed, "it is a great thing! And since your mouth is closed and you cannot thunder forth the greatness of Greece, I shall proclaim it for you, and for myself as well! Until this moment I thought it was my duty to look after my little group of people and my crops and livestock, and I have enjoyed the days I have spent here. But now there is a greater obligation and I shall fulfill it Alexis, do not fear."

And he fell into a deep sleep.

He opened his window wide and the stinging cold of the Thessalian winter struck his bare chest and face. He glanced at the faint December morning light and saw the leafless trees, the dark evergreens, the hungry sparrows darting about in search of a bite to eat. Far away in the distance smoke was rising from the chimney of a house. For nature and for the birds life rolled on. For men too it rolled on somehow since in the grey, cold mist smoke was rising from that chimney.

He shut the window, lit the fire, and started to make his coffee. Life rolled on for him too. And, after all, it was not so bad. He was enjoying it and the future might be much brighter. Perhaps the thoughts that had worried him last night were exaggerated. Perhaps in the darkness of the long and lonely winter night his anxieties had been magnified beyond reason. He must think things over calmly and objectively in the light of day, in the warm comfort of his fireside.

Why should he get mixed up in that filthy business? Why should he disturb the peace and harmony of his days at Pteliona? Phrosso was quite right. He was not a Vlach and no one was bothering him. Until they had told him about it last night he hadn't even known that there was propaganda in the area, that there were pro-Rumanians and traitors. What possible reason could he have to proclaim himself a Vlach, to get mixed up what was happening in Larissa among men who were strangers to him.

He ceased to think for a short time and sipped his steaming coffee and, as often happened in idle moments, he remembered Alexis. What would Alexis have done? Ah, there was no doubt about that. He wouldn't stay out of it. He would fight the traitors; he would tear them apart with his bare hands. He remembered then that during the night he had contemplated his own intervention as an obligation to Alexis. He remembered that he had made Alexis a promise. He was ashamed of his present hesitation, but he felt so comfortable by the fireplace, so contented with his beloved ranch, that he still hesitated.

"It's a long time since I've seen Father Modestos," he thought. "Maybe I should go and ask him."

But again he was ashamed. Should he intervene only because Father Modestos might advise him to? Where duty was concerned, couldn't he make his own decision? And if he saw that it was his duty to intervene, should he avoid doing so on the grounds that his Vlach ancestry was remote, or because nobody had disturbed him?

He was angry with himself for having hesitated. "My redemption is not complete," he reflected. "It is not others who force you or summon you to do your duty. You go ahead on your own. Even if I'm not a Vlach at all, I've got to become one now."

He started for town without quite knowing how he would tackle this problem which was so alien to him. Maybe he should go to see Katie. Suddenly the thought came to him that Katie and her father had quarrelled with Nikos Manoussis. That must have been because of his part in this dirty business! Perhaps this was what prevented her from accepting his proposal and made her find all kinds of ridiculous excuses! Could she have been ashamed to tell him? Even so he couldn't go to her to get information and plan how to attack her uncle! That would be most improper. He would talk to Katie later and quite differently on the subject.

Now that his mind was active and alert he thought of the right person to see. Mitsos had spoken about Dr. Raptis. He remembered him from the dinner at Katie's home and from a consultation to which the doctor had been called when he was ill. He would go to him first.

In the waiting room at the clinic loud voices could be heard coming from the doctor's office. Someone stopped Nikita and without asking for his name said, "One moment, please; I'll inform the doctor."

The voices ceased and he heard the doctor say: "If he's not sick tell him I've no time now. Later."

Nikita insisted and gave his name. The doctor came out at once and led him into his office. The men there, all of whom looked tired and worried, were astonished to see him. Could it be, they wondered, that he had been annoyed too? What had they done to him? Modestly and awkwardly he said that he wanted to help. No, he hadn't been disturbed.

But then, they enquired, why was he getting involved? Neither he nor his parents had been born in a Vlach village, nor had they ever spoken Vlach or had any kind of connection with the Vlach people. Nobody would ever ask him to join the Legion. So what was he after? Was he looking for trouble? The environment was entirely unfamiliar to him, these men were strangers, he had hardly any experience with this type of people. He found great difficulty in explaining.

It was true, he said, that he was not a Vlach, or at best a greenhorn Vlach. But at this time he felt he ought to say he was a Vlach. He insisted. If it did not bother them he would stay and listen, and if they permitted he might say a word or two. The wrinkled faces looked at him strangely, then looked at one another, then politely they asked him to take a seat. Thus he learned that everything Mitsos had told him was true, that in fact the situation was much worse than he had known.

In the first place the Legion's army was leaving no stone unturned to discover arms to hand over to the Italians. Men were beaten and tortured, their houses plundered, and they were forced to give information. Even more brutal treatment was meted out to anyone found with a rifle in his possession. If you were a good patriot and refused to join the legion, and they could get no evidence against you, a pistol would miraculously materialize in your cellar.

Fear spread through the villages that were also struck by another kind of calamity. The prefect who had come to Larissa after the defeat of the Greek armies by then had discharged the village headmen one after the other. In their place, had appointed the dregs of the communities who helped to find hidden arms and proclaimed the village a "Latin", even though there might not be a single Vlach in the whole area.

"That's the way they're enforcing their 'from the frontier to Domokos' policy," said one of the men.

"The bastards! They're a godless lot," said another.

"But what shall we do? What can we do?"

"We must hold our heads high. We must give courage to as many as we can. That's all we can do."

Then Nikita spoke. He spoke shyly in a soft voice, but his words changed the whole tenor of the discussion. He said that they must protest to the Italian authorities. It was possible that they might get protection and, on the other hand, by protesting they would refute the allegations that the Vlachs were not Greeks.

"If we just sit with our hands folded," he concluded, "we shall become accomplices in this betrayal."

"What sort of accomplices could we be," one of the group protested indignantly, "when we're being threatened and when we've been given a time limit to conform? The others have thousands of bayonets behind them while we haven't a single one."

Nikita begged their pardon, he took back what he had said about their being accomplices, but he insisted on the substance of his proposal. He suggested that if they remained silent this might be interpreted as acceptance. Wouldn't it be shameful if not a single Vlach raised his voice in opposition? He would be willing to do it alone.

The discussion grew lively and heated. Opinions were divided. One view was that if they protested in any way, they would be arrested, and then the majority of Vlachs who were powerless would be frightened into conformity. Another wondered whether a protest was really necessary. Wasn't it enough that no one conformed? A third asked who would feed their children if they were caught. Most of them lived from hand to mouth and depended on their daily wages. Another said that Nikita could make any protest he wanted by himself. But in that case he oughtn't to be seen in their company.

The discussion continued with increasing heat until a tall, middle-aged man began to speak in a calm, low voice. Nikita recognized him at once. It was the lawyer who had spoken to him so harshly at the station when he had arrived two years ago. He agreed with Nikita's opinion and supported it with further arguments. He suggested that the general might not be aware of what was going on and that certain officers in league with Diamantis, and out for illicit profit, might be concealing the truth from him. He thought it was necessary that they should see the general. That was the right thing to do.

Hadjipyrrhos spoke so convincingly and so calmly that he won the others over to his point of view. It was decided that the Bar and Medical Associations would ask to be received by the general in order to protest against the threats levelled at several of their members. On the other side, Nikita, who must be known to the general because of his predominant position in foreign literary circles, would ask to be received separately and would denounce the dangerous violation of international law that was being perpetrated. He would speak in the name of "a group of citizens." The discussion had ended and they were getting ready to leave when Nikita asked to say something on a different subject.

"I have heard, he said, "that Mr. Manoussis, the banker, and his brother the lawyer, have had a serious quarrel and that the latter has left their home. Was their quarrel about the Legion? Oughtn't we to suggest to Mr. Manoussis that he persuade his brother to withdraw? The resignation of the President of the Legion would make a tremendous impression."

Before he finished speaking he saw that his words had produced general astonishment. Some exchanged glances and smiled others looked at him as if he had said something outrageous. A painful silence prevaded the small smoke-filled office.

"Anyone who knows Vassili," one of the men said sharply, "knows that he hasn't quarrelled with his brother. They're in cahoots and are putting on a show."

These words pained Nikita, but he reflected that they came from one of the men who had objected to everything. Perhaps he was a negative sort of person or was prejudiced. But then, what about the sarcastic glances and smiles of the others? Hesitantly he continued and said that he was acquainted with the banker's daughter. He could speak to her.

Then Hadjipyrrhos spoke in his usual quiet manner. "Mr. Coletti, above all you must avoid speaking to her. No one can foretell what harm might come from speaking to her about the

Legion or from telling her that you have talked with us on this subject. She is very pretty and very clever, but she's possessed by the devil. And since you're a friend of hers you must learn something else. It's true that Nikos left their home, that they avoid seeing one another, and that they say that they have quarrelled over the Legion. But it's also true that all those who know them suspected from the first moment that the whole thing was contrived. And if at first these suspicions were indefinite, now there is evidence to substantiate them. A few days ago, Vassili's daughter, Katie, went to Nikos' office and stayed for some time. She took some precautions, but she was seen. Yesterday around midnight, Nikos with his collar drawn tightly around his neck and wearing a hat—a thing which he has never been known to do—went to Vassili's home and stayed two hours. That's the kind of quarrel they have.

Nikita was exhausted when he arrived at Pteliona. His head ached, his mouth was dry and his heart was heavy. He wanted to lie down, to close his eyes, and empty his mind of every thought in order to ease his pain. But he wasn't to be left alone. Police Lieutenant Skourtis was awaiting him. He was a coarse man, a typical country policeman, but a couple of incidents during the war had brought them together. He was passing by on his way to Larissa and had stopped uninvited to spend the night at Pteliona.

They talked about the betrayal. Skourtis said that at Trikkala there was no Legion. Yet many Vlachs lived there who had come down from the surrounding Vlach villages. Why had the Roman Legion chosen Larissa where the Vlachs were comparatively few in number and the Vlach villages in the area few and far between?

"Something's up, Christos," Nikita said. "We'll soon find out. Maybe they're getting ready for a coup at Trikkala." And he told him everything that he had learned about the Rumanian corn.

"A tragedy," Skourtis said, "a real tragedy. Naturally those who accept the corn will be made to sign a declaration that they are Rumanians. And because they're starving, they'll sign. And you know something? Many of them for the first time in their lives will be grateful to Rumania for looking after them in the hour of their great hunger, when Greece cannot or will not provide for them." And he told Nikita about the appalling conditions in his disrict.

The authorities acting with the utmost severity were trying to get all the grain they could to send to Athens where people were dying of starvation. But the mountain villages were poor, they had no crops, they too were suffering from hunger and did not know how they would get through the winter. So the mountain folk were cursing the Greek authorities because they did not take care of them and, above all, because they did not allow them to carry food to the hills. Men and women would go down to the plain trying to find half a bag of any kind of grain to carry back, by night, over hidden trails, through wolf-infested regions and in every kind of weather, in order to bring their starving children something to eat. Many were robbed of their precious burden before they reached home. Some who resisted were killed. In this tragedy the old adage "Your death is my life" became a grim reality. It would have been more accurate to say "Your death is the life of my children."

"Three days ago," Skourtis said, "an acquaintance of mine from Metsovo, a giant of a man, loaded two mules with wheat and corn. We found him dead outside Grevena. He was still holding his axe in his rigid hand, and next to him was another man's severed leg. Who knows how he struggled to save his children's bread. In such circumstances, Coletti, you understand what will happen if the Rumanians send plenty of corn and distribute it free to all who are willing to sign a piece of paper. It's a calamity, I tell you, calamity."

Nikita forgot his headache and his grief and said earnestly, "Look here, Christos, the grain must never reach its destination. I've thought of a way."

Christos pricked up his ears, the distressed look faded from his face. He was like an animal ready to pounce.

"How? Tell me!"

"You will know when the Rumanian corn is due to arrive and you will know how much there will be by the size of the warehouses which they erect . Even if the Italians guard them, it will be easy for you to pass the word to the nearest mountain villages and to arrange for the warehouses to be plundered. Then you'll see that the Vlach villages are told that nothing happened and that the story of the Rumanian corn was just a propaganda myth."

"That's just what I want to hear! I never thought of this before but now you've given me the idea, I'll see to everything. I'll rope in my men and a few hungry veterans and we'll do the job. Don't worry. They won't get a single signed statement, however much grain they send. I guarantee it."

They were both relieved that they could take some positive action in this unequal struggle; they relaxed a little and forgot for a while the evils that had come upon their enslaved land, and thought back on the time when they were free, when they fought and risked their lives, but were full of high spirits and hope.

VII

He had to do something. That cowardly braggart, Alcibiades, had panicked without reason,, but the matter had to be handled carefully. And it was his business to see to it, not so much as President of the Legion, but as the only man among them who acted with intelligence as well as with forcefulness.

The Chief of Staff of the Division had been alarmed at the requests for an audience and had informed Diamantis. He had been particularly alarmed by Coletti's written request, because he could not bury it. Some ridiculous underlings of his misled by the poet's fine Italian style, had accepted the request, had entered it in the files, and had already sent it on to the general's aides. And the general knew very little about the Legion...very little indeed.

What disturbed Nikos Manoussis was that the whole Division was not on their side; it's commander wasn't. They had not been quite frank with him and the facts on which Nikos had based his action were undergoing a change. But he couldn't retreat now; he was committed. So he must take certain measures. First of all he must see three people that very day and set them in motion in three different directions.

"We're all very pleased with you, Vassilaki," he said to him as he came into his office at the Legion. "I hope that we may soon get the approval of the Division to appoint you General of the Legion. For the moment however, two things are necessary. The first is to deliver more arms to the Italians—beginning tomorrow, if possible. Do you think you can do this?"

"Of course I can."

"How can you be so sure?"

He sat down in front of Nikos and looked at him with his small, cunning pig's eyes. "You may have conferred military titles on me but I'm a born general. I'm Ropotikas—the man who has organized seven bands. Every day one of them goes out on the prowl. The others attend to their private business. Tonight I'll order all seven of them to go out. They'll deal out seven times as many beatings as usual, and get paid for their trouble out of the loot they'll take in." He winked knowingly. "Tommorrow you'll have seven times more weapons."

"I have to admit you're a great general, Vassilaki," Manoussis said. "But we don't need that many weapons. Double the amount will be enough."

Ropotikas laughed with the self confidence of a man who knows what he can do.

"Why? Why are you so stingy, my friend? Have you any reason for this?"

"Yes, I have. First of all it wouldn't pay us to use up all our efforts at once and then begin delivering fewer arms again later on. Then again, something may come up later and we may need to increase our deliveries once more."

"You politicians are full of cunning schemes," Ropotikas remarked. "I'm only a general. I'll do as you say. But you mentioned two things. What's the other?"

"The other is that the President of the Legion wants some information about certain Communist elements that had disappeared years ago and have now turned up again. What have they been doing, and what are they aiming at?"

"We've got enough troubles already," Ropotikas answered. "Why are you looking for more? We're annoying the people enough going after arms, signed statements, milk and a little loot. Must we now bother them with other things which are none of our business?"

Manoussis remained silent for a while. He wore the self-satisfied expression of one who knows what he is doing.

"Can't you imagine," he said, "what an important organization we shall become in the eyes of the Italians if we reveal the existence of a left-wing revolutionary group, directed maybe from Moscow or Athens, about which they themselves have not been able to discover anything?"

Ropotikas looked at him in astonishment. "By God you're right, Nikos!" he exclaimed. "That would be great! I'll beat the daylights out of ten times as many bastards as usual. It's worth while, to get the information. I'll put all I've got into it. Don't worry about a thing!"

"I was counting on you because I know what a splendid fellow you are and what you can do when you want to. Thanks."

Ropotikas rose to leave, but sat down again.

"Since you thank me and I'm such a splendid fellow, tell me the truth about what I'm going to ask you."

"I always tell the truth, Vassilaki."

"The hell you do!" he laughed. "But just tell me what I want to know. Is it true that they want to turn us into a principality?"

"They certainly do," he answered briskly. "Why do you ask?"

The 'general' paused. "Most people say it can't be done. I, with my dull brain, think that it's in their interest to do it. But sometimes I wonder whether they're fooling us and saying this just to get us to help them."

"They're not fooling us. But why do you ask? Is the question being discussed widely?"

"Certainly it's being discussed. A clever man doesn't think about today only. He also thinks of the future. But, Nikos, do you know what I say when I can't figure out whether they will or won't set up a principality? I say to myself, 'So what?' This damned life is nothing but a crap game. Well, we've rolled the dice that'll make us lords and princes." He gave him a wink and got up. "Meanwhile," he said, "we're having a good time! Ain't that so? You bet it is!"

As he was going the old bandit chief turned back and complained. "Come to think of it, you've never been out to one of our celebrations. We have a hell of a good time."

"When things settle down, I'll come. I'll come without fail."

When night had begun to fall, Phoula came to his office in answer to his summons. She was paler, more troubled, and more frightened than ever. She didn't fall into his arms as she usually did, but sank into a chair and gave him a look full of love and hopelessness.

"My darling Nikos," she said, "what have we gotten ourselves into? I can't bear it. Life is becoming more and more difficult for everyone. And for me there's the added worry of your situation. I'm going crazy with anxiety. I can't stand the things I hear people saying against you."

He remained silent for a moment. Then he came to her, embraced her and kissed her on the neck. She leaned her cheek against his face and felt better. Like the sudden breath of a spring breeze, a wave of optimism came over her and she brightened up.

"Are you going to leave, Nikos?" she asked. "Are you going to leave?"

He sat down beside her and calmly and quietly told her that he would not leave. He explained why. He gave the usual reasons about his duty to the Vlachs, the salvation of Salonika, and so forth. Without being dramatic, he said that he wasn't the sort of man to abandon a struggle simply because people misunderstood him at the beginning.

"Unfortunately some excesses have been committed which have hurt us," he went on. "The incident with our friend Nikos Raptis should have been avoided, and Ropotikas' behavior is inexcusable. But I'm doing all I can to put a stop to these stupidities. I need two things to succeed. The first is your love."

She looked at him strangely. Her look betrayed love, surprise, disappointment, and doubt.

"Why are you looking at me like that?" he asked, aggrieved.

She was confused. "I'm afraid that you're not...Why do you say...?" Then, pulling herself together, she asked, "Are you telling me the truth, Nikos?"

He explained to her that he couldn't be doing anything but

telling her the truth. Whether it had been necessity or missionary zeal that had prompted him at first, and whether or not the outcome of the venture might be good, the fact was that just now all were casting stones at him. He was hated and rejected. All his friends had abandoned him, and even his relatives would have nothing to do with him.

Once more she looked at him strangely.

"Don't you know what they say about your quarrel with Vassili?"

No, he didn't know. He hadn't heard anything.

She told him, and also mentioned the secret visits at night.

"The only thing that's true is that Katie called me on the 'phone and came here once. She's worried about me and has her own troubles too. This gossip, as well as everything else, shows you how much I need your love. How can we manage to see each other more often?"

After a while she said, "It's difficult. And what I'm doing is dangerous for me and my family. You told me you were in need of two things. What's the second?"

"I've got to do something to mollify Nikos Raptis. I'm not suggesting that I can win him over, but I must placate him and in this way the others will become more friendly. After all, we're not persecuting them. I insisted that they should be left alone. If they resist, they'll force the Legion to strike and then we shall go from bad to worse."

"But what are they doing?"

"They are doing a lot of talking. Propaganda. They refuse to say good morning to me, their protector. And now they want to go and see the Italian general. How do I know what Diamantis will advise the general to do? He may have them arrested. It would be a thousand times better if they kept quiet. You realize what friction may ensue, and what bitter hatreds will develop. If only they would behave better in public we could guarantee that nobody would bother them."

A heavy silence followed. After a time he asked her, "Can you help me?"

"How?"

"Ask the doctor to persuade him. Raptis listens to him. If only he wants to..."

"He won't want to, and apart from that, how can I possibly speak to my husband?"

"Why?"

"I don't want to. He'll understand that I'm doing it for you and I'll hurt him even more than I have already. Besides which, he admires Nikos."

He caught her by the hands. "Phoula darling," he said, "you must do it. If Raptis calms down and decides to call in the others, I'll get some breathing space and I'll be able to prevent excesses from being committed. You must do it, Phoula. Do it for me."

She lowered her eyes. "I can't. I can't."

She was ready to cry. He gave her time to recover, then got up and stood behind her chair, leaned over and kissed her several times on the neck. She shut her eyes and again put her cheek against his face. How lovely it was to lose herself so. He took her in his arms and carassed her passionately. He let his hand slip down to her breast.

"No, not that, Nikos!"

He kissed her hard and drew her tightly to him. He felt no response and whispered in her ear, "Come, let's lie down on the floor like we did the other night."

She refused once more. He became insistent—his voice was warm and his breath came faster. He lifted her from the chair.

"Come, I want you, I want you!"

But she wasn't willing. And again she seemed on the point of crying.

His tone became forceful and he drew her to the mat.

"This isn't love, Nikos," she murmured. And before they reached the mat and he felt that his knees would give way, she let out a cry which sounded like a sob, saying that she couldn't, then slipped away from his grasp, unlocked the door and was lost in the cold night.

* * * * *

She waited a little while for the child to fall asleep and got ready to return to the living room. She knew by heart the hopelessly monotonous evening that lay before her. The doctor would be in his large velvet armchair, reading some medical book. He would say a few words to her, and she would sit opposite him with her embroidery. They would pass one or two hours in this way and then her husband would suggest that they go to bed. Every evening it was the same routine, almost the same words were exchanged—every evening, through the winter months at least. There was little variation in this pattern of utter boredom. She had gotten used to it and she put up with it. She had her child, and she had her hapless love affair and the guilt which came with it. It couldn't be helped. It was fate, the cruel unchangeable fate of a woman in the provinces.

But tonight it was different. She couldn't control her emotions. She had to help Nikos—at least she must try. Whether he was sincere or not in everything he had said, he needed her help and she could not refuse it. And, she thought, wasn't it in everyone's interest that the fierce quarrels between old friends should cease? However, it wasn't easy for her to talk to her husband. How would he react? That was the question. He might be hurt and annoyed, and she didn't want this. She was sorry for him—truly sorry.

Dr. Vaidis lowered his book when he heard her enter and smiled at her. He was short and bony and he seemed lost in his enormous armchair. On his sickly face even the smile seemed unhealthy. She couldn't help noticing the contrast with Nikos' virile and dynamic looks. As usual he asked if the child was asleep and she answered perfunctorily. Then they turned to their habitual occupations. As she embroidered, she began to talk to him about the Legion. She repeated what she had heard about it, told him that everyone she met talked about it, and said that people were frightened, that terrible things were being done, and that the general feeling was that a stop should be put to all this.

The doctor stopped reading and listened to her attentively. He always liked to talk with her; tonight what she said was particularly interesting. She was actually speaking against the Legion. That was strange. When she had finished, he spoke in his customary calm manner. "Of course all this must stop; but how? What can be done?"

"If only our friends stopped criticizing in public, and if they told the others that they were going to stop, maybe the Legion would change its tactics."

"Do you really think so? I don't believe it. Behind this treason there are compelling interests—money, power, the principality. To put an end to the treason the motivating causes it serves must first be eliminated."

"Maybe you're right. But with all the horrible things that are happening, even a temporary reconciliation would be worthwhile, even an attempt at reconciliation."

Quietly and calmly he asked, "What sort of attempt? How do you see it?"

Glancing at him from time to time as she went on with her embroidery to hide her embarrassment, she tried to speak as reasonably as she could. He was calm and wise, she said, and was a friend of Raptis who was the most active of them all. Couldn't he advise him to try to achieve a temporary reconciliation, or at least to get his associates to abstain from resistance for a month or so? That would give them time to see how the others would behave. If they too calmed down it would be a great thing. There was no one else at all except the doctor who could intervene with any hope of success. He should however...

He had let her talk without interrupting her, but now he did not let her go on. Without raising his voice, he said quietly and firmly, "I don't propose to do any of the things you say. I may be weak and I may be afraid, but I admire the stand our friends are taking. I don't pretend to be a great patriot, Phoula, and I don't believe it is patriotism that makes me say this. How can I describe it? It's a matter of dignity.

Instinctively she lifted her eyes from her embroidery and looked at him.

"Don't be surprised," he said. "That's how it is."

And with some embarrassment and hesitation, he added something which she never expected to hear.

"Don't be surprised that I've never wanted to talk about our situation—I mean about the malicious gossip that has been going around. There is the child to consider, and I don't want to lose you. It is, how shall I say, it is a private matter, between us alone, and I am free to face it as I myself choose. But this, Phoula dear, is different. It's something that involves others. I don't know if I can explain it clearly. It's a community—a public—a national question, so to speak. One's responsibilities are not limited to oneself alone. I don't know if I am making myself clear. It's not a question of doing this or that because it suits us. It's entirely different. In this case it's not just a handful of neighbors and busybodies prying into a private affair. The eyes of the future, of our children, of history, so to say, are upon us in this question which is public question, and the responsibilities are immense. Do you then expect me, who am afraid to act myself, to discourage those who dare? Never! I may be weak in many ways, but not in this. I don't know if you understand me."

Phoula did not understand. She was confused and upset. As she held her embroidery her hands trembled so violently that she set the canvas down on the table and hid them between her knees under the fringe of the tablecloth.

She listened to him, looked at him, and didn't know what to do. She knew that she was staring at him with a blank expression. She was terrified and she tried hard to appear natural, but she knew that she wasn't succeeding. How could she? Never before had he given her so much as a hint that he suspected her liaison, and now he mentioned it openly. Why? why? she wondered. Did he guess that Nikos had told her to speak to him? Might he have known about her recent visits to Nikos' office? Maybe now he hated Nikos doubly because of his involvement with the Legion.

She could not find words to answer her husband. She was increasingly upset by all that she had said before. She didn't dare look at him. The doctor stopped speaking and the silence which followed weighed heavily upon her. Then he got up and came and leaned against her shoulder.

"Don't worry dear," he said. "I don't want you to worry. If you only knew how much I love you."

She turned and looked up at him. She felt a compulsion to look at him with compassion and gratitude. But at the first glance she saw a change in him. He was less ugly and sickly and a quality of kindness suffused his features. She found him almost handsome and strong. She looked at him with deep affection and with a trace of sudden admiration.

"Come," he said. "It's late. It's time to be going up."

At that same hour Katie was arguing with Nikos Manoussis at his office. Without resorting to the caution and evasions he had used with Phoula, he told her everything. He told her the things they were afraid of and asked her to help him. The best thing, he suggested, would be for her to marry Coletti, on condition that they would live in Athens or, better still, abroad. If she couldn't manage this then she must persuade him to stop meddling in Vlach affairs, by resorting to the threat of breaking off relations with him, or even by going as far as actually breaking with him in order to force his hand. Katie agreed. She sensed that he was anxious and insecure and did all she could to give him courage for the future.

"By the way," he said pensively at one point in the conversation, "granted that we succeed in removing the danger I was in on account of my old involvement with the reds, do you still think we did right in getting mixed up in this business?"

"What strange creatures you men are," she answered at once. "The strongest among you have a childish side to your nature which makes you vulnerable and naive. You are like a bunch of grapes that doesn't ripen all round. Only we women mature completely. Of course we were right. Remember what we've been saying all these years. We used to curse our fate and deplore the fact that no great opportunity ever came our way. Well, the greatest opportunity one could dream of is here; the only trouble is that we're gambling heads or tails on who will win the war. But millions of people are making this gamble—many without any advantages and some with their lives. Whole nations and tremendous vested interests are in on the game. But the important thing is that the side we have chosen is winning. We couldn't have done better than to throw in our lot with the movement, so stop having any doubts."

"As for myself," she continued speaking with greater deliberation, "I shall do what you want not only because you need me to, but also because a number of things lead me to believe that I can't change Coletti's attitude. The time has come for me to settle it."

"You're right," he said firmly in order to encourage her.

"I've noticed him several times, and he certainly is a different man from the perfect gentleman whom we entertained at dinner a year ago. The way he walks and the way he dresses like an ordinary farmer...I'm surprised you have anything to do with him."

"Well, there are times when I like him like this—only like this."

"Katie! I don't recognize you!"

"You'll recognize me soon enough. But at certain moments I like him as he is, just as in the past I've liked one or two other men. Usually though, when I feel myself to be nothing but a human being living among other human beings, I loathe him and Pteliona and Larissa and everything else. I loathe it all and I'm afraid of the future."

He watched her as she continued to be absorbed by her thoughts, lit a cigarette, and then asked her casually, "Have you heard of a man called Castelleone?"

"No. Who is he?"

"If you haven't heard of him, you must have seen him. Haven't you noticed a very tall, handsome young Italian officer who rides around on superb horses, and occasionally in a peculiar one horse carriage?"

"I don't think so...Oh, yes, I believe I did see an Italian officer driving a small two-wheeled carriage like a madman."

"Well he, Katie dear, has heard about you. The other day he said to me, 'Mr. President, I hear you have a niece who is a beautiful singer and a most charming girl. Why do you keep her locked up? We're not cannibals.' "

He watched her with interest and continued. "Do you know who Castelleone is? He's a count, the son of a multi-millionaire. Imagine! He brought his own horses from Italy for riding and for his carriage. Besides, his family is very close to the Duce and he himself is a fanatical supporter of our principality, a great admirer of the Legion, and is forever urging us to intensify our efforts. He's a clever and charming man, around thirty-five, and a bachelor. You must get to know him."

It was late afternoon when Katie arrived unannounced at Pteliona. Nobody answered as she knocked at the door of the once proud mansion, so she went to the small iron gate which separated the garden from the farm area. She saw Nikita at the other end in the shed where he was helping two men to take apart a four-wheeled cart which needed repairs. They didn't see her coming. They were absorbed in their work and hardly spoke.

It was bitterly cold. Nikita wore a woolen vest, his sleeves were turned up to the elbows, and his shirt was open in front revealing the thick hair on his chest. He was struggling with one of the men to lift up the cart and was telling the third man how to prop it up so that they could remove the wheels. He was covered in mud and grime, and in spite of the cold he was perspiring.

He wasn't aware of Katie's presence until she came up to him and greeted him. He returned her greeting without interrupting his work. She stood a little way off and watched the men at their task.

''He's become a real farmer,'' she thought. ''Whatever has become of the Paris glamour-boy?''

She caught a whiff of odor emanating from his body, and remembered that this was the man who not so long ago was pommaded and perfumed with delicious French lotions. Now he smelled of sweat and the odor of damp earth, leather, and animal rut. She blushed as she realized that she liked this smell—that it actually excited her. She was disturbed by the conscious feeling that desire was taking possession of her, that she wanted to take this sweating man in her arms, to kiss him passionately, and to press her hungry lips to the damp hair on his chest. Suddenly she remembered what her mother used to say, which always sounded to her like the voice of doom. ''You'll come to a bad end because you don't know what you want.''

What did she want, really? Did she want the refinement suggested by the delicate Paris perfumes, or did she want her man like this—sweating like an animal? The fact was that she wanted both with equal intensity. That had always been her tragedy. Three years ago, when she had been under the spell of Alexis' robust virility, she had nonetheless run after a stupid young fop in Athens—the son of Spyros Coletti. She was utterly miserable because she lost him, or rather when she saw that she had lost the chance to lead a life of ease and luxury in the city. Yet it was

Alexis who had kindled her desire—she had been mad about him. And now she was violently attracted to this man.

Her reflections were cut short, because Nikita had finished the work on the cart.

"Take the key to the house," he said. "Go in and light the fire. I'll be with you in a few minutes. I have some instructions for the boys and I have to wash up."

This suited her, for she needed time to think over her plan of action. Nikita had made a strange impression on her today, his manner was somewhat peculiar—not quite the same as usual. It would have been more natural for him to have greeted her with a shout of joy and a hearty laugh, making some joke about his ability as a cartwright. But instead he had been reserved, and had spoken to her almost as a small-town husband might have spoken to his wife. Perhaps he had behaved like this because the men were there.

Whatever the case, she couldn't follow her uncle Nikos' advice to tell Nikita to withdraw. She couldn't press him to stop fighting the Legion. She had no legitimate excuse for doing so. It would only make him suspicious. Only a play for marriage combined with a demand for their immediate departure from Larissa could serve her purpose. That was the only logical course of action which was left to her, and in pursuing it she must be very careful, very self-controlled—above all very careful.

In reality, she would need to be even more careful than she knew, because just as Nikita started for the house, a young man on a bicycle rode up to the shed and asked to speak to him privately.

"If I'm caught," the young man said, "I'll say that Takis Hadjipyrrhos sent me to tell you that he's found you the seed for the chickpeas you want to plant in the spring. But what in fact he wants me to tell you..." He hesitated a moment in order to collect his thoughts. "This is what he said: another of the visits he spoke to you about took place again last night, just before midnight at the office."

'Another of the visits he spoke to you about'. That was Katie's visit to her uncle, Nikos Monoussis, at his office, he reflected and he felt his heart contract.

"Anything else?" he asked the young man.

"No, nothing else."

"Will you repeat the message, please?"

He repeated it and saw that Nikita was looking at him absently.

"Do you want me to tell him anything?" he asked.

"Tell him that I thank him very much."

"And if it's necessary, don't forget the chickpeas," he added with a smile. "Takis always finds magnificent seeds."

The youth departed.

From the moment he entered his room the atmosphere was tense. They spoke formally; their conversation was strained and contrived. The light-hearted good fun they usually had when they met was absent today. Each sensed that the other was hiding something. Nikita could not hold back.

"Katie, I wasn't expecting you today, and you don't seem to me to be quite yourself. What's wrong?"

"I might say the same about you. You seem different to me."

"Maybe," he answered enigmatically. "But tell me first what's wrong with you."

She took on an embarrased air, simulated perplexity, hemmed and hawed a little, and told him what was the matter. She wanted to escape from the moldiness of small-town life which was choking her; she had to leave with him—go far, very far away.

He looked her straight in the eye and asked her slowly, "Is that the only reason you have for wanting to go?"

She reflected that she had no reason to avoid the question, seeing that Coletti knew about the Legion, but she must weigh her words very carefully. She was on slippery ground.

"I have another reason too," she answered.

"Your uncle?"

"Yes."

"But your family has broken off with him."

"Yes, we have broken off, but what good does it do? He thinks of himself as a missionary, but everyone condemns him because, it seems, terrible things are taking place. I can't bear to hear all the accusations. This small-town atmosphere always got me down, but now it's three times as bad. I can't stand it any longer."

"What sort of missionary does he think he is?" he asked.

"He says that he will save the Vlachs and keep Salonika free from the Bulgars."

She realized that she had slipped on the dangerous ground, but it was too late. He realized it too.

"How do you know he feels and talks like this?"

"Friends of mine have told me and father has heard it from clients."

"Why don't you try to bring him back to reason, for your own sakes and to save him from this filthy business?"

"How?" she asked hopelessly, "He has left the house and spends all day at the beastly Legion with all those awful men."

Nikita averted his eyes, took out a pack of cigarettes, and tapped one against the pack. Katie looked at him intently. She was suffering agonies. Something was bothering him; he was very thoughtful. Did he or didn't he believe her? Where was she heading? For a fine marriage with this man who attracted her so powerfully? Or would she have to start all over again—go through all the disillusionment, bitterness, search for new prospects, suspense, rebellion and despair?

Everything would depend on what was said in the next few minutes. She saw him put the cigarette in his mouth and bend toward the fireplace to take out a burning stick. She had time to wonder why his movements impressed her; why they were so full of grace and nobility, and they were so strangely deliberate. She hardly had time to think about this, for as he leaned forward he said, "So he's at the Legion all day, but doesn't he ever go to his office in the evening? You could see him there."

She froze at the question. She understood that he had bent over the fireplace so as not to look at her and give himself away. So her visits were known. She must have been followed. The way the discussion was going, only a bold move on her part would avert the final slip which she felt coming very close.

"I have seen him, Nikita. You are the only one to learn this. No one else knows. I saw him only last night. I scolded him, begged him, cursed him, flattered him. But he wouldn't listen.

He says he has a sacred mission to accomplish and, if necessary,he'll sacrifice himself and us too. It's just my luck, my bad luck!''

And she hid her face in her hands. She appeared to be weeping or to be keeping herself back from weeping.

What she said could be true or false. Her voice sounded genuine and her desperation seemed real. What was he to think, and what conclusions could he draw? 'She's very clever but she's possessd by the devil' Hadjipyrrhos had said. 'To her above all you mustn't say a word. Great harm could come of it.' And everyone agreed, everyone had said that the quarrel between the two brothers was a put-up show. But what about her spontaneous confession, and the reasonable explanation of her meetings? What about her desperation, and her suggestion that they should go away together? Again he considered what he had heard at Raptis' clinic.

He couldn't make head or tail of it. It would be impossible to get at the truth. There was only one way. He sat beside her and put his arm around her shoulders.

''When things settle down'' he said, ''I may be able to go to Athens once or twice a year and sometime to Paris, although not so often. I've become an inseparable part of Pteliona, and it is here that I'm going to live and here that I'm going to die. If you wish to live here, fix the date and we'll get married. I'll remodel two more rooms in the house and build a new, comfortable kitchen. We'll make a fine life for ourselves.''

Her face was still hidden in her hands. Now there was no doubt about it, she was crying. Between her sobs she said, ''I can't...I can't stand Larissa, I can't stand the mud here, I can't stand my uncle...''

She was weeping genuinely because she realized only too well that Truth, which on ordinary days is more or less indifferent, in the critical hours of life is exacting. And if in those hours it finds one wanting in character and integrity, it cuts one to pieces with a fiery sword. She realized that she was being cut down thus for the third time in her life, and that now her predicament was worse than ever before.

For his part, Nikita found the scene unpleasant and painful—very painful—but he was sure that he had followed the only course possible in order to find out where he stood. He stood in front of her and drew her hands away from her face. Deep pain lined her features and tears ran down her cheeks. He had never seen her in such a state. She looked up at him and something within him stirred. He took her head in his hands and bent down towards her tragic and lovely face; he looked into her eyes with deep love. He was about to kiss her on the mouth and tell her...

But she didn't give him the time. She threw her arms tightly around him, thrust her face through the opening in his shirt, rubbed it against his chest, kissed him passionately, and suddenly tore herself away, running like a madwoman and crying out despairingly, "I can't! No, I don't want to! Impossible!"

He ran after her and saw her going off at top speed on her bicycle.

The bare trees of Pteliona, and those which despite the winter remained green, hid her from his view.

VIII

The winter of 1940, the year of the war against the Italians, was a heavy one, but the winter of 1941, the first year of the occupation, was heavier still. A cold and rainy December ended in snow and ice.

With gusto the heavens poured out snow. The peaks shone white and the mountain slopes were covered; the ravines were long white streaks while the plains were buried deep.

On the great plain not an inch of ground remained uncovered. In places the snow was more than knee-deep, and all the crops and shrubs were shrouded. The whole of Thessaly had turned into an immense, white, cold, and silent sea.

Then came the great freeze—a rare experience for Greece. For seven weeks the thermometer never rose above ten degrees below zero; at night it sank to fifteen and sometimes lower. The schools were closed. Children and those in fragile health fell ill. The sick and the old were dying and it was difficult to bury them under the hard snow in the earth which the ice had turned to stone.

Communications were hampered and movement was reduced to a minimum. The state, powerless and disorganized, was in no position to give much assistance. It was impotent to act, to command, or even to signify that it was alive. It was nothing but a spectator, a shadow.

There was trouble everywhere, trouble of every sort, prodigious, unprecedented trouble, bringing misery to the cities and villages all over the country. The greatest misery, to the point of desperation, came to the stock-breeders. There was not an inch of pasture left anywhere. So few were prepared for such a calamity that to all intents and purposes there was no hay available for feed. In makeshift stables, and more often in open sheep-folds covered with sloping roofs of matted twigs and straw, the sheep stood motionless, suffering from the intense cold. They grew weak and wasted away and after the first days would gnaw at any piece of wood they found. Many went out into the frozen snow, scooping it out madly, in search of a bit of grass to eat. On and on they went in their vain quest until, exhausted and numbed, they returned to their wretched shelters. One or two would bear young, but nearly all the lambs perished, and the shepherds were hard put to milk the mothers, not for the poor milk they would get, but in order to prevent them from becoming sterile against the day when they would be able to graze again and begin to give good milk.

General despair and fear of the future was such that no one would lend money or feed. Worse still, none of the merchants who every year preempted the milk for their cheese production would make the usual cash advances which enabled the stock-breeders to get through the winter.

How could anyone make advance payments? Not so much because prices were rising every day, and no one could know what the cost of the milk would be in the end, nor because there was a lack of money and the banks did not make loans easily. These difficulties might have been remedied to some extent by the compassion born of general calamity. But reason was that cheese could not be made without salt, and the Italian authorities had placed an embargo on salt which was now only issued on the order of the Roman Legion to merchants who agreed to collaborate. Except for two or three adventurers who had no money and could not borrow any, no serious merchant approached the Legion. So how could advance sales of milk be made and from whom would pre-payments be forthcoming? In all the villages and farms the prospects for the future loomed black and despair reigned.

How long would this terrible winter last? When the earth grew green once more, how many sheep would still be alive? And then how would the stockmen sell the little milk they had, since no cheese was being made? How would a farmer make even a pittance to scrape through to the next year with his family and animals?

This was indeed a thrice-accursed winter for those who lived off their quiet flocks! Black, black as pitch, was the night which this unbearable slavery had cast over them! And in this night of horror, the Legion, greatest blight of all, lightened and thundered!

In very truth, the Legion stormed through the night. Its army now amounted to more than three thousand men and was made up of a collection of the most impudent adventurers and worst vagrants in the area. Most of them were criminals who had managed to escape from the prisons when the Germans invaded the country.

They wore arm-bands on the sleeves, carried truncheons in their hands pistols in their belts, and, occasionally, light Italian rifles on their shoulders. They strutted, well-fed and clothed, among the starving and ragged population and spread terror around the plain.

Reports came in from every village of brutality, insults, beatings and torture; of people being hung by the arms or legs from trees in the public squares so that whole villages might witness the tyranny and humiliation.

There was nowhere to turn for protection. No one dared to ask for protection for if a court decision was issued against the offenders, they would pay the victims back with more beatings and with even more ferocious persecution. And it was clear, as shown in the matter of cheese production, who was now the master in all things small and great.

So the small fry and the weak tried to keep out of the way, and if they were forced, sometimes they declared allegiance.

What else could they do? On the surface they acknowledged the power of the Legion but, underneath, in their innermost hearts their hatred steadily grew.

A small minority in Larissa refused to stay out of the way and to keep silent. But their opportunities and means of resistance were very slender. Wherever and whenever they could they tried to get in touch with the people and to open a discussion with as many as they could, especially with the Vlachs. They said whatever was most suitable to the occasion, and they used both truth and lies in their propaganda. They said, for example—and this had terrified many of the bullies—that since the Italians and the Rumanians had sent an army against Russia, they would also send the army of the Legion to the Russian front. They said everything they could to frighten their enemies and to uplift the morale of their friends. But these were just words. There was no substance to them and they provided no solution to the problem of the winter privations. Whatever they might attemt to do, they could offer no remedy for the milk situation, and that was the most urgent and serious matter.

What were they to do? What could they do?

Now they all agreed that in the *impasse* in which they found themselves, they must at least try to establish contact with the Italian general, all the more since the protest of the Bar and Medical associations to the Chief of Staff, Colonel Pazzipolini, had not only been unsuccessful, but had actually resulted in a rebuff. The colonel had received them promptly, but did not allow them to finish what they had come to say. In a cold, cutting, arrogant tone he had informed them that Commendatore Diamantis enjoyed the complete condfidence of the Italian Army. He said he would examine their complaints but that they must realize that there was a war on and that the occupation forces would tolerate no obstruction. So saying, he had brought the meeting to an abrupt end.

But wouldn't the general be aware of all this? It was more than likely, but in their despair a meeting with the general offered a ray of hope—it was their only hope. But how could they get to see him? They knocked on every door only to find rebuff. The Greek prefect was friendly to the Legion and he turned them away in the most hostile manner. They fared no better at the headquarters of the Commandant of the City, and at the administrative headquarters of the Division. They had tried to approach the general one day as he left his office, but to no avail. What else was there to do? They were at their wits' end and despaired of finding any solution to their problem, when suddenly, out of a blue sky, a *deus ex machina* appeared.

Giulio Vianelli was an old inhabitant of Larissa. He had inherited vast estates from his father and, up to the time of the expropriation of the large manorial properties, he had lived more in Greece than in his own country. Since the days of his youth he had been honorary Consul of Italy in Larissa.

He was tall, well-dressed, with a carnation always in his buttonhole. In the winter he wore shining black top-boots, in the summer impeccably ironed white gaiters. and he carried an ornate whip. He was always full of high spirits, not very intelligent, but generous and well-disposed to everybody. He showered compliments on the men and kisses on the women and was universally popular. Before the war he had come regularly to Larissa to see the places he loved and to meet old friends. That was the reason why he returned now.

Nikita remembered him well. How could he forget the charming and original old man who in the old days used to visit Pteliona with his family, driving his smart tan carriage, or alone riding his spendid white horse. As soon as Nikita heard that he had arrived he hastened to call on him at his hotel. He might be very useful to them. The old gentleman put on his robe and received him in his bedroom with open arms.

''*Carissimo! Figlio mio!* You're the image of your grandfather! I can't tell you how you remind me of him! What an extraordinary old man he was. *Un gran signore.* Where are the aristocrats of those good old days? Even in Italy the *nobilità* is receding. You only have to look at the *gloriosa Casa di Savoia*, giving way before a paltry schoolteacher. I will say he has fashioned us into an empire, and from charming guitar-players he has changed us into a people respected by our friends and and enemies alike. *Ma per carità, per l'amor di Dio*, the aristocracy shouldn't be trampled upon. O what a noble old aristocrat you were, Nikita Coletti! What an impression you made on all who knew you! I remember once, your father gave a ball at Pteliona, and guests from Athens, landowners from the area, officers from the garrison in dress uniform filled the gardens. Chinese lanterns twinkled in the trees, and one band from Athens and another which specialized in waltzes, made music. *Un vero sogno.* Naturally this was planned in the abscence of your grandfather. But suddenly Grandfather appeared at the height of the ball. He got down from his carriage and stood still. We all bowed before him. He returned the greeting, looked around him, and departed. He sent word with your mother a little later that he wasn't feeling well, but requested that the dance go on. I can imagine what a lambasting your father must have gotten the next day! But your grandfather was right. It was wartime. This happened in 1917. Ah, war, war, *amico mio,* yes, we're winning on all fronts, but...

And so Vianelli rambled on in an amiable monologue, praising the Italians and praising the Greeks, and following his reminiscences of the 'good old days' in Thessaly, in the time of the great landowners, with observations on the progress of the war.

Nikita began to be afraid that he wouldn't be able to get in a word. He was hard put to it, but after a considerable time, he interrupted his chatter and told him what he wanted. The Italian was dumbfounded, and grew purple with anger.

"Diamantis!" he shouted. "*Un mascalzone, un villano!* I remember him. When he was an agent for the Rumanians, he came and called on me in my capacity as Italian Consul, and asked me for money, saying that he was heading a Latin movement. I sent him packing. The only thing that fellow is interested in is money, nothing else. A low, contemptible fellow, *un contadino volgare*! And what does he say he wants? To become a Prince? *Ma lascia mi ridere, caro!*"

"Mr. Vianelli, I'm afraid this is no matter for laughter," Nikita said.

"My dear boy, I'm quite sure it isn't; it's rather a matter for tears. But Fuggiero is good friend of mine. He'll put an end to this business. He is a sensible man and furthermore he is *un nobiluomo*. I am sure he doesn't know you asked to see him; he would have responded at once to such a well-known *nomme due monde* from Paris. Vianelli stopped suddenly and stepped back.

He examined Nikita from head to toe with an air of great displeasure.

"If you weren't the spitting image, but the spitting image of your grandfather," he said, "I would hardly believe you were a Coletti at all. What are those clothes you're wearing?"

Nikita was startled and smiled. This infuriated Vianelli.

"Do you remember how beautifully your dear mother used to dress? Do you remember how *soigné* your father was? Do you remember those silk waistcoats made exclusively for him? You, their son, can't go around dressed like a peasant. If you're doing it out of *genre* it's a very bad idea. If a Coletti shows himself in public looking like a peasant, who is going to set the example of respectability and good taste? Don't smile, *carissimo*, what I'm telling you is very serious. 'If the salt be lost wherewith shall they be salted?' If the aristocracy is going plebeian, what is there to hope for? Tell me what's happening."

Nikita laughed heartily. The kindly Italian didn't understand. He looked worried and bent over him with benevolent solicitude. "Are you in such great need?" he enquired. "Do you need money...or maybe some clothes from Italy?"

"No, no," Nikita replied. "I have everything I need. You must come to Pteliona and there I shall explain to you why I dress in this way. But what is important now is that you should help us get an interview with the general."

"*Ma certo, certo*. I'll see him this morning, and this afternoon or at the latest tomorrow he'll receive you. But don't come dressed like that. In the eyes of an aristocrat like Fuggiero, such a vulgar appearance would take away all the glamour from the darling of the best *salons* in Paris."

For an instant Nikita's mind went back to the refined society of the French capital. He remembered how many people had tried in vain to gain entrance to the circles he frequented. He remembered also the boredom he felt going from one reception to another, and marvelled that such a useless life had once meant so much to him. And even now in the midst of this great calamity, his old friend still thought of that kind of life as ideal. Could there be people so far removed from reality? Turning to Vianelli, he said very seriously, "Mr. Vianelli, the refined *salons* of Paris are being swept by a great wind blowing down from icy mountains and fiery plains. The clothes I wore then couldn't stand the blast. Only these rough clothes I'm wearing will."

In spite of the earnestness of his manner, the old man failed to understand.

"The war," he said, "*Maledetta guerra*! Yes, of course, war is bad for everything. But it will pass, it will pass. And then, *figlio mio*, you'll see that very many things will depend upon the survival of the aristocracy."

"But which aristocracy, sir? The aristocracy of clothes?"

The loquacious old gentleman was silent. It was evident that he was puzzling in his mind to find some epigrammatic answer which would make an impression. But soon he laughed and slapped Nikita on the back. "I see that you're in a mood for a philosophical discussion while *nous avons d'autres chats à fouetter*. Now let me get my clothes on. Come back at noon and I'll give you the answer *del mio caro Fuggiero*...But wait a moment. Let me embrace you, *carissimo*. You've given me a great deal of pleasure by coming. I've been deeply touched."

Diamantis broke the silence by banging his fist angrily on the table.

"And to think that just as everything was going so well, the presence of this old nincompoop in Larissa threatens to upset the apple cart."

"Don't get so dramatic," Nikos Manoussis observed coolly. "They managed to get one interview. That's not so terrible."

"You're a peculiar fellow," Diamantis answered with annoyance. "When there's no reason to fear you're afraid, and when our schemes go wrong you stay cool. I tell you that the general gave orders in front of that puffed up turkey to inform Coletti and Raptis to go to see him tomorrow morning and to take along any others that wished to go. I tell you that the general made a great fuss, that the Chief of Staff is worried to death and sent all over town to find me to give me the news at once. What more do you need to start you worrying?"

"Listen to me. It's not a pleasant situation, but don't forget that the general has aides and that they have some influence and moreover are the ones who will enforce the order. The way an order is enforced is much more important than the order itself."

"But I've already told you that his principal aide is out of his mind with worry."

"Possibly because he may have come in for a drubbing, and possibly because his own hands are not so clean. But you forget that we have a lot of friends in the Division who can be counted on for help. They'll help because they want to make money. The Second Bureau is on our side because we've handed over enough weapons to equip one or two divisions. Do you realize what this means in terms of their security? And lastly we have the support of the idealists, those who have visions of the grandeur of Italy, who believe in our principality, and are ready for any sacrifice and any excess in order to establish it. There is quite a number of these, and they hold key positions. Take Castelleone, for example. Such men will react on our behalf and they are in a position to make themselves heard in Rome. What can the general do when he's short-circuited in this way?"

Diamantis looked at him and after a moment said, with obvious relief, "We are going through some bad moments, but you've made me feel better about things."

Then he added with some animation and a crafty gleam in his eyes, "You mentioned Castelleone. How is he getting on with your niece?"

"The matter's practically settled. They're getting engaged."

Diamantis pushed his chair back violently, "Engaged? Seriously?"

"It's only seriously that girls of good family get engaged," Nikos replied coldly.

Diamantis leaned across the desk and took his hand. "For God's sake, Nikos, you're not going to misunderstand me. I was only asking if it was certain because you used the words 'practically settled' and you said they were 'getting engaged', not that they were engaged. I'm asking again, because I'm interested."

"Judge for yourself. He came to the house and asked Vassili for her hand. He only said that in order to make the announcement simultaneously here and in Italy he must have the consent of his father, according to custom, as well as the permission of the Division, according to regulations. I don't believe there will be the slightest objection.

Diamantis was enchanted. He got up and took him by the shoulders.

"Excellent! Excellent! A splendid marriage from every point of view! Tell me, how did it come about?"

"Love at first sight, on both sides."

"Well, I'll be darned! This is a great stroke of luck. He's a big shot in Italy. And he's got a title, hasn't he?"

"He's a count and his father is a marquess."

"So it'll be Countess Katie! And later Marchioness! When will the wedding be?"

"I don't know yet. But it won't be long. They're both in a hurry."

"I don't blame them, and you should be in a hurry too. And by the way, what is his job in the Division?"

He commanded a unit, and his war record is excellent. For some months he has been holding a confidential post at the Division."

Diamantis' look became craftier than ever. "Well, then," he cried joyfully, "the new son-in-law is falling straight into our lap!"

"When you were telling us about your troubles, it occurred to me that Katie ought to call him in tonight, so that I might have a talk with him.

"And you're still sitting here, Nikos? Get going at once. In any case tomorrow's visit to the general must be handled with great caution."

His beautiful niece took a lively part in the conversation because Nikos' French was not too good. Castelleone listened to them carefully, and then with a carefree expression he said, "You did well to inform me, because the general, when he's not on the battlefield, is overfond of courtesy and protocol. But we'll see to it and set him right on the matter after the others have gone, and so, after a little thunder and lightning, the skies will clear up again. Don't worry, Mr. President."

"The trouble is," Nikos observed, "that there have been some excesses on our side."

"In this contingency the Pontius Pilate of Thessaly might say, 'what is excess?' When you are at war, my friend, and decide in cold blood that you are going to kill human beings, there's no such thing as excess. Everything is permitted. We avoided excesses and as a result we haven't discovered a single rifle. But you, with your excesses, have found ten thousand and we want you to find more. Because no matter how many were lost, the important question remains. What has happened to the several hundreds of thousands of rifles which the Greek army had? Then there is also our great dream—the empire of Rome extending to the Aegean once more after two thousand years. So why speak to me about excesses? One might also ask the general question: where does the norm end and excess begin? To what extent do present circumstances extend the limits of the norm, and what is normal for one man and what for the next? What I have been saying can be summed up in the question I put to you again: "What is meant by excess?"

Katie leaned over to her uncle with a facetious expression.

"You see, uncle, what a luminous dynamic intellect will produce. A single ancient Roman query: What is excess?"

Her fiancé took her hand, and looking at her sweetly, said, "My darling, I'll tell you of another area in which there is no excess. Love. Don't you agree?"

They laughed, but the Italian became serious again. "By the way," he said, "you mentioned a poet. I'm told that in the group which is fighting us there is a French-speaking poet, an aristocrat who dresses like a peasant. What has he to do with the group? And explain something to me. I understand that these people haven't been disturbed much. Why are they agitating? Why are they against us? Aren't they Vlachs too? Haven't they any sense of their Latinity?"

Uncle and niece exchanged a quick glance and Nikos replied. "The question requires a more general analysis of which all of you should be aware. A small minority among the Vlachs was led astray by Rumanian propaganda and was convinced that the Vlachs were Rumanians. A few, a very few, through the study of history, were inspired by the greatness of Rome. The great mass of the Vlachs has not national sentiment. Because of the language, it has always had a vague feeling of racial solidarity and, in order to survive, has attached itself to those who happen to hold the power. A smaller group, for various reasons, has attached itself to the Greeks and either believes in Greece or has sold itself to it. The little group that is fighting us belongs to the last category."

"Ah, now at last I understand. I am beginning to see many things clearly," Castelleone said. "I had oversimplified the question in my mind and was confused. Naturally these Latins, poor and uneducated as they are, abandoned and continuously in bondage, cannot be expected to have a lively Latin consciousness. Now I understand. It's a great undertaking, Mr. President, to reawaken them and to have Latin brothers as far as the shores of the Aegean!"

"It is a great undertaking, and we're going to see it through."

"Indeed we are. And as for that small group, if it gives us any more trouble, we'll have to neutralize it."

"What do you mean?" Katie asked.

He smiled at her lovingly. "That's our business," he said. "There are a thousand and one ways. So far we have ignored these gentlemen."

"I think my uncle will agree, that you shouldn't talk about them in the plural. Only one is dangerous. The French-speaking poet. His family was wealthy and powerful under the Greeks. He himself is trying to fill his useless life with this cause so that he will be able to talk about it in Paris after the war. That's the man that must be humiliated and neutralized."

She looked at her uncle intently.

"My niece is right," Manoussis said. "He is the stumbling block. He and, possibly, two others."

"Vedremo, vedremo," said Castelleone as he got up to go. Resuming in French he added, "I have to leave now to get in touch with my colleagues about tomorrow."

He said goodbye to Nikos, kissed Katie, walked to the door and suddenly turned back.

"To think that I almost forgot to tell you," he said joyfully, "that a short time ago I received the good news I was expecting. Listen to this telegram and see what a wonderful father I have."

He took a piece of paper from his pocket and began to translate, beaming with joy.

WHATEVER MY BRAVE SON DECIDES CANNOT BE WRONG. YOU HAVE MY CONSENT AND BLESSING AND THE CONGRATULATIONS OF THE FAMILY. WE ARE IMPATIENT TO MEET THE GIRL WHO CONQUERED THE CONQUEROR.

He laughed like a boy, kissed her again, and left hastily. From the front door he turned to her and sang the first lines of a well-known Italian song: "We'll be married in May With the roses in bloom, The roses in bloom..." He left and Katie embraced her uncle.

"Prime Minister," she said gaily, "I think I'm about to go crazy."

He disengaged himself and smiled at her sarcastically.

"Something you said earlier about the instigator of the resistance, and the way you said it, prompt me to ask whether you are about to go crazy with love?

She did not answer and avoided his eyes. Then, as if in a trance, she said, "Now for the wedding...Later...This kind of marriage sometimes brings love with it."

IX

On that icy January morning, at about ten o'clock, the handful of people passing through the central square of Larissa stopped to watch a small group pass by. The evening before the news had spread that the Italian general would at last receive the small group which had dared to oppose the hated Legion. And now six of that group were leaving divisional headquarters and crossing the square. They must be going to Dr. Raptis' clinic which was their center of operations.

The few passers-by saw them and followed them with their eyes, and felt for a while that it was not so cold. In spite of the freezing weather, something within them was warmer. The six men were smiling, their eyes shone, they walked with a brisk step, and held their heads high.

"God be praised!"

"Up with the Country!"

"Bless you, boys!"

At the clinic the others were waiting. The six told them quickly in a few words how the meeting had gone and then began to relate in great detail what had transpired.

The general, a tall, proud, courteous man, had received them standing behind his desk, surrounded by his staff and officers of the Second Bureau. Among them was the 'son-in-law.' Giulio Vianelli was also present. Every now and then he put in a word in favor of the petitioners and punctuated the proceedings with exclamations and grunts of approval or disapproval.

Dr. Raptis spoke first and an interpreter translated his remarks. The general showed great astonishment at the outrageous things that were going on. He asked for clarifications several times; he wanted to know if soldiers and carabinieri were involved. More than once his face flushed with anger and he turned to glare furiously at his officers. He also took notes. Finally, his annoyance was so great that he indicated that he wished to terminate the discussion. He assured the petitioners that he would put a stop to the misdeeds they had reported. He spoke eloquently of the high aims of the Italian Administration, and then and there instructed Lieutenant-Colonel Pazzi to take the petitioners under his protection and to receive them whenever they had anything untoward to report. If necessary, he would receive them himself.

But the general did not intend to leave matters there. He had his own counter-accusations to make. Food supplies were not coming in satisfactorily, he said, and he inveighed with particular vehemence against the operations of the black market. It was the duty of every good citizen to fight the black-marketeers. The group offered various explanations, but the general wouldn't listen. It was his turn to point the finger of accusation. "If the good citizens of the area were willing," he said, "there would be no black market."

Nikita asked permission to speak. The general looked at him attentively and asked, "Is it you who speak Italian so well?"

"Yes, fairly well."

The general continued in faultless French. "I believe I'm right in saying that you write poems in French. Let us continue the discussion in French."

"The lack of supplies," Nikita said, "is due mainly to

reasons which are beyond remedy: imports, lack of fuel for the tractors, and other things. It is also due to the black market. I don't know what is happening elsewhere, and particularly in Athens where people are dying of hunger, but here, for nearly all the operations of the black market, the fault lies with the Prefect and the Legion."

The eyes of the Italian officers who were listening to him flashed with anger. Castelleone made a spiteful gesture which the general noticed. With an arrogant, ironic smile and with a Parisian turn of speech he said: *"Vous faîtes flèche de tout bois, Monsieur.* That is dangerous. You make use of your beautiful French in order to accuse your own authorities."

"No people, including ours, is made up exclusively of angels."

"Could you give us instances in support of your accusations?"

"Many, I assure you. The most outstanding is that of the cheese production. In their attempt to exploit it the Legionnaires have destroyed the industry. This year the cheese produced in the whole district will amount to less than one tenth of the usual annual production."

The general opened his eyes wide and turned to his officers. "You told me about some plan which would ensure that the cheese production would stay out of the black market. In fact I signed something about it. What is happening?"

Captain Angelo di Castelleone stepped forward: "You signed an order, sir, putting an embargo on salt. As regards what is happening, it is my duty to report that the Greek citizens here present are distorting the significance of that measure, just as during today's discussion they distorted many other facts."

While Castelleone was talking, the general tapped the table nervously with his fingers. Finally he told the 'Greek citizens' to send in a memorandum to the Second Bureau about their views on the cheese production, and instructed his staff to bring the matter to him for discussion on the following morning. The interview ended.

* * * * *

They all thought that the news was excellent. At least they

saw a ray of light and, for the first time, there was some hope.

"There's no cause for celebration yet," Hadjipyrrhos said. "The officers are all in a vicious mood. What we have to do now is to try to get as much good as we can out of the small advantage we've achieved. First the people must learn what has happened, and second we must bolster their morale."

"How can we do that?"

"Those of us who were at the meeting should publish a letter of thanks to the general in the local press; that way we can say whatever it suits us to say."

"Why shouldn't we all sign?"

"Because we don't want to look like an organized job. I propose that his letter should be drawn up by the man to whom we owe the interview, our good friend, Nikita Coletti." They all agreed with a warmth which indicated their feelings. Nikita was deeply moved.

The letter he composed contained an abundance of courtesies which cost them nothing. It also contained the statement that 'as to the pressures and propaganda of certain Vlachs, we declared that we Vlachs are unalterably loyal Greeks,' and that General Fuggiero 'assured us that no one will exert pressure on us to change our Greek ethnic character.' He added more in the same vein, and made three copies. The six delegates signed the sheets and the letter of thanks was sent to the newspapers.

Stretched out on the couch near the fireplace Nikita was reading. The book was a good foreign novel with many descriptions of incidents of the first World War, and it had kept him awake. Some years ago he had disliked this kind of book, but now he sought them out because in their pages he constantly found characters who reminded him of Alexis, or episodes which brought back to his mind the hours they had spent together, at Pteliona and at the front, or those dawn hours—Alexis' last hours—on the ninth of May of the previous year.

He looked at his watch and saw that it was past midnight, an unusual hour for anyone to be awake at Pteliona. He felt chilled and realized that all the time he had been reading he had not been warm. And yet the fire had been burning brightly all evening. It must be a very cold night, he thought. He placed the thermometer outside the window and took up his book again. He smiled to himself: "I wonder if it's an excuse to read a little more, or if I'm really curious to know what the temperature is?" When he took in the thermometer he was surprised, and became anxious. It indicated eighteen degrees below zero.

Would the beasts be able to endure such cold? He didn't know. And supposing a door or a window had been left open in the stables? He was particularly worried about the horses which had less natural covering than the other animals—and about Pegasus whom the College had placed in his care.

He jumped up from his seat. The beast that Alexis adored must come to no harm! He put on his cap and a thick coat and took a storm lantern from the corridor. Why hadn't he remembered to change the wick? He had been meaning to do so for days and now it was nearly burned out and glowed only faintly. He couldn't do anything about it now; he must make the best of the poor light.

The cold was more bitter than ever. He turned up his collar and pushed his head as far down as he could but that made no difference. The cold was terrible' it stung his eyes and drew tears. His nose and every part of his body exposed to the freezing air smarted and he thought how much the animals must be suffering.

He hastened forward and when he came near the stable he heard Pegasus. He recognized his way of stamping his feet, and his whinny. But he was not neighing in his accustomed manner, brisk and loud, sorrowful or playful. It was a different kind of whinny.

"He must be cold," he thought, "and yet everything seems to be closed. Anyway I did right to come."

He entered and held the lamp up high. In its weak, trembling light he saw a tall figure standing near the grey horse, more a shadow than a man. As he closed the door, the lamp went out. He stood still, frightened.

"Who is it?" he asked.

He was answered by a joyous whinny and a lively stamping of hoofs.

"Who is there?" he asked again louder.

There was no reply and he stood motionless. Behind him an

icy breath of air whistled through a crack in the door and made him shudder. His whole body trembled.

Again he called out: "Who are you? What are you doing here at this time of night?"

This time his question did not remain unanswered.

"I was expecting you."

He seemed to recognize the voice of Alexis, faint and tenuous—but it wasn't possible. Something was happening to him. It must be the tension, the privation, the loneliness... being so long without a woman when in former times he had one with him almost every night...Something was wrong.

But the voice spoke again slowly: "You're not mistaken. It is I. How could I fail to return to the great plain? But tonight I've come for you alone."

The voice was still faint but the words were clear, so much so that Nikita forgot his fears and doubts and shuffled forward a couple of steps in the dark.

"Alexis, you did well to come," he said. "I have shed so many tears for you! I have learned to love you so much!"

"I know it very well, Nikita, my brother."

"Without you..."

He was not allowed to continue.

"Many disasters...Beware...all of you beware.

"Of what?"

"Beware...Manoussis...Notis..."

His heart thumped wildly; his mind faltered. He tried to see in the dark, straining his eyes to the utmost. He saw nothing but pitch darkness. But this wasn't possible! This conversation with his dead brother must be the figment of his imagination—a touch of madness.

He was carried away by his feelings once more and cried out with warmth. "Stay with us, Alexis, stay! You will be as the sun to us in the night of our oppression. Stay!"

But without warmth, almost without expression, the voice replied, "It isn't possible. Beware...you lack strength."

Nikita spoke with animation. "You don't know how much I've changed, Alexis. You don't know."

"I know...Great strength..."

"Alexis, I don't understand. My brain is reeling!"

"I'm going, Nikita..."

Nikita cried out imploringly, in anguish. "No, Alexis, no! Stay, my beloved brother."

"I am going, my beloved brother! Farewell Nikita Coletti."

He heard not a step nor a rustle, no sound of voices. He cried out in the deathly silence, "Alexis! Alexis! Where are you? Speak to me."

A whinny and the stamping of hoofs was the only reply to his call.

He turned to the door abruptly, wrenched it open, and shouted wildly into the darkness: "Alexis..." He waited in desperation and called again: "Alexis, my brother!"

He hears a voice in the darkness: "Alexis, my brother!"

Was that the echo of his own voice or was the night haunted? He was sweating, and he realized that the freezing air chilled him more than ever. He went back into the stable and stood there dazed. What had happened to him? How had he suffered this illusion? What was the meaning of the 'appearance' of his dead brother...and of his words?

He took out his matches and with difficulty managed to relight the lamp. He paid no attention to Pegasus, or to the other horses, or the windows. He went to the far end of the stable to see if anyone were lurking there or if he could find some clue. Then he went out again into the cold night.

As he passed in front of Mourayias' cottage he saw a light in the window of the small parlor. To him, in his confused state of mind, this flicker was a hope, a joy, a kind of truth. He knocked on the closed shutter and the light went out at once. "They must have been frightened," he thought. "Who knows what they suspected?"

He stood close to the shutter. "It's me, Nikita; let me in."

The window opened and he heard Phrosso's voice. "I got out of bed," she said "because I heard a cry in the night. Just a moment, I'll light the lamp and open the door for you."

As soon as the front door had closed behind him, they looked at each other in frightened silence. Phrosso's hair, drawn straight back from her forehead and tied behind her head, fell loose down her back. The freshness and color had faded from her cheeks and she had lost her smile and her usual cheerful animation. She was wrapped to the neck in a dark blanket, and all that was visible was her beautiful face which might have been carved from dull marble—a face that reflected infinite anxiety.

Nikita looked at her in the lamplight and, still under the influence of his harrowing experience, asked her dreamily, "Are you Phrosso?"

His eyes were vague and his face was deathly pale. Phrosso was very frightened now and cried out in alarm, "Nikita? Don't you see me? What's the matter?"

She put her free arm around him, held him close, and drew him into the room. Again she asked him, trembling, "Tell me, what's the matter?"

"Something unbelievable," he replied. "But first light the stove. I'm cold, terribly cold. I'm shivering all over."

When the stove began to roar the tiny parlor warmed up quickly. Nikita told her in detail all that had just happened to him. The only thing he did not mention was Notis' name. Phrosso listened to him spellbound.

"I know it was a delusion," he said, "but everything was so vivid! I could have sworn he was there and was talking to me!"

Suddenly he turned to her. "Phrosso! Do you think something's wrong with me? Ought I to see a doctor?"

She laughed to give him courage: "There's nothing wrong with you," she said. "For the moment you're upset; and this can happen to anyone. What you need is a double shot of brandy."

She brought it to him, and standing beside him as he sat drinking it, she wiped his forehead with her handkerchief

"You're perspiring a lot," she said with a tremor in her voice.

She took off his cap and stroked his hair as she might have stroked an unahppy child who was about to cry, and then sat down again beside him. Nikita felt better. He cheered up, lit a cigarette, and said quietly, "Your warmth and kindness have brought me back to reality. But what do you say? Why did this happen to me? The illusion was so very vivid."

"If I were a doctor," she laughed, "I might be able to answer you. What can I say? Was it the cold, worries, bitterness?"

She stopped suddenly and looked at him pensively. "But still, who can assure us that it was just an illusion?"

Nikita jumped up from his chair. "Are you crazy? Do you believe that Alexis really came? Do you believe that it is possible for a dead man to return and to talk?"

"I don't dare believe either that it is possible or that it is not. Maybe the soul fades away and is lost. Maybe it doesn't fade and wanders around the places it loved, or maybe it doesn't wander at all. Who can say for sure what happens? I myself often feel that Alexis is here, near us. Is that because we loved him and he is in our thoughts, or does he come and watch over us from time to time?"

Once more Nikita showed how much her words startled him. "But he was killed!" he cried. "I myself buried his lifeless body. I buried him with my own hands!"

"And how do you know that you buried his soul? Father Modestos will tell you it was only his body you buried. It may be a sin to doubt, but I do not presume to say whether the soul does or does not exist. But if it does, can you imagine the kind of soul a man like Alexis must have, and how it must strain to break its bonds? My father once told me an odd thing. He said that Alexis himself was one of the voices of the earth. I didn't ask him what he meant, but his words seemed to me to have a strange unworldliness about them. There was a vague faraway look in her eyes.

He asked her shyly, as if ashamed of what he was going to say, "Since we're talking about such things, tell me something. Do you believe that the earth has a voice of its own, a real voice?"

"I don't know," she replied. "But so many people say that they hear it. You should know better than I, because father and Alexis said that the earth spoke to you clearly."

X

The country festival—the *glenti*—was in full swing and was wilder than anything Nikos Manoussis had ever seen.

When Vassilaki Ropotikas had invited him he had not shown much enthusiasm because he did not enjoy vulgar merrymaking with crude people. But he accepted the invitation because he realized that the 'general' was beginning to take offense at his repeated refusals. And there was another reason too. He was a little ashamed of himself, but he had to admit that he had been greatly influenced by the news that they were bringing women along.

But when the *glenti* got under way, he felt uncomfortable again. The old brigand chief, once a shepherd, had repaired and elaborately remodelled his farm-house. The wooden ceilings were new; so were the doors and windows. There were carved wooden ornaments and fleece coverings on the couches. Outside it was snowing and very cold, but the house was overheated. There were stoves in every room, and stoves and fireplaces in the two big halls. All this was good and pleasant, and the rooms had an old-world air of graundeur about them.

But these surroundings were not at all suited to Ropotikas and his toadies. Manoussis knew hardly any of them; most of them were ex-convicts from other parts of the country. They were rough and tough and, for the most part, young with forceful and cunning faces. Uncouth creatures worthy of their leader.

He felt even more uncomfortable when the gypsies arrived with their instruments and the women. What place did a proud and cultured man, a gentleman by education if not by birth, have in this den of bandits? For a moment he thought of leaving, but there was no way of doing so, so he stayed against his will.

But now the *glenti* had reached its peak and he forgot his scruples. He was enjoying himself. Was it the plentiful wine, the food and the heat? Was it the boisterous conviviality of the whole party? Was it the half-naked women who were free with their kisses and caresses? He didn't know. All he knew was that he was in high spirits. Now and then he too would let out a yell. He felt primitive instincts welling up inside him which could only be expressed with noise. He was possessed by a kind of frenzy which had to be let loose in order to subside. And let it loose he did in wild carousing as, like the others—even more freely than the others—he gave vent to his instincts without a thought or a care.

The food was good and there was plenty of it, and the wines were strong and heady. Everyone—and especially the women—ate and drank without restraint. Now they had removed the tables from the big hall; they had only kept the bottles and glasses on the sideboards and shelves and in front of the fireplace, and the dance began.

Hardly a dance—but the travesty of one. Each dancer tried somehow to keep step with the primitive music as he concentrated on showing off his strength and agility, the power of his voice, and the shrillness of his whistles. Those who were not dancing sang, whistled, clapped their hands, yelled and bellowed.

The first dance lasted some time. The 'general' led it with verve and vigor, frequently changing the pattern of his steps. He would hold his body straight, thrusting out his broad chest, so that he looked like a sturdy column as only his feet, encased in shining black top-boots, seemed to dance. Or he would hold his hands at his waist, swaying his body to right and left as his glistening boots continued their mad cavorting. Then again, he would double over, as if he were about to charge into someone head first, and would suddenly snap back, his head held high atop his bull's neck.

The dance went on and on. The floor groaned under the tread of stamping feet, the movements of the dancers and the singing and shouting grew wilder, and all the time the men called to the gypsy players, "Hit it, fellows, faster, faster!"

When the music struck the highest pitch, the 'general' bawled out pretentiously in Vlach: "Long live our mother, Rome!", a phrase which he seemed to have adopted as his special battle-cry. Everyone shouted and yelled and some threw their glasses into the fireplace.

Then the younger men took over. One of them bent his knees until he could strike the ground hard with his palm, and then with a sudden swift movement sprang up erect and leapt up to strike the ceiling with both hands. Another from time to time showed his skill at turning cartwheels round the room. Then he walked on his hands waving his legs in the air and with a deft movement found himself on his feet again and went on with his frenzied dance. Yet another danced in a sitting position, bumping the floor with his bottom and singing a popular bawdy song at the top of his voice

How do monks the pepper grind—
The Devil's monks? With their behinds!
(Chorus) With their behinds
They grind and grind.

and then, like lightning he resumed his sitting position and started to kick his legs Russian style. Every time he shot his legs out he let forth a howl.

And so the orgy reached a *crescendo* amid yells and howls which, the men let out to whip up the excitement. They drank down gallons of wine, stuffed themselves with food, and threw themselves on the women who were ready for them with open mouths and open arms.

"To the flower of Vlach youth!"

"To the Legion!"

"Long live mother Rome!"

"Samarina, pride of the world!"

The hall was in an uproar and the house echoed with the noise. The night wore on. They were all drunk and too tired to go on dancing, and Vassilaki put on the final show. Masses of dry wood were thrown into the fireplace to keep the fire going, the lights were put out, he set the women to do a belly-dance.

They too were drunk, dizzy with the heat and the orgiastic atmosphere, and they threw themselves with gusto into the center of the room. If any one of them chanced to wear anything which concealed the alluring rotundities of her body, she quickly discarded the offending garment as she danced.

No one took the trouble to notice if the plump forms were pretty. They were flesh, living flesh, warm and soft—that was enough. And now as the naked bodies were swaying lasciviously and the dancing flames of the fire illumined them with a strange light full of mystery—maybe the mystery of insticnt—an eerie feeling crept over the onlookers and grew more intense by the minute. They vaguely sensed that before them lay a composite image of exotic lands, hell, and paradise. And the women danced and danced, slowly grinding their hips and bellies, playing with their breasts, and passing their hands with lewd, snake-like movements over their undulating bodies which were reflected in the flickering glow of the firelight.

The men shouted, or rather bellowed, applauded and

stroked the women as they went by. Their eyes bulged with desire and expectation, and they clenched and unclenched their fists as they breathed in the air heavy with wine, smoke, sweat and human flesh in rut.

Then as the hour grew late, the party broke up, and each man took a woman with him to the bedrooms where they lay down under heavy fleeces.

* * * * *

The horse was sturdy and spirited and Ropotikas had to be in Larissa early. But they were going very slowly because the road was in wretched condition. Some of the holes were so bad that the axles or wheels were in danger of being smashed. The 'general' was in no mood to have his smart gig ruined; it was his pride and joy and he drove it for pleasure.

The going was rough. As they jerked and bounced along he thought his guts would fall out, and his head was heavy with wine and lack of sleep. Heavy was hardly the word to describe the racking pain that throbbed in his head. Under the hood, protected from the snow by a black oilcloth but exposed to the cold air which struck him in the face, Nikos sat, pale and wan, his eyes closed. He looked sick...exhausted.

Ropotikas had lowered the oilcloth half-way so that he could hold the reins. The cold, the holes in the road, and the effects of his debauchery didn't trouble him so much. He was used to the mountain snows. But he was terribly bored. He longed for a little conversation to pass the time.

Nikos opened his eyes and Ropotikas said, "You shouldn't fall asleep. Sleep is bad for you in cold weather."

"I'm not asleep, but I'm very tired."

"You're new to it all," he said. "It was a wonderful party. But we ought to have slept through the afternoon. That's what we usually do. But the Leader called us in at the last moment. There are important questions to be discussed, I'm told."

Nikos remained silent. Ropotikas guffawed. "Important questions. If only my old man was alive. He used to say that I'd never amount to anything! But did I ever expect to be the ruler of the plain, to have the whole world trembling wherever I go, and to take part in meetings with men like you? Well, the wheel turns. The wheel turns: These things are natural for you, Nikos, my boy. But for me?''

He got no reply and answered himself. ''Years up in the mountains, a bandit, and years in prison. Then my luck turned. But when I came back to these parts one of my men told me that I was due for deportation to an island. I was supposed to be a menace to public safety.''

He laughed boisterously. ''Well, so I was. Ropotikas was an eagle. He caught birds in the air everywhere, and had his eyries on every mountainside. At night he was in the east, at dawn in the west. An eagle, I tell you, an eagle. And suddenly I settled down. What a turn of the wheel! And do you know how this came about? Deportation to an island was worse than jail. I would have been a stranger lost in a small place surrounded by the sea, like an eagle in a cage. I'd have belched to death. I saw this was the end, so I went around and knocked on doors that refused to open to me, until, as a Vlach, I knocked on old Grandfather's door (he made the sign of the cross), may God rest his soul!''

'' 'I'll save you from deportation', he said to me, 'because I think you are a man. Maybe you weren't given the opportunity to live like a good and honest fellow. I'll give you this opportunity. I'll get some sheep for you, and if you're on the level, later I'll help you buy a meadow. But you've got to be honest with me, and if at any time I need information to go after bandits, you'll give it to me. Is that understood?' ''

''I couldn't believe my ears. As he stood there in front of me, tall and stately with his white beard, and dragged me out of the grave, I thought that God was talking to me. I bent down and kissed his hand. I pressed my forehead on it too.

'' 'The kiss is your thanks, but your forehead on my hand is your bond as an honorable man. Is it a deal?' ''

'' 'It's a deal, master.' ''

''And that's how I became domesticated. And with the exception of one or two parties with old friends in their hideaways, I kept my word through and through and led a quiet life. Until mother Rome came along.''

Nikos Manoussis turned his head a little and gave him a

sidelong glance. He smiled at him sarcastically. Ropotikas looked back at him mockingly, gave him a wink, saw the sardonic grin on Nikos' face and burst out laughing. He flexed his broad body on his knees once or twice and, laughing louder with renewed animation, said, "Nikos, my lad, I say to myself sometimes, 'We have brains and know what we're doing. But do those fellows have any brains?' "

"Who?"

"The Italians. Who else?"

"Why d'you say that?"

"Dammit, man! What sense is there in trying to make out that the Greeks are Vlachs and the Vlachs Italians?"

"Latins," Nikos corrected him without looking at him.

"What Latins, Nikos, for God's sake? When did we ever hear of Latins? The propaganda used to tell us we were Rumanians and made us furious."

"Then what do you think we are?"

"How do I know what we are? We're Greeks."

"So you think we're Greeks?"

"Come on, Nikos! Just between us, aren't we? Well, for the sake of old mother Rome, let's say we're slightly mongrelized Greeks."

"Then why do we speak Vlach?"

"How should I know?"

"Well, the fact is we do speak it."

"Then we're Vlachs of Thessaly, Vlachs of Macedonia and all the rest. How did we discover Rumania, or Latinia? When did we ever hear of Rome before?"

He laughed. "Where does that mother of ours hang out? Around Trikkala? Around Volos? There's no end to the mysteries of life!"

Nikos turned to look at him. He wasn't laughing.

"Mysteries and betrayals," he said.

The words didn't bother Ropotikas, but the icy tone did.

"What do you mean?" he asked.

"Don't you realize that what you've just said is treason?"

"We were talking confidentially—just between ourselves."

"But walls have ears, as the proverb goes."

"I don't see any walls here," said Ropotikas. He was angry.

"We opened our hearts to each other. We're all alone. Completely alone!" he insisted.

"That doesn't make any difference. You denied and made fun of the ideas for which we are fighting. In other words you betrayed us."

Ropotikas was at a loss. He remained speechless and seemed to be frightened. Then he said vigorously, "I betrayed you! Who was it that smiled when I spoke about mother Rome?"

"I smiled in order to test you."

Ropotikas didn't understand what Manoussis was getting at. But he realized very well that his cold expression was not something just to worry about. It was deadly. He had the same feeling he used to have when he was up in the mountains and was surrounded by the sheriff's posse. Either he would get out of the trap immediately, or he was lost.

He dropped the reins and turned sharply, taking Manoussis by the lapels of his coat.

"You're a goddam liar!" he shouted shaking him hard. "You laughed because you don't believe in mother Rome, and I talked the way I did to see how you'd react and how you really feel. You're not getting away with any of your tricks. D'you hear me? D'you hear me, you old communist whore, or shall I bash your head in for you?"

The horse had stopped, the snow was falling faster, and as the oilcloth had slipped over the edge of the carriage, the flakes were coming down on them.

In his tired and frightened mind, Manoussis conjured up a picture of that moment as a third party might see it.

The grey and wet desert...A carriage standing abandoned on a road full of holes and mud...In the carriage two people full of hatred confront one another, almost on top of one another. In the cold and dank fog these two souls who could warm themselves by huddling together, freeze in the grip of their fear and hatred. The cold stabs them increasingly and the thin snow spatters them, as though preparing the shroud they deserve.

Such ideas never crossed the old brigand's mind. Straight and simple talk was all he knew. Now he was infuriated at the mistake he had made which had suddenly put him in a dangerous position, and he sought to repair the damage by shouting, by giving Manoussis a rough shaking up, and by threatening him with blackmail. He stopped shouting and shaking Manoussis, and glared at him in silence for a few moments, fixing him with his black eagle's eyes. He was still in a great rage.

But Manoussis' attitude began to change. He was smiling. Ropotikas was puzzled: was he scared, or what was he driving at now?

As soon as Ropotikas let go of him, he said, "You blockhead, can't you take a joke?"

"This is no joke!"

"Don't you understand, you idiot, that among us no one breaks away from the others, and no one can speak against another?"

Ropotikas looked at him, sullen and suspicious. "No I don't understand. Spell it out."

"It's very simple, Vassilaki. The Greeks and the Vlachs detest us. If they could, they would hang us today. Can we afford to start a quarrel among ourselves? It would be fatal."

"That's how it is," he observed, disgruntled.

"We're on top, but only because we have power and force behind us."

Ropotikas livened up again. "Ha! We've got power all right. And we'll keep it. We'll give them hell till they come crawling on their knees, those devil's bastards! Old Ropotikas knows what he's talking about!"

"Start the horse up again. We'll be late."

They advanced without speaking—the gig jolted them terribly. Nikos Manoussis broke the silence: "About the other danger—you told me you didn't discover anything. Have you tried again?" The 'general' grunted and gave an angry lash to his horse.

"Have I tried again? And how. But I can't find anything. My men saw some strangers go into some 'red' houses at night. They called me at once and I hurried to the scene. I got there at dawn. Nothing! You'd think the night had swallowed the strangers and that witchcraft had struck the villagers dumb. But, oh brother! What a beating we doled out!"

"And what do you make of it?"

"How should I know? Something's cooking. But not for us. For the Italians. If they were after us they'd come out in the open, just like the other clods did." After a while he continued, "It beats me! I can't understand it! Those who hide and those who roam about in the open are persecuted, hungry, with everything against them, yet they stand up straight and hold their heads high. How is that possible?"

Nikos turned and gave him a long, sorrowful, almost blank look.

"Why are you looking at me like that. It's the truth I'm telling. How do you explain it?" And he went on stubbornly. "And yet we haven't struck hard. We could have eliminated quite a lot and that would have taught the others a lesson. Elimination is the best method for bending bodies that stand up too straight and bowing down heads that are held too high. I wanted to get rid of five or six, but they didn't let me."

"Well now it may be necessary to eliminate one."

The old bandit suddenly brightened up and he said briskly, "Who? Tell me and I'll take care of him right away—tonight."

"Nikita Coletti."

Ropotikas pulled hard on the reins and the gig came to an abrupt stop. He looked at Manoussis in amazement. "I've heard of him. I don't know him. But that's one I refuse to eliminate, and what's more," he added stubbornly, "I won't let anyone else eliminate him." Manoussis remained unperturbed. "Colletti is fighting us," he said. "And there's something else. Do you remember telling me that you heard years ago that there's a cache at the monastery of St. Elias?"

"Yes, I remember. People said that at the time of the Macedonian struggle old Grandfather used to conceal weapons there."

"Well, that cache is not likely to be empty today. Who knows whether there are not two hundred, five hundred, a thousand rifles hidden there? If we find it we'll be able to hand in weapons to the Italians every day for weeks. With one operation we'll be riding high for a long time."

"So?"

"Two men at least must know the secret: the abbot and Nikita Coletti. If the one is eliminated it won't take much pressure to make the other talk."

"No, no," Ropotikas broke in, "I refuse to kill a Coletti. Name anyone else. Not him."

He struck the horse hard and the gig shot forward. Sullen and determined, he drove at full speed not caring about the jolting and the danger of his carriage breaking up. He might smash it, but so what? Of course what Nikos said made sense, but he was not going to break his pact with Grandfather. He was a man, wasn't he? Nikos Manoussis could no longer keep his eyes closed. He looked at the road ahead because he was afraid that at the speed they were going they would meet with an accident. The horse's hoofs, and the wheels of the carriage churning through the muck, spattered muddy water in all directions.

Nikos' eyes were wide open. They reflected all the greyness and the wet misery of that day, as they rushed forward on their fatal course.

As soon as they finished their work at Legion headquarters, he hurried to the little house he had recently rented. He felt tired, unwashed, needed sleep and was a trifle hungry, but he couldn't rest or wash or eat. He felt an imperative need to be alone, to think things through.

Everything was going better, and yet he himself felt worse every day.

The Legion was gathering strength, and the scare the general's interview had given them had burst like a soap-bubble.

The small group of dissidents continued its propaganda, but the majority conformed.

The fame of the Legion was spreading to other provinces and other cities, and from everywhere came offers of collaboration.

The Italian authorities were, more than ever, active on their side.

Their bellies were full while all the others went hungry.

The cheese production had not yet gotten under way because credit was lacking, but it was obvious that a solution would be arrived at with one of the banks. And even without the cheese, a tidy little flow of money was coming in. What with his law practice, and with the deals that were fixed for him, he was earning in a month more than he used to in two or three years.

It was true that the puppet-government in Athens had

changed the prefect and that the retired officer who had been appointed was in contact with the others. But they would either bend him to their will or else short-circuit him. This was the onlv obstacle and it was not too significant. Everything else was going well.

Even Katie's affairs which had troubled them for so long, had now taken an amazingly satisfactory turn. She would be married in Turin in two or three months and would become a great and wealthy lady. And she was happy.

So, what more did he want? Why was he so worried? What was the matter with him? Try as he would he couldn't find any reason.

Could it be the distant future, the eventual outcome of the war that bothered him? Nonsense! Such a question hadn't crossed his mind for months. Besides, only the other day the most competent officers of the Forli Division had proved to him with solid arguments that by autumn the Axis would win the war. At the most it might take one more summer. No, it wasn't the outcome of the war that preoccupied him. He didn't even think about it.

What then was wrong? All his life he had been looking for a great opportunity. Now it had come, he had seized it, and it was greater and better than any he had ever dreamed of. He was annoyed because he couldn't find the reason. He was always good at finding reasons when he set himself to analyse situations. Surely he was not losing his intelligence now. What could possibly be the source of his discouragement? For the first time in his life he felt that his mind had come to a standstill.

He sank into a vaguely pensive and enquiring mood, and began to recall, one after the other, the events and persons that had come into his life during the past two or three months. At one moment when his mind went to his old friends who now belonged to the group that was opposing him, he thought he saw a light slowly breaking through the thick fog around him.

Whenever he happened to meet those old friends of his in the street, or to follow what they were doing, he always found them united, determined, strong and almost gay. Only the other day, he had hidden behind a window-curtain to watch the Greek Independence Day thanksgiving service and see how it would go. A tremendous crowd had gathered in front of the church. When the service ended the crowd made way for the authorities to pass. The new prefect appeared, deliberately accompanied by the small group of Vlachs. They were all radiant. On the right hand of the prefect was that detestable fellow, Coletti. For the first time in months he did not wear his farm clothes. He was dressed as he used to dress before—better than anyone in Larissa or even in Athens. These must have been Parisian clothes, because the stores in Larissa and Athens did not stock such fine materials, such stylish Homburg hats, nor scarves of such quality.

Nikita's expression too had changed. It was not bored and melancholy, but showed gaiety, strength and determination. He no longer stopped but stood upright, chest forward, head up, a proud and free man. The rest of them had the same confident expression, as the crowd proceeded down the hill to the plaza.

Nikos remembered Ropotikas' remark that morning. Even that primitive man had noticed the attitude of these people. They hadn't enough to eat, their business was bad, and the bayonets were not on their side. The prospects for these people, and for the communists who were secretly active, were black indeed, and yet they did not appear to be discouraged, weary, or despondent. How could that be? He knew them well enough to know that it was ridiculous to attribute light-headed bravado to them.

So then? So then there must be something else. There must be. All of them must have some kind of truth working for them. And in addition to this, the small group of Vlachs had something more on their side: the respect and love of their fellow-citizens. He had neither truth nor love on his side. His banner was one of hatred and lies. What was worse was that the banner did not float over his enemies alone, but over everyone including his friends.

That morning in the gig, when he had cunningly tried to find out what Ropotikas thought about mother Rose, that was the lie in operation. Later when he had schemed to get him into his clutches by taking advantage of him, Vassilaki had reacted with violent hatred, forgetting all about their friendship and the *glenti* they had shared. So there was lying and hatred among the closest of comrades. Truth and love brought joy and strength to the others even while they were being persecuted, even when they were in misery.

The basic values and the symbols of himself and his friends, with all the power they wielded and its rewards, carried with them weariness, doubt, and distress. Thus the darkness which had clouded his keen sight parted, but the returning light revealed nothing but chaos to him.

''Damn their eyes!'' he swore. ''We've got to break them!'' He smote the table angrily with his fist. He began to walk up and down the living room, and his customary sarcastic smile returned to his lips. ''To hell with all this!'' he thought. ''Love and truth, lies and hatred! A lot of nonsense! A figment of my overwrought mind! If I don't look out I'll begin disintegrating in a welter of petty bourgeois narrow-mindedness!''

He stood still, his hands behind his back. He didn't know why, but his thoughts went unconnectedly to the shame he felt and the precautions he took on nights when he left the brothel. And indeed a man of his age and his position should be ashamed of going to a brothel. But what was he to do? Parties like the previous night's *glenti*, in company with so many people of that kind, were certainly no better.

He began walking up and down again. A new train of thought came to him. No, it was not truth and lies and all that stuff which had discouraged him. That was nonsense. In life the lie was supreme. There was not a man alive who didn't tell lies several times a day. What upset him was that everyone had cut him, and he had lost the company of his friends. What upset him still more was that his sexual habits had been disturbed. He would have to see to that.

He thought of Phoula. He had not seen her since that December night when she had fled, running from his office. And now he realized that he needed her physically and because he loved her. Phoula was a sweet woman. She was sensitive and cultured, delightful to be with. He had gone for so long without seeing her. Hadn't he realized that he missed her, that maybe she was the only one he missed in this difficult life of his?

He looked at his watch and saw that it was a few minutes past noon. The doctor would not be back yet and she must be at home. He called her on the phone and she answered.

"Phoula, my darling Phoula," he said. "Why have you disappeared from my life in this way? Why don't you ever come to me, why haven't you called me one single time?"

He got no answer and was anxious lest he might have called a wrong number.

"Who's there?" he asked.

"It is I, Nikos," she said in a very faint voice.

He spoke to her passionately, tenderly, sweetly. But she said nothing.

"Why don't you answer me? Why don't you say anything?" And with growing anxiety he went on. "Is there anyone in the room with you?"

"No, I'm alone. The child hasn't come home from school yet."

"Then why won't you speak to me?"

Still no answer. Then in a very soft voice, unusual for him he said, "Phoula, have you stopped loving me?"

"If I had stopped loving you, I could speak to you more easily,"

"And I love you too, Phoula, I love you madly!"

She didn't answer at once, but after a while, she said to him tonelessly, "You seem to be telling the truth. Never were your words and your voice so warm."

"It's because I love you and I want you terribly."

"Then why didn't you call all this time?"

He hesitated for he had no ready answer. He thought fast.

"I felt very bitter after our last meeting. You behaved as though you were leaving me for good. I was hurt, and at the same time I didn't know what you wanted. But you see, I can't bear it." Then more insistently he added, "I've got to see you. I am at my new house. Come as soon as it gets dark."

"No, no, impossible," she said. She seemed scared.

"Why? I do want to see you so much. You used to come to the office."

"Impossible, impossible!"

"Phoula, dear, I beg you."

"It can't be done, Nikos, it's not possible."

"Well, then, come to the office."

"Don't insist Nikos. I can't." Then with a change of tone she added quickly, "If you need anything, I'll be only too happy to help. Just tell me on the phone."

He replied somewhat harshly at first. "I don't need anything, I swear to you. Not a thing. It's your love, it's you I need."

Another silence. He waited a moment and then spoke again. "If I can't see you alone, then I might come this evening at dinner time to pay a call. At least I'll set eyes on you."

She replied sharply. "No, for God's sake, no! The doctor might do something to insult you. No, Nikos, it's impossible."

That abortion insult *him,* that washed-out creature? He felt like laughing, and at the same time he was getting angry. He restrained himself however, and said quietly, "In other words, Phoula...in other words we're not going to see each other again?"

"Yes we are, Nikos, we are," she said animatedly. "We shall see each other after this accursed war and occupation are over. Then we shall see each other. And in whatever condition you are then, however much you are persecuted, I'll always be at your side."

He laughed harshly. "I persecuted? Tell your friends who say those things that they are making a very great mistake, and they'll soon realise it." In a calmer voice he continued. "But let's leave all that, Phoula. It has nothing to do with our love, which is not only real but grows stronger every day. It will be so sweet to be together again When are we going to meet? Won't you change your mind?"

"If I do I'll call you," she said and hung up on him.

He put down the receiver and sat thinking.

"The beasts!" he said to himself. "The beasts! They are poisoning the whole world against us. Even Phoula who is melting with love. Castelleone is the only one who sees straight. They must all be arrested and shipped to Italy. At any rate they must be arrested."

He smiled sarcastically, he murmured to himself. "And together with the others sir husband must be arrested too so as to stop being a thorn in my side." Then talking louder to give himself courage, he said, "Go ahead, Nikos! You are clever, strong, and ambitious. Don't hesitate any longer over the proclamation. Circulate it and go forward toward the great goal. And for a little while more put up with the filthy brothel and Vassilaki's parties. Don't be stopped by silly nonsense."

Suddenly he stood up. If anyone who didn't know him were to have seen him at that moment he might have been taken for a madman. He stared fixedly before him, clenched his fists, and spoke in a loud voice. "Soul? Conscience? You don't exist. You are the creations of the cowardly petty-bourgeois, but at last science has exposed you. You are nothing but an electromagnetic vibration of our cells, and these are matter and can be handled. You are nothing!" And bracing his body and holding his head up high, he shouted wildly like a madman. "Nikos Manoussis, Prime Minister of tomorrow, all-powerful dictator of tomorrow, govern without fear and forge ahead!"

XI

Alexis' favorite horse, Pegasus, was at Pteliona.

In the first days of the occupation the Director of the Agricultural College had called Nikita in and said, "I have reason to believe that the Italians will seize all the animals in our stables. If our horses pass into private hands there is a good chance that they may not be noticed and, even if they are, they may be spared for fear of the bad impression it would make if they were confiscated. I have decided to entrust them to people who will take good care of them until such time as they can be safely returned. In the meantime I've arranged with my staff to say that our best horses were stolen during the bombings. The best horse of all is Pegasus, and our dear friend Stournaris loved him very much. I am asking you to take Pegasus."

He had left the College with the proud grey stallion and Pegasus had become the pride of Pteliona. Everyone living there was fond of him. Nikita adored him and always took him when he went out on the plain or paid a visit to St. Elias.

Nikita was not a very good horseman. The riding-parties at the homes of his rich friends in Paris had been contrived and tame affairs: the horses were quiet, well-trained, and mature. They were good-looking and graceful, and ran around the corrals or along the private riding trails as though they were performing a service the details of which had been planned with care. Naturally that type of riding had nothing in common with the horsemanship to which Pegasus was accustomed.

This six-year old still had the cold winds of England and the scorching *hamsin* of Arabia in his veins, legacies of his forebears. In his nerves and sinews he had all the spirited liveliness of Greece where he had been born and bred. Anyone who rode him sensed at once that he was asking for thrills—speed, jumps, rearing up on his hind legs. But he was disciplined, and showed it even when the rider gave him freedom. And he was an intelligent beast, quick to understand what was required of him; he was sure-footed and never stumbled. For all these reasons it was a delight to ride him.

This master was a good man. Of course he was not as good as the other one and, above all, did not ride as surely and boldly. But he smelled like him, was kind, and from his eyes, his mouth, and his whole body there came a warmth which reminded him of the warmth of the other. Pegasus loved him.

Now Nikita had him saddled and held him by the bridle as they started out, Pegasus prancing gaily at his master's side. They came to Mourayias' cottage and Nikita called out to Phrosso. She appeared at the window and he imagined that he saw her blush, but he decided that she had probably only been startled at seeing him suddenly in the gathering dusk.

"Where on earth are you going with Pegasus at this hour?" she said.

He glanced furtively to either side, and she realized that this was no time for banter.

"What's the matter?" she asked. "Don't be afraid to talk. Nobody's around."

"Something's going on, but I don't know what," he replied. "One of the three monks at St. Elias just came over with a message from Father Modestos who wants me to go up there now without fail. All three brothers are out foraging for food. They're running out of supplies and having a difficult time. Does Father Modestos just want me to keep him company, or is he organizing something—some special meeting, maybe? I don't know. But I feel I have to go."

"Of course you have."

"If anyone turns up here asking questions, say that I went over to buy some clover, since our grass is almost gone and we have very little feed left for the animals. Say I was probably delayed and it was too late for me to ride home tonight—and you don't know when I'll be back."

"By the way, it wouldn't be a bad idea if you did get some clover. We need it anyhow."

"Yes, I shall, and tomorrow or the next day I'll go and bring it in. I want you to tell the same story to everybody here. We two alone know the reason why we have to be very cautious about our contacts with the old abbot."

It was not for the reasons he had imagined that Father Modestos wanted to see him.

"My son," he told him as soon as he arrived. "My monks have no idea of the existence of the crypt. We have here a lot of weapons hidden in the monastery now. You and I must get them into the crypt, and they will have to be sorted out and stacked carefully in order to fit in. There is a quantity of arms and a lot of ammunition too."

"What if someone comes along?"

"Oh, the outer wall is very high. I'll bar the doors and let the dog out in the courtyard to warn us."

You say the monks know nothing about the crypt, but they do know about the guns."

"Yes."

"But then, won't they ask what's happened to them?

"Yes, and I don't like it, although I trust all three of them. They may suspect that your presence here tonight has something to do with the disappearance of the weapons, but what am I to do? All day yesterday two strangers were wandering about on the hill. I don't know what they were after. Maybe nothing, but it's best to be careful. I don't want anything to happen to the monastery or to the arms—they'll be safe only in the crypt, and I haven't the strength to carry them alone, to go up and down those steep steps so many times."

Nikita smiled. The abbot noticed this with some anxiety and maybe a touch of displeasure.

"What's the matter, my son? Don't you agree?"

"Of course I agree, Father. You have very wisely thought of everything, and I'll carry down anything you want. I smiled because here you are collecting weapons, and I remembered what you told me last time I was here—that they will be needed in the hour of rebellion. In other words, you the man of God and of brotherly love, are preparing for killings as you did once before. I have often smiled at the thought that priests of the same religion but differnt nations bless the arms of rival combatants in the name of the same God. Once I didn't believe in religion and God. But faith came to me in Albania when I stood face to face with death. But even now when I have come to believe in the supernatural, all this seems to me...well, strange, to say the least. I approve of what you are doing with all my heart. But what is strange to me is that the man who is this is you, whom I regard as a holy and wise man of God."

The abbot listened to him calmly and attentively. When he had finished he said, "You are quite right. For me, a conscientious priest, there is a problem when I gather and bless lethal weapons. I'll explain it to you some time, but not now. We have work to do. We must put away the arms."

They got down to work and toiled until midnight. The old man had collected an large quantity of weapons, for the most part taken from soldiers during the collapse of April and May, 1941. There were a great many rifles, light automatic rifles, some machine-guns, unopened cases of every kind of ammunition, and a number of hand-grenades. All the arms were well-greased and in excellent condition. It looked as though Father Modestos had been shrewd in his calculations because, when all the arms were carefully stacked, they fitted into the crypt with no room to spare.

When everything was in place, the hardest task remained to be done. With two heavy crowbars they struggled to move the long, narrow stone block and put it over the entrance of the crypt, where it lay looking like a piece of chiselled rock rooted in the earth.

As they were having something to eat after their labors, the abbot said, "It has often been asserted that historical causes have blended the Orthodox Church indissolubly with Hellenism. There is a lot of truth in that, and I know that many of our people feel that they are Greeks in the same degree as they are priests, and sometimes Greeks first and churchmen second. I too have a deep love for the nation, but whenever I have become involved in anything other than peaceful, I have never followed my sentiment; I have always followed the guidance of the Lord. And I have never gone forward without first receiving a message that the forces of good must strike down the forces of evil. War is bad, horrible, with its slaughter and destruction. But even more horrible is the triumph of evil. You said that it often happens that churchmen also bless the forces of evil. I know this and it grieves me deeply. These churchmen are led astray; they neither examine the facts nor their consciences to find the truth. With truth as their guide, they might find it necessary to oppose their own country, if necessary. I have not always been in agreement with my country and have not always prayed for everything it did. But my conscience has always agreed with its national struggles because we have never waged any wars that were not just."

"Are you sure, Father," Nikita said, "that you have never been led astray by your sentiment?"

"I'm quite sure," the abbot replied firmly. "The voice of the Lord has always spoken to me as I knelt on the floor of my church. Apart from the Albanian campaign in which we were defending our homes, what other wars did we fight, my son? We fought the wars of the 'Great Idea'. Now the 'Great Idea' is extinct. Its roots have been torn up, and the premises upon which it was founded have vanished. You are too young to have known the 'Great Idea'. Have you any notion of its mission and the vision that inspired it? We, who were few in numbers and lacking in strength, dreamed of liberating all our brothers around us and building a powerful and just state which would enclose within its boundaries all the lands inhabited and dominated by Greeks. The chosen people which speaks the language of the Gospels, almost in its entirety was to be included in one country with the Queen of Cities on the Bosporus as its capital. Whole generations of famous or humble men forgot their own troubles and anxieties and lived and toiled only for their enslaved brethren and God's State.'' After a pause, he continued with increased fervor in his voice. ''The periods of greatness, for the Greeks of today, Nikita Coletti, were the War of 1821, the struggle in pursuit of the 'Great Idea,' and the Albanian campaign.''

To Nikita the abbot's words came as a cool, refreshing breeze on a broiling summer's day.

''Father,'' he cried, ''do you believe that this war is as important as all that?''

''To me this struggle shines like a beacon over the progress of the Greeks. It resembles the War of 1821.''

Whether by conviction or to spur the old man on, Nikita, in high spirits, challenged his opinion.

''I don't think you're right, Father. This war is not like the War of Independence. Then the aims were different, the sacrifices were greater, and the duration of the struggle longer.''

''And yet the circumstances are similar. And I'm sorry Alexis is not here to hear this. He gave his splendid life for one of Greece's finest hours...Just think. In those days, after the fall of Napoleon, the fate of Europe was in the hands of the Holy Alliance, a combination of all the mighty of the earth. And they agreed with Turkey, then at the height of her power, that her subject-races should not be freed. And the slaves, weak, hungry, and barefoot, insisted nonetheless. They insisted, they fought, and in the end they carried all the great and powerful nations with them and brought the mighty empire of the Sultans to its knees. Two years ago, in 1941, two mighty powers over-ran Europe. All the nations of the continent, helpless, enslaved, and discouraged, submitted to their yoke. No one resisted any longer. But at this very time, the selfsame people of the war of '21, the Greek people, comparatively few, hungry and barefoot, almost as it was then, stood up and said 'no' to those who humbled and enslaved all those other nations...And the Greeks were victorious for six whole months...A beacon, Nikita, a shining beacon as bright as the beacon of '21. And as that beacon illumined and inspired our hearts for more than a century, so this one will light our path for a long time to come.''

The flickering flame of the lamp cast a feeble light over the abbot's cell. But the old priest's face shone with an inner light of intense spiritual strength.

Nikita was deeply moved as he drank in the old man's every word. Spontaneously, as if he were doing the only natural thing the moment called for, he slid from his seat and knelt before the priest and kissed his hand. Lifting his eyes, with arms on high, the abbot prayed: "Lord of the Powers! Lord I pray Thee, vouchsafe that two souls that have been received in Thy kingdom may look upon us and hear us; the soul of my honored father, the lord Nikita, and the soul of my beloved child, Alexis. Lord, Lord, we pray Thee, hear the supplication of Thy humble servants Nikita and Modestos!"

The old man lowered his arms, took the young man's head in his hands and kissed him on the forehead. Then he wiped his eyes and got up.

"Well, enough of that," he said. "In this difficult time we must be strong. We have a great and hard task to accomplish. We have to set in motion a new 'Great Idea.' "

"How is this possible?" Nikita asked in surprise.

"I don't mean the same one. Another. When we are liberated we shall work toward the making of the 'Great Idea' of the soul and the intellect. That will come to pass one day in Greece. I'm sure. I'm quite sure of it. Let's get to bed now. You'd better leave early tomorrow."

He woke him up as dawn was breaking. "You must go before the sun comes up, but first I have something to say to you."

Once again they sat by the fireplace in the abbot's cell.

"I told you yesterday, my son, that in all the moving experience that came my way I was guided only by the great light of God. In following His light there was one instance when I deviated from the narrow rules of the Church and brought great sorrow to a dearly beloved person, sorrow so great that I may have caused him to abandon prudence and go to his destruction. I want to tell you about this."

Nikita was embarrassed. Whatever it was, it obviously weighed heavily on the old man's heart. Why should he take him as a confessor? Why should he humble himself? Nikita did not want this to happen.

"Father," he said, "don't tell me. This is something that

grieves you deeply, and I don't want you to tell me."

"No, my son," Father Modestos replied calmly. "I don't want to tell you this in order to relieve the burden on my heart. There is no weight on my heart, because what I did, I did guided by the Great Light. And when that lights the way, one doesn't feel any burden afterwards for anything that may happen, not even for the worst misfortune." He paused and looked earnestly and intently at Nikita. Then he continued. "I want you to know what I'm going to tell you for two reasons. First because it concerns the most dearly beloved of all my children, one who has departed into the bosom of the Lord, and secondly because you now are living very close to the other person concerned. You must be told. You must."

Then he related the conversation he had with Alexis on St. Mary's Day in 1940, when he dissuaded him from marrying Phrosso.

His body ached from the previous night's effort. He was tired because he was no longer accustomed to late hours and had slept badly; but he had to go to the clinic that afternoon.

The meeting had been arranged several days earlier and there were matters of importance to be discussed. They were to debate once more their reply to the proclamation, and that was indeed a very important subject. The proclamation had made a bad situation immeasurably worse. From the day they had gone before the general, the situation had steadily deteriorated.

For many days their letter of thanks had not been published; then suddenly it was printed in all the papers in a prominent position, in large print. Instead of the names of the six signatories, those of the whole group had been inserted, and the text of the document had been altered unscrupulously. It read that "all the nationalites which lived under the general's jurisdiction would enjoy his protection." and instead of strengthening their movement it weakened it. It was the Italians themselves who had given the altered text to the papers with the strict injunction that it was to be published without the change of a single word.

They tried to protest but they were refused a hearing. After some days, three of them were summoned to appear at the Second Bureau of the Forli Division. Lieutenant-Colonel Pazzi, looking especially at Nikita, spoke to them politely but in no uncertain terms. He told them that they had to search for and deliver arms. If they succeeded better than the Legion, the role of the Legion would decline. But if they didn't hand over weapons, "their fate would be decided by their resistance to other measures." They had replied that they did not associate with people who possessed weapons, and consequently had not handed any in.

From that time on, the attitude of the Italians had become more hostile. Giulio Vianelli had disappeared without saying goodbye to any one, and nothing more had been heard of him. The raids on the villages had multiplied and had become more savage. More frequently than before people were strung up by their hands or feet, and often straw was ignited under them. Terrorism was rampant in the plain and, out of fear or broken by torture, many were putting their names down for membership in the Legion. The new prefect treated them well but had no power, and the Italian authorities worked secretly against him.

The cheese industry was the one area in which things did not go well for the Legion. Legionaires and Italians scoured the sheep-farms, sometimes beating the farmers, but little milk was forthcoming. The quantity was so inadequate that cheese could not be made. There was no money for the smallest amount of credit, so the business failed to get off to a start.

But if, perchance, some farmers were lucky and got paid, general conditions were getting very much worse. The morale of the people was sinking and the small group of patriots found themselves helpless to stimulate reaction.

And now, on top of all these troubles, there was the proclamation. This was triggered by three courageous articles, denouncing the Legion openly, which appeared in a Volos newspaper. For a time men's hearts were uplifted and a current of patriotic fervor ran through them. The author of the articles was sent to prison for a short term, the paper suspended temporarily, and then the matter was forgotten.

But forty-five days later, on April 2, the Legion published a reply. It was the first public formulation of the great betrayal. It stated that the Vlachs were pure-blooded Latins and that they had always had their eyes fixed on mother Rome and on their brothers across the Adriatic and the Danube, that 'the wings of the Roman Eagle were once again spread over the whole world' and the the Greeks should be sensible and work with them. There was more in the same vein.

The document was signed by Diamantis,as Commander of the Vlachs of the Balkan Peninsula, by several others representing the Vlachs of neighboring countries, and by about forty Greek Vlachs. The latter gave their professions in Italian and italicized their names: Avvocato: *Nico Tullia Manoussi;*Dottore: *Costa Naha*; Professore: *Giorgio Caloianni,* and so forth. Two colonels and one major of the Greek army supplied their ranks in Italian.

Surely it was not possible that all these men had signed. Diamantis and Manoussis must have appended the names of men who were absent or of others who would not have the courage to protest. And so it turned out. The alleged signatories said secretly that they had known nothing about the proclamation, but in the meantime the damage was done.

People became increasingly indignant, but they were afraid. The Legion, they realized, must feel secure and very powerful to dare to publish such a proclamation.

The group of patriots had to do something to raise the morale of the people. Moreover, action must be taken for another reason: it was the first time that so many intellectuals and proffessional men had allegedly signed a public statement that the Vlachs were not Greeks but Latins. From an international standpoint, if the statement remained unchallenged, there might be serious consequences for the future. It was their duty as patriots and as intellectuals to counteract the effect of the weaker colleagues with a strong declaration of faith. Such an act would actually obliterate a declaration extorted by force since it would be performed in defiance of the enemy's power.

That afternoon they all gathered at the clinic. Nikita had already made a draft of a proclamation replying to every point advanced by the Legion. The traitors were branded for their betrayal, and the faith of the patriots was proclaimed in words which ended with the phrase: "We were born Greeks and Greeks we shall die."

Everyone agreed that their reply should be impressive, and they found Nikita's text excellent. But the meeting broke up without a decision.

If they gave their declaration to the Division it might have an historical value, but it would never reach the public. If they submitted it to the papers, it would never be published. If they printed it in pamphlet form and circulated it themselves, they would first have to overcome the difficulty of finding a willing printer and, secondly, they would all be arrested. Their followers would lose their leaders and suffer all the more at the hands of the terrorists. Some proposed that the declaration should be delivered to the prefect and the mayor as a matter of record; others suggested that they organize a demonstration, to which the objection was made that the Vlachs in Larissa itself were very few and, of these, very few would dare to show themselves?

Since they could not agree, they decided to meet again. The same difficulties arose at the second meeting, and after much discussion Hadjipyrrhos remarked, "We don't seem to be getting anywhere, and the matter is a very serious one. Either we shall have to split up and each one of us go it alone as he thinks best, or else, if we are to continue to act as a group, we must widen our circle. So far we have been right in taking action by ouselves as a group of Vlachs, but now it is in the interest of everyone to fight treason. We must address ourselves to non-Vlachs as well. So let's find out what the other doctors, lawyers, and property owners in Larissa say. After that we can decide whether or not it will be necessary for us to resort in individual action."

They agreed, and one of the group added, "I don't see why we need be in a hurry to deliver our reply or why we need answer them at all. Let them proclaim whatever they want. We refuse to submit. Our behaviour is our reply."

Then Thanassis Phassoulas, a sturdy, well educated stock-breeder, who was well liked and respected in the community, said, "It seems to me that the most important thing at this moment is for us to tackle the cheese question. The people at the Legion are beating their brains out trying to get money. They are threatening the Agricultural Bank and the other banks in town, and I hear that they are hopeful. If they find somebody to finance them, they'll get somewhere. This will bring them great prestige with the masses and put a lot of money in their pockets. This is the first thing we've got to hit. Because it speaks louder than words, which are alright to let off steam with or for diplomacy about which we know nothing. The cheese business is something every stock-breeder understands—it hits him in the pocket." Phassoulas was a man who liked to joke, so he added in a mock-Vlach dialect a phrase to the effect that 'business was business, and proclamations were for the birds.'

And that evening, too, they parted without having come to a decision.

Nikita returned home after nightfall and was surprised to find Dr. Vaidis waiting for him at Mourayias' cottage.

Tall and sallow, his horn-rimmed glasses disproportionately large on his thin, bony face, the man was an object of pity as he stood there wrapped in his heavy overcoat. In the dim light of the oil-lamp he looked frightened and sick. He asked that they be left alone.

"I saw you passing in front of my clinic. If anyone asks questions say that you went in to tell me that Phrosso was suffering from sharp abdominal pains. It would be natural for you to call me since I'm a gynecologist and an acquaintance of yours. I've spoken to Phrosso. The man who drove me here can be trusted."

He smiled timidly, and it was evident that he didn't know how to begin. Nikita felt sorry for him. He had heard about his wife's affair with Nikos Manoussis. He wondered whether anything had happened,, whether the doctor wanted to speak to him about that. He said to him warmly, "I'm entirely at your disposal. I shall be very happy to help you in anything I can."
"No thank you, Mr. Coletti," he replied shyly. "I'm not in need of anything. I came to offer... I wanted to tell you...you are fighting a good fight. I know that you are, how shall I put it—the most liveliest one in the group. You haven't any relatives or close friends here. I see that things are getting rough.That terrible proclamation...I think...in my opinion...this means that they are changing their tactics. And they are determined, unscrupulous criminals."

He paused and hesitated to continue. Nikita listened to him attentively, and the pity he had felt for him was changing to a feeling of irritation because he began to suspect that he may have come to warn him to be more careful. He wondered whether he was motivated by fear or whether his wife had put him up to it.

Nikita broke the awkward silence by saying coldly, "I am well aware of the kind of men they are, and I agree with you that they may be changing their tactics. But what do you expect us to do?"

"Oh, nothing, nothing. Go on resisting them even more forcibly than before. I mean to say...No, I'm not the one to give you advice. You must do as you think best."

He appeared to be making a great effort, and he went on. "This is what I wanted to tell you. Nikos Manoussis used to be a close family friend of ours. We have severed all relations with him, but people don't know this. They think we are still friends. I am a weak and sickly man and, apart from my work, I have no interests. I have never been involved in anything, and so no one is suspicious of me, and no one will interefere with me. So, I want to tell you, if ever you find it necessary to hide anything, or if you should have to go into hiding yourself, my house would be the safest place and it will always be at your disposal."

Nikita remained speechless.

"My clinic too is safe enough, but still a lot of people go in and out. My house, I think, might be considered the safest hiding place in all Larissa."

Nikita could hardly keep the tears back from his eyes. Tears did not come to him easily and he was disturbed by his unusual emotion. In his troubled state of mind, and in the tremulous light of the lamp, the doctor seemed to have changed. His ugliness and his sickly aspect were gone. All Nikita saw was two eyes, very strange eyes, filled with fear and courage, humility and pride, and with a steadfast flame. Nikita got up, and as the doctor rose too he seized his hand.

"Doctor..." he said. "Doctor..."

He wanted to thank him, but the words would not come out. Impulsively, he put his arms around him, and the doctor returned his embrace. The two men stood locked in each others arms, the tears streaming from their eyes, and not a word was spoken.

When they went outside, the doctor spoke for the coachman to hear: "You were right to call me, but don't worry; it's nothing serious. The girl will be all right."

"She's like a sister to me, and I was alarmed by those sharp pains."

"It's nothing. Just woman's troubles." And then, in a different tone of voice he added, "Many times, Mr. Coletti, a sharp pain brings about a salutary reaction in the organism. I hope you never experience this, but it's true. And don't forget what I recommended."

Nikita stood by the gate and watched the carriage as it vanished into the night. A breath of spring air brushed his cheek. Unconsciously, as though searching to see where that fresh and fragrant caress came from, he gazed into the night. What he saw was an infinite expanse of murky blackness and, in the distance where Mt. Olympus stood, he noticed a star which twinkled in the unfathomable gloom of the sky. It seemed to him that this star illumined the doctor's carriage in some mystical way, and that he could catch a glimpse of it, although all it was now was an insignificant dot in the deep gloom. It seemed to him that all the darkness in all the world was striving to extinguish the small twinkling star, but did not succeed in doing so because it was determined to cast its radiance on something beautiful lying hidden in the impenetrable blackness of night.

XII

The Legion Headquarters at No. 6 Athanasios Diakos Street were inundated every day by a rowdy mob, but on this particular morning an unusual quiet reigned. Conversation was carried out in hushed tones, and several of those present went out onto the sidewalk where they walked up and down, smoking nervously. They had been cowed into silence by their 'general' who had come out of the committee-room in a furious temper and had bellowed at them to shut up. There was a serious discussion going on inside, he said.

Present at the meeting were Diamantis, Manoussis, Ropotikas, the most dynamic members of the central organization, and forty trusted representatives from the districts of the province—one from each district.

"Things are going well," said Diamantis. "Very well. Most of the people are joining and the rest are beginning to waver. I didn't expect them to swallow the proclamation so easily."

"Have they really swallowed it?" one member said.

"The only thing they have done is to ask all the signatories to deny that they signed. Apart from one out-of-towner not one dared to make a denial. And I ask you, is that resistance to such a blow? Its been over two weeks since the proclamation was issued. Are these the so-called heroes, the lions? And they don't say a word?"

"Let's wait a while," Manoussis remarked. "They may reply to us one of these days."

A man from Tyrnavos spoke. "That was a good proclamation. It has cowed them all. But I'll tell you one thing, If they publish a haughty reply, it will create a greater impression than the proclamation itself. It will show that they still dare to hold up their heads."

"Don't worry," Diamantis answered with conviction. "We've taken all the necessary measures. They can't get anything printed in a newspaper, they can't circulate pamphlets because we control the printing establishments in all the towns in the plain. We've also got other secret weapons, which it's best not to divulge."

"We don't want to know about these. You do what you think best, Leader," one man said.

"And a champion leader he is too!" another exclaimed. "Fine, fine. He's absolutely right. We couldn't be doing better."

But another member, who seemed out of sorts and sat with a stern, unsmiling expression on his face, was of a different opinion. "Damn it all! Are we going to tell the truth, or are we going to kid ourselves with lies?" he asked.

They all turned to look at him. He was known as a serious and strong-minded man.

"Who is telling lies?" Diamantis asked coldly.

"I don't know who's telling lies, but I know that things are not going well for us. The people don't want to have anything to do with us, but they've been intimidated into submission. There's one way, and one only, by which we can impose ourselves and that's the cheese business. If that fails we'll be the laughing stock of the town."

Nikos Manoussis replied sarcastically. "We have set a great enterprise in motion with a whole foreign army behind us, and you want to put all this into a cheese-churn?"

"Look here, Nikos," the man said angrily. "I don't know anything about great schemes. Proclamations and all that guff are for you pen-pushers. They don't impress the little people. Where there's nothing to give there'll be nothing to take. Today the little people have their eyes on the churn. For months we've been saying in the villages that we would be buying the churn. And what have we managed to do so far? From all sides we take in nothing but dribbles, and it's only our own milk that we give out, and that too without getting paid for it. The others are all laughing at us and we're the ones that are being fooled worst of all because we're giving our milk away for free. We're sunk."

"We'll sell the cheese and you'll get paid." Diamantis said.

"A likely story!" the man said angrily.

"You've a right to complain, but we are going through a difficult period. That is my principal reason for calling you in today. What do you want me to do?"

"To find money. A little money, anyhow, so that we can make a down-payment for a month, or two weeks at least. What the hell good is a Principality and a Legion which can't pick up a little money? Where is our power, since the Agricultural Bank and all the other banks—even Vassili's bank—are resisting us."

"He doesn't own the bank." Manoussis said stiffly. "He's asked for authorization to lend a hundred million drachmas to the merchants, and I hope that he'll get it. However, I must tell you that the news got out and Coletti, on behalf of the opposition, went to see Vassili and asked him if he had reported to the central offices that the money was to go exclusively to the Legion's cheese producers, and also if he had explained what the Legion was. Vassili answered him that the money was for a sound commercial enterprise and that was all that interested the bank.

But Coletti was rude to him, and his uncle is the governor of the bank. How do I know what he may write and tell him?''

''How can he reach him?'' Diamantis asked. ''We control the telegraph and post offices, and it won't be easy for him to find a special messenger.''

Kopotikas moved in his chair and coughed. He wanted to say something. His black top-boots were brightly polished, he was wearing new clothes, his freshly died mustache was waxed and curled up at the ends, and his eagle eyes glinted in his coarse and heavy face. His air of authority made him stand out among those present.

''Everything is going fine,'' he said ''I see it wherever I go. But I also see that the cheese production is not doing well. We depend on it for our success and security. The trouble is that if we don't do something about it now, immediately, we've lost the deal. We're almost at the end of April. In a month, at the latest, half the sheep will be out on the mountains. The others which remain on the plain will go dry in two or three months. The opportunity is slipping away from us. If we miss, it won't come back.''

Coldly sarcastic, Manoussis said, ''You're the great military chief, why don't you seize it? You wield your sword. Go ahead and force the breeders to hand over their milk.''

The Legion's 'general' was greatly annoyed.

''Whatever I have to seize, I seize. I don't set traps. I haven't any. In this case money is the trap. Are we going to lose the game for a few pennies, for money? Vassili has got to hand it over.''

''Without authority from the central office?''

''To hell with authority. What authority? Who needs the central office? Vassilaki, when Coletti approached my brother?''

''I don't know and I don't care.''

''Well, you should care and you'd better find out. He was coming out of the bank when he met you in the plaza and gave you hell and spat on you.''

The old brigand chieftain stood up and stamped his foot on the ground. ''He never told me to go to hell! He didn't spit on me!''

Some of the others started in on him.

''We heard something. What happened?''

''Did he really spit on you, Vassilaki?''

''Gosh! Did this happen right in the plaza?''

''And you mean to say you didn't beat him to a pulp?''

Diamantis banged his fist on the table. ''For heaven's sake, shut up! Calm down. Sit down, Vassilaki. Tell us what happened. I did hear of an incident, but I didn't know it occurred in the plaza and that he spat on you.''

Ropotikas was enraged. ''He never spat on me. He never spat on me.''

''Listen here, Vassilaki. We want to help, We're not making accusations. Tell us quietly what happened. Then we'll see what we'll do.''

Ropotikas was embarrassed. He held his knees in his hands, coughed two or three times, and spoke with his eyes on the floor. ''I was in the plaza, in the corner near the bank talking to Doulas. A peasant came up and interrupted our conversation. 'Mr. Doulas' he said, 'I've been waiting for an answer. Are you or aren't you going to give me that hay?' I got angry and told him, 'Shove off, you!' I couldn't believe my ears when he answered back. 'I'm talking to the gentleman', he said, 'I wouldn't think of talking to you, you old bastard!'

''I got mad as a Turk. I lifted my stick to break his skull, but Doulas caught it, and I heard him say, 'Mr. Coletti, go away, please go away.' I looked at him. He was the spitting image of old Grandfather. I lowered my stick.'' Ropotikas stopped. He did not lift his eyes from the floor.

''What happened after that?'' Diamantis asked. ''Tell us the whole truth, Vassilaki. You are our general. We must know everything if we are to decide what to say and what to do. You're among friends.''

He looked askance at Diamantis, glared at Manoussis, and dropped his eyes again as he continued. ''My heart softened, I laughed, offered my hand and said, 'I'll be damned! So you are the Old Man's grandson!' He looked at me with hatred and said, 'Down with your paw! I don't want to dirty my hand.' ''

''How do I know whether there were any people? Somebody may have been passing by. But I didn't let him get away with it. I answered back, 'Your grandfather who was twice as big as you used to shake this hand.' 'Today he would cut it off,' he replied. 'He shook it then because you were a different man.' "

Ropotikas stopped again. The Leader insisted gently, "He must have said something more than that."

"He added this. 'In those days you weren't a traitor.' I got angry and shouted: 'I'm the same man. I haven't changed.' Then I pointed with my stick in the direction of Trikkala and said in a loud voice for all the hear, 'I always looked toward mother Rome. We Vlachs have always looked toward mother Rome.' He glared at me again with hatred and shouted back, 'Both you and the Vlachs like you never looked toward anything but money.' He spat on the ground and went off. He spat on the ground, not on me."

An uproar greeted his last words. Almost everyone in the room was shouting.

"And you mean to say you didn't crack his skull, Vassilaki?"

"We've been made fools of in public."

"What do you mean, he didn't spit on you? It's as if he did."

"To think that we have to swallow such an insult!"

"Some general we've gotten ourselves!"

"An insult like this cancels out ten proclamations!"

Diamantis and Manoussis were silent. With some anxiety they followed the discussion, and became alarmed when Ropotikas really exploded.

His eyes flashed and his every movement seemed to be imbued with a dynamic energy. He leaped to his feet, stamped his foot on the ground, gestured wildly with his hands, punching the air in front of him and right and left, and let out wild inarticulate howls. He sounded like a wild beast at bay, and flayed the air with his hands. He would not stop shouting. His eyes blazed and it was evident that he wanted to impose silence in this manner.

The leader whispered to the Prime Ministers.

"The son-of-a-bitch is some actor."

"More like a professional wrestler. But he's wild and he may do some harm."

The rest of the group were silenced by the bandit chieftain's maniacal outburst. When they were quiet he said to them threateningly, "It's all my fault for telling you things that none of you knew. And you have the gall to tell me that I have made you look ridiculous! Without me you'd be beating the air. Who was it, you fools, who built you up an army which is now the terror of the plain? Who was it who collected so many weapons that the Italians are coddling us? You all need educating. Well, you'll get your education from me. You call me a general. Very well then, I'll become a real general. I'll take my boys and found a Legion of my own."

He noticed tha Diamantis and Manoussis exchanged anxious glances; he also noticed that the others were not pleased by his words, and he got up to go. At the door he delivered his parting shot. "We'll see which Legion has the real power and which one the Italians will support! Mine which makes fools of you, or yours with its white collar dummies who have nothing but fresh air to sell!"

Diamantis jumped up to stop him. He threw his arms around him, flattered him and assured him that their indignation was directed against Coletti, not against him. But Ropotikas was not easy to placate. "I'll go my own way," he shouted. "You're sore at me because you can't get the money to finance the cheese making. Well, OK. Forward! I'll collect the arms, you go out and get the money."

He turned to Nikos. "You there, you fake Prime Minister, you just get that brother of yours to cough up the cash. Who does he think he is, marrying his daughter to an Italian millionaire while people are laughing at us for giving our milk away for free?"

"He's right about that" one of the group muttered, "It's Vassili's duty to give us money."

Another cried out, "A loan. Why can't he make us a loan?"

"The money won't be coming out of his pocket."

"Put your foot down, Leader. Make him do it."

Ropotikas had calmed down. He had let off his steam and had directed the discussion just as he had wanted to. "What's come over Manoussis," he wondered. "We're good friends. We've been on so many binges together. Why is he trying to put spokes in my wheels now?"

Suddenly the reason came to him. "I'll be damned! He's

afraid of me! He's the Prime Minister, but I hold all the power, and I haven't realized it til now. He's terrified of me. That's it."

He plucked up his courage, and was about to start bellowing again in order to humiliate Manoussis, and to say that he would leave them if the money was not found within a week. However, all the others were shouting and, while the hubbub lasted, he thought of a crafty plan. He had great power, very great power. It wasn't in his interest to break with the white collar fellows who talked with the top Italians. He only had dealings with a few sergeants. He rarely came into contact with an officer and then it wasn't one of the higher ones. They might pull a fast one on him; they might turn him out. There were plenty of willing and sturdy mountain boys to choose from if they wanted to replace him as general of the Legion.

He indicated that he wanted to speak and everyone stopped talking. In a calm voice he said, "Nikos once said something very sensible to me. He said that there are difficult times ahead and that, whether we like it or not, we must avoid disputes. You insulted me without reason and I lost my temper. I'm willing to forget everything and join you in the uphill trek. In that long climb, the first obstacle to be passed is the money for the milk. So let's break up all these discussions and let the Leader and the Prime Minister go right now to find out what the hell can be done. They must go to Vassili first and then to the Division to tell them that they must put pressure on the Agricultural Bank, or else the Italians must give the money themselves."

As the two of them walked along, Diamantis said, "It seems that even the wildest of men can achieve political maturity. I never thought I would hear such conciliatory words from Vassilaki. There are the makings of a politician in the truculent brigand."

Nikos was silent, and Diamantis asked, "Don't you agree?"

As they approached the bank and Nikos replied thoughtfully, "No I don't. He is primitive, rough and wild, and is guided only by the instincts of the wolf and the fox. He has no political qualities. His attitude was prompted by some crafty calculation."

Diamantis stopped, clasped his hands behind his back,

looked Nikos in the eye, and observed, "If he wasn't sincere, if his remarks were prompted by cunning, then he's more of a politician than I thought."

"You're indulging in political philosophy," Nikos Manoussis said, trying hard to conceal the sarcasm in his words.

"I don't know what I'm doing, but I do know that if he doesn't believe what he said, he's up to something."

"Possibly."

"What could it be?"

"I really don't know. I can't imagine."

They took a few steps. The Leader stopped again. "We've got to get to the bottom of this. We've got to find out. It might be dangerous."

"With the power he's got in his hands, he not only might be, he is dangerous."

Diamantis frowned. "What do you mean by that?"

"Exactly what I said."

"No, you're leading up to something. First, you said 'it might be dangerous'—then you said 'he is dangerous. If you do believe he is dangerous and say so, you must be leading up to something."

"No, I just made an observation."

Diamantis took him by the arm. He was frightened. "For God's sake, Nikos, what are you hiding from me?"

Nikos felt a secret satisfaction. Diamantis had won him over by threats related to his communist past, and by false promises regarding the future. It did him good to be scared and worried now, cowardly show-off that he was. He threw him a cold glance.

"I'm not hiding anything form you," he said smiling enigmatically.

"Please, Nikos, please. You know something. That wild man is planning something. What is he up to? Who is he working with? What do you know about it?"

"I don't know anything."

"Well, what do you suspect? What do you suppose he's thinking of?"

"How do you expect me to know what a wolf is thinking of?"

"What are we going to do? We must do something."

"Beg for money." he replied coldly, "because your Principality is on the rocks."

They walked on in silence, each wrapped in his own thoughts. Nikos recalled the reflections that had come to him about a month ago, when he was alone at home after one of Ropotikas' binges...They were all enmeshed in hatred, suspicion fear and lies. And on the other side, the patriots had...

They had called the Second Bureau from the bank, and all the 'key' men were expecting them: Pazzi, the director; Bignoli, his deputy, and Castelleone, the hard-boiled ideologist of the Axis. They stated their problem, and explained its seriousness and the need for a quick solution. They pleaded with intense urgency.

The Italians listened to them with interest and sympathy, but Pazzi and Bignoli were not at all optimistic. What more could they do? They had already brought pressure to bear on the Agricultural Bank and had gone so far as to take part in discussions at the bank with the higher executives and representatives who had come from Athens. The Bank had produced all kinds of alibis. They had written to Army Corps Headquarters to bear down on the competent functionaries of the puppet government and of the banks. What else could they do? They had no authority to give orders.

At one point the Italians observed, "Why are you in difficulties? You have a bank of your own under your control."

They explained the situation. They said that one of the bank's principal shareholders was Coletti's uncle, and they related the details of Nikita's visit to the bank. In order to show the fanaticism of the opposition, they also mentioned the incident between Nikita and Ropotikas, doctoring the facts to make the latter come out a hero.

Castelleone asked to speak. "We shall have to deal with that gentleman, and the sooner the better. But as for the money, I think, Colonel, that we ought to find it. The Roman Legion is our creation. It is dear to us and valuable. Its prestige is in jeopardy. We must find the money."

"I quite agree. But how shall we get it?"

"Army Corps Headquarters can issue an order to the State Bank or the Agricultural Bank in Athens. In a pinch we could give orders to one of their branches here."

"My dear Captain, we should be exceeding our powers. We are the occupation army of a civilized country, and we have to abide by certain general rules. Italy's good name cannot be jeopardized."

"If I may be permitted to say so, Italy today is primarily concerned with the attainment of its objectives. And here the attainment of a great objective is being impeded at its outset by a matter of a few pennies. Are we going to lose the game because of a few insignificant regulations? If you will permit me, I should like to ask, if the Duce were to learn of this, would he allow our prestige to suffer? Wouldn't he order these subjects of ours, who now resist, to conform? He would break their ribs!"

Pazzi raised his hands in gesture of agreement. "Ah, the Duce, with his dynamic authority, would be able to do anything, I agree."

Castelleone replied coldly. "If we believe that that's what the Duce would do, then we have to do it too. But, another thought has just come to me. If none of us in Greece has the courage to act as he should, why shouldn't the Duce himself be apprized of the matter? He might even send the money from Rome, althought I find it outrageous that we should spend our good *lire* when we can lay hands on filthy drachmae locally."

I'm sure the idea would bring results," Bignoli observed. "But first, is it worth the Duce's while to go into such a matter himself? And, secondly, how can the matter be brought to his attention?"

He thought it over for a while. "It's a pity that when I go to Italy for my wedding it will be too late. But," he added with alacrity, "if I have your approval I can write to my father and ask him to mention the question to the Duce."

They all agreed and the two visitors were about to leave when Castelleone stopped them.

"Sit down for a moment, please," he said. "We have to talk about the case of that fanatical landowner, Mr. Coletti."

The two heads of the Legion portrayed Nikita in the worse possible light.

"I cannot conceal from you," Nikos Manoussis said, "that the members of the Legion are so enraged at him that I shouldn't be surpised if he met with a bad accident one of these nights."

"I'll never tolerate that," Pazzi said. "You must prohibit any violence."

"For heaven's sake!" Manoussis hastened to say, "It's not something we want. We're only afraid of what our men might do behind our backs."

"This has got to be prevented!" The Italian colonel repeated severely. "If anything happens to him I shall be obliged to hold an enquiry, and that will be very bad for us as well as for you. Mr. Coletti is a man of great prestige."

Nikos smiled. "He knows about fifteen or at the most twenty people around here. It is only his name that enjoys prestige."

"That makes a difference. There are other ways of neutralizing him. And I'll tell you something confidentially—for your ears alone—so that you can take the appropriate measures and help us. We have reason to believe that various secret organizations are being formed in Greece. One of these will address itself to officers and non-commissioned officers, while another is inspired by the Communist Party. We are going to smash this business at its very inception. We'll seize this occasion to arrest the reactionary Vlachs at the same time. Give us a few names."

After a brief pause, Manoussis told what he knew about the organizations and what had been done to discover them. He spiced his story with details of his own fabrication in order to appear well-informed. "However," he admitted, "we haven't been able to find out much as yet. They are extremely well organized and work in great secrecy. Arrests are the only means of neutralizing them. But I am sure that Coletti must belong to one of those organizations. He is a violent fanatic. And his ranch would make a good place for meetings and for concealing weapons. In my opinion, he should be arrested as soon as possible."

Pazzi turned to Bignoli. "Have we or the Roman Legion searched the ranch?"

"Not yet."

"The place is not to be searched and there is to be no surveillance because, as the ranch is so isolated, he will have time to protect himself. As soon as he is arrested you are to order a thorough search. Not before. If the slightest incriminating evidence is found, he is to be shipped to Italy with the others for summary court-martial."

He turned to Diamantis and Manoussis. "Our information is that he fought in the front line on the Abanian front and was awarded the Medal of Courage. What do you know about his war record?"

Again Nikos Manoussis answered, saying that Nikita had been ill and had not been drafted but that, nonetheless, he had volunteered and had fought in the front line.

"Do you know in what sector of the front he served?"

"I have no general knowledge. I only know that on the first day of your March attack, he held a key position with a single heavy maching-gun on the slope of hill 731 known as *Collina Monastero*.'

As soon as the name of the bloodiest battlefield in Albania was mentioned, the two higher officers turned and looked at Castelleone. At the same moment he stood up abruptly. His arms were taut, his fists clenched, and he took on a strangely hard expression. His eyes were wild like those of a madman. He started to talk and as he blurted out his remarks, he became more and more excited.

"No," he cried, "it was not the machine-gun alone. There were many automatic rifles, many guns. An extraordinarily great number of them. And they wouldn't stop firing! And yet on the first morning we fired one hundred thousand shells along a front of one kilometer. General Ganbara told me so himself. The heroism of our infantry was unbelievable, their spirit legendary. We had been reviewed the day before by the Duce himself. For all that, we could not make headway. We were stopped after the first few meters of our advance. The small ravine at the foot of the hill was filled with the bodies of Italian boys stretched out in their final sleep. On the seventh day of the battle this rugged slope with its sharp, jagged rocks, was covered with more bodies than stones! It was horrible! I cannot forget that terrible scene. It rises again before my very eyes!"

They all looked at him in startled sympathy.

"Calm down, Captain," said Pazzi. "After all you were the only one on the first day of the attack who was recommended for a Medal of Honor by the Duce himself."

Castelleone sank heavily into his chair. He was calmer but seemed tired. He began to talk again, quietly at first, but he whipped himself up into a frenzy as he went on.

"Yes, I commanded Gambara's own guard. In the early afternoon, the Duce alone and thoughtful, was eating lunch when Francesco Pricolo, Chief of the Air Force, came to tell him that all the reports were good.

"Mussolini was sullen, and didn't look at him, but said, 'The attack has failed. I was an infantryman and I know that an attack which does not attain its objectives in the first three or four hours is not going well.' I was next to them and heard it. Impulsively, I stepped forward, stood at attention and said, 'The artillery will shortly make new preparations. I command the First Company. On your orders I can take it out and we'll attack too. We'll reach the top of the hill. I can promise you that, Duce!' So we too attacked and we got half way up the hill...but only half way...it was too much...Out of all the company, I alone remained unscathed. Around me lay all my men, all my brothers, bathed in blood, all of them!"

He stood up again and shouted wildly. "But how did they manage to go on firing? How? The whole hill had been reduced to dust by our shells and we fired obstinately at their nests!...How did they do it? Their wounded men must have risen to fire at us, those we butchered just before they died, even the dead. Yes, even the dead must have been firing!"

It was difficult to tell if the drops on his face were sweat or tears. And it was difficult to tell whether it was out of shame or rage that he suddenly turned and left the room.

XIII

He awaited them at Pteliona with little enthusiasm. He was not looking forward to the meeting.

At first he had shown some interest in the affair, but later he realized that he had probably been mistaken in his original appraisal of it. Something lay beneath the surface and he didn't feel comfortable about it. Early in April, as he was buying a farm implement, Augustus Callaris had come up to him and said: "You fought in the war, you're prominent in Vlach affairs. You ought to belong to a secret society."

"What secret society?" he had asked.

"A liberation organization."

He had laughed. "Unarmed and cut off from the rest of the world as we are, how are we going to free ourselves? What can we do? Now that we are dying of starvation it seems to me that it is our duty to cultivate as much land as possible so that the hungry can eat."

He hadn't told the whole truth. He had received a message from his uncle Spyros in Athens to be ready to support some military organization. He had sent Nikita instructions and had urged him to act with the greatest secrecy in collecting weapons and ammunition for an uprising to take place one or two months before the landing of the allies. At the same time he had recommended the utmost caution and the avoidance of any untimely action which might increase the sufferings of a people who already had one foot in the grave.

Augustus Callaris had insisted. "Land cultivation is a duty, but the war is going on and we must do our share."

"But how is this possible?"

"There's a way."

"What way?"

"Are you interested?"

"Of course I'm interested."

"I want to entrust you with a great secret. Do I have your word of honor that you won't talk whatever happens?"

So the next day Callaris had come to Pteliona with another man whom he introduced as Kisavitis. Nikita didn't like him but he listened to him attentively. Kisavitis had told him that a nationwide organization had been formed under the name EAM, the National Liberation Front. Its headquarters were in Athens, but there would be local branches in every provincial capital, town and, eventually, village in Greece. These branches would enroll members. The purpose of the organization was to uplift morale, to give assistance to patriots, and to organize an army and guerilla bands for sabotage and armed resistance to the invaders.

"Great and difficult objectives," Nikita had remarked. "How do you expect the Germans and Italians not to get wind of the movement?"

They had discussed the project for some time, and Kisavitis had given him further information. Then he had said, "The local committee of EAM believes that it would be very useful if you joined, and they have sent me to invite you. You will be given an important position in the organization."

Nikita had shown some hesitation and had asked to see the charter. Kisavitis was surprised. Neither he nor Callaris knew of any charter. They had been approached by friends and, as it was an organization for liberation, they had joined. Nikita had insisted. Since it was a nation-wide organization with broad aims, it must have a charter, and if he couldn't study it there was no question of his joining.

Somewhat acidly Kisavitis had then said, "I shall report to my superiors. They will find your condition strange. It's the first time such a request has been made. However, we shall see. They may comply, because they very much want to have you."

He had given him a meaningful look and had continued, "They are counting on you for hiding-places for arms."

A cold shudder had passed over Nikita as he thought of Modestos and the monastery, but he had laughed. "If that's what they want me for, they are making a mistake. If they consider Pteliona to be a good hiding-place, that's all right. But I have no arms."

Nikita had laughed, but Kisavitis was serious when he replied. "If you become one of us, I'm convinced that you will provide us with good hiding-places and plenty of weapons."

Nikita had not relished this talk. It had made him suspicious, and his suspicions grew stronger after they had left and Phrosso had come in to see him.

"What did they want?" she had asked anxiously. "Do you know them?"

She knew them. Kisavitis was one of Notis' fanatical comrades, a man of lesser status in the organization.

"Be on your guard" she had told him. "Please, please take

care. Maybe they are patriots. Maybe there is a good side to their ideas, but they are hard and determined men. They will sacrifice anything to attain their objectives."

He had been startled by her intensity. He wondered whether it was induced by bitterness over her first love. He didn't want to probe further. But together they probed into something else—the innuendo about hiding-places and weapons—and they agreed that Father Modestos ought to be informed.

In order to avoid any suspicion that might arise if Nikita went to the monastery, he decided that Phrosso should go. She would take a little bottle of oil to light an offertory lamp at St. Elias. When Phrosso returned she had brought disquieting news. An unknown stranger, accompanied by a lawyer known to Modestos, had called on him and asked for weapons for a revolutionary organization. Modestos had pretended that he knew nothing, but the stranger had insisted and seemed to threaten him, for he had told him to take good heed while there was still time.

"The trouble is," the old abbot had said to Phrosso, "that they may know about the weapons from some of the soldiers who have given them to me. As for a hiding-place, they may suspect that there is one but they cannot possibly know." The old man had added, "One of my monks thinks that he recognized the stranger. He was one of those, he says, that was recently wandering around the monastery. Another monk who was with him at the time says it was Notis." This was bad news.

All this business had left a bad taste in his mouth and so, when one day Callaris handed him the 'constitution' of the EAM, Nikita was not too pleased to take it.

And now he was waiting for them, as arranged. Callaris and Kisavitis were to come with the 'high-ranking agent who had come from the city especially to see him.'

This man had a peculiar face. It was gaunt, frozen and bony. The forehead was high, the eyes and chin determined. It was difficult to decide at once whether it was attractive or repulsive. It was the face of a man who might be admired for his strength and intelligence and feared for a hardness that had the quality of steel.

As soon as they entered the living-room, the only well-appointed room in the house besides the bedroom, the stranger looked around with a searching glance.

"You have some nice pictures and furniture," he said.

"It's all that was saved from the old house," Nikita observed.

The stranger said nothing. He fixed Nikita with a look that seemed to register the contrast between the rich furnishings and the owner's peasant clothes.

As soon as they sat down the visitor said, "You don't know us and you don't even know our names. Augustus brought Kisavitis first, and now me, because we want to rent a part of Pteliona for cultivation. You asked for a rental of 40 percent of the produce, we offered 20 percent and went as far as 25 percent. That's the excuse for our presence here. If the Italians happen to come, what we say about ourselves is our business. Now for the purposes of our conversation, my name is Voliotis. You owe me a paper and an answer.

Nikita took a piece of paper out of his pocket and gave it to him.

"For the most part, I like it. It is very well drawn up. But there are some points which disturb me, and one in particular which makes me shudder."

"Your criticism will come later. Tell us first if you will join us."

"I think not."

"I am not sure that I understand you. Does 'I think' mean 'perhaps', or is it a French way of saying no politely?" Voliotis asked sarcastically.

"It does not mean 'perhaps'. It signifies a refusal. If my way of putting it offends you, I'll give you a straight no."

Voliotis was taken aback and withdrew his glance from Nikita. Was he dealing with a refractory person or could it be that Coletti was a 'disguised aristocrat' as a comrade familiar with Pteliona had told him?

"Until now, no one in Larissa has seen our constitution. You are the only one who has read it and yet you refuse to join us. That is irregular and dangerous."

"It is indeed irregular, because it would be right for all your members to be familiar with it. But it isn't dangerous."

"Let's not discuss it. Now for the heart of the matter. Why won't you follow us? Because of the constitution or for other reasons?"

Nikita did not answer at once. This inquisition annoyed him and especially the stranger's tone of reproof.

"You will pardon me, but it seems to me that you are questioning me as though I were under obligation to reply, as though I were a defendant." Changing his tone of voice completely, he added, "We have a particularly good mixture of roasted seeds; it is 10 percent of real coffee. Shall I tell them to bring us some?" Voliotis was silent.

"But it makes an excellent brew of coffee. And you're lucky. I have some cigarettes."

"We didn't come here for coffee and cigarettes. We came..."Voliotis stopped short for the door had opened and an old man stood on the threshold.

"Later, Mourayias," Nikita called to him.

"It is urgent."

"Later, later."

"Something's happened to Pegasus."

"Excuse me," Nikita said to his guest and rushed out.

When he got to the stable he found the grey horse standing firmly on its feet. It pawed the ground with its right hoof and gave out a slow whinny. Next to it stood Phrosso who looked frightened.

"Are you both crazy?" he said. "There's nothing wrong with the horse."

"Nikita, " she said in a trembling voice, "Nikita what have you gotten yourself into?"

"What are you talking about?"

"I saw the men that came. Do you realize who's in your house?"

"No. One of them I don't know at all."

"He used to be far higher up than Notis in the Communist Party. Now he may be at the very top. He's and extremely clever man, but he's beast, a wild beast."

Nikita paused for a moment before he spoke, then he said, "I suspected as much. He's a capable man, but hard as nails."

"What are you getting yourself into? Why are you doing this?"

He noticed her deep anxiety and he thought that there was love in her eyes. He was disturbed, and answered gently. "Don't be afraid. I shan't get involved."

She talked quickly, breathlessly, as though something were impelling her to speak fast and get her message out in time. "Mere contact with such people is in itself an involvement. You don't know what kind of men they are. For them friendship, love, human feeling only exist if they conform with their objective, for only their objective exists for them. In the face if that, everything else vanishes! It's completely gone. You would think that they have hearts and brains of stone."

She took his hand in both of hers. They were warm and they trembled. He felt her squeeze his palm and his fingers tightly, and a familiar, almost forgotten tingle ran through him.

"Take care, Nikita, I beg you, take care."

When he returned he found the two men seated at the table as he had left them.

"Please forgive me. That horse is our joy and our pride."

"The pride of the Agricultural College from which it was stolen during the bombings," Voliotis said with a thin smile. "Well, to get back to business, we did not come here for horses or for coffee or for cigarettes. We came for a matter of the greatest importance. In regard to your last remark, I will say that of course you are under no obligation to reply to my questions. I, for my part, seeing that I am addressing myself to a patriot and am asking him to help us in a great undertaking, must do my best to persuade you. That was the purpose of my questions. Do you refuse to discuss it in this context?"

His manner was gentler, the argument was reasonable, and Nikita felt that stubborness was out of place. He replied, "No, I won't refuse to discuss it."

'What was the point in our constitution which caused you 'to shudder'? I might be able to explain it to you."

"You say that when the country is liberated, the organization which you will have created in the meantime, and which will have fought the enemy, will seize the government in order to protect it against any kind of usurpation.''

''That is quite a natural provision. What's so strange about it?''

''And who will protect the government against usurpation by you?''

Voliotis appeared to be genuinely surprised.

''I don't understand. We shall be the People.''

''What if other revolutionary organizations are formed which also claim to represent the People?''

''That's impossible. We alone have given a wide popular base to our organization.''

''It's not impossible that others may make the same claim too.''

''Yes, they may make the claim, but they will never be able to give effect to it. The whole Greek Communist Party has already joined EAM, together with other large popular groups. Take this area, for instance. Augustus is not a Communist, neither are you whom we are inviting to join us.''

''Anyway, if another organization should make the same claims that you do you will clash with them.''

''Furthermore there are our forces abroad with the King at their head.''

An icy smile stole over Voliotis' lips: King, Metaxas, dictatorship...let's not talk about that mess. As regards the forces abroad, there is this to say. They fled and didn't have to endure the starvation, the slavery, and the revolt. What right have they to take over the government of the country when a nationwide organization with hundreds of thousands of members liberates it?''

''The country will not win its freedom alone. It will be saved by the issue of the general conflict in which the Greek forces abroad participate.''

''Without starving and without fighting.''

For an instant Nikita was at a loss. Then he said, ''What do you mean, without fighting? What about our destroyers, our airplanes, our army—are they not fighting?''

''Look here, Coletti. First and most important, they have no popular foundation as we have. Second, it is a very small army commanded exclusively by regular officers. We saw it in Albania: the regular officers don't fight. They capitulate."

Nikita had heard that myth before, he had read about it often, and it always infuriated him. "In what unit did you serve, and in what sector of the Albanian front did you fight?" He asked Volliots.

Voliotis was taken aback but he recovered quickly and said, "The illegal dictatorship didn't give me a chance to fight. I came back from abroad in the summer of 1940 and they arrested me at once. I was in prison."

"I was at the front," Nikita said with new zest in his voice. "In my unit not a single officer, regular or reserve, survived in the end. Non-commissioned officers had to take over. Listen here, Voliotis, at the front I saw pamphlets urging us to throw away our arms and come to terms with the Italians because Russia, then friendly to the Axis, would protect us. I've read many foul things of that sort, but the foulest of all is the slander about the regular officers. And I will also ask you this: would you have asked us to fight by your side and bring untold suffering on the country, if the Ribbentrop-Molotov pact were still in force? Would you have made common cause with us if Russia were not today at war with the Axis?"

He was angry and spoke heatedly. The visitor did not join issue with him and seemed to give way. He resumed in a firm voice. "I might have much to say in answer to you, but I haven't come here to dispute details of the past. I have come to reach an agreement with you on the broad lines of action. We want you as a fellow-combatant. We are making a great effort to get you.You have read a document which very few people have set eyes on, and you stop at one article which, after all, need not be interpreted too rigidly. And it does not seem to me that this is enough for you to refuse, now and in the future, to join us in fighting for the freedom of this oppressed land. Have you any other reason for not wishing to join us?"

"Possibly."

"Would you mind telling me what it is? I might be able to give you a satisfactory answer."

His tone had become softer and his manner was almost

polite. It was difficult for Nikita to cut short the discussion.

"What exactly is the position of the Communist Party in EAM?"

"I expected you to ask something of the sort," Voliotis said. "The position of the Communist Party is that of any group of fellow-combatants, with one difference: we have not hesitated to lay aside our ideology in order to bring about the success of this nationwide effort. The struggle, aid to the Allies, and liberation must come first. Our sincerity is evident from many indications. The name of the organization is already a great concession on our part. It begins with the word 'national', a word completely alien to our theories of world rule, and one which is significant. We accepted it so that you should all realize that national liberation comes first, and that we must all work for it together. On the other hand, you have just had proof that we are making every effort to recruit patriots who, like you, are not communists. You ask me about the position of the Party in EAM. I don't know. It will depend upon its evolution. If you all come into the organization our position will be relatively small and weak. If you don't join, it will not be the Communist Party's fault if it dominates. And why shouldn't you join? We're engaged in a common struggle in which Stalin, the socialist and revolutionary, has joined hands with Churchill, the imperialist, and Roosevelt, the plutocrat. What prevents you from temporarily working with us? Where the liberation of the country is concerned how can you hesitate?"

Augustus Callaris broke in enthusiastically. "You're quite right. We must all join, and especially the young people. You must come with us, Mr. Coletti. It's no longer a question of Communism and non-Communism. It's a question of the Greeks and their fight for freedom. When the struggle is over we'll settle our accounts with Communism which I can't stand any more than you can."

Nikita didn't answer. He wasn't sure what impressed him most—the genuine and ardent patriotism of the young merchant, or the arguments of the stubborn ideologist most of which were well founded. He didn't have time to consider his doubts further because his attention was drawn to an incident which now arose between Callaris and Voliotis. The latter had just said to Augustus: "My fellow-combatant, your views on the reasons for joining the movement are sound. But there is something I should like to know. True, EAM has no objection to your not being able to tolerate Communism. That is your right. But I, Voliotis, would like you to tell me why you can't tolerate it."

Callaris was taken aback and found difficulty in answering. Voliotis profited by his silence to give the answer himself.

"Just prejudice. You haven't any good reason."

Callaris, who was unprepared for this challenge, struggled to find an argument, and said sullenly, "Communism does away with property. Without private property, and without an interest in increasing it, there can be no progress and no business activity."

Voliotis did not have to struggle to find arguments. He had them ready-made, and he spoke with confidence: "What you advocate is the very foundation of every form of human misery. Private property and the craving to increase it is what makes man vile to his fellow-man. Only if private property is abolished can man become good."

"The desire for private property is instinctive in man," Callaris insisted.

"It has nothing to do with instinct. In the beginning a few powerful men imposed the system on the majority of weak ones; then the evil took root and spread to the whole world, and became the cause of every conflict and every disaster." Uncertain in his replies and lacking Voliotis' confidence, the small-town business man tried to argue.

"Without private property," he said, "whoever has power or holds any government position will have a better life than the man without power — a hundred times better."

"That's not so, because we are going to make man good."

"Are you going to turn him into a saint?"

"Yes, we are going to turn him into a saint," Voliotis replied with conviction.

Nikita joined in the discussion saying simply, "In a society of saints all social systems would work perfectly. It is important to know which system is the most practical for a society of human beings."

Voliotis answered him sarcastically. "It is natural for you with all your acres of land not to be fond of us who believe in abolishing property."

"You're mistaken," Nikita said quietly. "I'm much more disturbed by the fact that you suppress it. For the general good the people will discipline their freedom."

"The point is: who are the people? Or rather who will represent the people so that they may exercise their rights in this manner?"

"No one represents the people. However, the sideline I embarked upon has caused us to deviate from our urgent theme. You have heard how our friend Callaris, who is not a communist, has stated the case. For the present let us unite to go on with the struggle. Later we'll clear up our differences. So then, will you come with us?"

"No, I shall not."

"I don't believe this is your final answer. We'll talk about it again."

Nikita replied firmly: "That won't be necessary. My answer is final."

There was a pause. Then Voliotis said, "Do you really imagine that a struggle will be going on and that you'll be sitting here idly refusing to help us?"

"It's possible that I may help you when the revolt breaks out, and when the Allies' landing is about to take place. Then there will be some sense in fighting. Now it would only bring reprisal to poor, peace-loving people who don't know how they'll manage to feed their children."

Voliotis replied sternly: "That's a terribly dangerous theory. There is sense to the movement because it will absorb enemy troops which otherwise would be used elsewhere. There will be reprisals, but in every struggle a few sacrifices, more or less, are of little account. And this will be a struggle with a great objective. You are now incurring danger in your efforts on behalf of the Vlachs, that is to say for an insignificant objective—one that will be swept away with the first gust of wind. We call on you to fight with us for freedom and for the honor of the country."

"I am not changing my position. Each one must fight according to his lights."

Voliotis' voice became as cold as ice. Each one of his words fell from lips as sharp as a razor's edge: "You are making a great mistake. In conflict, a man is never free to do as he wishes or to remain neutral. Above all, those that are able to contribute effective help are not free to do as they wish. You can help effectively."

"Let me get this clear. Are you threatening me?"

"I'm telling you a few home truths. If you join us you will be among our top people. If you don't, we'll go all out. The absence from our ranks of a man of your position and dynamic qualities will not only deprive us of substantial help but will also lead others along the same negative path. This we shall not tolerate."

He leaned toward Nikita and, in the same cutting tone but speaking faster, said, "There's something else. As soon as we have fought one or two battles we are sure that plenty of weapons will reach us from abroad. We want to get the business going quickly, and at present we are poorly armed. We have practically nothing. You can help us with weapons. It will be treason on your part not give them to us."

Nikita was annoyed by the man's tone and by the word 'treason', but he forced himself to laugh: "Kisavitis said something of the sort the other day. You can search the whole of Pteliona but you won't find a single rifle here."

"Possibly, but others are holding guns for you."

"I don't understand what you are talking about."

"You understand very well. The second reason for which I've come to Larissa is to get the guns. We need them."

Nikita decided that it was best to feign anger.

"What sort of behavior is this? First you tell a lie, and then you use it to make demands and threats."

Voliotis leaned across the table towards Nikita and spoke in a harsher voice. "Coletti, I'm not playing games. I need those weapons, I need them quickly and I'm going to get them."

Nikita got up. "I think we've said all there is to say."

Voliotis grasped the table with both his hands, and gave Nikita a determined look. There was a glint of hatred in it.

"Yes," he replied. "I've said all I had to say. I wash my hands of the consequences. I advise you to get on your beautiful horse as soon as we leave, get on it as soon as we leave. Immediately."

He got up abruptly. Callaris rose too. Voliotis stopped to look attentively at a painting, then at one or two others.

"Fine pieces," he said. "I can't stand this crazy modern stuff, but I can take the impressionists. Everything that comes after them makes me want to throw up."

Nikita found these words strange coming from Voliotis.

"Are you interested in art?" he asked.

"I've also read your poems. I like most of them. Anything that has to do with the arts interests me."

"Strange that you should like works that are more or less classical in style. Your politics are avant-garde, yet avant-garde art makes you want to throw up."

"Anarchy, too, claims to be avant-garde, but it isn't. It is a sterile form of disorder without purpose. Everything in life requires discipline. Art too must have discipline, otherwise it expresses nothing and doesn't serve its purpose."

"And what might the purpose of art be?" Nikita asked.

Voliotis looked at him and grinned. "You're starting a big argument, and we'll disagree once more," he said. "Let's leave it for another time."

Now, he was relaxed in his speech and the harshness had gone out of his face. He took another look at the paintings.

"This one is a masterpiece. Only in Paris have I seen its equal. Is it a genuine Manet?"

"Yes."

"And these by Lembessis and Savvides are superb. They are both great masters — giants by international criteria. It's a shame that only a dozen people are aware of them! You must have inherited them from your grandfather."

With simulated nonchalance he added, "Wouldn't it be a pity if all these went up in flames some night?"

Nikita felt that he ought to say something in reply, but he was choked by the fury which came over him at the open threat. He could not find the appropriate words, so he pretended not to hear. He moved towards the door.

Before leaving the room, Voliotis stood in front of him, held him by the lapel of his coat, and with a gleam of kindness in his eyes, said to him;

"You're a very nice fellow and you've got guts. If only you

would join us we would see a lot of each other and would become real friends.''

Nikita smiled: ''Quite possibly. But I'm not joining you.''

Voliotis froze again. ''I know,'' he said. ''But I'll get the guns anyway. My advice to you all is to help me get them quickly and quietly. I don't like bloodshed.''

Again Nikita did not reply, but he looked him steadily in the eye. What put him out more than Voliotis' threat, was his expression and his conviction that EAM was strong and that everyone else was weak. He felt like slapping his face, like tearing him to pieces, because Voliotis seemed to relish his own words with such conceit and disregard for the words of others.

After a pause Voliotis continued: ''From now on, Coletti, many nights will be pregnant. I want you to know that.''

Nikita smiled sarcastically:

''Pregnant nights, eh? And can you tell me what they'll being forth — boys, girls or abortions?''

Voliotis thrust his hands into his trouser pockets and looked Nikita up and down as though he were taking stock of him and then, in a provocative manner, he said, ''They'll bring forth males with triple sets of kidneys.''

Nikita could stand it no more. He preferred quiet arguments. He hated shouting and believed that to lose one's temper was a sign of weakness. But this was too much! This man thought that he would crush him by intimidation, that everybody had to bend before his words or at the slightest show of his strength. He could not bear it. He had to give vent to his feelings.

In a furious rage he drew near to Voliotis and shouted in his face:

''Since you insist on imposing yourself by threats and violence, you can take it from me that you're no good to free men, whatever it is you're fighting for.''

Both of them were strong, strapping men and both were angry. Their faces almost touched and each could feel the other's hot breath upon his face. And yet they appeared to be separated by an unbridgeable gap, because it was an immaterial force that kept them apart, something that could not be measured in terms of matter.

Voliotis answered coldly: "What you have just said, taken by itself, is almost a confession of faith. But you can take it from me that your faith is crooked and sterile. The means by which an end is reached are soon forgotten. The end, when it has been fashioned and stabilized, remains."

And he left quickly without waiting for a reply.

Nikita looked at his watch and saw that it was only ten o'clock. His first reaction was to ride over and see the abbot. He could be back before noon.

But it was not right for him to go, nor to send Phrosso. If they were being watched and someone was seen going to the monastery at once, the others would understand. Their suspicions about the weapons would be confirmed. This might bring on speedy action on their part.

He would go on the following day, not in the morning but in the evening, preferably at dusk. But at all costs Modestos must be informed not later than then. He would have to decide how to protect his monks from being tortured and how to prevent them from confessing that there had been many arms at the monastery which had disappeared. That he had to go on the next day was made clearer that evening. At nightfall he was called to Mourayias' cottage. The doctor wanted to speak to him.

"I have taken all precautions in coming here. My excuse is that I had to see my patient and I have hired the same carriage as last time. I came without warning you because something happened today which you ought to know at once."

He looked around cautiously and lowered his voice. He smiled modestly.

"It will appear strange to you," he said, "but I'm afraid of speaking, I'm even afraid of knowing the things I know."

"Doctor, you are afraid of nothing," Nikita said. "The proof is that you have the courage to come here and tell me."

Dr. Vaidis looked at him gratefully. "And yet I am afraid. I'm terrified. Listen to this horrible story. A member of the Legion who is a good man, poor and miserable and the father of a large family, has been troubled with his wife's health for many years. I look after her. I don't charge him much, in fact nothing, so he's obligated to me. He is also indebted to Father Modestos. The abbot once helped him with money and food, and takes one of his children who suffers from glands, every year to spend the summer at the monastery."

He looked around again and lowered his voice still more. "He came to me this morning and told me that the Legion believes that the abbot possesses a great quantity of hidden arms. They are trying to find a way of getting them. They called in my informant who knows the monastery, asked him a lot of questions, and told him to be ready because they would need him at any moment. He came to ask my advice because he wants to protect the holy man. I told him to say that there are no weapons at St. Elias and, if his comrades go up there, to go with them and see what he can do to help. They are also saying at the Legion that you must know about the arms at St. Elias. That's why I came to warn you."

As he was about to leave, the doctor closed the door again and stood silent. He looked at his feet, hesitated, raised his eyes, and coming very close to Nikita whispered, "Am I entitled...May I ask you something? Is it true about the weapons?" The doctor's eyes were shining.

Nikita was deeply moved as he looked affectionately at that haggard face. He noticed that it glowed with a strange spirituality. But he did not answer.

"I know, I know," the doctor said in a trembling voice. "These are terrifying secrets. I must not ask questions. And it's terrible of me to speak of concealed weapons, even to know of such a suspicion...No, no, don't tell me. I'll be even more frightened if I know. I don't want to know, but you understand my curiosity. It's a stupendous thing, a wonderful thing, the War of 1821 coming to life again. To be involved in something like that by chance, wonderful...terrible...."

Once more Nikita's eyes had filled with tears. The emotion was sweet, but it made him angry. There were other occasions, far more tragic and intense, when the tears had not come.

The doctor looked at him. He was scraggy yet noble, sickly yet strong, though he trembled he was firm and upright on his feet. He didn't want to know about the weapons, it was obvious that he was scared, but at the same time he was yearning to find out if he, even in the slightest degree, was part of some great undertaking.

"Doctor," Nikita said, "apart from the abbot and myself no one knows the secret. You are the only person worthy of hearing it. Only you. 1821 is coming to life again, with all its glory and with all its suffering. Don't ask anything more, but I want you to know that you are part of this."

The doctor embraced him, kissed him on the cheek, and left hastily.

XIV

The evening was waning; dusk had not yet fallen. Nikita galloped towards St. Elias. He had lain awake all night thinking and had spent the day talking with Phrosso.

Two different but equally determined enemies, with the same purpose in mind, were bearing down upon St. Elias. The danger was great and something had to be done. Not that there was any fear that the crypt would be discovered. But if those who were after the weapons were frustrated in their search, the people at the monastery, and above all the abbot, would be in dire peril. Nikita had gone over the question thoroughly with Phrosso, examining every possible solution. It was imperative that he see Father Modestos immediately and that they reach a decision concerning the wisest course of action. These were the thoughts that preoccupied him as he started out for the monastery.

As he galloped across the verdant plain its beauty enchanted him and caused him, momentarily, to forget the Legion, yesterday's visitors, and the dangers ahead.

On this late-April evening the scents of spring wafted on the gentle breezes and the plain, as far as the eye could see, was decked in a shining robe of emerald green. Thousands of delicate little flowers of every hue adorned it. Here and there flaming poppies marked it with brilliant splashes of red.

Now and then a lone tree in full flower would appear, lifting high its tufted head above the green sea and driving its hidden sap far above the earth, where its blossoms shone today in joyous tribute to the glory of nature and where, tomorrow, fruit would grow, a welcome offering to man. The scented branches tossed and bent scattering over the ground the flowers, wearied by the kisses of the breeze, which sought a cool refuge in the green grass that awaited them.

Everywhere around him, as he rode on, the hidden sap of the earth swelled the crops and drove them upwards.

Today the plain had taken on a different aspect. The wheat, the barley, and the other crops were no longer the short, stubby stalks he had looked at for so many months. They had grown tall and thick, and stood straight and motionless until a breath of wind gently caressed them. Then they all quivered and undulated in unison under gleaming radiance which passed over them in its headlong course, onward and onward to the far horizon—maybe to the end of the world.

Deeply moved, he brought Pegasus to a halt and looked out over the view.

What he saw, he reflected, was not merely the growth of the crops. It was the warm April wind that vitalized innumerable secret forces. It was the shudder of earth conscious of her pregnancy. It was the joyous stirring within her womb, now that the crops, under the sun's kiss, sprang lustily upward. It was a dance, the youthful, festive dance of the crops, initiated for the first time to a sense of their own strength, to the light of the sun, to the warmth of its kiss, to its intoxicating golden caress.

It was a song of youth, joy, and promise. The youngling crops were as yet unaware that the rainstorms or hail of May could break them, that the hot south-winds of June could wither them. In the innocence of their youthful immaturity, they were confident in their infallibility and believed in the promise of the future. And so they danced carefree, trusting in the wind under the blue skies above them.

Nikita felt the whole plain quivering under the caress of the creative breath of spring, and opened his shirt wide to receive the warm breeze on his chest. It came from Olympus, the home of the gods, and from the plain, the mother of men. He felt it ruffle the hairs of his chest and creep up his sleeves to his armpits. He opened his mouth and took a deep breath of it.

What exquisite joy!

He closed his eyes to savor it better.

What was the secret of this extraordinary phenomenon? This unbreakable bond, this oneness of man with everything around him—with all things living and inanimate? It must be, in simple language, what was called love of country, attachment to the land of one's ancestors. It must be the inexpressible beauty of Nature which beguiles a man into thinking himself a part of her. It must be the vitality of the earth as it rejoices and strains to bring forth millions upon millions of trees, plants, and grasses, from the greatest to the most insignificant, from the proudest to the most humble. It must be the knowledge that the earth nurtures all men—every single one—even those who had no love for her, who paid no attention to her, who behaved toward her as though she did not exist.

Or could it be, could it be just simply the call of the earth, which he had always felt within him, sometimes strong and sometimes faint, ever since the blessed hour when he had first heard it?

"Oh, my dear brother, Alexis," he thought with a deep yearning. "If I only had you here now."

. The thought of his dead brother dissolved the enchantment of the moment. His thoughts reverted to all the problems which he faced to the fact that he was alone, unaided, and in danger. The holy man was in peril. He must give him the news, tell him about the solutions he had thought of, and come to a quick decision.

Leaning over and speaking to Pegasus in his own language, Nikita spurred him on and started toward the hill at a gallop. He had discussed his thoughts but the enhantment of the plain would not be broken; It filled the air with an eerie atmosphere of magic and illusion.

Now Nikita was riding up the slope. The fine old monastery came into sight. There was the wooden bell-tower—but what was that, in front of it, over the doorway? Something hanging there, long and white. It was as though an angel hovered over the portal. Yes, an angel. Nikita was not close enough to make out in detail what it was. It looked like a white angel, hovering in the air over the monastery.

How very strange! He really did see the angel. This was no vision.

He halted, opened and closed his eyes, and looked again intently. And again he saw the long white form, motionless, suspended above the courtyard door of St. Elias. Pegasus too must have seen something, for he began to stamp the ground where he stood, and to neigh in a peculiar, mournful fashion.

But still it could not be true. It must be a mental aberration! He must be intoxicated by the beauty of the green plain! He did indeed see something up there that looked like a white angel, but it wasn't possible...His eyes fixed on the vision, he tapped Pegasus with his riding-crop, and advanced. He was breathing heavily.

When he arrived at the last hillock leading to the entrance, he stopped short. Horror of horrors! Now he saw clearly what it was. The worst of all that could happen had happened.

As he stared before him with wide-open eyes, his heart contracted and he felt a sharp pain. It seemed to him that the world had come to an end.

The angel... the angel... It was the abbot who had become an angel. Over the monastery doorway hung the body of Father Modestos, stripped of its robes, almost naked.

A sob shook him, choked him. But tears would not come. His eyes remained dry. He felt the numbness of paralysis come over his whole body.

What good could he do now? All was useless, all was lost. The holy man was gone. And who could know what torture he had suffered, that good man who had been the guide of his beloved brother and, until now, his own.

At the thought of Alexis, buried far away on an Albanian mountain, Nikita roused himself from his state of shock. No, he would not give in! Everything around him cried 'Vengeance! Vengeance'! He must avenge the old abbot. It was his sacred duty.

He remembered the lines of the poet Valaoritis, about the hanging of the Patriarch of Constantinople by the Turks during the War of 1821. When he was a boy he had thought them beautiful:

> Strike, gallant chieftains, strike!
> Let rack and ruin loose from coast to coast.
> The Patriarch hangs dead!

He had thought the lines beautiful when he was a boy, but later had found them cheap—an exercise in sensational versification. Now he found them beautiful again.

"Strike, chieftains! Strike without pity! Strike our own traitors and foreign foes! Strike! Strike!"

Pegasus was restive and let out a succession of short, mournful whinnies. Nikita led him to the portal and dismounted. For a moment he considered untying the abbot's body and burying it, by he reflected that it would be better to leave it for the constables to find when he sent for them. He approached and made the sign of the cross. The lean body was frozen and stiff. The crime must have been committed the night before or perhaps dawn.

He remembered Voliotis' words. "Get on your horse as soon as we leave. As soon as we leave. Immediately."

He remembered the doctor's words: "They told him to be ready because they would need him very, very soon."

He ought to have been more alert; he ought to have come yesterday morning. The thought shook him. But how could he have thought—how could anyone have imagined...

He examined the abbot's face close by and saw that it bore the marks of beatings, that his mouth was bloody, and that the toes of one foot were crushed.

"The weapons!" he thought, and ran into the church. He found it in a state of upheaval. The pew had been moved and underneath it many slabs pulled out of the floor. The large slab of rock which led to the sanctuary had not been touched, but the two steps on either side and another further off had been pried out of their sockets.

With the sanctuary, the altar had been overturned, and at the base of the enclosing wall pick-axes had been used to break through the plaster. The stone structure stood bare.

He went over to the monastery building. In the yard, in the corridor, in the cells, and in the abbot's quarters he saw bloodstains. Not many, a few drops here and there, but everywhere there was destruction. Benches and closets were pulled away from their places and floors torn up.

He called the monks by name, but no voices answered him. He went through the whole monastery finding ravages at every turn, but no sign of human beings living or dead. Suddenly he caught his breath. A cold sweat came over him, as he remembered the words of his dead brother on that freezing night in the dark stable:

"Beware...beware all of you...I see disasters coming..."

His clothes, drenched in sweat, stuck to his body. He was seized with a sudden fear. What if the place was being watched? What if they had foreseen that he would come and were waiting to extort the secret from him?

It was still light outside, but within the monastery the evening shadows had deepened. What was done could not be undone. Now, Nikita thought, he must look out for himself. He was alone and unarmed. He hurried outside, made the sign of the cross in front of the church and the body of Modestos, mounted his horse and left at a gallop.

He looked around him and saw that the place was deserted. He felt a little more secure and began to turn over in his mind the horror that he had just seen. He held Pegasus back and advanced at a slow trot.

What a calamity! The abbot was dead, the monks were almost certainly dead or carried away to die, and the monastery was in ruins. And with the poverty and starvation everywhere it would have been devastated even more. How could it be protected? Who would protect it? And even if anyone cared, what good would it do since its soul was now dead?

"A curse is on the land." he reflected. "The curse that has fallen upon it time and time again throughout the centuries."

Why had they hanged Father Modestos? What was the reason? Vengeance or punishment? There was no sense to either since with his death, they lost the key to the secret. But did they know that he had held it? Why should they have supposed that the abbot alone knew the secret?

The it dawned on him. The must have tortured all of them to extract the secret, and that was the meaning of the bloodstains he had seen all over the monastery, and of the bruises on the abbot's body. Obviously none of them had confessed, and they had killed one to terrorize the others. They had killed the one who was the least likely to talk. They must be holding the monks somewhere, torturing them, and then they would kill them too, to prevent them from revealing what they had seen and suffered. Thus another secret—the secret of the preceding night—would be buried in some unknown place with the dead bodies of the martyred monks.

Who could have done this? The cultured Voliotis or that wild beast, Ropotikas? It must have been Voliotis, for it was easier to kill for an idea passionately served than for sheer self-interest. Caught up in abstract ideology, a man could become hard and indifferent to concrete obstacles, even to the obstacle of a human life. It must be Voliotis.

But what did it matter who had done it? It only mattered for the revenge that he would take, that he must take.

He realized that Pegasus had stopped. They had come to the small piece of flat ground just before the last slope. There he had often stopped to enjoy the view of Pteliona, the College, the river, and the city of Larissa. From there everything could be seen clearly—the forest beyond, and the small wood in the foreground.

"Ill-fated country," he reflected, "how many times have you been invaded and ravaged by foreign foes, and outraged even by your own people? Poor country, prostrate under the curse of slavery, lovely country enfolded by the sea, bathed in sunlight, stretching out under the shadow of Olympus,yet ever tormented by human jackals!"

He was about to go on, when he noticed a carriage advancing toward the small wood. It seemed strange to him that a carriage should be there at this late hour and he observed it carefully. when he realized who it was his heart stopped and he felt a sharp pain. But this time the pain was not the same as before.

He recognized the smart little tilbury of the arrogant Italian. He was driving and next to him sat Katie. They disappeared into the wood. Dusk was falling and they were alone, the two of them in the deserted wood, his own wood on his own ground. There he was, the arrogant foe, going openly, for anyone who should chance to see him, to be alone with a Greek girl, and to...

He struck Pegasus with his heels, tugged hard on the bridle and rode headlong down the slope. He did not feel sure of himself and held onto the horse's mane, but did not check his breakneck gallop. On and on he rushed, determined to reach them as soon as possible.

Why? What was he going to do? Nothing.

He did not know.

An enemy on my land, my land...with one of our girls...He must get to them at once. That was all that was in his mind. When he came to the edge of the wood, he reduced his mad gallop to a moderate trot and went forward through the trees. From afar he saw the tilbury. It was empty and the horse was grazing.

He quickened the pace unmindful of the branches in his way. Pegasus slipped nimbly between the trees, and soon Nikita found the pair lying on the ground in each other's arms.

By the time they heard him he was very near. He leaped off his horse and rushed toward them in a fury. They both got up flushed and dishevelled. Nikita looked at Katie with hatred. "Whore!" he cried out. Two resounding slaps brought the blood to Nikita's cheeks, as the Italian shouted something in Italian. Nikita paid no attention to his words but struck him back.

The Italian stepped back and drew his revolver. Nikita jumped him, tore the pistol away from him, and threw it away. He approached Castelleone and shouted at him in Italian, "This is my property and I don't allow anyone to bring his whores here."

A hard blow struck him in the face. He was stunned and reeled backwards. He had never been struck so hard in his life. Castelleone was very strong. He leaned against a tree for a moment and heard the Italian saying to the girl, "Get into the carriage quickly and wait for me. I have an old account to settle with this gentleman."

Katie joined her hands together in a gesture of supplication and said to him in French, "No! No! Please don't. Let's go!"

Then he advanced toward Nikita. He did not say a word. He moved forward with his clenched fists extended and a vicious glint in his eye.

"He's very tough, and he's probably and expert boxer," Nikita thought. "I know nothing about boxing." To give himself freedom of movement he came away from the tree against which he had been leaning. With an evil grin, Castelleone said to him in Italian, "You're scared. Are the heroes of Greece all scared?"

Nikita sprang at him and tried to strike him with all his strength, but Castelleone warded off the blow and brought down two punches on his face. He must have been wearing a ring, because Nikita felt that the skin beneath his eye had been torn. Warm blood was flowed down his cheek.

From the carriage Katie again cried out in distress, "Please! That's enough! Let's go!"

Nikita, feeling dizzy, had fallen back a few steps. Castelleone stood waiting for him with his fists outstretched. "Maybe you don't know," he shouted, "but we've already met at Hill 731—at Collina Monastero—but then the mountains were fighting on your side. Now," he went on sarcastically, "we're fighting man to man. There's no blood on my face, but yours is streaming with the blood of heroes, no doubt."

Nikita boiled with rage but realized that he was in a tight corner. His opponent was stronger than he and he knew how to fight and defend himself. He must find another way to fight him and avoid humiliation. He too extended his hands as though in readiness to strike but, as the Italian advanced he hurled himself at him with his whole body. Castelleone was taken by surprise and lost his balance. He fell and Nikita rushed at him and struck him in the face.

Katie called out, "no, Nikita, no! I beseech you," and in French she cried, "Angelo, my love, come, let's go!"

"Shut up, you whore!" Nikita cried savagely.

Arrogance in victory had always been distasteful to him. In the past, whenever he had seen or read about an arrogant winner he had been disgusted. A victor might feel a natural elation at his success, but arrogance cheapened the triumph.

But at this moment, the hard facts of experience were stronger than words. The natural reaction of the present overcame the convictions of a whole lifetime. He held his enemy pinned beneath him, and an invincible feeling urged him to revel in his temporary triumph, to gloat in vulgar exaltation.

He utter a loud cry, and instead of a blow, he gave him a slap in the face, and shouted to him in Italian. "The blood of heroes you said? What would you know about the blood of heroes? If your blood flows it will be the blood of a coward!"

But the Italian was in a fury. With a sudden effort he pushed Nikita on to his side and their two bodies, tightly clasped together, rolled on the ground. Nikita was on top again, gave Castelleone another hard blow, and shouted savagely once more to press his triumph further. He turned toward the tilbury and cried, "Your hero is nothing but a limp ball of meat, you whore! He's a piece of rotten flesh!"

But Castelleone was not a ball of meat. He took advantage of the moment when Nikita relaxed his grip, to punch him violently on the chin. Nikita lifted his head and chest to recover from the blow and the Italian swiftly pushed his hands against his opponent's body and ,with an abrupt and vigorous shove, threw him off. Then with an acrobat's lithe movement he leaped to his feet.

Nikita got up too, but Castelleone had no intention of losing the advantage. He saw that Nikita was unsteady on his feet, came up to him quickly and, finding no resistance, delivered a succession of powerful blows to the jaw and temples.

Nikita was dazed and fell to the ground. He felt a sharp pain, and blood ran down his face. He realized that he would not be able to get up at once and was overcome by a sense of shame and humiliation. There he was beaten, bloody, and prostrate, in front of Katie and her fiance, the arrogant staff officer of the Italian Second Bureau. What a humiliation!

The Italian, self-confident and proud, dusted off his clothes, picked up his cap, drew out his gloves from his belt and prepared to to put them on. He looked at Nikita contemptuously. "I presume you've had enough punishment," he said. "I could kill you if I wanted to, but I won't, because Italians don't kill weaklings who pick quarrels with women. Italians only kill brave men in battle."

He was about to go but stopped as he saw Nikita getting up. "I advise you," he said, "to stay quietly where you are. If you get up I'll give you such a beating that you won't be able to get yourself home."

At the spot where Nikita had fallen there was a big branch that had fallen from an elm. He seized it, got to his feet and, holding it firmly in both hands, fixed his eyes upon Castelleone. In a paroxysm of rage and hatred, he said, "One of us is not going to go home tonight. One of us is going to die."

Once more Katie cried out, but he did not hear what she said. His ears buzzed from the blows he had received, and his heart was in turmoil under the lash of his hatred and humiliation.

"You're crazy," Castelleone said.

"One of us is going to die here and now!" Nikita took a step forward.

"You're crazy. Mad!"

"I don't want to kill you unarmed. Pick up a stone or stick or anything you want, pull out a knife. I'll wait."

Katie screamed. Nikita advanced another step and stopped. The Italian did not move. He had lost some of his arrogance, but he stood erect and looked straight at him. He remained unperturbed even when Nikita shouted at him, "We're going to fight. You won't get out of it. Take whatever weapon you can find."

Castelleone answered him superciliously. "Throw away that branch, and we'll fight."

"Coward! You know you're stronger than I. With equal weapons—we'll fight to the death! Come on! D'you hear me?"

The blond foreigner neither moved nor spoke. He stood there staring at Nikita.

Nikita now addressed him again in lower tones, but the words were full of venom. "I told you to pick up a weapon. You don't want to. I'm not going to wait any longer. One of us has got to die tonight. There's no other way out."

The Italian bent down suddenly and picked up a sharp rock. Nikita lifted high the branch he was holding and advanced toward him. All the hatred born of the months of resentment at the slavery imposed by the foreign occupation welled up within him and was concentrated in the grimness of his expression. The Italian still did not move, but realized that his opponent was in deadly earnest. In an instant one of them would be dead. He risked dying ingloriously, without reason, in a ridiculous manner. Katie would be left alone in this deserted spot with this maniac who was driven by hatred and humiliation. If he managed to kill Nikita he would have to explain his action. How could he explain it? He would have committed a queer kind of murder.

Slowly, ominously, and with a grim determination, the Greek moved forward. They were now only two or three paces apart. One of them would fall to the ground with a cracked skull. Maybe both of them.

Suddenly the Italian dodged to one side, ran to his carriage, jumped up into the seat, whipped up his horse and went off with Katie.

Nikita was on the verge of letting out a great shout of triumph and relief at his release from humiliation, but he restrained himself. Was this really a triumph? he asked himself. Yes it was, because victory in the true sense is not the victory of the stronger over the weaker. When you are weak and hurt and afraid, and still stand up to fight, and are prepared to face death, that is victory.

He sat down on the ground. He was in pain and his head reeled. No sound came out of his mouth. He leaned back against the trunk of an elm. His mind was completely vacant. It was not the pain and dizziness which distressed him as much as the events of these past hours which were beyond the capacity of the human brain to absorb. And his mind remained empty and grey as the grey dusk which now filtered into the forest.

For a moment he thought he was the victim of a hallucination. There was hot breath close to him, warming his face. It was no hallucination. It was Pegasus caressing him, gently rubbing his nose against Nikita's injured cheek.

He felt better. He got up, mounted with difficulty, and Pegasus bore him slowly and carefully, as though conscious of his plight, to Pteliona.

His appearance was lamentable and gave the impression that he was in much worse condition than he actually was. His torn clothing, his bleeding face, the blood all over him, his dejected expression, and his bent body made him look as though he were seriously wounded. The moment he saw Phrosso he realized that there could no longer be any doubt about her.

She was beside herself with anxiety. Her every word, her

every movement, everything she did to help him showed him that these were not merely gestures of interest and warm friendship. Deep love, beyond reason and affection, an upsurge of her heart and her whole being went out to him.

Weary and injured, he abandoned himself entirely to her care. It was so good, after all he had gone through, to let someone else take over. She lighted the fire, for the nights had become chilly, she helped him to undress, and when he was stretched out on the bed she washed his face and hands and disinfected his slight wound.

Because he didn't want to startle her late at night, he had said, in reply to her query, "I met with an accident." When she pressed him, appearing to suspect something more, he had said, "I'll tell you later. Tomorrow." And she had not insisted.

She made him a warm drink laced with a good measure of brandy, and placed hot poultices on his blackened eye. He didn't want her to take all this trouble, but at the same time he didn't want to disappoint her. Also he felt much better, almost well again.

Now that he was clean and lying in his own bed between freshly laundered sheets, comforted by the friendly warmth and bright flicker of the fire, and basking the the atmosphere of tenderness and love he actually dismissed from his mind the horrible events of that terrible day. He felt so comfortable, so relaxed. The warmth of the moment was so soothing. Nothing else mattered. Phrosso sat by him and , from time to time, changed the poultices on his eye. A few drops from a poultice ran down his cheek. She wiped them off gently with her hand and he felt a thrill, infinitely sweet, run through him. He lifted his hand and stroked her cheek lightly.

And so love came to them on that warm spring evening. The world and its troubles faded away as, with eyes sparkling, they looked at each other, together and alone in a paradise of loveliness and truth. Hand pressed in hand, with fingers intertwined, they savored the fleeting moments in silence. There was nothing to say, for they knew that no words could express the exquisite richness of the golden hour.

He stroked her cheek again, and then brought his hand slowly down to encircle her soft neck, then down to her trembleing breast.

The he kissed her and she responded with passionate tenderness to his kiss. They kissed again. She slipped into his bed and they fell asleep in each others arms.

In the middle of the night Phrosso was awakened by Nikitas wild cry. "Strike chieftains! I have conquered!" She tried to calm him, kindled the fire and gave him a sedative. Before he fell asleep again he told her what had happened. She listened to him. Pain and anxiety, desperation, rose within her. She said nothing. A few muted cries came from her lips which she bit convulsively. There were moments when she dug her nails into her palms.

After some time Nikita's words began to trail off. Sleep gradually gained on him. But he roused himself suddenly and said, "Darling little Phrosso—St. Elias crypt. Only you and I know the secret now. If anything should happen to me it will be up to you to decide whom you must tell, when the general uprising of the people comes.

He closed his eves and sank into a deep sleep.

XV

When they knocked loudly at his door the sunlight was streaming into the room. Mitsos came in and stopped short, startled.

"What happened? What happened to you?"

Nikita said that he had fallen from his horse, that he was very tired and had slept late.

"Where's Phrosso?" he asked Mitsos.

"She left early."

"Why did she leave?"

"One of her aunts fell ill and she said she was going to stay with her."

Nikita raised himself up. He was greatly disturbed. "Dr. Vaidis is here," Mitsos said, "and wants to see you. He's in a hurry. That's why I knocked on your door."

"Tell him to come in."

As Mitsos was leaving, he stopped and bent down. "A letter," he said "It must have been slipped under the door."

While he waited for the doctor to come up he opened the envelope and read, "I have no regrets. None at all. But I'm leaving because you are in love with another woman. Phrosso."

At that moment the doctor entered. He looked more frightened than ever.

"Once again I used Phrosso as an excuse for coming, but she's not here. This time I shan't be able to explain my visit. I'm lost if anything happens and they investigate me."

"Why, doctor? All you have to say is that you didn't know she was away and came to see your patient. It's a legitimate explanation."

The doctor appeared to be somewhat reassured.

"Sit down," Nikita said, "and tell me."

The doctor's face brightened. He was a different man. "My friend, Raptis," he said breathlessly, "asked me to come to see you because nobody suspects me. Didn't you sent a message to your uncle in Athens about the cheese production?"

I sent two, one with Golemis, the engineer, and the second with Dotiadis an old friend of mine."

"Well, today your group heard the wonderful news and they send you their congratulations. The day before yesterday two telegrams from your uncle came to the bank. One forbids the extension of any financial aid to cheese producers unless they bear certified statements for the Agricultural Bank and the Police that they are *bona fide* and honorable businessmen with no black-market connections. The other telegram notified Vassili Manoussis that he is being transferred to Almyros."

Nikita forgot all his trouble. "Good old uncle Spyros!" he shouted.

The doctor was jubilant. "Just think of it!" he said, "over ten years as manager of Larissa and now transferred to an insignificant little town! He's to take over the Almyros branch office within forty-eight hours! Our friends are celebrating and the whole town is talking about it. Greece isn't dead. She's fighting back. Everyone in Larissa is full of smiles. And just imagine! Diamantis and Vassili Manoussis have just left for Athens by car to try, no doubt, to countermand the order. Splendid! Splendid! Larissa is celebrating!"

He was weary, in pain, and anxious, and at the same time he was overjoyed. But he did not want to go into town that day. It would be better for him not to be seen in his battered condition. He went around the property, inspected the sheep that Mourayias had brought in during the afternoon, and worried all day thinking of a way to find Phrosso. He went to bed early. But he could not sleep. All the events of the past days ran through his brain, and he turned and tossed restlessly on his bed. Two thoughts in particular bothered him. He realized that he wouldn't be able to get to sleep, so he lit the lamp and crossed his hands behind his head.

Last night with Phrosso had been wonderful. Sweet, infinitely sweet, strange and unexpected. How had it all come about? She had been in love with him for a long time. He saw it clearly now: many little details pointed to it. But what about himself? His mind was a void. What a change had come about. Until she had come to see him when he was ill eighteen months ago, she had been nothing more to him than the daughter of his plowman. Then he had begun to pay attention to her. Later still, after the war and the destruction of Pteliona, she had begun to interest him. He had observed her, depended on her, suspected that she might be falling in love with him, and was sometimes disturbed by this suspicion. At the same time he had rejected the notion of this love; he hadn't wanted to have anything to do with it.

The realization came to him like a sudden beam of light. A surge of joy sprang up within him. But how was it possible? What about Katie and the torment she had caused him through all those months. But the radiant joy in his heart was so simple, so clear, so pure that it illumined the depths of his conciousness. In his loneliness and desperation he had been drawn to Katie by the remnant of his former superficial and degenerate self which had grown up between stone walls and every kind of futile blandishment devoid of human warmth, in the days when he slept on the soft beds of tedious pleasure—a pleasure without the spontaneity of real passion. His loneliness had made him prone to carnal longings which aroused acutely by Katie's vigorous lasciviousness.

Thus a cloud had come over his senses and he had not realized that his new self, his true and manly self, was reaching out to the other woman, beautiful and strong, who did not spend her time belaboring life in order to extract from it false and devious values, but saw it as it really was, as something sweet and strong, full of meaning, mystery, and passion. He had not hitherto understood that from the time when he had at last found out that he was himself an inseparable part of the life of the great plain, it was Phrosso he had sought, for she was cast in the mold of all that woman should be, companion, lover and mother, a man's joy and loyal ally. She too was part of the plain and a part of the call of the earth.

At this thought his heart leapt. "Naturally," he reflected, "I never believed that the earth had a voice or speech of its own. What it does have is its own vibrant vitality and a message which comes, perhaps, out of the vapors of its torn entrails, of its plants and its crops, and from the men who have lived with it and understood it. Phrosso, my little Phrosso, is part of the call of the earth, and without realizing it I fell in love with her gradually and very, very deeply, until understanding came to me and we were united, as it were, by the will of God."

His tender meditations were interrupted by the sudden grief he felt as his thoughts turned to Modestos. That good man, that dear old man, was gone leaving behind him an irreparable void. Nikita's sorrow was deep and genuine, but he was also perplexed and worried by the mystery surrounding the old abbot's torture and death.

If Ropotikas had committed the murder—which was unlikely—the matter was of relatively minor importance. The man was a bandit and had many other murders and acts of brutality to his name. One additional murder for a treasonous cause was not significant particularly as that cause may have appeared highly promising at first, but, as Voliotis had said, was really an insignificant thing which would be swept away by the first contrary wind. But if it was Voliotis who had ordered the murder—and that seemed more probable—the implications were many and extremely disturbing. Such a killing would not have been committed by a common murderer. It would mean that a fratricidal struggle was beginning and that good men, patriots, and warriors would be killed.

He let his thoughts wander to the historical precedent of the internecine fighting among the mighty heroes of 1821, to the conflict of ideologies and the conflict of the great powers which might soon rage over the tormented land of Greece.

He did not persist in these meditations. "Such questions are for other people and other times," he reflected. "I have matters to attend to here and now. As things are going I can't follow the advice uncle Spyros gave me in his letter. We cannot afford to wait until the Allied landings are imminent. The trouble has started and nothing will stop it. We are going to be torn by civil strife and we'll begin killing one another. Those who are not alert to the danger will be lost, and with them Greece may be lost too. Either we must all—every single one of us—join EAM, or else all of us who disapprove of it must organize swiftly. In Athens they are surely not aware of what is going on here, and in a few months it will be too late. I must find some way of getting to Athens to talk to them. Looking after the property and resisting the Legion is all very well, but now something a thousand times more important and serious is starting. Yes, I have to go."

Now that he had come to a decision he felt better. He blew out the oil lamp, and lay back in bed to go to sleep. He was awakened by a knocking on the window. He lit a match and saw that it was past midnight. His heart missed a beat. "It must be Phrosso," he thought. "She couldn't stay away any longer. She had to come back."

He went to the window. "Who is it?" he asked eagerly.

A man's voice answered—the vaguely familiar voice of an interpreter for the Italians.

"It's me, Tsirios, Mr. Colletti. Open up, we need some information."

"At this hour of the night?"

"Yes, yes, it's urgent."

He put on a robe and opened the door. The interpreter, an Italian sargeant holding a revolver in his hand, and two soldiers carrying rifles entered.

"Get your clothes on," the sergeant said. "We're taking you in for interrogation."

"Can't it wait until tomorrow? I've had an accident and I'm not feeling very well,"

"It can't wait. It's urgent. Anyhow you'll be back almost at once. So get dressed. Don't take anything with you.

He hesitated. Then he said, "Step outside please while I change. I shan't be a moment."

"Get you clothes on now," the sergeant said roughly. "You're not shy, are you? Come on, get moving."

He had believed them when they said they wanted him for an investigation and had wondered whether it was about what had happened at the monastery, or about the incident in the wood. Now he realized that the investigation was only an excuse and that he could not refuse to go.

At the front door of the house Mourayias was waiting for him. His eyes seemed to be damp. In a trembling voice, he said: "Master, son, where are they taking you?"

"Cheer up!" he said. "What can they do to me? You take good care of the ranch, and above all take good care of Phrosso. Tell her that was my last word to you."

Mourayias bent and kissed his hand. Nikita felt the old man's tears on it. He embraced him and moved forward. As soon as they got to the head of the outer staircase, a wild neighing rent the air. It was sharp and vehement, straining to make its urgent message heard afar. And it went on without stopping as though the horse never paused for breath, as though, in its whinnying, all the winds it has ever breathed in from the great plain were pouring out of its burning mouth.

Nikita was deeply moved. He spread out his arms and held the others back, and in response to the cry of his beloved horse he shouted as loudly as he could, "Come, Pegasus, come!" The Italians were alarmed. The two on either side of him seized him by the arms and forced him down the stone steps. At that moment, a command in Italian rang out in the garden, and he heard the clicking of rifles being loaded.

Coming out of the darkness into the starlight he could see Italian troops stationed along every path in the garden. There were others farther off. They moved about and some nearby bushes stirred strangely. He supposed that they had attributed some ominous significance to his shout and were taking protective measures. They had brought masses of troops and had surrounded his house. He felt rather pleased.

He stood still for a moment, looked around him, laughed

out loudly and derisively, and then shouted, "*Molti nemici, molto onore*!" using a well-known phrase.

Two days later, around noon, all Larissa poured down to the plaza near the Railroad Station. A report had been circulated that the prisoners were going to be transferred to a train leaving for Italy. A little later two cyclists who, just after midday, had passed in front of the concentration camp at the other end of the town had said that they had seen the prisoners from Larissa and about fifty other citizens being loaded onto trucks. They were all handcuffed.

Furthermore a train with sealed windows had come into the station. People were saying that there were prisoners in it. Some said thirty, others fifty. They were being transported from Athens and other points.

The confirmation of these rumors came at about one-thirty when it was learned that the prisoners' families had been told that the closest relative of each prisoner must go at once to the station. The Larissans were to go in separately through the iron gate leading to the tracks where the farewells would take place.

And now the whole town was running—men, women, old men, even children—running anxiously to get there in time. They wanted to show their sympathy, esteem and, above all, their solidarity. They had not done anything, had not exposed themselves to danger and they lived undisturbed. But they felt it was their duty to show that they were on the side of those who had risked everything. The town wanted to send them off with a resounding "Well Done!"

And so they ran as fast as they could. The old and the infirm ran with the others forgetting their fatigue, for they had to be on time.

The Station Plaza soon filled up and the crowd overflowed into the adjoining gardens and streets. They waited and waited. Hours went by. At five o'clock no truck had appeared. Had it not been for the deportees' relatives who were there with a handful of Italian guards, they would have begun to think that it was a false alarm. Then at last, at around seven o'clock, shouts rang out.

"Here they come! Here they come!"

The crowd made way for a line of big trucks to pass. They came to a halt at the station but, instead of the prisoners, troops clambered down and began to evacuate the plaza by force. This done, they took up positions along the sidewalks standing at attention with fixed bayonets.

The people who had gathered there were filled with a sense of pride.

"They must have been afraid we'd set the prisoners free."

"They were afraid of a riot."

"We were right not to leave."

"Let the Italians learn that we're good Greeks."

Again there was a whirr of engines. More trucks appeared, but these were open. They were filled with soldiers armed with rifles. The third and fourth trucks in the line turned sharply to the left and drove up to the station railings. They had canvas tops and sideflaps. They were going to the left, where the relatives were standing! There was no doubt now. It was the prisoners!

Behind the lines of troops guarding the plaza, the people held their breath, standing on tip-toe and straining to see if they could recognize their fellow-townsmen, straining to hear a word or two of what passed at this tragic moment of parting.

The scenes on the platform were heart-rending. Women and children wept; wives embraced their husbands, little children clung to their fathers, terrified at the evil that they sensed but did not understand.

Dr. Vaidis' wife said, amid her sobs, "Everything's going to be all right; I know it, I swear it. Don't worry about anything. Take care of your health, my love, my dearest, dearest husband."

Only one of the prisoners stood alone. No relative had come to see him. He stood apart from the others and followed the harrowing scenes. He avoided looking at the Italians who were standing by. One of these was Manoussis' arrogant son-in-law, and the others were non-commissioned oficers who had given all the deportees a bad time during the interrogation at the camp.

After a time the Italians began to separate the couples. There were more cries, tears and sobs, and now some of the prisoners wept. A sergeant said to one of his comrades, "Ha! See how the Greeks cry! Are these the sort of men we beat in Albania?"

They both laughed and turned toward Nikita and gave him a sarcastic look. Castelleone too looked at him. It was the first time since the day in the wood that their eyes had met. Castelleone's glance was hard and cold.

Nikita's blood began to boil. Near him on the ground there chanced to be a good-sized block of stone. He got up on it and said to them in Italian, "The men who beat *you* in Albania." And with a sudden movement he lifted his manacled hands to his mouth, cupping them to his lips, and shouted to the crowd with all the strength he could gather from his lungs. "Aerrrra! Long live Greece!" He was going to repeat his cry when one of the Italians gave him a violent shove and pushed him to the ground.

But he had been heard. The signal was taken up by the crowd and from far and near fierce and angry shouts went up. "Aerrra! Aerrra! Long live Greece."

Nikita was flat on the ground. One of the sergeants kicked him; the other fell to his knees and began to beat him. Nikita paid no attention. He laughed out loudly, hysterically. It was difficult to tell whether his laughter came from some inward satisfaction or whether it was put on in order to annoy his enemies.

Abruptly Castelleone appeared. He took one of the assailants by the arm, and the other by the shoulder, and pulled them away. He ordered them to go away.

Nikita got to his feet.

The two men looked at each other. There was no hatred in their eyes now. They were both self-assured and proud—the Italian as the master who had performed an act of chivalry and Nikita because he had been given the strength to find himself in chains and not be daunted, to be persecuted and reduced to servitude and yet able to give courage to his fellow-slaves and to insult his enemies. Most of all he was proud because now at last, a prisoner, he felt more clearly than he had ever felt before, that his country, even in defeat, knew how to wear a crown of victory.

His heart warmed as he remembered his beloved friend, and

something he had said now resounded within him. "The greatness of Greece," Alexis had said, "is measured by the greatness of her mind and heart."

Now the Italians were shouting to the prisoners to board the train. They rounded up the stragglers, gesticulating at Nikita who had remained outside the railings. As they looked in his direction they were astounded by what they saw. As the last Greek passed in front of him, handcuffed, the arrogant captain, almost involuntarily and as though forced by some inner compulsion, stood at attention and saluted him.

In the third class carriage they were so crowded together that they could not lie down; they could not even stretch out their legs. By a stroke of good fortune Nikita found himself next to Dr. Vaidis.

On one night of the long journey, when everyone seemed to be asleep, the doctor leaned toward Nikita and spoke in a low whisper. "I want you to give me your word of honor that you'll answer the question I'm going to ask you with absolute sincerity."

"Certainly, doctor, I will."

The doctor hesitated, looked about and, whispering in Nikita's ear, asked, "Why do you think they arrested me? What was the reason?"

Nikita was surprised. The doctor looked troubled.

"I understand why they took you and the others," the doctor continued, "but why me? Why?"

"I don't get you, doctor," Nikita said.

"I don't see the reason," Vaidis said. "And I beg you to tell me the truth specifically about my arrest. Do you think there is some secret attached to it?"

His voice trembled, especially as he uttered his last words, and Nikita realized the agonizing suspicion which troubled the doctor. The doctor was surely afraid that he had been arrested in order to leave the field free for Nikos Manoussis; maybe he was also afraid that his wife might have conspired against him.

"Yes, indeed, there was a secret reason," Nikita replied firmly. "I'm sure they were following you. They considered you a go-between on very important business."

The doctor looked at him suspiciously. "What go-between? The others didn't carry messages. They were active. And yet they were not arrested. So why me?"

Nikita again spoke steadily. "I suppose they must have taken us at random, otherwise why did Hadjipyrrhos escape? He was among the most fanatical and the most active. Besides, most of us didn't do so much after all."

The doctor stared at him hopelessly. "But I did nothing! Nothing at all! They must have arrested me for some other reason. Don't you think so?"

Vaidis seemed on the verge of tears, tormented by a desire to utter the suspicion which so deeply distressed him. Nikita felt the greatest compassion for him. Maybe he thought that on the very night of his arrest his wife. . . Nikita purposely assumed a severe tone and said to him, "First you asked me whether there was a specific reason for which you were arrested. I told you there was. But you don't seem to believe me. And so you force me to tell you a terrible secret, one which I did not wish to tell—a secret in which the Italians think you are involved. Well I'll tell you anyhow. The abbot of St. Elias was hanged and the monks abducted. By this time they too must have been liquidated."

The doctor was dumbfounded, he looked about fearfully. "How? When?"

Nikita gave him some information, and told him that that was all he knew. They would surely learn more in letters from home.

"Did the Legion do it?" Vaidis asked.

Nikita hesitated for a fraction of a second and, then, dismissing his private thoughts, replied firmly: "Certainly. Who else?"

"Can you tell me this? Had it something to do with concealed weapons? Was that why I found you so bruised the other day when I came to call?"

Nikita hesitated again, but replied in the same tone. "Yes. And now you must realize the nature of the affair in which you have been involved. You came to my house the day after the hanging, the day after I was beaten. They obviously think that you had an important part in this business; that we were both mixed up in it."

"I see."

His expression changed. The anguish faded from the doctor's sickly face and it took on an almost happy look.

"So that's why they took me. You're quite right, of course that's why. I didn't know. Now it's crystal clear. . . But. . ."

He paused, deep in thought, and a worried look came over him again. "But then, he said, "This means that I must have been in danger. It's better that I was arrested, otherwise I might have been court-martialled. I would have been terrified. And how would I ever have been able to prove. . ."

As he uttered the last words, he straightened up, his eyes brightened, and he caught hold of Nikita's hand. "No, Mr. Coletti, pay no attention to that. I could have gone to court-martial. And how would I have been afraid? It's 1821 all over again! Astonishing! Unbelievable! How could I have been afraid? I would have been standing beside you. A new 1821. I shouldn't have been afraid!"

After a little while he let his head fall on Nikita's shoulder, and for the first time since they boarded the train, he fell into a calm sleep with a tender smile on his lips.

XVI

What a strange feeling it was to be in prison!

It seemed that the whole world—the outside world—was something very far away, almost non-existent, as in a dream. When one thought about it one knew it was not so. One knew that everywhere, outside the prison yard, people did as they pleased, woke up whenever it suited them, ate whatever they chose. There were perhaps a few restrictions but, on the outside, in general, everyone could do as he pleased.

One knew this and yet it seemed unbelievable. Everyday life appeared to be so distant, so intangible, while the prisoner's life was so real and so different, that without wanting to one felt that one's confined existence was the only reality. Everything else was an otherworldly dream of a lost paradise.

When, after two months, they were released from the prison, somewhere in northern Italy, and were told that they would be transferred to a concentration camp, they thought that the feeling of isolation would pass. They imagined that they would move around more, that maybe they would not suffer so acutely from the pangs of hunger, and that maybe they would not be made to sleep on flagstone floors, with only two thin blankets for mattress and covering. And, certainly, conditions improved when they found themselves among so many other foreign prisoners, when they had a little more to eat, and had wooden cots to sleep on.

But their feelings about the reality of their circumstances, as opposed to the dream of the distant outer world, hardly changed. All that had happened was that the confines of their own world had widened slightly from the thick stone walls of the prison to the mesh of barbed wire which surrounded the camp. Inside was reality, the only reality and truth which they could experience. Nothing existed for them beyond that.

But a day would come when they would leave the wired enclosure and return to their fairy-tale cities. Yes, possibly. But it was not so certain. First of all, when would that day come? The fires of war had only just begun to flare up in Africa and Russia and, for the moment, seemed to be causing more damage to the Allies than to the enemy. Would it be three years, or four years, before the blessed day of liberation came? And then, how many would still be alive to enjoy it? How many would have succumbed to their privations? In what state would they find the world to which they returned? And their own cities, villages and homes? And what about the destruction and anarchy left by the war in a defeated country which had aspired to empire? How would they manage to escape from a country in the throes of anarchy? How many would fall by the wayside?

If only they could escape. Things would be different then. But how could they escape? They had discussed it often enough. Even if they succeeded, how would they manage to survive in a strange land, penniless and starving?

No. They had to resign themselves to it. On this side of the barbed wire lay their own special reality. Everything else was faraway, intangible, almost non-existent. Here the only difference for them was that, instead of being shut in by cold, damp walls, they were kept within the limits of a multitude of harsh, impassable barbs.

While some details of their captivity had improved, others were worse and taxed their bodies and their souls. The camp, in southern Italy, was designed as a base for the draining of a great swamp. During the day, it was intolerably hot and humid; the nights, as on the opposite African shore, were bitterly cold. When the evening breeze blew from the part of the swamp which was less drained a succession of small, dark clouds wafted across the camp. They were swarms of mosquitoes, and woe to him who found himself in their path. Everyone made for the narrow barracks with the screened windows, and there they had to say until morning if they wanted to escape the poison of this living cloud. And a curfew prevented anyone from leaving the barracks at night, so the choice lay between the voracity of millions of mosquitoes and that of thousands of bed-bugs.

Sickness took its toll. The old, the feeble, and those who had some lurking disease, fell ill during the first weeks. Many were consumptive and spat blood. It was heart-rending to visit them in the makeshift hospital and to try to give them courage. One's own courage was drained by the very sight. With what nourishment, what strength, what fortitude would one be able to face the disease that was lying in wait?

One looked at the patients and turned cold. One looked at those who still stood on their feet, or at oneself in a pocket mirror, and was filled with fear and disgust. All the men in the camp had had their heads shaved; they were nothing but skin and bones, ragged and crumpled, wearing wooden shoes on their naked feet.

Worst of all was the infinite boredom for which there was no cure. What was there to do? What was there to say? Everything had been said, repeated a thousand times. They stretched out on wooden cots and let their thoughts roam over the past, shifting their positions frequently to find relief from the monotony. But the only relief from boredom and sickness was to be found in the grumbling and petty hatreds born of hunger.

Every afternoon there was a break in the long stretch of boredom. This came with the arrival of the mail. For while prisoners were allowed to write only once a week, they could receive any letters that were sent them. So, every afternoon, they rushed out in a frenzy of anguished expectation, hoping to hear their names called. Those for whom there were no letters returned saddened to their bunks to save their strength and think over a thousand reasons why they had been forgotten.

But those whose names were called went forward eagerly, tearing the letters open and reading them where they stood. . . reading them again and again overjoyed, for news from home or from friends was always good, for letters always brought messages of love.

Nikita was among the less fortunate, for during all that time he had received one letter. It was indeed a precious letter—from Hadjipyrrhos—who told him cautiously but surely that everything was going very much better, that their exile instead of dampening the people's spirits had, on the contrary, made them more fanatical in their determination. Lastly, he said that Phasoulas had undertaken the support of the families of all those who had been arrested in Larissa. That was a wonderfully encouraging letter.

But the one he anxiously awaited did not come. It would have been worth a thousand others to him, but it had not come and he had not received any other. But, he reflected, that was only natural. His friends abroad did not know where he was and anyway would not be interested in him. Maybe from time to time, at a party, someone might ask, "I wonder what's become of Coletti?" Or another might say with a sarcastic laugh, "I'd like to know how that difficult fellow is making out now that he's trapped in the Greek squirrel-cage!"

That would be the extent of the concern of those people with whom he had spent so many years of his life.

Uncle Spyros was different. He certainly must be concerned about him, and would do everything he could to send him money, and would surely write. But he would not have learned his address yet. No one else in Athens would be interested in writing to him. And from Larissa he didn't expect any letters except the one precious letter he was longing for. Those who would have written to him were all dead, and others who might have were here in the camp with him. No one else was close enough to him and would not dare to write without a specific reason.

It seemed that the world had written him off, that the people of every faraway city he might dream of had conspired to keep him enveloped in a heavy, unbreakable silence which bore down upon his weary heart. What would he not give to receive one letter every week? In the midst of the suffocating blight of utter boredom and physical deterioration, he would have given anything to be able to communicate once in a while with the outside world that now seemed so unreal to him—to feel that someone wanted to get in touch with him and him alone.

On that day as they went for the mail, Nikita moved aside from the others. He was sorry to have to admit it but, when he saw them greedily reading their letters, their faces lighting up, he felt jealous and distressed. He walked away and sat under one of the few trees in the camp. He would stay there dreaming of the lofty elms of Pteliona, and when the others returned they would tell him. If his lucky day had come. If his name had been called then he would run to the post office.

But the others passed by. Nobody said anything to him. Only Dr. Vaidis came and sat beside him. Skinny as he had always been, he had not changed much. He seemed troubled, as though he wanted to tell him something.

"Did you get a letter, Doctor?" Nikita asked.

"I got two. One from my wife, my darling Phoula. She writes me every day, you know. I also had one from my assistant at the clinic."

Nikita did not ask what was in the letters. He felt that their contents could be of no possible interest to him. But the doctor kept looking at him and seemed all the time on the point of speaking. Nikita was sorry for him but at the same time felt like laughing at his bashfulness. He was sure that the doctor had something to tell him. At last, to help him out Nikita said, "Is anything wrong, doctor?"

"Yes," Vaidis replied at once. "My assistant has written to me about one of my patients who is pregnant. He advised her to get rid of the child but she refused." What a bore the doctor was with his little worries!

"Well then, let her keep it," Nikita said indifferently.

"Yes but with such a lack of everything. . ."

"Why worry, doctor? We have enough troubles of our own."

"But the girl is not married."

Utterly bored, and at the same time inclined to tease the doctor, Nikita said, "Well then, let her get rid of it."

With a tone of almost childish despair in his voice the doctor said, "But she doesn't want to. She won't hear of it."

"In that case why do you worry? And if your assistant can't convince her himself, why does he write to you about it?" The doctor seemed confused, gave Nikita a quick look, shifted his glance, looked at him again in an embarrassed way, and then, as though he were making a super-human effort, whispered, "Only you could convince her."

Nikita was startled. He raised himself up abruptly and asked, "I? But who is this girl?"

"It could only be you. It is. . . well, it's Phrosso."

For a fraction of a second Nikita felt his senses reeling. Then he sprang to his feet. What strange sensations ran through him! He felt weak in the legs, but now as his feet struck the ground he felt that the earth shook under them! He was suddenly filled with joy, vigor, and happiness!

"Do you mean to say that Phrosso's pregnant, doctor?" he cried.

"Yes, she's in her fourth month."

"For God's sake, doctor! She mustn't lose the child! For God's sake, no!"

"Don't worry. I told you. She herself doesn't intend to lose it."

"But your assistant insists, and writes to ask for your help. Listen here doctor. I haven't written a letter for two weeks. You can make use of my quota. I want you to write to your assistant. Get up!"

He gave him his hand and pulled him up. He continued, panting with eagerness. "Write him two letters in case one should get lost. Tell him that we were married secretly. No, that's not true. Tell him that I'm going to marry her as soon as I get back. Tell him that on no account is he to let her lose the child. I'll never forgive him if he does; I'll hound him all the days of my life. On the contrary he is to look after her well. He's to visit her every day, to give her all the care she needs, and to let us know how she's doing. I'll write a long letter later, but these letters of yours are urgent, very urgent."

The doctor had never heard him talk so fast and so vehemently.

"I'll write to him. . . I'll write to him," he murmured.

"You are not just to write to him. You are to order him. Tell him to do everything he can. I'll give him half Pteliona for his trouble."

"Yes, yes, I shall write to him."

"Not 'shall'. Go right now and write the letters, doctor. Hurry. We must get the letters in the mail this evening, I want to read them first. Hurry now. I'll wait for you here. Please, doctor, don't lose a moment!" He started to go, turned back, looked at Nikita with an expression of deep affection, was about to speak, thought better of it, and ran off.

What joy, what unutterable joy he felt!

A baby, a child that would grow up beside him, flesh of his flesh, a continuation of his life. This was real happiness. Was there truly such happiness on earth? He had been talking of faraway dream-cities. But here was the realization of all dreams. Here was paradise.

Now at last he had been completely redeemed. How could he have talked of rebirth at Pteliona? That was only the beginning. His beloved brother Alexis had shown him the way, had opened it up for him, and in the hour of his death had thrust him onto it. Now he was nearing the goal. From afar he could see the true light—the light of resurrection. Now there was Phrosso, and perhaps, a son.

He leaned against the tree.

No, he was not leaning against a tree in an Italian swamp. As in a dim vision he seemed to be supported by the thick trunk of an elm.

And not far away rose the enormous elm, grandfather's elm, whose foliage was richer than that of all the others, which watched the whole plain, gazed proudly at the river and at Mt. Olympus, and drank in the rays of the sun.

The vision was still dim, but he saw clearly that now his son was standing beside him. How old was he? What did it matter? This was his boy; and what a fine young stripling he had become—handsome, well-built, and strong.

Now a bird appeared on the distant horizon. What bird was this? Was it a sign, a portent? But no, it was not one bird. His tear-filled eyes deceived him—there were many birds, a whole flock of them. Of course, of course, now he understood. These were the birds starting out on their migration. Here came a great arrow-head of the familiar sky travelers.

He turned to his son and said, "Do you see them, my son? Do you see them? Once your father bent his head in shame when he saw them. Now you, the extension of his body and soul, stand here beside him. How could he ever bend his head in shame now, when with you at his side he is becoming strong, almost immortal!"

He gazed at the birds coming from Olympus. As they approached they cried aloud, "The shelter of the reed-thicket is not for the conquered. Let the victors go forward! Forward! Let the others die! Let them die!"

He grasped his son's shoulders with one arm, and stretched the other toward the heavens and, looking up at the proud birds, he cried out with all the power in his lungs:

"Let them die! Let them die! To you welcome, and a good journey, conquerors of the storm, mighty of the sky! We salute you standing by Grandfather's elms, rooted with them in the soil of Greece, we salute you from the blessed spot where first I heard the call of the earth."

NOTE

The names of Guilio Vianelli, Nikos Raptis, Thanasis Phasoulas, Takis Hadjipyrrhos, Alcibiades Diamantis, and Vassilakis Ropotikas are those of real people who have since died. The last two died traitors' deaths.

As a result of Hadjipyrrhos' systematic representations to a pro-Rumanian relative of his, the Rumanians were convinced that Diamantis had abandoned them in favor of the Italians. Thus, in the summer of 1942, he was invited to Bucharest "for consultation," and was not allowed to return. With the change of regime in Rumania after the war, he was comdemned to life imprisonment as a fascist and died in jail.

Toward the end of the Occupation, Ropotikas was caught by the EAM. He was bound naked, put back to front on an ass, and paraded through the areas which he had terrorized with his hordes. No eye-witnesses to his end have been found. Two rumors were circulated. According to one, as he was being taken through a ravine, he leaned toward a precipice and fell over, together with the ass on which he was tied and was killed. According to the other rumor, he was tied to the tail of a horse and dragged through two villages until he died. It was said "that the mountains echoed with his cries and groans."

The names of Golemis, Dotiadis, Scourtes, Nikos Manoussis, Bignioli, Pazzi, Pazzipolini, and Fuggiero, have been changed slightly but represent real people. All other personages are fictional.

Also fictional are such events as are not directly related to the activities of the Roman Legion and the Italians, or to the resistance offered to them.